MW00893989

ALSO BY KASSIE J RUNYAN

This is 2020: part two

Their Footsteps: a collection of travel poems and

photographs

This is 2020: a poetry collection

Enjoy the Journey!

THE
DEATH AND
LIFE OF
JOHN DOE

KASSIE J RUNYAN

Happy Bird Publication - New York

Happy Bird Publication

New York, New York 10036

Cover design: Kassie J Runyan

Cover model: Travis Allen Patten

Editor: Brittney Marie

Invisible Man Song: Kyle Dean Patten

Library of Congress Cataloging-in-Publication Data

Names: Runyan, Kassie J, author.

Title: The Death and Life of John Doe / Kassie J Runyan

Description: First edition. I New York: Happy Bird Publication

Identifiers: LCCN 2021923433 I ISBN 978-1-7355140-8-6 (paperback)

Classification: LCC

LCC record available at https://lccn.loc.gov

Our books may be purchased in bulk for promotional, educational, business, or book club use. Please contact your local bookseller or Kassie J Runyan at kassie.runyan@gmail.com

www.kassiejrunyan.com

Follow at Instagram @kjrunyan I Facebook @KassieJRunyan

to my mom

who taught me to love the written word

to my dad

who taught me to love the people

to my husband

who taught me to love the world

CHAPTER ONE

THE GOODBYE

I DIED TODAY.

I FOUND MYSELF slowly falling to the earth, feeling weightless as I floated down and down, stopping with a light thud to enter the body that was laying on the bed. I kept my eyes squeezed tight and watched the black turn to red as the daylight hit my closed eyelids. How long could I delay? Deep breath in. Long sigh out. I smelled the sheets as I breathed in again, a mix of fabric softener and morning musk and the color grey. The color grey... It floated around in my mind trying to make sense of how to describe the scent of a color. It smelled like the dust that had built layers on a counter for more than a year. Or maybe like the pile of clothes that sat forgotten in a garage. Pushed into a box with the word 'Donation' scribbled roughly on the side with a thick black marker. I kept searching for the word. Stale. The color grey smelled stale. My throat and lungs were dry as I took another deep breath in.

I continued to lay on the bed that had seen too many years of my life. I read an ad once that claimed that an adult should change their mattress every seven years. I meant to. We spoke of it a few times but just hadn't gotten around to it. This one was still comfortable and molded in just the right spot where my heavy body lay. It was warm under the soft comforter that she had purchased months ago. Or was that years ago? My left eye opened slowly and glanced at the wall that was lined from the sun starting to pierce its way through the slits in the blinds. Enough to make the room look dusty and the paint on the wall show its age. I slowly pulled my arm out from under my soft pillow and opened my other eye. My arms bent to push my body to a sitting position. I swung my legs around so that my feet could land heavily on the cold plastic floor, and I flexed my toes up and down trying to work the stiffness out of them. Looking down at my feet. Those are my feet? The nails are too long. The dark hair that grew on the top. Was that always there? I flexed my toes again and watched them move at my command. Those must be my feet. I looked at the cold floor that sat beneath them. There used to be carpeting in this room. It was an ugly brown carpet that was made in just the right way to hide years of wear and spills. I loved that carpet. It was worn where I walked and soft under my toes. Then we remodeled. She wanted a project to throw herself into to get her mind off… it didn't matter. Out with the carpet. In with plastic slats that were carved and painted to look like wood. For a moment I saw her standing there. Giggling at my frustration as I tried to hammer the damn things together. "Easy installation" said the guy at the flooring warehouse. Depends on who you ask, I guess. I shook my head, and the image was gone, replaced by the present. I looked at the hands resting on my knees. At least they looked like my hands. They moved like my hands. But they didn't feel like my hands. Deep breath in. Long sigh out. And still I sat. I heard the groan of the pipes as the shower turned off down the hall. A mower engine roared to life outside of the window before slowing into a steady purr. The birds were chirping away on the tree outside. I watched the minutes click away on the clock next to my side of our comfortable bed. Click. Another minute passed. Click. I stood up.

The soft sounds of every morning followed me as I stumbled down the dark hall towards the bathroom. Hung along the way were photos of a smiling couple. At times joined in their posed moments by friends or family. Every one of them also smiling. Some mornings I would pause and stare at the eyes of the people behind the glass, looking for the truth or pain that existed hidden behind the smiles. This morning I walked past them. I knew the truth that lived there, masked by smiles of the past.

I made it to the closed door of the bathroom and paused, closing my eyes as a memory played in the darkness. I looked down at the hand from the memory as it turned the knob. I walked through the doorway to find my freshly washed and damp wife standing there, naked and trying to unsuccessfully dry her long hair. Water dripping from the tips of it down between her breasts and tracing its way down to her belly button. I watched her for a moment before moving close and wrapping my arms around her, not minding her dampness. She turned and smiled before leaning in for a kiss, having to stand on the tips of her toes to reach my lips. The first kiss would turn into another until I finally pulled her back behind the sliding glass door to join me for my shower. I shook the memory away and opened my eyes with a hint of unexpected hopefulness as I reached towards the knob and wrapped my hand around it. It didn't turn. I let go of the cold metal and stood there, eyes closed again to shake the fog out of my head before closing my hand into a fist and tapping lightly on the door. There was the sound of movement on the other side and the click of the door unlocking. It swung open slowly revealing her standing there wrapped like a tiny burrito in her soft grey robe. The light shone through the window behind her and for a moment the sun shone through her like she wasn't even there. My wife. A soft smile in my direction. A dry kiss on the cheek. Then she shuffled around me and down the hall towards the bedroom I had come from. Our bedroom. Always walking away from me. Quietly in our own worlds. I walked into the light of the bathroom and closed the door before pushing in the button on the knob. That little movement of my thumb and I locked out the memories. The past that no longer existed.

I stood in the shower, the hot water stinging my face as I watched the steam lazily float away and work its way along the corners of the ceiling. How long could I possibly stand in here and avoid the next moments of my almost finished life? Five minutes? Fifteen? Before long, she'd be back up here, knocking on the door and questioning what I'm doing or how much longer I'll be. I turned the water off and grabbed the oversized grey towel with the J on it. Everything was labeled in our home. I used to find it endearing. The laugh when I bought her a label maker to continue her obsession throughout the house. The water trailed down my body and I raced to pat it off before walking over to the double sink vanity. Methodically putting a small peak of white cream on the bristles before trying to scrub away the fuzziness that grew over my teeth each night. I stood in front of the mirror, toothbrush hanging between my lips, looking at my reflection. The odd shaped folds, the patchy hair, the splotches of freckles. I recognized myself in the glass. Like I recognized myself in a photograph on the wall. I knew I was looking at a reflection but found myself mouthing the words, "who are you?" I didn't recognize the eyes of the man looking back at me. They belonged to a stranger living in the empty shell of my worn-out body. I was nothing but a host. The strange eyes stared back at me as I leaned my face closer to the glass, caught in their gaze. There was nothing living behind them. I leaned closer. Maybe if I could just see something within them. A spark of life. A reason to stay. I blinked and the eyes blinked back, emotionless. And I leaned back to finish scrubbing my teeth.

I know it's hard to believe, but there was a time when I had trouble engaging with situations or people I didn't trust. So, I chose to stay hidden and aloof amongst people until one day, a teacher told me that it came across as 'cocky.' He told me to smile. If I felt that I didn't trust the person in front of me, sad, angry, or even felt nothing at all – I should smile. That the perception of seeming happy for others will start to make me seem more relatable and would even help me feel happy inside. I knew it was bullshit, but it stuck with me and became a part of my routine. So, like every morning, I finished getting cleaned up and looked back into the face in the mirror. My lips widened and I smiled at the man in the mirror. The stranger did not smile back. Asshole. He watched me, emotionless, as I walked out of the bathroom and down the hall. I looked back once to see if I had left him standing there; alone in the mirror without me. But just like every day before he followed me out.

She was already dressed and gone from the bedroom by the time I opened the closet. Her side of the bed always freshly made; the blankets pulled tight. I pulled out the outfit of choice today… the same as every Tuesday. Grey slacks. White oxford. Dark tie. She used to tease me about my routine outfits but didn't say anything about it anymore.

I walked down the stairs to the open kitchen and saw that she had filled my cup with black coffee and placed it on the counter for me. The steam still rose from the ceramic mug that used to be white but was now stained with age. I heard a soft noise behind me and turned around to see her putting on her grey jacket, just a peak of orange coming out the bottom where her dress lay against her legs. She gave a little wave as the door opened. And she was gone. I looked back at my coffee sitting on the clean counter. How long had I stood here? I took a sip of the cold coffee before pouring the rest of it down the drain. The brown liquid disappeared as my head filled with a single thought, "how could anyone miss something that was already gone?" Deep breath in. Long sigh out.

I SAT UNDER the florescent glare of the light that hung above my cubical, staring at the bright computer screen. I shook myself and rubbed the dryness from my eyes. What had I just been working on? Oh yeah. I looked down at my hands as they typed out the words, *I'm sorry. J.* I had drifted off, thinking about the life that I used to have. That we used to have. The hope and desire and the belief that I had a purpose. That we would do something amazing. Was that so long ago? We weren't those people anymore. She might still be more than a host, but I was not. I looked at the fabric on the cubical wall. A small piece of paper stuck to it with the four simple rules of client management. My eyes drifted to the photo that sat directly next to the monitor. I glanced at her before moving my eyes to the man. That's me. I leaned in to stare at the smile. Was that real? Her smile looked real next to his. How long would it take her to move on? To find someone that made her smile like that again. I leaned back in my chair and focused on the light shining above me. I looked past the glow and saw the corpse of a roach, long dead. It had had been there for at least the six years I have. I named him in my first year. Phil the Roach. In those six years did anyone else ever noticed the little empty shell of death named Phil? No. No one notices the dead once they are gone. I focused back on my screen. The silence only broken by an occasional distant conversation between people who were never my friends. I tapped the mouse and waited for the question to show. Would I like to print? I looked around me. Deep breath in. Long sigh out. There was nothing in this cubical I wanted. I left my computer on, the cold coffee sitting in the mug and waiting to form a green moss over the next few weeks, the jacket on the hook, the photos in their frames and I clicked the mouse as the arrow hovered over 'yes.'

Slowly standing up from my worn desk chair, keys in hand, and I grabbed my note from the printer on my way to the elevator. No one stopped me from hitting the down arrow. Hell, I don't think anyone looked up from their fucking desks. How long would it take for any of them to notice that I wasn't there the rest of the day? How long before they noticed that I wasn't coming in anymore? A week? Probably more. The most likely scenario is that no one notices until she calls looking for me. Then they will turn to each other, confused, and say "No. I don't know when we saw him. Last week maybe?"

I stepped off the elevator and walked through the revolving door, unsurprised when the man at the front desk pretended that I wasn't even there. Not even a slight raise of the head from his paper. Hell, what did I expect? I never even learned his name. I had named a fucking corpse of a bug and couldn't tell you what the security guard's name started with. I doubt he'll even remember my face when I'm gone. I stepped outside and my eyes narrowed against the blinding sun before walking towards my little silver sedan and sliding into the driver's seat. I liked this little car. We had bought it together. It will be a shame that it will probably be sold at a fair price to some kid who is just learning to drive. Hands at ten and two. I remembered my uncle yelling that at me every single time I left the house when I was a teenager. Driving the same truck that he drove each night after a few too many beers. He wasn't worried about driving drunk, but he sure was worried about my hand placement. Still must have stuck with me – because even when I wasn't thinking about it – there were my hands. Ten and two. It didn't help to keep me from forgetting to look behind me before I crawled backwards out of my space or get me to pay attention to anything going around me during my autopilot drive. But dammit my hands were at ten and two. As I drove, I tried to think about what I was about to do. I should have felt sad or ashamed or disappointed in myself. I was giving up. I knew that. But I felt nothing. My hand instinctively clicked the button to open the garage door and the car pulled into my spot. I left the car running as I sat there wondering if I would ever feel regret for this. Not waiting to see if this life would get better. If I would start feeling something again. I looked at the hands that looked like mine and pulled them off the grip on the steering wheel. The key turned and I slid out of the quiet car, leaving the keys swinging in the ignition and the garage door open.

It was time to prepare. How does one prepare for something like this? I changed into my routine Saturday clothes – my grass tinted jeans and a worn-out shirt with a logo of a college I never went to. I walked through the house that we had built for our future family that never came. That would never come. I said goodbye to the walls and useless items that we had collected through the years. I refused to look at the smiles that would remain locked behind the glass and waited for the reality of the situation to hit me. I waited for the guilt or the second thoughts. The desperation or realization that maybe I was having a mid-life crisis. Nothing. I shrugged. I took the cash out of my wallet and put the wallet on the entry way table along with the typed note. I forced the gold ring off my finger – no longer a symbol of anything but a simple circle – and sat it on the note. It looked strange and lonely sitting there on the white. The house echoed with the emptiness that I felt as I stood in the entryway. I saw us walking into the house for the first time. Her immediate joy over it before detailing the shades of color that we would paint the outside. We faded into the dust, and I looked up to see the stranger staring back at me from behind the entryway mirror. Deep breath in. Long sigh out.

I opened the front door, and the empty sounds were replaced with birds chirping, another mower running, the world passing. I hesitated. Is this right? There was no answer and my right foot stepped out the door and into the light.

AND I DIED.

CHAPTER TWO

THE SCREAM

THERE WAS NOTHING but a hollow feeling as I walked down the clean paved road and away from the home of the man who died. I was waiting for an immediate change or revelation, that would turn my feet and send me running back towards the empty house. But none came. I was still a shell. An empty host who was still waiting to feel something remotely human. My body slowed and I stopped moving, standing in the middle of the empty road. Anyone watching would have thought that my battery had died. My eyes closed and opened, and I breathed in and out. I looked down at the feet beneath me as they straddled the middle of the pavement and I willed one to move; almost relieved that it listened to my command. Then the other. Focusing on them as they started moving quicker as if they had a life of their own. I didn't turn to look at the home fading away from me in the distance as I broke into a run. Images flashing before my eyes. Painting the outside so that it would stand out just a bit than the other houses that bookended it. I kept running. Jogging past the rows of grey box houses that I recognized as near mirrors of my own. The images faded and I remembered that I was making the right decision... I had to die. Shit: I had already been dead for months. I had to leave all resemblance of that life that had existed before my death. Before his death. I had to embrace the anonymous host that I was meant to be. Because there just wasn't anything else. Fuck. Is that right? I slowed to a walk and looked back down at the feet. Right foot then left foot. Moving forward through the dead man's neighborhood.

The sky was as grey as the pavement beneath my feet. Walking past the old man who always seemed to be mowing. I looked over at him wondering if he would notice me and wonder why this body was walking past him in the middle of the day. He glanced in my direction for just a moment before turning his eyes back down to his row; not even pausing to meet my stare. I don't think he ever saw me. Did I ever talk to him? I couldn't remember. Does he enjoy his life or is he an empty host as well? I think I remembered hearing his wife passed a few years ago. Bright red birds flew over my head; yelling at each other as they flew. I kept walking. My breath had turned shallow. I made it to the end of the road and froze. Left was another row of houses stretching as far as I could see. Forward was nothing but a field. Right headed towards the buzzing sound of the interstate. Right was the fastest way away from people who would recognize the dead man and try to get me to conform back into his life. Or even to a new grey box where everyone tried to get me to feel something. I turned my body right and my feet followed. I was walking towards an idea. A thought. The closest thing that made sense. Deep breath in. Long sigh out. I walked and waited for the surge of emotion that refused to come.

IT TOOK DAYS before I started to feel something. The feeling came on slowly. I felt fucking cold. Not the kind of cold that makes a nose rosy and eyes sparkle and kids want to run out and experience the joy of building a man of snow. No. This was the kind of deep and resonating wet cold that makes a grown man want to bash his own face against the side of the building just to feel the warmth of the blood. I sat huddled under an awning not nearly far enough from where I had first started. I had walked in circles for days, questioning and going back closer to the dead man's home before continuing in another direction. And I had ended up here. My legs were pulled deep into my body and my arms held them close as I shivered into a brick corner. I had made it to a row of brown stores that lay hidden away from the road just a bit. The interiors were dark, and the parking lot was empty, so it seemed to be a safe place to shelter for the night. I hadn't prepared for the ice from all directions. It was pelting against my poorly clad body; the cold material sticking to my back as it tried to protect the rest of my body. My eyes closed against the cold, and I tried to remember how I had gotten here. I hadn't really thought about what this would be like before I left. The decision had been made around the leaving and there wasn't much imagination left in me anyway. But somewhere in the back of my mind this small thought must have lived, and it came to the surface in the first day. I had an image of what I thought it would be like; thumb out on the highway and drifting quickly to a new world in a car of stoned teenagers that listened to alternative rock. Driving me away from this place to someplace new. Someplace that could make this all matter. Someplace that would make me feel.

It took six hours for me to give up on hitchhiking on day five. I think it was day five. Every time I would see a newer suburban I would hide from the potential recognition of an acquaintance. Every time I would hold my arm out for a beater nothing would happen except my arm grew heavy and I was met with blank stares from the drivers. Halfway through yesterday, the storm from hell hit. A storm this time of year is a bad omen. And it wasn't just any storm. It was a fucking blizzard. My pace slowed and my clothes dampened. I thought I would have weeks before the weather changed back to winter. I thought I would be gone from this area before then. Eyes still squeezed shut, I heard a noise come from my mouth. A noise that was full of scorn and disdain. I had finished my granola this morning, I think, and as I sat there lost in myself and sitting in the storm, my stomach grumbled.

I had a small amount of cash, now surely a wet wad of worn paper stuck down into my pocket. And even if the lights were on in the stores next to my hidden brown brick spot, I didn't think I could find the energy to uncoil and purchase anything resembling food. So, I sat. My eyes squeezed closed tighter. I shivered and starved and leaned my stocking capped forehead into the rough brick corner of the building.

I could feel the outlines of the surface of the brick indent the skin that wasn't covered and tried to focus on that to make the other pains go away. My goal wasn't to see how long a shell of a human could live outside in a blizzard. Shit. I don't even know what my goal was. I tried to picture her, but she was already fading into the background. Focus. Try to focus on something, anything, to keep me from thinking about the cold and the hunger. I pushed my head harder into the brick but the pain from the stone had been replaced with a numbness. I saw my dad. The sun shining behind him as he grilled in the backyard. That was odd. I hadn't really thought about him for years. His big hands holding a small jar filled with bugs that lit up in the darkness. His face floating in the air swaying back and forth. My eyes shot open and fluttered a few times before I forced them closed again. Don't think about that. Don't think about anything. Focus on why I shouldn't just lay down and let my soft fragile shell disappear under the white snow. I couldn't answer why I didn't give up, but I knew that it wasn't what I was looking for. I pictured the sun and warm water and leaned my head against the cold brick again;

and tried to replace the razor of cold that beat against my back. The snow piled against me as I just tried to stay alive while I waited for it to pass.

The cold pierced into my bones and I tried to imagine what that looked like. The cold was made of tiny knives that stabbed deep, each thrust sliding into the white bone. And then the bone started to bleed. Like it was skin. The blood oozed bright red from the punctures and warmed the bone around it as the knives disappeared. My body started to warm from the inside out while confusion ran through my mind before being replaced with a memory of an article read about how a body feels warm shortly before freezing to death. "This is the end. This is how it ends," I whispered into the wind.

The shivering stopped and I could feel my back growing warm… almost hot. It felt like the sun was shining and warming me. I sat for another few minutes, trying to slowly warm like a lizard in the sun that was created by my dying mind. The sun made the pains in my stomach feel a little more bearable. The black behind my eyelids started changing to red and I slowly opened my left eye. My head was not leaning against the brick wall any longer. I was no longer even looking at a brick wall. Maybe I already died. I shrugged my shoulders at the thought and opened my other eye. Nope – no brick. At this moment, one might start to worry. But there was no worry in any part of my warming body. I stretched my arms out slowly like a cat and arched my back. Finding myself sitting in a clearing made in a field of grass. Brown and green grass like what one would see when they go for a drive in the country. So tall I could barely see anything around me. The sky was almost orange like right before a storm but without a cloud in the sky. Deep breath in. The air that filled my lungs was thick and sweet... almost like molasses. I thought molasses before even reminding myself that I had no idea what molasses would taste like. Interesting. I unfolded my legs and slowly started to rise. My stomach was no longer growling as I leaned towards the sky to peer over the grasses. Trying to see if I could find anything beyond. Nothing. The left and right were both the same. The grass moved against me and tickled my neck. The quietness sat thick in my ears as I breathed slowly trying not to let my emptying lungs make a sound. I rubbed my ears to drain whatever must be blocking the sound of the earth around me. Nothing. I turned around expecting to see more grass coming from the other direction as far as I can imagine. There in the middle of the emptiness was a town. I forgot that I was dead for a moment. I could feel and smell and taste the world that I was in. I rubbed my tired eyes and looked back at the town in the distance, leaning towards it as if that would make it come into focus. I couldn't place the feeling that was trying to take hold in my body. Was this what 'peaceful' feels like? Standing in a field that's not there and staring at town that lives only in my mind? Maybe. I started making a path towards the town. Swimming through the grass, eyes on the town that I worked towards. I walked slowly and steady, as my dad taught me, to watch for snakes and holes in the grass. This field seemed to have a shortage of both. I stretched towards the warm sky and breathed in the sweet air and walked. And walked. I felt more of this… what was this feeling? I think it must be a comfortable death with each step and with each breath. I slowly made my way to this imaginary town. It wasn't that far away, was it? I peered over the grass and noticed that I hadn't made it close. I hadn't even moved at all. I looked behind me and saw the clearing that had been made by my crouched form. The ease of the dream quickly dissipated as a dull panic set in. I lifted my arm to slide through the grass, but nothing happened. My eyes moved down towards my arms as I willed them to raise but they refused to lift from the side of my body. I pushed my right foot through the grass in front of me, but it wouldn't leave the ground. I realized that I no longer had control of the host body that I was in. Was I imagining that I was moving this whole time when really, I was just standing here? Why couldn't I wiggle my toes or fingers? I closed my eyes and tried to focus on just one finger on my right hand. Move dammit. MOVE. Nothing. Wait. Did it move? I tried to force the eyes to look down and check on that finger, but they refused to follow direction. What was happening to me? I closed my eyes again and tried to focus on my big toe on my left foot. Move. My breathing became shallow, and I tried to focus on going back to a feeling of ease or fullness instead of the panic that started to choke the throat of the man who was dead. I opened my eyes again as the grasses shifted so that I could see the town sitting there still far away. It was no longer inviting but had now become a ghost town waiting for me in the afterlife. Maybe if I screamed someone would hear me. I had no idea what I wanted but I knew I didn't want to die alone in this field more forgotten than I was before. Or was I already dead? I couldn't remember. What happened before I was standing here in this suffocating air? I opened my mouth to scream. Nothing. Not even a whisper or a moan. A wave of panic washed over me, and I closed my eyes as my breath shortened to a level that must have been just above a panic attack. Breath trying to shoot into my lungs and emptying before I could draw again. Calm down. Think. What was going on? Deep shaky breath in. Long raspy sigh out. A scream pierced the dead silence.

My eyes shot open and tried to focus for just long enough to realize that the scream didn't come from me.

I was forced back into the painful cold and hunger much quicker than I left it. By a kick to my lower back. I was lying down half covered in snow and between me and the snow... a blanket? Where did that come from? I quickly sat up and saw a looming shadow standing over me and wearing enough layers to have kept us both warm against the storm.

"What are you doing, trying to die in front of my store? Go! You can't sleep here!"

As he pulled back his meaty leg to swing at me again, I painfully jolted to my feet and awkwardly ran down the snow-covered sidewalk away from the man. The blanket left to rot in the pile of snow behind me. I could hear his steps as he chased me, probably thinking I needed another lesson in where to sleep during a blizzard. It was now completely dark, and I ran... mostly slid... over into the parking lot being lit up every ten feet by the circle of lights that were scattered in the lot. I held my bare hand in front of me to protect my eyes from the intermittent blinding light and piercing snow. My body moved quicker than it should have in its frozen form, fueled by confusion and fear. Fear of death. Fear of not being dead yet. Fear of the unknown assailant lumbering after me. I finally saw a break in the brick façade of the strip mall. Somehow, I knew that beyond that there would be an open space and I ran towards the gap making it through the buildings before pausing for a moment to let my eyes try to adjust to the darkness. A sound thudded behind me, and I ran painfully away into the dark cold night.

CHAPTER THREE

THE DOG

A GROAN FELL out of my mouth as I thudded to a seating position on the hot gravel and waited hopefully for a wind to cool the sweat that ran down the side of my face and into the rough hair that grew around my chin. No wind came. I sighed audibly to no one and watched the trucks speeding past my resting spot. I could almost see the thoughts behind the wondering eyes of the drivers as they thought, *who is this idiot sitting on the side of the road*. I tugged at the sleeve of my faded sweatshirt and pulled the fabric from my right arm and then my left. Then grabbed at the damp hole that hung around my neck and slid the shirt over my head, making sure not to let the rough fabric turn inside out. An obsessive habit of the dead man. One that had stuck with me even after he was gone. I didn't know why I kept this action when the shirt smelled of sweat and a little bit of piss, and was faded to exhaustion, but it gave me a small piece of normal. I folded the shirt and set it next to me on the rough ground. The sweat rose on my arms and started to cool the hot skin beneath it. My legs folded up against my chest so that I could reach down to unlace my right shoe. Teeth pressed against each other in anticipation of the pain to follow and I slowly slid the shoe from my foot. The sock followed immediately, and my vision blurred as the frayed fabric pulled the skin that peppered my swollen feet. I looked down at my naked foot and noticed that it was no longer blistered but completely raw. Skinless flesh where the blisters had lived just a few short days ago. No wonder it hurt so badly. I touched my finger to one of the openings and pulled it away quickly. Fuck that hurt. I took off my left shoe and sock and performed the same meticulous inspection with the same results. My face turned towards the cloudless sky and the piercing sun, and I tried to take my mind off the pain in my feet. The air providing minimal cooling relief as a heartbeat thudded through the open sores. I sat in my own sweat attempting to ponder the meaning of life and what I was doing sitting on the side of this semi-truck filled highway. How did I get here? It was a useless task. There were no deep revelations, so my mind kept making its way back to the throbbing feet and the strands of sweat that tickled my back.

I have to get up. I must keep moving. I haven't found what I'm looking for yet. Shit, I don't even know what I'm looking for. I could feel a new line of sweat make its way down my back and my mind focused on the path it was creating. It started under my right shoulder blade and charted its course towards the middle of my rapidly thinning back while running down towards my tailbone. I could see it in my mind, leaving a faint streak of pink and tan under the brown layer that covered my skin before meeting up with the other wet tracks of sweat. I looked at my feet again and dreaded the moment I was leading up to. But I was driven by a reminder that I needed to move. I couldn't sit out here in this heat forever. There had to be an end. A goal. Otherwise, this whole life was completely pointless. I sighed against my own inner voice and grabbed the first sock.

I ground my teeth together to keep from yelling out in pain as it slid over my foot, the rough fabric stinging against the skin. Covering up the red nakedness with the dirty brown sock, yet again. Another truck cruised by. This time it was a little too close and the gust from the tires sent my other sock flopping merrily away from the doom that was my foot and its fate. I snatched it and slid it up over my other foot before sitting for another moment trying to slow my breath against the pain. It was time for the shoes. In the dead man's life, these were the most comfortable shoes he owned. That life no longer existed. They were now the shoes that the devil made you wear for all eternity to cause irreparable pain and suffering. I loosened the laces as far as they would go and still hold some purpose and slid the shoes on my feet; letting the noises come when the pain was too much for my mouth to keep quiet. Now all I had to do was walk. I had thought I was getting closer to a town. Maybe I could spend some of my remaining funds on a small hotel room where I could clean up and soak my feet. I didn't think I had that much left. Maybe just a beer in a nice cool bar and a hidden nap in a corner booth until they kicked me out. That I had enough for.

I rolled over onto all fours and slowly started to right myself into a standing position. Hands on knees for a second longer than what was truly needed in this moment. I stared down at the dirty shoes that hid so much pain and for a short moment I felt another pain. A pain from somewhere deep inside of the dead man as if the physical pain had been a switch to turn it on. I couldn't catch my breath against the sob that started to fill my throat. Where was this coming from? I forced air into my lungs and forced the sob back down to where it came from and pushed my body upright. I turned and faced the direction that the trucks kept coming from and took a step to steady myself before starting to raise my thumb.

I FELT THE slam and cold before I saw the open window with the sneering face. I heard high pitched laughter fading behind me as I saw the cheap plastic cup lying on the ground in front of me spilling the last of its sticky contents onto the hot gravel. Assholes. The soda dripped from my beard, a drop at a time, onto my soaked and stained t-shirt. I didn't mind the sweet smell or the cold of the ice so much as I did knowing that these clothes would stick to my skin for the next two weeks or at least until I found something to wash them in. The pain from my feet and the unknown sob forgotten in the moment and replaced by an undeniable 'fuck all.' *Screw this,* I thought as I watched more trucks approaching on the road. I lost the energy to lift my thumb and wait for a stranger to not be a complete jackass.

I looked behind me to see a wall of trees beyond a small walk through a field. Maybe there was a stream or something that I could just clean up in for a minute or two. Cool down and maybe take a nap. I limped slowly down into the ditch, watching my footing, knowing that if I fell that I may not be able to get back up. My left arm held out in an awkward attempt to steady myself as I made it to the flat piece of land before almost falling face first over a flimsy wire fence. No barbs. That was good. I raised my right let over the useless wire and followed with my left. Then continued slowly limping, trying to find just one way to walk that brought about the least amount of pain. The trees were close, and I made my way to the edge of the thick growth and looked around for just a moment before disappearing into them. The sound of the highway was immediately gone. The glaring heat of the sun was immediately gone. Any hope of a breeze was also gone. The ground was soft as I shuffled through the overlay of fallen pine needles and old leaves. I continued walking slowly, focused on the dead man's feet as I pleaded with them to continue to do my bidding and move me in a direction. I felt like I barely moved at all before I saw the sun shining through the dense trees ahead of me. Maybe a clearing with water? I looked down at the feet and told them to move that direction. The air thinned and a breeze picked up the strands of hair that were sticking to my forehead as I walked towards the white light that was framed in the distance.

SHIT. I FROZE. Immediately, I was standing at the edge of a small clearing with tall trees towering around the edge. There was no water, but a small cabin sat directly in front of me. It was covered in warning signs that were yelling at me about dogs and guns and reminded me that I was an unwelcome traveler. My brain raced as I stood frozen waiting for a gun welding person with crazy eyes. I was going to get fucking shot for entering this piece of forbidden land. I hesitated. Maybe being shot was ok. My feet throbbed. I stood still for moments more but aside from the slight rustle of leaves blowing against the grass, it was silent. I finally breathed out, slowly, and relaxed my tensed muscles. No one was home. I lifted one painful foot and stretched it out to take a step.

A branch snapped on the ground behind me, and I spun around with my arms coming up to protect my face, waiting for the shot that would end my shell of a life. No shot came. I slowly lowered my arms from my face and stared… into nothing. My gaze traveled closer to the ground, and I saw the large brown eyes that were staring back at me. As I leaned down to pick up the sweatshirt that I dropped in my panic, the owner of the brown eyes padded over to me slowly, not breaking eye contact. I stood up quickly and the dog froze. It didn't seem aggressive. No growling or hunching. That's what dogs do before they attack, right? Was it scared? Scared and hungry? I could see myself in the sunken eyes. A lost and empty host with an equally empty stomach. My bones creaked as I slowly crouched down to eye level with the shrunken beast and ignored the pain that screamed from my feet. If it lunged at me, I knew I couldn't move quickly enough. So, I waited. It lowered to the ground and slowly started crawling towards my outstretched hand. I looked away; I would rather not see it bite my fingers, but I had made my decision to be the first to say *Hello*. Finally, I felt its cold nose brush against my fingers and low whine start in its throat. It looked back up at me and started waving its tail back and forth like it was on a hinge, dust rising into the air from the sweeping motion. I dropped to the ground with a slight thud and reveled in the contact with another life form as the dog stood and ran into my open embrace, shaking from fear or hunger or the same desire I was consumed with. I pet the greasy fur and felt the bones beneath the slacked skin. The rough sandpaper wet my face and cleaned the dirt and soda from my cheeks. A sound came out of my mouth that I wasn't expecting. Not of pain. But a sound that held desperation and joy and relief… all in one groan. I held the dark quivering mass of fur like I hadn't held anything in my life. We sat like that barely noticing the sun going down overhead or the chirp of crickets slowly awakening in the night.

Shit. What if the owner was coming back? I looked down at the now calm dog that was lying in my arms. How could this dog be here, and so skinny, if the owner was nearby? No lights came on in the house and no sounds came from outside the clearing we sat in. The dimming light was still bright enough for me to notice that there was decay and plant life growing over what looked to be a gravel path to the house. I moved the dog off my lap and slowly crept into a standing position. The dog whined at my side for the loss of touch in the moment. We walked towards the house in the slowly darkening night. Not a sound but the hum of nature and the soft footsteps of my new friend. I made it to the porch and swept away a web that was blocking my entry. I wiped the sticky strands down the front of my shirt and took a deep breath. The narrow porch creaked beneath my feet as I reached towards the rusted knob. It turned and the door unlatched, coming away from the frame. Dog pushed past my legs and nudged the door open before disappearing into the darkness within. I reached out and pushed the door open further and stood in the safe zone just outside of the deep darkness. Deciding to go in or stay out when I was smacked in the face with a smell that reminded me of the things that live in the dark. Things that nightmares are made of. It smelled like death. I folded in half and tried to empty my stomach. Wheezing and hacking up the food that didn't exist there. Then there was deep whine that came from within the dark. Dog. He was in pain. He needed me. Something needed me. I launched past the smell that rolled from the house and the fear that was building within me, and over the threshold towards the sound of my new friend. Barely able to see my hand that was guiding me as it hit a wall and hurried me towards the sound that was coming from past the hall. I made it to the room, but I couldn't find dog. I reached out blindly in front of me towards the sound and touched soft padding. A bed? I groped the fabric and worked my way around to a corner and a side and then felt something different. A hard sort of different. I rubbed my hand around the hardness and my hands sent the picture to my brain. A shoe. And beyond the shoe an ankle and the start of a leg. Hard as a rock and cold as ice.

A leg? A leg. I shot back, falling over something that had been hunched behind me and my head slapped against a wall. Shit. I knew why this cabin seemed empty and Dog was starving and alone. His owner was in that bed. All alone with no one to care enough to find him there. Like me. I tried to pull in a heavy breath and gagged on the death floating in the air around me. I had forgotten the smell in my rush to find my new friend. "Dog" I whispered. "Dog" louder. I heard his soft cry and the padding of his feet right before I felt his face against mine. I wrapped my arms around his thin ribcage and picked him up as I awkwardly pushed to my feet. Left arm clutching at him and trying to tell him it would be OK. Right arm reaching out in front of us and trying to find our escape from the death within this room. I almost fell when I finally found the opening and quickly launched us out of the room and closed the door behind me.

What now? I dreaded going back outside but didn't know how long I could stay in this dark purgatory of a home, clinging to this dog. We found our way to a soft cushioned seat and sat down. My body was shaking as I held a quivering Dog in my lap, and we rocked back and forth both moaning in our own separate pain. So much pain. I moved my hand down the coat that covered his back and moved my face down to hide my eyes in his fur, "What are we going to do Dog?" There was only a whine in response. I breathed in and tried to focus on the smell of the fur; musk mixed with dirt; instead of the smell of rotted flesh that was hidden in this house. The pain and confusion rolled over me. I felt everything. And I did something that I hadn't done in years. I cried. The tears kept coming as I wept for the dead man at my old house and the dead man that died alone in this house. I wept for the desperation of Dog and myself. I wept out of pure hunger and exhaustion. I kept crying into the fur of the moaning dog and we clung to each other as we rocked back and forth in the dead man's recliner.

CHAPTER FOUR

THE LETTER

I OPENED MY eyes to see the tall grass swaying above me; the orange sky above it. How many times have I been here now? I was so exhausted that I didn't jump to my feet to try to desperately to make it to the town I could never reach. Instead, continuing to lay there gazing at the sky and allowing myself to enjoy the lack of physical pain in my prematurely aging body. This dream allowed the aches of the previous weeks to drift away. Or was it months now? This time I didn't feel the giddy adventure and desperation that I was used to feeling before; this time my heart ached with a pain that I couldn't describe. The tears welled up again as they had done when I was awake, and I didn't have the energy to contain them. I was forced into a seated position as my body shook with sobs and I felt the full pain that my life has been devoid of for so long. The empty nothingness was gone for this moment and was replaced by unbearable loneliness and sadness. What was I doing here? How did all of this happen?

My thoughts drifted to the dead man's mom. My mom. Her body shivering as she lay crying on the bathroom floor surrounded by pills that dropped from their small container. I cried with her now. I forced my thoughts back to my dad smothering his cries as he lay alone in his bed. I cried with him now. I thought back to the dry eyes of the same man as they floated in the air. I cried with the boy, sobbing on the floor of the basement with the feet swinging above him. I cried until I had no more tears to shed, and I began to feel the hollowness creeping in again. The feeling I knew. This I could deal with. I opened my swollen eyes to look at the grass around me. I breathed in the sweet air and pushed it back out of my lungs, exhausted from my drying tears. I sat and breathed and then realized that I had been here for too long. The scream that alerted me that it was time to wake up must be coming. I pushed to my feet, and I waited, not sure I wanted to wake up again. Nothing made a sound. I furrowed my brow and squinted towards the town. Something wasn't right here. I knew I've had now been here longer than any of the times before and the orange sky had started to fade into a pink. I took a step knowing that my body wouldn't move. Then another step. My eyes widened realizing that I was no longer stationary. Well now, this was different. I took another step and moved a foot closer to the forbidden town. I stared at the hazy buildings in the distance for just one curious moment before I started running. Grass stung against my face as it flew past me. I worked to keep my footing in the slick ground as I got closer to the town desperate to find what my subconscious had been trying to hide there.

I WOKE UP to the sound of a water drizzle and the smell of newly recognizable decay. The sun had started to lighten the inside of the cabin to a dusty haze, and I could see the source of the water. Dog was standing in front of the closed front door relieving himself. Shit. I didn't even remember closing that door last night before falling asleep. I rocked the recliner forward to touch my feet to the ground and felt the sharp pain radiate from the back of my head where I hit the wall the previous evening. Everything slowly came back to me; not nearly as quickly as the pain had. I looked at Dog sitting next to his wet puddle of piss, and he looked back at me as if to ask "well, what now?" I pushed myself to my feet and felt every muscle ache as I moved to stand. The searing pain in my feet and my head were quickly forgotten as my stomach painfully started to growl.

Looking behind me, I saw the dusty kitchen in the dim light of the morning. The cabinets showing the signs of regular use where the oils of skin had darkened the unvarnished wood. I limped over to the faucet, knowing before I even got there that nothing would happen when I turned the knob. No stream of water. Not even a hiss of a sound with the hope of water. The once silver spout now had a film over the top fogging my reflection. I opened one of the cabinets, expecting nothing but a swarm of bugs working their way into the freedom. Instead, there was row upon row of slightly dusty cans peeking neatly at me from the shadow. I reached in and wrapped my fingers around the closest can and pulled it to me, looking down to see that I was in proud possession of a can of dark red kidney beans. It had one of those pull tops that meant I didn't even need to hunt for a knife or an opener to get to the sweet insides. My mouth started to water as I grabbed another can with a matching label and walked over to the front door of the cabin, barely missing the puddle of dog piss. The door swung open, and Dog leapt past my legs and into the damp grass. I leaned against the wood of the door and slid down into a seated position on the porch before scooting forward so my legs folded over the worn top step. I looked down at the precious can that was clutched in my right hand before sitting the other down on the wood plank next to me and squeezing my finger beneath the tab. Pulling until the whole top of the can was open to me. Savor, I told myself. Enjoy this moment of found food and shelter and the new friend who was rolling in the shimmering grass. The need overrode the goal as I turned the opened can upside down and guzzled the contents like it was a cold beer on a hot day, almost choking on the slimy beans as they slid down my throat.

I heard a whine in front of me and saw the eyes of Dog sitting there when the can lowered. He had lost all desire to roll in the grass the moment he had heard me eating. The sun shone off his patched fur that was now wet with dew. "Sorry Dog." I dropped the can into the grass in front of him and watched Dog clean it out with his rough tongue while I worked open the second can. This time, I reached my fingers into the slimy mush and pulled out a handful of red beans and sauce to slowly slurp it from my fingers. I pushed to the side of the step as Dog came and sat next to me; the clean can forgotten in the grass. I reached my fingers into the can again and held it towards him, letting his sandpaper tongue lick away the beans and sauce sitting in the cup of my hand. We took turns until the second can was empty and I let Dog clean out the remaining salty sweetness from within the metal canister. As I sat, the food pains slowly receded from my stomach and were replaced with something resembling a normal hunger. We watched the sun shift through the leaves above us and listened to the wind blow.

We couldn't sit here all day. The sky was quickly getting brighter, and I had work to do. I pushed up and looked into the darkness of the house behind me. I had to force myself to stumble back inside the rot. The door was left open as I started on the living room. Pushing the flimsy material to the side of each window to let just a bit of light in. There was a small space in the worn wood, just under the bottom glass pane. I tucked my fingers under the ridge and pulled. Nothing happened. Moved one hand so that my palm was above the bottom pane and pushed while my other hand pulled. The window shifted slightly. The worn muscles of my arms pulsated as I pushed and pulled. Suddenly it gave and the window shot up with a loud thud as it leveled with the top pane. Reluctantly I let go. It stayed in place, and I stuck my head out of the opening letting the soft breeze brush against my face before forcing each of the windows open to let the breeze push into the room and back out, pulling the rotten smell with it. Once I finished with the main room, I looked down the dark hallway towards the bedroom. I dreaded walking down that tunnel, imaging the monsters waiting for me in the shadows. But it had to be done. Forcing one foot slowly in front of the other, I walked down the hall with Dog trailing silently behind me. My breath was locked behind my throat as I slid my fingers around the doorknob and turned. The smell smacked me in the face and my eyes started watering before they even had time to adjust to the dimmed room. The sun was blocked by the same flimsy material covering the windows in the other room and the walls were untouched wood like the rest of the house. They had faded to a light orange over time. Determined… or just trying to avoid looking at the bed… I moved directly to the window and pushed the curtain back and pulled the window open. It slid easily, not allowing me more time to gather myself before the next step. My head hung out the window for a moment to clear my lungs and my mind. I breathed in and turned back towards the room, ready to take in the sight that had been waiting for me.

THE MAN DID not die naturally. He sat in his bed up against the wall with his feet straight out in front of him, like the position of someone who is reading a book. He wore what seemed like his everyday clothes: jeans, a button-down flannel shirt, brown work boots. In his right hand was a revolver. But the most apparent sign of his suicide was the blood and brain that was splattered on the wall behind his slumped head, turning it a dark ominous black in the shadowed room. The newly acquired beans were trying to force their way out of my stomach and I sucked in my breath to try to keep them from emerging. I turned from the body and quickly walked towards the door, patting my hip for Dog to follow me out of the room. Taking just a moment to grab the pair of sandals that were sitting next to the closet on my right before walking out.

I made my way back to the dead man's recliner and sat, my mind working through what this day would look like. Dog sat faithfully next to me as if he understood that I was his only living friend in this world. I hunched over and pushed the licking tongue from my face as I slid off my worn shoes and painfully tugged at my red stained socks. The raw flesh was trying to heal, and the old socks painfully pulled at the new skin as the fabric came away from my feet. I needed to clean them off but first things first. I slid my feet into the worn leather sandals, relieved that only a few of the red sores were touched and stepped outside into the carefree sweetness of nature again. I stood for a moment listening to the birds in the trees and pretending that this day was going to be different than it really was. I shook the thoughts from my mind and Dog followed me as I worked my way through the overgrown grass that engulfed this hidden cabin in the woods. I started to give up hope by the time I made it to the third side of the house. But there was what I was looking for. A wooden shed was attached to the back side of the cabin. I walked over and yanked on the small door, barely nudging it open at all. I pulled harder and it finally gave, revealing exactly what we needed. I grabbed the wood handle of the shovel and dusted the remains of webs from the shaft that now sat in my hand as well as my arm that held it. As I backed out and closed the door, I noticed a bright piece of blue peeking from behind the overgrowth on the other side of the shed. I peered around the edge of the worn wood and tried to keep my hopes from climbing as I saw the barrel with a spout leading from the roof of the cabin into the top of the plastic tub. A metal ladle hung from a rusted chain and rubbed against the bright blue side. How had it remained so bright when everything around it had rotted and rusted?

I dropped the shovel in the grass behind me and reached towards the lid. It fell to the ground as I pushed it off to the side. Waiting until just the right moment to look down into the container. Breathing quietly, as if that would determine what was in the tub. I leaned over and slowly peered into the blue. In awe, I reached both hands down into the tub and slowly cupped the cool water to my face, rubbing it against my worn skin and moaning as the water flowed through my beard. I grabbed another handful and brought it to my lips, not caring that the color was a little less than clear or it smelled like musk and dirt. The man that I had been before had cared about those things. Drinking water from a filtered container or from a new plastic water bottle to ensure it was fresh. The man who stood here now: hell, I just cared about the fact that it was water. I slurped through another handful and then with my next glistening bounty I turned to the dog that I knew would be right behind me patiently waiting. I let him lap the wetness from my hands. We took turns, filling ourselves with water before lying down in the soft weed covered ground behind the cabin. The clouds drifted lazily overhead, and we enjoyed this piece of normalcy that I had taken for granted for so many years.

Finally, I got back to my feet and grabbed the shovel from where I had tossed it aside. Glancing around me, I looked for what seemed like a good spot to start digging. I drove the shovel into the ground at my feet, stepping on the edge to get more depth, and pulled the dirt from the earth. I continued to dig, taking breaks for another handful of water or a short sit and tongue bath with Dog. The sweat ran down my face and I felt useful as I moved, making a hole in the earth with a friend by my side. The sun crossed so that it sat straight above us and then it moved over to the other side marking the entry into the afternoon. Finally, I had a hole that was deep in the ground. It was the size of a man.

Walking back into the house, I noticed that the smell of decay was stronger, even with the pull of air from the open windows. I made my way to the bedroom and pushed the door open to reveal the man there, still frozen in his last moments, alone and resigned to his fate. The sun had brightened the room as I slowly walked to the side of the bed and gazed down at the man, taking in the detail. He stared back at me, right eye white and stubborn. Left eye pointed awkwardly to the side, past the trickle of black that had made its way from the wound in his head. He looked to be in his seventies and had a slight shadow of grey hair thrown across his chin. His slack mouth was hung open revealing an almost neat row of white bottom teeth. He didn't look much different from me, probably about the same height and weight that I was now. I looked towards his hands. The revolver was clutched in his right and as I looked closer, a bit of paper sticking out of the grip that was his left. My hands moved towards his and carefully slid the crumpled paper from the unwavering grasp, managing to only create two slight tears in the words. Without reading it I carefully folded the paper and slid it into my back pocket. My eyes continued to take in details as I noticed the mess beneath him. I made my way down to his feet and tugged on his ankles, trying to pull his stubborn body down further on the bed to the part that was covered by the thick blanket. Finally, his head perched away from the wall, unmoving.

Dog was weaving around my legs whimpering at both me and at his lost owner. I shooed him away so that I didn't trip over his quivering body and pulled at the corner of the blanket that was closest to me. I pulled it straight up and then over the wooden body that sat in front of me, following with the other three corners, trying to cocoon the death inside the rough grey fabric. I leaned over and held my breath as I squeezed my arms between the rigid flesh and the crusted mattress. And I lifted the man, one arm under his back and one under his thighs, holding him like a giant stubborn baby. I walked to the door with Dog jumping around my legs trying to figure out what was happening. Turning sideways as I carried my charge from the room that saw his death, I hit his outstretched feet against the wall. "Shit. I'm sorry" I mumbled. We slowly struggled to the front of the house and down the steps and worked our way over to the hole I had made to contain this man's body. I tried to slowly creep to my knees and lower him into his grave, but the blanket slipped, and he fell into the bottom of the hole with a thud.

The blanket floated in after him and covered most of his body. One lifeless eye and the hand with the gun were exposed. I looked away in shame; I wasn't sure if it were shame for the man or for me; and reached towards the shovel that I had stuck into the mound of dirt next to the open ground. I started pushing the dirt back and tried to avoid looking at the man I was covering up. Dog crept around the opening making sounds of pure pain as I kept shoveling the black dirt into the hole. They were sounds that I hadn't heard from him yet, even in his starvation. I looked down at the cloudy eye staring at me right before it was covered with dirt and tried to ignore the truth that I saw in it, reflecting my own life. The sun was getting closer to the trees when I finished patting down the earth with the back of the shovel, and then dropped it where I stood. Limping over to the blue barrel and dipping the ladle in, drinking all its contents when it made it to my lips. I turned around to see Dog lying on the fresh mound of dirt in the ground, his chin resting on his soft paws as he looked at me with his sad brown eyes. I walked towards him tugging the piece of paper out of my back pocket. And I spoke the words of the dead man as if it were tribute or a prayer.

M –

I know you won't understand this. I know you probably will never even know this happened or find my body and this note will never find its way to your hands. I just can't live in this world any longer. I have been stranded in an island for so long. I don't know how to go on. I don't think that there will be anything after this life, but it has to be better than the pain of living each day knowing that I caused so much pain to those I loved. So much pain that no one noticed when I left or came looking for me. I felt nothing then, I was an empty shell of a human, a host.

I stopped as the word caught in my throat. I took a shaky breath in and kept reading, trying to ignore my own words reflected in this stranger's writing.

But now I feel all the pain. I have the dog and I think he loves me as much as a dog can, but once I'm gone, he'll find another human to feed him and he will shift his love and forget about me too. I wish I could have known your kids. I hope you told them that your mom loved you. I hope you told them that your dad wasn't such a horrible guy and he did the best he could. But that wouldn't be the truth and your kids deserve the truth. I hope you find happiness and forget about me – if you haven't already.

T

I folded the letter back into squares and leaned down towards the mound, trying to shake the feeling that I read a letter that could have been written by my father. Or by me. My fingers scraped against the fresh ground as I made a small hole and pushed the note into the dirt. I covered the note to bury its contents along with the man who wrote them, knowing that no one would ever find it and hold it against him. I stood and left Dog alone in his mourning as I went back into the house to start my next task.

I walked down the hall and closed the door to the bedroom. I would deal with that tomorrow. That was enough of death and decay for today. I went back to the kitchen and opened the cabinets to take inventory of what existed. There was instant coffee, cans of vegetables and soup, pots, and pans, and in the last cabinet there was a bag of kibble. Dog would be thrilled. I opened the drawers to reveal rows of utensils and one drawer filled with candles and boxes of matches. I grabbed two of the candles and a small container for them to stand in along with a box of matches. I laid them on the table next to the recliner in preparation of the deep darkness that would be brought when the sun finally fell behind the trees. I walked down the hall again and found another door. It pushed to reveal a tidy but dusty bathroom. I turned the knob in the small tub hoping that my good deed in the burial of the man would have an otherworldly result and I would be blessed with magically running water.

Not a drop. I opened the small door next to the shower and found what I was originally looking for. I grabbed the box of bandages and soap as well as a rough grey towel from the small shelf and I closed the door. Walking back towards the front of the house, I noticed another small door and pulled it open to find a reward I wasn't expecting. I was faced with folded jeans, flannel shirts, and faded grey underwear. I grabbed one of each and carried my full load with me out the front door and into the slowly fading day. Slowly, I worked my way around the house to where Dog was still lying in the dirt that housed his dead friend. I knew his eyes followed my every move to the still mostly full barrel of water as I dropped my goods to the ground.

I PULLED OFF my shirt first, not even caring that it was inside out, and tossed it on the ground reveling in the fresh air against my skin. I slowly undid the buckle of my pants and peeled the dirt-soaked jeans down my legs while slipping the leather sandals from my feet. I pulled the pants off over my right foot as I balanced on my left and then followed with the other leg, trying to ignore the searing pain coming from my feet. I tossed the stiff denim to the side watching its attempt to unsuccessfully fold to the ground. And then followed with my boxers that were no longer the soft grey they had been when the I had put them on back in that suburban home. I stood in the clearing in all my nakedness, not worrying about the brown eyes watching me from behind, just feeling the skin prickle beneath the soft breeze. I dipped the ladle into the murky water and tossed it onto my body, my skin dimpling with the coolness of it. I leaned over and dumped another ladle over my head and felt it trickle down my body as the wet strands of hair fell over my eyes. I grabbed the soap from my pile of items on the ground and started meticulously rubbing it over every spot of my skin and into my rough beard and hair, lathering every inch as I went. The soap fell into my eyes and down into the sores at my feet and stung both in different ways. I kept scrubbing away the dirt and the sticky soda and the blood. And the pain. As I ladled water over the soapy covered areas,

I saw the slack skin turn to a peach color and the darkness run down my body and back into the ground where it belonged. "Dog, it's your turn" I called. Dog looked at me wearily but stood slowly and padded over to stand obediently in front of me and we washed and lathered and rinsed all over again. Once I was done, he backed up a few steps and shook, hitting me and my pile of clean clothes with the spray. A sound came from my mouth and stopped when I realized what it was. It sounded strange: almost foreign. I couldn't remember the last time I had laughed. Dog wagged at me and jumped around in a little semi-circle and shook again. I chuckled and this time it felt good. It felt normal.

I stepped into the damp but clean pile of clothes that had belonged to the man I had buried and as I buttoned up his flannel shirt, I felt more alive than I had in years, the irony not going completely unnoticed. I sat in the grass and bandaged the sores on my feet before slipping back into the sandals and walking back into the house. My new friend walked by my side only stopping for a moment to look back at the mound of dirt with the shovel now stuck in at the head like a marker. The dirty clothes of my previous life lay in the ground to be forgotten just like the man who had worn them. The man who had been me. The night was closing in, and the sun was disappearing beyond the line of trees behind the house as I lit one of the candles that I had set out. I found two bowls and filled one with cold soup and a spoon and the other with kibble. Balancing them in one arm, I grabbed the candle with the other hand and walked out the open door into the dark night and sat on the steps. Dog sat next to me patiently waiting as I sat his dinner down in front of him and we ate, listening to the hum of crickets and the crunch of kibble. The stars and moon were gone from the sky, but the night was occasionally lit with the distant shot of lightning striking from the clouds. I hoped it would work its way in our direction and fill back up the blue barrel to replace the water that we had used today. We sat, full and tired and clean, watching the storm getting closer as the orange flicker of the candle slowly burned out.

CHAPTER FIVE

THE TEAR

EYES SHUT TO the world, but awake. Trying to delay the start of the day. I heard a slight scratch and opened my eyes to see Dog sitting by the door scratching the wood frame and watching me expectantly. "Yeah yeah, I'm awake Dog." I pushed down on the footrest of the faded recliner with my legs; shoving the orange blanket off to the side to create a pile on the floor. I stood and grabbed a shirt that had been tossed carelessly over the back of the recliner as I shuffled to the closed door and pulled it open to let Dog run outside to relieve himself. He circled for a moment as I slid my head through the hole in the cotton before walking away from the open doorway and towards the kitchen. I grabbed the dented pot that I had filled with water the night before, turned the nob on the front of the stove, and struck a match to light the small burner. I discovered three propane tanks on day two and found that it was relatively simple to get one hooked up to the stove once I worked my way through the faded instructions written on the back. I stood, trying to wake up, as I watched the water slowly start to steam and create tiny bubbles along the bottom of the pot. I turned and grabbed the small coffee cup that I had claimed as mine and poured some of the heated water into it trying not to let it slosh out the other side. My hand wrapped around the glass container of instant coffee and as I dug the spoon down into the gravel, I realized that the container was almost empty. The metal spoon hit the bottom of the glass and I stood for a moment looking at what could maybe make two more mornings. A sigh escaped my lips.

Something nudged me from behind and I dropped the grounds into my cup and stirred, letting the steam become aromatic before I turned to the brown eyes patiently waiting for his breakfast. I pulled the kibble from the bottom cabinet and filled Dog's bowl watching a few stray pieces scatter around on the floor. There was another bowl sitting on the counter and I grabbed it to place it on the ground next to the first. The second bowl was filled with water and Dog went back and forth between the two as if he was still starving. I sipped my coffee and watched my friend; noticing that I could no longer see the bones that covered his lungs, and his fur was growing even thicker.

I walked over to the open door and sat on the top step listening to the breeze work its way through the trees surrounding me. The coffee warmed my body and I sat in peace. Somehow in my time here, I had yet to see another soul seeking asylum in these woods. The dead man must have made sure of that when he came here. His private and hidden cabin in the woods. He must have owned the land; no one came looking for past payments or debt owed. I didn't even know places like this still existed in our overcrowded world. I sat quiet, breathing in the air, putting my arm around Dog after he finished his breakfast and came to join me. He eventually got bored and ran out into the grass, rolling in it and chomping at the weeds, checking every few rolls to make sure I still sat there watching his fun. It had become a comfortable routine. One that I knew had come to an end. This wasn't where I was meant to be. It was just a short reprieve from the hell that had preceded it. Today would be a good day for us to prepare. I investigated the sky and saw the clouds rolling in. A storm was coming.

I finished my coffee and stood at the top step, wanting to spend more time watching Dog have his fun, but I was just delaying the necessity of the day. I turned to the little house and walked back towards the bedroom. The room now smelled of soap and no longer held the sight of death. I still couldn't bring myself to sleep on the bed, but I did enter the room to see what I could discover from the man who had died here. Now the bed was made with a clean sheet to cover the stains and there sat a duffel bag that I had pulled from a closet just days before. It held a mound of extra shirts, socks, and underwear. I dug through its contents and pulled out the pile of bills that I had found scattered and hidden around the home and added to my meager bills. I sat on the edge of the bed and opened the stack of cash to count. The pile now totaled over a hundred dollars. I looked towards the ceiling as I heard the rain start to hit against the roof. Dog would be a mess. I put the money on the bed and stood to go find him. By the time that I reached the front door the rain was coming down hard and I saw Dog running around the clearing trying to catch drops in between his teeth. "Dog come on – inside time now," I called to him. He ran to me, tail wagging, and shook the water off while only still being halfway outside. The inside half splattered the walls and windows with sweet and musky water. I laughed and fell to the floor, covered in a wriggling and wet Dog as he licked my face. This must be what "happy" feels like.

WE SPENT THE day working together to search the final nooks and crannies of the house, making sure we weren't missing anything that we could use in the upcoming weeks or months. The cans in the cabinets were down to just a dozen and six of those went into the duffel bag, two were saved for tonight, and the rest would remain in the cabinets for the next hungry soul who might find this house and in need of saving grace for a night or two. I took three of the long candles and two boxes of matches and folded them into the clothes of the bag to keep them safe. As we worked the rain pummeled the house from above as if to remind me that I have shelter here and should stay. But I knew it was lying to me. I lit another candle and poured some of the wax on the table next to the recliner before pushing the unlit end down. Letting it harden and make a permanent spot for the new candle. The main room stayed lit as I took the other candle and went back to the bathroom. My feet were now healed into rough scars, but I grabbed the remaining bandages knowing that there would be a time soon that they were raw again. I went back into the bedroom and pushed the box of bandages down into the duffel along with the sandals before walking back to the living room and sinking into the recliner with Dog jumping faithfully to my lap. We sat and thought as my hand made its way lazily back and forth across the soft brown fur. Finally, I stood, shooing Dog to the floor, and made us some dinner. Soup for me and kibble for the dog. I took my time eating and realized this might be my last warm meal for a bit as I slurped the broth in silence, the candlelight flickering against the walls.

I finished the warm soup and rinsed the bowl leaving it drying in the sink. Falling back down into the recliner, I pulled the lever to raise my feet and blew out one of the candles. Leaving the other to dance orange through the room as I pulled the blanket up over me and drifted into a dreamless sleep, lulled by the sound of Dog's soft snores next to me.

THE NEXT MORNING, I woke, just as I did each morning before it. I sat on the front step staring at the water dripping from the trees and the clouds floating away into the brightening sky. Dog rolled and jumped through the grass. I sat for longer than any morning that had preceded it and my bones groaned when I finally stood to go back into the house for the last time. I walked towards the bathroom after grabbing the scissors I had found in the kitchen drawer and undressed in the tiny room. I stopped and stared at myself in the mirror. I no longer looked like the stranger from the suburban home. Now I looked like a different stranger. Worn and dark with a beard and hair speckled with grey. My skin clung to the bones beneath my face. But those eyes. The eyes were the same hollow that they seemed to have always been. How had none of the recent laughter made it to those strange eyes? I picked up the metal shears in my right hand and held the hair straight up as I started to hack at it. It wasn't anything to be proud of but at least it would stay out of my face for a while. I looked at my beard and grabbed a chunk with my left fist, but the scissors stopped short. No. Not yet. I sat the scissors down on the ceramic sink with a little ting and stepped into the bathtub next to a bucket. The bucket had been filled a few days ago and I grabbed it with both hands and lifted the water over my body, the skin dimpling under the fresh coldness. Soap and lather followed, washing away the final stray hairs from my hack job of a haircut and the minimal dirt that had built since my last bath. Once I was clean and rinsed, I stepped out of the bath and patted myself off with one of the grey towels, a rougher version of the grey towel that had existed in my past. I shook my head to rid myself of the thoughts of a previous life that kept sneaking up on me. A life I barely recognized. Towel wrapped around my waist, I walked over to the bedroom and put on the clean clothes that I had laid out the day before. Jeans and undershirt on. Flannel over the top. Socks and shoes over my calloused feet. I looked down at the shoes, the only thing I had owned prior to finding this house. They had been scrubbed and cleaned and now just had a slight off-color to them. I grabbed the open duffel bag and closed the door behind me. I could still hear Dog jumping around the front of the house when I sat the bag on the recliner. I pulled the money out of the pocket of the bag and slid two tens into the back pocket of my jeans. I stuffed the rest of it down in a clean sock roll to hide it from the world. Working my way over to the kitchen I grabbed the bag of kibble from the cabinet and worked it into the remaining space in my bag. One final walkthrough making sure I had put everything away and zipped up my bag. Leaning over the kitchen counter I peered out into the yard and watched Dog running around without a care in the world. I grabbed the pen and the scrap of paper I left on the counter and started my rough note.

To anyone who finds this home –

I found it in a time of need. It became a haven. I left you food in the cabinets and candles in the drawer. If you need water – there is a bin out back that catches the rain. If you are looking for the man who used to live here, he is gone, died in his sleep and he is buried in the back yard beneath the shovel. There is nothing of value in this house if you are looking for something to steal.

I put the note on the end table and put a can of beans on the corner of the paper so it wouldn't be swept away some night and never found. I had thought about how I would share the news of the death of the man if his family ever did come looking for him and found this hidden spot. As soon as they dug him up, they would know that my letter told lies. But if they left him where he lay, they might be able to move on to the next day thinking that he died in peace, and it might give them a feeling of comfort. The strap of the duffel bag went heavily over my head and dug into my shoulder as I took one last look back down the hallway towards the room that shone orange in the sun before walking out into the day and pulling the door behind me.

Dog stood looking at me, frozen in a playful stance and ready to pounce on me if I said the right words. I looked at his eyes and he stood straighter, solemn as if he knew that we were being serious today. He ran over to stand by my side, and I rubbed his head and looked down on him. "Ready Dog? "He wagged his tail in response. I started walking towards the edge of the trees in the direction that I knew the highway sat, Dog stepping quietly by my side. We stepped into the dark cover of the forest, and I resisted the urge to look back at the clearing that had once been so frightening. I had a new fear that if I looked, I would immediately go running back to its safety with Dog at my heels. Time to push forward. I was ready to restart to this journey and this time I was better prepared and had more accurate expectations. I felt something that almost reminded me of confidence. I kept working my way in the direction of the highway.

I didn't remember the trek in taking nearly this long. I had to be going the right way, right? I couldn't see the sun above me. What if I was going the wrong way? Were there enough woods to get lost in? I spun around trying to get my bearings and noticed that Dog was no longer trailing behind me. The panic of my location was immediately lost and replaced by a new panic as I tried to think of when I saw him last. He was walking next to me into the forest. Are there animals here? No, I would have heard him if he was attacked. I turned around again and yelled "DOG?" Nothing. "DOG COME HERE!" Not a sound. I started running back towards the direction of the clearing, the bag banging against my side. My foot caught on an upturned branch and sent me sprawling against the leaf covered ground. I waited for the padded steps and the rough kisses on my cheek to say 'don't worry. I'm here. You just didn't see me.' Nothing came. I jumped to my feet and ignored the searing pain that began to rip through my knee as I continued to run shouting for Dog, the duffel trying to knock me over again as it slammed into my side. I neared the clearing and burst through the trees scanning the ground for the sight of the brown fur. I saw no sign of him and looked towards the cabin. The door was still shut. I ran around the side slipping on the damp grass.

I stopped suddenly; the bag hitting my backside and knocking me forward another step. There was Dog. Lying on the uneven mound of earth that he had ignored since the first day we created it. His chin was resting on his crossed paws and his big eyes looked up at me. He didn't lift his head even as his tail faintly moved across the ground. "Jesus Dog, you scared the shit out of me. It's time to go," I patted my hip. The tail thudded the soft ground, but he made no other movement. I pulled the bag strap over my head and dropped it on the ground next to me before slowly walking over to the mound to sink into the grass in front of him. "Dog?" It wasn't really a question. It was a plea. It contained my life in that one syllable. Don't leave me. Don't do this. I'm alone too. Can't we just go together and at least not be alone. Thud thud thud. The tail continued its slow motion against the ground. We sat and stared at each other and without another word I knew what he meant to do. I reached out my hand and patted the top of his head rubbing across the spot at his right ear that he liked. He finally lifted his head just enough to wrap his tongue around my fingers in a sloppy goodbye. I leaned forward and put my forehead against his and we looked into each other's eyes, each seeing the pain that we had forgotten for the short while in our time together.

I stood up and walked back over to the duffel bag. I opened it and grabbed the kibble from it before moving around the house and up the steps to push open the door. My note fluttering on the table. I pulled all the bowls from the shelf and filled them with the remaining water from the bucket in the kitchen then picked up the bag of kibble and turned it to pour all the pellets on the floor of the kitchen in the furthest corner. I picked up the pen from earlier this morning and went over to the note and added a line to the bottom of it.

If the dog is still here – please take care of him – he is a good dog and a good friend. He doesn't bite.

I left the pen sitting next to the paper, made sure that it was still secure beneath the can and walked back out the front door, this time leaving it open just enough for Dog to make it through. He might need shelter or would come in here looking for food and water. I just hoped he wouldn't eat it all at once. I walked back around the house to see him still in the same spot with his big eyes watching me as I picked up my bag and threw it over my shoulder. It felt heavier, even without the bag of kibble in it. I looked back once to see his head back on his paws and his tail thudding quietly. The dead man had been wrong. He hadn't been alone. The dog wouldn't forget about him. But maybe he would forget about me.

I WALKED BACK the same trail I had run just a short while ago. More solemn and less assured of my steps. I could hear every leaf rustle and the breath going in and out of my lungs. I breathed quietly so that I could listen for the padded steps running up behind me. The steps that I knew would never come. Finally, the trees cleared, and I saw the flimsy wire attempting to block my path in or out. I stepped over it, pain shooting through my leg as I bent it over. I made it over the fence, and I looked down at my knee, remembering my sprawl against the ground. There was a bit of dark red soaking through the denim. Not a lot though so it couldn't be that bad. Most likely just a decent cut. The numbness crept back into my mind as I stared at the dark spot. It had been a while since it had taken over, but there it was. I looked in front of me and continued to walk towards the sound of the highway; lacking the desire to stop and clean up my knee. Knowing if I stopped, I would run back to the little hidden cabin and the brown beast that guarded it and never leave again. I struggled a bit trying to climb the damp grassy hill leading up into the road, but I finally made it to the gravel. It seemed like a different life when I was last standing here, sweating, dirty, and looking at the blood on my feet and the sticky soda running down my front. I adjusted my bag and stuck out my upturned thumb at the truck that was getting closer. Whoosh. Right by me. I looked down the road and saw another car coming and left my thumb out knowing that this could take a while.

I saw the hand sticking out of the passenger window and the pimply teen behind the wheel and I braced for a hit with a cold drink. I refused to stand down and left my hand upturned towards the car. The empty hand waved, and the car slowed as it pulled into the gravel, sending puffs of grey dust up from behind the tires. I walked over, pulling the bag over my head and tossing it into the backseat, sliding in behind it. Two pimply faces turned back towards me and grinned nice enough.

"Where ya going stranger?" teen one asked in a deep voice, obviously trying to sound older than his face let on.

"Nowhere in particular, where are you guys going?"

"The city" teen two said, as if I knew what that meant.

"OK, great by me."

"What's your name?"

I lied without hesitation, "My friends call me J."

"Welcome Jay! We should be there in about two or three hours I think."

Both teens turned back around, and the driver floated back into the road and picked up speed as the other kid started jabbing the buttons in the console looking for a song. I watched the trees of the little home fade away with my friend hidden in their depths as an unexpected tear made a path down my face.

CHAPTER SIX

THE DRESS

I SAT ON a wooden bench that someone had attempted to create for lounging comfortably. At least for ten minutes at a time. Stuffed in between two of the wood pieces next to me was a cigarette butt. I looked a little closer and shook my head. No. There wasn't enough left to get anything good out of it, so I left it stranded; a reminder of the smoker who sat here before me. I looked up at the green leaves that sprawled over my head hiding the bench from the hot sun above. There was a musical giggle and I turned towards the sound. A small child was running across the pavement with a woman trailing behind pushing an empty stroller that was the size of a small car. Bags were folded and pushed into every available space with only the small spot remaining for the child to sit in once her legs were tired. Brown hair shining in the sunlight; the child ran past me and over to the small man-made ravine. She ran to the edge and stuck the toe of her little pink plastic shoe into the water before squealing and jumping back. Again, inching forward, she stuck her foot in further this time, laughing and jumping back. She turned to make sure the woman was seeing all the fun that she was having. She did this a few more times before seeming to become bored. A determined look came over her small face only a short second before she jumped into the shallow water with both feet. The water barely came to her knees, but the splash was great, and the girl stopped laughing to turn and run back to the woman, crying about the water on the lace of her dress. The woman laughed and looked over in my direction. Our eyes met and she gave a little smile. I smiled back as if we shared some silent connection about kids being kids. Behind her eyes I saw a flicker of something as she took in my appearance before she looked away.

I moved my gaze over to the table that sat across the pavement from me. Two men were involved in a serious chess game with other men watching and providing occasional support. This had been going on for about an hour already and the game had increased intensity. One bystander whispered in one into another's ear and made a sweeping motion at the board while the player moved a knight to a new space on the board. Every few minutes a stray person would stop for a moment and watch or take a photo of the group or ask a question. But otherwise, they were in their own world of serious battle. I could see the younger of the two players getting heated for a moment as his ears turned slightly pink and he furrowed his brows at the board before making a hasty move that made the other men laugh.

Beyond the group of men was a crowd of people, getting on or off one of the tour boats that floated lazily as they got into line next to the park. The people in this group looked to be mostly made up of families. Annoyed looking parents tugging on kids' arms. Kids screaming about one thing or another. Adults talking to their partners in hushed angry tones or jabbing at a map. All standing in the middle of the sidewalk not paying attention to the chess game or water sports. Most of them had wide Canon or Sony straps holding their cameras around their necks. Announcing to the world that they were visiting here and didn't belong. Just like me. Although I hoped I was more private about it. I watched as the families slowly walked in an organized line to enter one of the large red boats that floated, waiting. Other families slowly joined another line to climb onto one of the red busses that stood patiently on the street. A few people in the lines would laugh. The others continued to look confused or frustrated. And all kept wiping at the sweat that was running down their faces.

The water of the river slapped lazily along the side of the wood planks that held up the park on this pier. It was a peaceful sound that almost couldn't be heard above the people talking and babies crying. The water was a matted grey that couldn't even reflect the blue that shone down from the sky. But the seagulls didn't seem to mind. They flew overhead, taking a moment to dip into the water before they would come back to the cement or wood and chase the scraps of food tossed from the people eating around me. I watched as two birds fought over the remains of a hotdog on the ground and saw the little girl standing next to me as she watched too, the damp dress forgotten in her fascination with the battle of the large birds. She lost her hesitation and stomped over to them, clapping her little hands, and giggling as they flew off in panic and left their food to be stolen by another once the threat of human child subsided.

I looked to the left where kids and adults ran over the cement and through water that shot without rhyme or reason out of small holes in the ground. All the water would shoot up out of the cement in a circle and fall back to earth splashing people who were trying to cool down in the warm afternoon sun. The adults would laugh like children at their damp clothes and the kids hunched down and stared at the holes in anticipation of the next untimed shoot of water. Some of the kids were braver than others and would get splashed in the face when the water finally decided to show again. Then everyone would laugh and run around again waiting for the following splash to come. I watched the water come out of half of the holes, arch at the top and come back down and I found myself smiling at the laughter that followed. The simple pleasure of a fountain in the heat.

I felt a nudge at my hand and looked down. The little girl stood in front of me, trying to push a rock into my fist. She pushed her tangled hair out of her face with one dirt-streaked little hand and looked up at me with big brown eyes. I opened my hand and accepted the gift. She smiled and ran back to her mom, peeking out at me from behind her safety net. The mom either didn't notice that the girl had wandered over here or was doing her best to not make eye contact again. I looked down at the hard surface in my palm and saw a perfectly smoothed grey rock. Where did she find this? I looked at the ground around the ravine and the bench but couldn't find any others. I rubbed my thumb across the smooth surface and then shoved it into the front pocket of me jeans, ignoring the fact that it almost reminded me of a rock that I had seen before. The girl grinned at me from behind her mother's arm as I looked her direction and thanked her with a smile and a nod. Such a strange kid. She must have brought the rock from home with her. She didn't find it around here.

I looked backed towards the fountains and saw a girl standing next to the fountain in a blue dress. She pulled out a small yellow camera from her bag and handed it to the man standing next to her, then posed. Snap, he took a photo, and the camera made a whirring sound. Pose again. Snap. Whir. Pose again. Snap. Whir. The wind blew and her skirt exposing her legs. She laughed and snap, he took another photo. Pose. Snap… there was no whir. Her smile frozen on her face. Her dress held by the air that had stopped blowing. Frozen.

Everyone. The people playing in the fountain, the girl with a thousand photos, the families looking at their maps, the chess players, even the water in the air. They froze and faded into silent grey. The stillness deafened in my ears as I seemed to be the only thing that was moving in this moment. Calm swept over me as quickly as the quiet did.

I SAW HER. She wove in between the groups of people, smiling at the maps in their hands and the kids playing on the ground. She looked up at the sun and closed her eyes for a moment, like a cat sunning herself in the warmth. She stood there for a moment, and I sat watching her, not breathing or making a sound. I turned my head to see a man stuck in time, in the air as he had jumped down from a bench. I looked back at the woman, the only other one unaffected by this moment frozen in time. She worked her way past the chess players and bent over, grinning, before she moved the white queen. She walked towards my spot on the bench and leaned over the metal railing to watch the water stopped mid-lap against the side. She stood on the bottom rail and the back strap of her sandal slipped off her heel as she closed her eyes again taking in the quiet and the heat. She stepped down and adjusted her sandal and then turned away from me. Walked past the line waiting to get on the boat, her orange dress moving against her calves. And she was gone.

I grabbed my bag and jumped to my feet as everything slowly came back to normal and the people around me resumed their activity as if nothing had just happened. I stood on the bench, scanning for the top of her dark head but seeing nothing. I must have dozed off or passed out. Had a dream. I heard an exclamation from the chess players. One of them was blaming the other for moving his queen. Shit. I jumped down from the bench and ran in the direction that she had disappeared. People yelled behind me as I shoved past the line of people waiting to tour the river. I made it to the other side and saw no sign of orange in the form of a dress or anything else. Where could she have gone? She was just here. I know it. Right? I was walking quickly towards the path that followed along with the river. She must have gotten in a car or a cab or something. To be gone this quickly, that would be the only explanation. It's for the best anyway. What would I have said to her if I would have found her? "Excuse me; did you see the time stop? Weird, huh?" Yeah, that would have gone over well. I tried to shake the fog from my head. She was gone. And so was the moment.

NOT WANTING TO go back to my semi-comfortable spot on the bench, I decided to walk further into the city. There was twenty dollars in my pocket and more in my bag. I should grab a beer, try to shake this feeling. This uncomfortable fog weighed my mind, like I was trying to make sense of something that wasn't meant to make sense. I walked up the street and away from the river, noticing very little on my walk except for the littered ground beneath my feet and the smell of fresh shit drifting from the corners of the sidewalk. I kept walking, forgetting to look for a bar and just thinking about the orange dress. Did I know her? I feel like I should know her, but she was a stranger to me. Maybe my subconscious was trying to tell me something in this strange dream. It was a dream... wasn't it? I was almost thrown back as a man ran into me not looking up from his phone or even glancing at the person he just ran into. Just kept walking. I looked at the people swerving around me not looking at anyone or anything around them. I kept walking forward towards the corner of the street, neon lights flashing at me in the dimming day. The sun was creeping to hide behind the buildings and the wind started to cool my arms. I stepped to side out of the way of the onslaught of foot traffic and unzipped my bag to pull out a flannel shirt. Awkwardly holding the bag in one hand I worked the sleeve up over my right arm and up onto my shoulder before rolling the sleeve up to my elbow. I switched the bag to my right hand and covered my left arm before continuing to head toward the walk symbol on the corner of the street. I stared at it for a moment – a man frozen mid-walk. His little white leg started to move as if he were going to take a real step. I closed my eyes before looking at the cement below him. I saw the amount of people on this sidewalk and turned right to avoid more people while I walked.

I took a left and jogged across the road to find myself in a street lined with trees and brick houses. It was as if I was immediately thrown into a different world as I continued to walk, paying close attention to the jagged edges of the broken cement; the grass sticking up between the chunks of stone. Pay attention, I told myself as I tried not to get lost in my mind again.

Focus. Focus on the sidewalk laid out in front of me. It took a minute before I realized that the street was quiet. The people seemed to have disappeared into their homes, happily greeting their families before a warm dinner or a cold drink. I stopped on the sidewalk and turned towards the buildings next to me. My eyes slowly scanned up the building and I found myself looking at a long dead man as he stared down at me. Judging me. I was standing in front of an old grey brick church. The color was coming from lights within, flickering against the stained glass of the man on the cross. His eyes didn't look sad as they stared into me, a drop of blood trailing red from the thorns at his head. His arms stretched and thin against the cross. What is he thinking as he watches me? This man made of glass and paint.

I jumped a little when something nudged my knee. I looked down looked into brown eyes framed by dark fur. I knew those eyes. "Dog," I gasped in shock. But then I saw the leash and the owner of the dog as he pulled it away from me with an apologetic look. Not Dog. Just a replica. A shell that looked like Dog. I sighed and glanced back up at the eyes of the glass man before turning back towards the far corner of the street.

My breath caught. I saw orange fabric and a foot covered in a thin sandal fade out of view as she turned the corner. My heart thudded against my chest, and I ran away from the quiet sidewalk and the dog that wasn't Dog. Instead to the apparition as if I was possessed. The end of the block seemed to get further and further away the faster I ran. I was out of breath by the time I finally got to the corner where she had been, and I turned right expecting to see her standing there waiting for me. There was no one in the darkening street. Just another row of houses and dark shops. Only one that had a light and a neon sign in the window that announced 'Budweiser.' She must be in there. She must. There is nothing else open in this damn street. I walked over in long strides and pulled open the heavy wood door to the music and bustling noise of the after-work crowd. The realization that I couldn't have really seen her hit me. Why would I have thought that anyway. She was a dream. A fuckery of my own mind sent to mess with me. Screw this. I walked over to the bar, sat my duffel bag down and perched on a worn bar stool that had seen its days of drunks.

BY MY THIRD beer, I had a decent buzz and had almost forgotten about the woman in the orange dress or the dog that wasn't Dog or the rock that had found its way tucked into my pocket. I sat and listened to the music playing in the background and the vapid discussions happening next to me while a man tried to impress a woman with his self-professed prowess in life. I knew assholes like this guy before. But listening to him, here and now, when my life had changed so drastically, it just made me laugh. Now he was trying to tell her all about how much money he made without mentioning a figure. His boat and his apartment and his… She just sipped on her drink and responded with an occasional "mm hmm." Finally, I couldn't keep it in anymore.

I laughed. Loudly. It must have been the third beer. I don't think I can handle my beer anymore. They both turned to me sitting on the stool next to her and while he looked annoyed, she grinned and turned her body towards mine. "Wanna buy me a drink?" Interesting. The beard and dark light must have suited me. While I knew that this would deplete the funds in my pocket and I would have to draw from reserve that lay in the sock in my bag, I agreed to save her from continued monotonous conversation and a hopeful reprieve from talking to myself in my head. The asshole walked away as we talked about non-personal useless subjects, and he looked back once with a glare. Another two beers later I was drunk. It was time to go. I needed to find a spot for me to hole up in for the night that was out of site and safe to allow me to nurse the inevitable hangover that would come in the morning. I apologized and wished the woman luck as she wandered over to a group of eligible looking men. I reached down and fumbled with the zipper on my bag, pulled out the full roll of socks and struggled to locate the extra cash. I finally found it and pulled out the stack as the bartender brought my bill. Shit.

That took a lot of my money. What was I thinking? I chastised myself as I put just over the total on the bar and shoved the rest of it, along with the socks back into the bag. I slung the bag over my head and pushed through the new crowd of people towards the door before the bartender could see the minimal amount left there for him.

I pulled the door, but it didn't budge. I sat confused for a second until I remembered and pushed at it, letting it swing heavily open into the thick night. I stumbled outside and walked a few steps. The dark pavement shone against the streetlights from above. The cool air hit my face. The scent of fresh urine. I only remembered. a moment of that street before something smashed across the back of my head. The warmth that followed from the blood was replaced by the sidewalk quickly coming up to greet me before everything turned to black.

CHAPTER SEVEN

THE SILENCE

MY LEFT EYE slowly opened, and I slammed it back shut as the sunlight bounced around the room blinding me and sending a searing pain through my head. I startled myself as I let out a deep and involuntary groan. Where was I? I tried to think back to the last moment I remembered. My eyes opened slowly as my arm moved up to block the light. I remembered that I walked into a bar. I had been talking to a woman. What else happened? I slowly moved my arm from my eyes and as I squinted and realized that it must be morning because the hazy light was turning the room a pale orange as the sun rose and pushed its way into the small room. My eyes started to focus, and I could see a white sheet directly in front of me. Beyond that a silver gate trapped me on this uncomfortable mattress. The wall further away started to come into view and

I could see a faintly textured beige wall. I think that is the right word for the color. Beige. The most arbitrary color that could be chosen for a wall if someone is trying to not pick white. Or off-white, I suppose. More was coming back to me. There had been a man who had been talking to the woman. He had seemed pretty pissed when I drew her attention. That's right. I focused on the faded orange couch beneath the window. It looked rough and uncomfortable to sit it. Just the right couch to put in a room to make sure that no one stays too long. I followed the lines of the rough fabric with my eyes and slowly started to drift back out.

I had drunk too much and spent too much of my money. My money. My eyes shot open. Where was my money? I rolled onto my back and sat up in the narrow bed and I almost fell back over from the pain in my head. My right hand shot up to my head, stopped only by the slight pull at the crook of my elbow. I looked down and saw a small bandage with a tube flowing out of… or maybe into… my vein. I followed the clear fluid filled tube with my eyes. Down over the side of the bed and through the prison bars then back up to a hanging bag where the clear liquid dripped. Drip. Drip. I had walked out of the bar and into the night. I think. Then… oh. I reach my left hand up this time and when I made it to my forehead, I felt a cloth surrounding my head tightly, my hair sticking out in all directions. My fingers slowly felt their way to around the bandage to the back of my head and when they found their mark, I yanked them away in pain. The cloth felt hard there and a little sticky.

I looked down by my left hand and saw a little remote with a red button stating "help." Well, if anyone needed help, it was me. And where was my fucking money? I scanned the room but saw no sign of any of my belongings. I pushed the button and waited while the sun brightened the room and I started to notice the scuffs in the beige wall. I pushed the button again and craned my neck to listen for the sound of footsteps walking my way. What kind of shitty hospital was this? Was this a hospital? I sat and waited and finally pushed the button repeatedly like an impatient person pushing the up button to call an elevator when they are late for a meeting. Like I think I used to do. No one came. I looked down at my right arm and grasped the piece of the tube that I could see before it hid under the bandage. I slid it out slowly like they show you on TV shows. It stung. They don't show that in the TV shows. Probably because in the grand scheme of being shot, no one gives a shit about a little needle in the arm. A small line of blood followed the needle out from under the tape that was holding it in place. I rubbed it away with my thumb and it was replaced by a smear of red pointing down towards my wrist. I stared at the mark of arrow shaped blood and tried to think back to a whisper about my walk in the city that was disappearing from my mind. Something that I had lost. Was it my bag? No. I had my bag in the bar. I pushed at the prison railing that was trying to hold me to this bed and turned so my legs were hanging over the side. There was a breeze against my back, and I realized that if someone would answer my push call for help right now, they would have a full view of my handsome rear end under this flimsy thing they must call a robe. I grinned a little at the thought of being able to moon someone without even trying to do so and looked down at the bare legs that were dangling off the side of the bed, not even reaching the floor. Those were not my socks. They were thick grey wool socks that went up to my calves and warmed my feet. I wondered whose socks those were. I also felt faintly happy that I didn't wake up with a tube installed to help me piss but now I had a sudden and urgent need to find the bathroom. I pushed myself from the bed and steadied for a moment as my vision faded to black and then came back to color. Slowly shuffling to the open door of the fluorescent lit bathroom in the new socks. Good sliding socks. The pain in my head stabbed me again every time I moved with any motion that was less than smooth. So, I slid in my new socks like I was learning how to ice skate. Arms out to steady myself. Right foot slide. Left foot slide. Finally, my eyes narrowed as I entered the white room and made it over to the sink and looked at my reflection.

I STARED BACK at the mirror in horror. There were dried streaks of orange across my swollen face. I was so concentrated on the pain in the back of my head I hadn't even realized that there should have been pain around my right eye and cheekbone, which were already a nice eggplant purple. My beard was crusty with what must have been my own blood and I could see more dried into the hair around the white headband when I turned to inspect the sides of my battered face. I reached my hands up to poke at my cheek and watched the finger sized circle fade back to purple from white.

I slid over to the toilet and used the silver bar to help me lower to the seat and started to feel each pain in my face as I sat relieving my bladder. I pulled myself back up from the stool and slid out of the room, not even bothering to flush. I needed to get out of here. I saw a clipboard hanging at the foot of the hospital bed and yanked it towards me focusing on the line that lists the name. John Doe. That's me, right? What was my name? Jay? John? I turned around and saw the closet with doors. Ah Ha. This would be where my bag was. I opened the door. No bag. The panic started to rush over me like a wave. I slid around the room searching for my bag that contained everything in my life. I needed that bag. I couldn't be alone again. I looked by the orange couch and in all the corners of the room. No bag. Defeated, I slid back over to the closet and pulled out the only things that were sitting lonely in the bottom. The clothes I remembered wearing last. The flannel was now hard with dried blood at the back but overall, they were in good shape.

I slid back into the blinding bathroom and shut the toilet lid to lay the folded clothes down as I surveyed the objects sitting on the sink waiting for me. Put there by some nice hospital staff that had now decided to take a coffee break along with everyone else in this god-forsaken place. I picked up the dull scissors and pulled a tuft of matted and hard fur away from my chin and cut into it. I kept going until I was left with just short stubble on my chin. It might not have been the best idea. It brought more attention to the beating I had received from the asshole that jumped me and probably stole my bag... maybe the beating had been from the cement... honestly, I wasn't sure. But it did make me look less menacing and it erased the extra iron from my face that would have been a bitch to rinse out. I picked up the small canister of shaving cream and put it back down. There was no reason to go that far. I reached my hands up and slowly started unwrapping the bandage that was around my head. Once it was bare, I reached back and felt the pointy edges of the stitches I knew would be there. The bow at the back of my neck was easy to untie and the thin fabric slid from my shoulders and fluttered to the ground. I turned on the shower and stepped into the mist once I could feel the heat. The blood washed from my hair and face; working carefully to miss the wound at the back of my head. I watched the water circle the drain, first red, and then brown, then eventually clear. The steam worked lazily across the ceiling and disappeared from the small room. I wanted to stay here forever. "You can't," I whispered to myself just below the drum of the water. I turned the faucet off and stepped out of the shower to grab the towel and pat myself dry while looking in the mirror again and noticing a slight improvement. A bit more human. Had a way to go though. I slowly slid into my slightly dirty but only clothes and as I pulled my jeans over my legs, I felt something in the pocket. Something that hadn't been stolen from me. My heart started to rise as I pulled the worn grey stone from the pocket. It felt lighter than I remembered. I rubbed it a few times. Maybe for luck but it felt like habit. And shoved it back down into my pocket as I finished getting dressed. I pushed my new socks into the back pocket of my jeans and pulled on my old everyday ones.

I moved slowly, my head still throbbing but now a little less, to the door of the room. No one ever came after the manic pushing of the little red "help" button. The button probably didn't work or was disconnected but I just wanted to get out of here. I needed to be careful. I wanted to stay lost. I pulled the door open without a creak and stuck my head into the hall. The hazy sun lit hall was quiet. Almost like a dream. I slowly shuffled from the room, waiting for someone to pounce or run around a corner and spot me. No one came. The hall was only filled with ghosts. I started walking towards a sign in the distance that shouted a red 'EXIT.' Look normal. Act normal. Just in case. What the hell was going on in this place? Where was everyone? I peeked in the first room I passed since the door was flung wide open. The bed was made. The room was empty. So was the next one. And the next one. I kept working my way down the hall, occasionally reaching out to the beige textured wall for support. I peeked into the next room as I walked past, having to turn back around when it finally reached my brain that there was someone laying in that bed. I froze and tried to collect myself. Maybe this person knew what was going on here. But maybe they didn't and there is no reason to get them all worked up. Deep breath in. Long sigh out. I turned into the room and stopped. Suddenly, I could not move forward towards the small woman who was lying in the bed. My breath caught in my throat, and I found a panic washing over me, this time from a lack of being able to control the movement of my own feet as I stared at the sleeping woman in the bed across from me. Had I seen her before? She seemed familiar. Maybe she was someone famous. Before I knew what I was doing, I was drifting towards her. Not walking or moving. Drifting. Being pulled through the thick air. Suddenly I was standing over her staring at the woman that I didn't know, mesmerized by the shape of her nose and the hair that was flowing around her on the pillow. I looked down and saw the clear tube that was flowing out of her right arm and the thick band that covered her left. I tried to reach out towards the band, but I was still frozen, as if I was in a dream. Or a nightmare. So close to being able to read the name that is printed there. But I couldn't move my toes or my fingers. My arms or my legs. I found that I could turn my head and I looked over at her opened closet to saw an orange dress hanging there. It was a familiar hue of orange, like the couch that was sitting back in the room I had come from. I stared at the dress and tried to place where else I had seen that orange. I had seen it. Hadn't I?

KASSIE J RUNYAN

I HEARD A noise that pierced into my heart and made my stomach drop. I looked over at the machine that was plugged in next to the strange woman and watched the straight line as the flat sound bounced around my brain. I found that I could suddenly move, and I turned to rush out the door and into the empty hallway. I shouted for help as I awkwardly ran down the hall back towards the room I woke up in, my hand catching against the wall to try to keep me upright.

"HELP!"

I turned a left and right and another right and I reached a desk with only those damn ghosts sitting behind it. There was no one. I had to save her. The thought was pounding in my head harder than the pain. I had to save her. I turned around and ran back the way I had come from, occasionally rebalancing against the wall to keep from losing my footing and falling to the ground. Save. Her. It shouted against the pain in my head. I finally made it back to the room and I rushed towards the bed where the woman was dying. Is dead. What could I do to help? I felt a panic rush over to me as I stared at the machine. I thought I could try CPR. I thought that was the only logical thing to do. I had seen it on television. I reached my hands out to her face to block the air from her nose as I bent down, ready to blow life back into her lungs. I looked down at her face and I froze, right hand inches from her nose, my face above her face. I saw her lifeless eyes staring back at me.

Out of the face of my mother that I could barely remember.

CHAPTER EIGHT

THE NURSE

MY LEFT EYE slowly opened, and I slammed it back shut as the sunlight bounced around the room blinding me and sending a searing pain through my head. I startled myself as I let out a deep and involuntary groan. Where was I? I tried to think back to the last moment I remembered. My eyes opened slowly; my arm moved up to block the light from my eyes. I remembered that I was sitting on a bench in a park. I had been watching old men play chess. What else had happened? No. That was all I could remember. I slowly moved my arm from my eyes and realized that it must be late afternoon because the hazy light was dimming into grey as the sun lowered and the last beams pushed their way into the small room. My eyes started to focus, and I could see a white sheet directly in front of me. Beyond that a silver gate trapped me on this uncomfortable mattress. The wall further away came into view and I saw a faintly textured and non-descript grey wall. They should have just gone with beige. More was coming back to me. There had been a woman in an orange dress. She had stopped time. Wait, that couldn't be right. I must be thinking of a dream. I focused on the dark grey couch that sat alone beneath the single window. It looked rough and uncomfortable to sit it. Just the right couch to put in a room to make sure that no one stayed too long. I followed the lines of the rough fabric with my eyes and slowly started to drift back out.

There was a church and a bar. Or a bar in a church? Did I spend some of my money? My eyes shot open. Where was my money? I rolled onto my back and sat up in the narrow bed and I almost fell back over from the shooting pain in my head. My right hand shot up to my head, stopped by the slight pull at the crook of my elbow. I looked down and saw a small bandage with a tube that flowed out of... or maybe into... my vein. I followed the clear fluid filled tube with my eyes. It traveled down over the side of the bed and through the prison bars then back up to a hanging bag where the clear liquid dripped. Drip. Drip. I had walked out of the bar and into the night. I think. Then... oh. I reached my left hand up this time and when I made it to my forehead, I felt a cloth surrounding my head tightly, my hair sticking out in all directions. My fingers slowly felt their way to around the bandage to the back of my head and when they found their mark, I yanked them away in pain.

I looked down by my left hand and saw a little remote with a red button with letters spelling "help." Well, if anyone needed help, it was me. And where was my fucking money? I scanned the room but saw no sign of any of my belongings. I looked at the little red button and hesitated. I sat with my finger poised an inch above the raised words. Help. I pushed the button and waited while the sun dimmed further and the scuffs along the worn grey wallpaper faded away. I prepped to push the button again when my door swung open to reveal a short wide woman in bright orange scrubs, a false smile plastered against her broad face. She waddled over to the side of my prison bed and beamed down at me.

"WELL GOOD AFTERNOON sunshine. I was wondering if you were going to wake up today."

I opened my mouth but couldn't push a voice past the gravel in my throat. I coughed a few times to clear the pipes as she waited patiently.

"How long have I been here?" I growled.

She looked a little confused and her eyebrows pushed together. "Honey, don't you remember asking me that yesterday?"

"I was here yesterday?"

"Oh my. Yes. You have now been here three days. You woke up yesterday and we took out your catheter before you went back to sleep. Don't you remember that?"

She spoke down to me like I was a slow child, and I could feel my annoyance growing. "No. I don't fucking remember that or else I probably wouldn't have asked."

"Hmmm." She pressed her fingers against my wrist and watched her tight wristwatch as she measured my pulse. "Well, you didn't remember your name either. Do you remember that now?"

"No." I lied.

"Well, your color seems to be better. Let's get you up and into the bathroom and if you feel up to it, then you can clean yourself up and get into some clothes. The shirt you were wearing had to be cut off, but we found you a replacement in the lost and found. Then the doctor will want to talk to you. And there will be some officers in here after dinner to ask you a few questions."

"What happened to me?"

"We think you were hit on the head with something. But you were found quickly and brought here. We stitched you up and you are doing fine minus the little bout of lapsed memory. The doctor will give you more information but it would be useful if you could remember your name so we could contact your family. I'm sure they're worried."

I'm sure they're not.

She padded over to the other side of the bed, the light from the sun lit her from behind. She pushed down the prison bar and helped me swing my legs down over the side of the bed. She pressed her thumb against the bandage on my right arm and slid the needle out almost painlessly. I felt a breeze against my back and realized that everyone passing the open door has a clear view of my rear end under this flimsy thing they must call a robe. She reached her arms towards me, and I let her bow my head to the ground. As she slowly unwrapped the gauze from my head, I stared down at the bare legs dangling off the side of the bed, not even reaching the floor. Those aren't my socks. They were thick grey wool socks that go up to my calves and warmed my feet.

"Whose socks are those?"

She giggled. It was an odd sound that didn't mix with her face. "Those are your socks now. The hospital put them on you to keep your feet warm and the circulation in your feet moving while you were asleep. Comfy, ain't they?"

She finished unwrapping and I could feel her prodding at the back of my head, sending sharp pains to the front of my skull.

"Looking good. Does this hurt?"

"No" I lied.

"Ready to get to the bathroom?" I put my hands into her outstretched arms, and she pulled me up as if I weighed no more than a child. Her head only reached the crook of my armpit, but she folded my right arm over her shoulder and fixed her left arm around my waist and we walked to the bathroom connected like we were finishing a three-legged race. When we entered the neon white room, I saw child scissors, shaving cream and a single blade razor, a toothbrush and toothpaste on the counter and the shower held canisters of soap and shampoo against the wall. She helped lower me to the toilet seat and then showed me the help button before double checking that I felt fine enough to clean up on my own.

"I'm going to put your clothes on the bed for you and remember to pull that lever if you need any help at all" She grinned as she started to slide the door shut. I smiled back and her eyes lit up before disappearing. I finally finished relieving myself and pulled my sore body up using the shiny metal bar next to the stool like she had shown me. I turned towards the mirror that sat over the sink and I looked at my reflection.

I stared back at the mirror in horror. There were streaks of orange dried across my swollen face. I was so concentrated on the pain in the back of my head I didn't even realize that there should have been pain around my right eye and cheekbone, which were already a nice eggplant purple. My beard and hair were crusty with my own blood. I reached up to poke at my cheek and watched the finger sized mark fade back to purple from white.

I surveyed the objects sitting on the sink waiting for me. Put there by Nurse Smiley I assume. Probably thought I would want to shave but knew sure enough that I wasn't a threat. I picked up the scissors and pulled a tuft of matted and hard fur away from my chin and sliced. I kept going until I was left with just short stubble on my chin. It might not have been the best idea. It brought more attention to the beating I received from the asshole that jumped me and the sidewalk that joined in. But it did make me look less menacing and it erased the extra iron from my face that would have been a bitch to rinse out. I picked up the small canister of shaving cream and put it back down. No reason to go that far. I untied the bow at the back of my neck and slid the thin fabric from my shoulders and let it flutter to the ground. Turned on the shower and I stepped into the mist once I could feel the heat. I washed the blood from my hair and face having to work carefully to miss the wound at the back of my head. I watched the water circle the drain, first red, and then brown, then eventually clear and the steam worked lazily across the ceiling and then disappear from the small room. I could have stayed under this spray forever. "You can't," I whispered to myself just below the drum of the water. Eventually Nurse Smiley would come back in to check on me and maybe with the police in tow, which I couldn't wait for. I turned the faucet off and stepped out of the shower to grab the towel to dry off. I looked in the mirror again and noticed a slight improvement. A bit more human. I wrapped the towel around my waist and then slid the door open to reveal the dim room behind it.

I slowly walked back over to the bed and stared down at the pile of clothes folded neatly on it. My jeans, socks and shoes sat folded with a stranger's t-shirt, underwear and a sweatshirt that had the name of a brewery I had never heard of, sprawled across the back. I started dressing and as I slid my jeans over my legs, I felt something in the pocket. I pulled the worn grey stone from the pocket and rubbed it a few times before shoving it back in place. I finished getting dressed and turned to the closed closet door to get the bag that must lay behind it.

I opened the door. No bag. The panic started to rush over me like a wave. I stepped around the room to search for the bag that contained my life. I needed that bag. I just couldn't be alone again. I looked by the grey couch and in all corners of the room. No bag. I patted the rock that was down in my pocket again. Maybe for luck or out of habit. I pushed the new hospital socks down into my back pocket and prepped to leave with the only possessions that I hadn't been stolen from me yet.

I moved slowly, my head still throbbing but now just a little less, to the door of the room.

I NEEDED TO be careful. I didn't want to give them my name. Not to Nurse Smiley or to the doctor or to the police that would follow. I pulled the door open and winced as it creaked loudly, waiting for someone to hear and come. Nothing happened and I stuck my head into the hall. People in colorful scrubs and normal clothes were all moving around in their own lives, not bothered enough to pay attention to me. I slowly shuffled into the hall and waited for someone to pounce on me and turn me back into the small room to await my fate. A few minor looks of curiosity and that was about it. I started walking towards a sign in the distance that shouted a red 'EXIT.' Look normal. Act normal. I walked past the doors of three rooms, occasionally reaching out to the grey textured wall for support. I glanced into the next open door I passed and paused, watching a man and woman cry while holding each other up and looking down into the drawn figure dying in the bed. A priest and nurse waiting patiently behind them. The woman looked up towards the door and I felt embarrassed like the intruder that I was as I stared into her tear-filled eyes. I slowly looked away and continued working towards the exit.

I made it to the door without anyone noticing the escaped patient and stared in horror at the stairs that lay in front of me. Holding to the railing with both hands, I took a step down. The moment the foot hit the step it shot a searing pain into my head and the stairwell faded into black for a moment. Careful. I took another step. Putting my foot down gently this time. I moved like that in a pace that seemed to last for hours until I finally to the door that led to the outside. A giant red sign yelled at me, "No Re-Entry." Good deal – I wasn't planning on coming back inside this godforsaken building. I opened the door and stepped out into the darkening evening. I looked right and then left trying to determine the direction I wanted to head. There was a bridge rising in the distance leading me away from this city on my left side. My feet turned left, and I walked.

I looked back at the bright lights once on the bridge and tried to remember what it was that I was still forgetting. Something that happened or something that I saw. Something other than my missing bag. My eyes narrowed and my head pounded, and I turned again towards the far side of the bridge and walked away into the fading night.

CHAPTER NINE

THE BEARD

I CLASPED MY hand to my stomach as it growled painfully. Trying to push the hunger away and stumbling down an empty gravel road to draw less attention to my head. My face had turned a nice yellow now and the swelling had gone down. It was still sore, but I counted myself lucky that it wasn't joined by a broken nose or teeth. The stitches remained in the back of my head, but they had stopped oozing some time ago and the only pain came from the sharp edges of the stitching material. My hair could lay over it nicely and helped to keep the stitches from drawing attention. Growl. My mouth watered as I pushed my hand harder against my stomach and thought about the cold canned beans that I ate not too long ago. Or was that a long time ago?

A truck sped by. The rotation of its tires pelting me with tiny rocks and sending a cloud of dust into the air. I stopped holding my stomach long enough for my hands to clasp my knees as I doubled over coughing before dropping to my knees. I thought about just laying down right here. On the side of this road. And letting the dust cover me amongst the rocks to be forgotten and tossed aside. I looked down towards my right knee at the overgrown grass that was scattered next to the gravel. Grass... My hand wrapped around a bunch of green leaves and pulled it from the ground, hesitating only for a second before shoving it in my mouth. Another fistful. And another. I paused for just a moment to catch my breath and felt the grass immediately try to push itself back out of my stomach. I fell back on my ass with a thud and waited for the nausea to pass. The realization that it might not have been the smartest idea I've had as I lay against the gravel and watched the sun move across the sky overhead and I finally started to stop feeling sick as the grass decided to stay down and slightly dampen the painful stab of hunger.

The crickets chirped in the long grass next to my ear, scolding me for eating their dinner, and I pushed myself to my feet. I slid my sweatshirt over my head and wrapped the arms at my waist. I wiped the sweat from my forehead with the back of my arm and started walking again. One foot in front of the other. I heard tires on the gravel behind me and braced for the sting of the rocks and the cloud of dust to follow. Instead, the red truck slowed, and I turned to glance into smiling eyes that shone out of a dark face. The black beard split as the man grinned and leaned towards the open passenger side window.

"Hey brother, you need a lift to town?" I looked at him wearily and he laughed in return, "I won't bite."

He leaned further and pushed at the passenger door to swing it open while I stood there staring at the dusty grey interior of the red truck. What did I have to lose? I was too worn to think. His grin widened as I grasped the doorframe to lift myself in and then slumped silently against the seat, working hard to not show him how good it felt to sit on the soft interior. The door closed behind me, and the bearded man reached towards my lap. I tensed out of instinct, but he continued reaching and hit the button to pop the door of the glove compartment. I sat, stressed and tired, as his hand rummaged around for a moment before pulling out a bag and tossing it on my lap.

"You look hungry, brother."

I looked down at the bag trying to recognize it. My eyes widened and I ripped open the top and pulled out the long piece of dried meat and shoved it in my mouth, trying to slow enough not to choke, but not caring about savoring the moment. My mouth watered as I kept shoving and chewing and swallowing and I barely managed a mumbled "thankyou" when I realized that the truck had started moving again.

"No worries, my friend. Do onto others, ya know?"

We drove quietly and I would catch him peering at me occasionally as we bumped along the gravel road to 'town.' I focused on finishing the chunks of savory meat from the bag and slid my finger into the greasy plastic so that I could lick away the last morsels. Finally, I sat back, hands still clutched the empty bag as if it had held my saving grace, and I closed my eyes. Slow breath in. Long sigh out. The world faded to black.

SOMEONE WAS PUSHING against my shoulder softly, "brother, we're here."

I opened my eyes and saw that we were parked in a small parking lot next to a building with a glowing sign that said 'restaurant.' I rubbed my eyes and focused on my surroundings. The restaurant looked like an old diner. Pickup trucks lined up next to the one I was sitting in. A handful of people sat and ate in the large windows that faced the parking lot. There was a big sign that said, 'Cash Only' next to another sign that said, 'Coke Products and PBR'. A small grey and white striped awning sat over the door, and it barely moved in the hot breeze. I looked around and saw that this view of the 'town' proved it to be closer to a city. The street we were on was small but towering behind the diner were office buildings and further still, more buildings climbed. Good. This should give me more of an opportunity to find some supplies, money, and food. Back on track maybe. Apartments and office buildings meant dumpsters. I remembered the life that came before and that people that live and work in areas like this throw away all kinds of useful things. Decent clothing, bags that still work great, and three fourths of a delicious steak all go into the trash. The bearded man got out of the driver's side of the truck, and I prepped for a long night on the street and exploring the dumpsters as I climbed down from the passenger side. My bones groaned in pain as I turned to say thank you and goodbye to the man. He stood there, poised to walk towards the restaurant and was looking at me expectantly.

"You ready?" he cocked his thumb towards the restaurant.

I looked down at the cement, suddenly and surprisingly ashamed of my lack of fortune, and mumbled a response back to him. "No man. I… uh… I can't afford that stuff. I'm just going to take off. Thanks for the ride though." I turned to walk away from him, head still hanging towards the ground.

"No shit, brother. I know a leather when I see one. Food is on me. You just have to keep me company while we eat and tell me a little bit about your story. I always enjoy a good story."

I didn't want to tell anyone 'my story' but I was somehow drawn to tell this stranger everything. All about my childhood, the end to my marriage, my shell of an existence, and my newfound and difficult life where I can sometimes feel again. I stared at the eyes smiling back at me and I nodded. When I made it to his side; he reached out and slapped me on the shoulder like we had been friends for years. I tried not to let him see the wince of pain.

"And when we're done eating, I can cut those stitches out for ya. I had to pull the stitches out for one of my dogs last month. I know how to do it." I froze for a second and watched him walk under the striped awning and into the diner. How the hell did he know about the stitches? How long did I sleep? They must've not been as hidden as I thought they were. I followed behind him and my stomach growled again as I was almost pushed over by the smell of hamburger meat cooking on the grill.

The sound and smells entered my body as if I were in a dream. Watching as my new companion grinned and shook the hand of someone that must be a friend before sauntering over to a booth. Drunk on the ambiance, I followed and slid into the side of the booth that faced him, leaving a smear of gravel dust on the clean plastic seat. He grinned at me. I grinned back.

His grin got wider, "Ha! I saw that!"

"Saw what?" the words roughly croaked out of my throat and sounded like the words of a stranger.

"You smiled and I was here to witness it."

I stopped smiling. "Yeah, well listen man. I really appreciate this."

"I told you. Dinner for your story."

I looked down at my dusty hands. Grass and mud beneath the too long fingernails. I stretched my fingers and tried to locate the words. "I'm not sure what you want to know. I mean I was…"

"What can I get you both?" I looked up at the pink face that was cheerfully facing at my companion. She wore a bright pink dress that made her face look a prettier shade of pink. She made me want to smile again. She turned her green eyes towards me, and I only saw the slightest hesitation to her smile when she took in my dusty and bruised face. I felt like a fool, grinning at her wide pretty face but the hesitation was gone and the smile she gave me back reached every corner of her eyes.

My companion boomed, "two cokes, two cheeseburgers, an order of fries, an order of onion rings, and I'm sure we'll want some pie once we're finished with that, sweetheart." She giggled and nodded and swayed her way back behind the counter. We sat in silence. I knew that if I would make eye contact, he would be sitting there watching me, patiently expecting his payment. A hand with pink fingernails came into my view and left a plastic glass that was filled with brown liquid. Little bubbles pushed their way to the top as I heard her steps moving away. I kept my eyes on the prize as I worked the paper covering off the cheap plastic straw and started sucking before I had it pushed past the ice. Crap. How could I have forgotten how good a coke could taste? I kept pulling the liquid through the straw like I was dying of thirst. Hell, maybe I had been dying of thirst. Pinky was back with another before I was finished. I stopped drinking about halfway through the second coke before taking a breath and glancing across the booth at the man that sat there. He sat watching me drink, hands on the top of the table, silently waiting for the story that I promised. Deep breath in. Long sigh out.

"I don't know where to start."

"Well, how about we start with you telling me what you are looking for."

I furrowed my brow, "I don't know what you mean. I'm not really looking for anything… I don't think."

"How did you get here?"

"You drove me." That earned a little smile.

"How did you get to the side of the road looking like you would fall over and die in the next moment?"

I looked at the straw sticking out of the cup and took a small sip. "There was a day where I decided it was time for my life to end." I paused. Why did I say that? "But really, I had died a long time before that. When I was a child…" the words flowed from me in a way that I hadn't experienced before. I told him about the dead man that I had been. The shell of a man that I was. I continued to stare at my hands, and I fidgeted with my straw, only taking small breaks for a sip of the sweet liquid. I kept talking and weaving through the story of my past without ever looking at my silent partner who listened to me without uttering a word. I was sure I was making him rethink his offer of dinner while listening to this shit spewing forth, but I couldn't stop. It was like a spell had been put on me to tell all my deep, dark secrets to this stranger that sat across from me.

I made it the part of the story leading up to the day that I died when pinky showed back up. She was balancing plates on her arms and put a steaming burger down in front of each of us. Then came a basket overflowing with heavily salted fries and another that had thick fried onions. My mouth watered and I tried to take my time placing the lettuce, tomato, and onion on top of the meat before bookending it with the top bun. Pink grease flowed onto the plate, and I couldn't contain myself any further. I took a giant bite and closed my eyes to try to memorize the flavor of the hot hamburger over every taste bud. The grease coated my throat and the cold tomato squished against the roof of my mouth. I swallowed the bite and finally opened my eyes to see him watching me before following suit with his own bite. I smiled and wiped the grease that was working its way in a streak through the stubble on my chin. I giant goofy grin of pure joy of the moment. One bite at a time, I worked my way through the burger and grinned at my companion as he matched me bite for bite. I felt like a perfectly normal human sitting and having dinner with an old friend... just for a moment. For that one moment I forgot the death that surrounded me. I forgot about the loss of love throughout my life. I forgot about the hunger pains after my 'death' and the loss of Dog and our momentary stillness. I forgot about the grass that I ate just this morning and the bruises that still scattered my face. I shoved the last bite into my mouth and licked the savory grease from my fingertips before leaning back against the booth, letting the plastic squeak beneath me.

He finished his last bite and motioned at the baskets of fried vegetables sitting in between us. I leaned forward to grab a, now lukewarm, onion ring and as I chewed, I made eye contact again and asked, "What is your name?"

He grinned and leaned back in the booth, using a napkin to clean the grease from his whiskers, "Well there, people call me a lot of different things… bastard, buddy, Phil… but you can call me 'brother'."

I laughed and it shocked me when I almost recognized the sound coming out of me, "Ok brother, enough of the past life shit. Would you now like the stories about what landed me in your truck and into this booth?"

"Hell yeah."

Over the last bit of fried food in the baskets, and then over coffee and pie, I continued to speak. This time he chimed in. He empathized over losing Dog, laughed with me over the countless times I've been pelted with a soda, laughed harder over my grass breakfast, sat quietly as I spoke of burying the lonely man, asked questions about the rain barrel system that I kept running, turned the grey rock over in his large hand and rubbed it with his thumb. And then I got to the dreams.

He sat back questioning, "What does it mean?"

"I don't know. I have had this dream for so many nights. I just can't figure out."

"Maybe it's about your journey. The town is what you are searching for, but you just can't get there yet."

"Maybe. But it doesn't feel like the town is a metaphor. It feels like the town is there and that physical place is where I should try to go. I just don't know where it is. And then there is the scream."

His brows pinched together as he leaned forward, "A scream?"

"Yeah. That's what wakes me up every time. The scream. It pierces me."

"It's a woman screaming?"

"Yeah."

"This is going to sound fucking insane."

I close my mouth, waiting to see where this is going.

"I think I've been in your dream."

"Bullshit" I laughed off his poor excuse for humor.

"It's not. Not really. About a week ago, I had this dream. Only I wasn't in a field. I was in a town. Maybe it is your town. Maybe not. But I was walking and there wasn't anyone in sight. It was a ghost town." Now it was my turn to stay silent and listen, leaning forward for the next words. "The sun was setting or rising. I'm not quite sure but the sky wasn't blue. It was more of a… I don't know…"

"Orange" I whispered.

We looked at each other; our smiles vanished from our faces. He nodded, "Orange. And I walked around this town. There was a warm wind, but it wasn't hot. It was sweet. The old pain in my hip was gone and I just kept walking down the street. I got to the end and the road just stopped. There was nothing beyond this town but tall grass. The cement just ended where I stood. I thought about walking into the grass to see what was out there but as I lifted my foot," He looked into my eyes. "I heard this scream. A woman. She sounded like her soul was taken from her. And I woke up."

"Holy shit," My mouth hung open and my throat started to dry.

"I almost forgot about it completely. Until you mentioned the scream." I took a sip of the cold coffee sitting in front of me and we sat in silence thinking through our own memories but stuck in the same place. I looked across the table as he asked, "What do you think it means?"

The shivers had already started to wear away "Honestly, I don't think it means shit. It's a cool coincidence that we had a similar dream. I mean, how many people probably have a dream like that?"

He looked disappointed but then grinned at me, the smile missing something from before. "Yeah, you're probably right.

Just a weird coinkidink." He glanced out into the darkened parking lot then looked back at the interior of the diner to wave over pinky, our comradery from before now lost. I tried to not let the knowledge of that disappoint me. It's not like we would be pen pals after we left this dinner or ever see each other again. Why did I care?

Pinky came on over and Phil bellowed, "well, how much do I owe you darlin'?" She blushed and handed him a slip of paper and walked away with a smile on her face. He pushed his way out of the bucket seat, and I followed him, letting myself fill the full pain of my body as I unfolded. He took out his thick leather wallet and laid some bills down over the receipt and waved as he walked out into the night. I followed and tossed a little wave and smile at pinky and there was no hesitation on her face as she smiled back at me. We walked over to the truck sitting under a light in the empty lot and I made my way to say 'goodbye' to the man who had been my confidant and friend for a fleeting moment.

He opened the tail of the truck and motioned at me to sit while he rummaged around in the back for a moment. I slid my ass up onto the hinged metal seat wondering what was going to come next but trusting this man without reason. He pulled out two beers and a small wire cutter. "Ok brother, you start drinking your beer here, I'll get those stitches out, and then we'll enjoy a moment of friendship before I ask you if I can take you somewhere or help out in any way and you tell me no." I laughed and reached for the warm beer. I took a gulp and let the warm liquid buzz its way down my throat before I turned my head away from him so that he could work. I felt him lifting the hair that I had thought hid the closed wound. Then the push of cold metal against my skin before the relief of a cut. A few snips and the odd sensation of something being pulled through thin skin, and my head felt better than it had in days. The truck creaked under him as he joined me on the tail bed and popped open his beer.

I looked at him, "Thank you."

"Anytime," he nodded, and I knew he meant it.

"I thought I might die on that road today. Death might have been a reprieve from where I was right in that moment. Maybe from where I am going." The words floated to the ground around us.

He reached over and patted my back, "Every now and then we all need help. When I have needed help, someone has been there." The wave of his arm told me that was all that was to be said on that subject. He took a swig, "So where are you off to now?"

"I don't know. You were right though. I'm looking for something. I just need to figure out what it is first."

I finished my beer. He finished his beer. And we both jumped down from the truck. Phil pushed the tail up and latched it before tossing our empty cans into the back.

He looked at me, "Is there any place I can drive you or anything I can do for you?"

"No but thank you. Brother."

He shook his head but was grinning the big eye-smiling grin when he looked up. I stuck out my hand to shake and he grabbed it and pulled me towards him, wrapping me in a musky hug, his beard still smelling of hamburger grease and beer as it scratched against the side of my face. He patted my back, and I patted his and he pushed away, giving a little wave and jumping in the driver seat of his truck. It roared to life as I realized that there was something sticking out of my hand. The headlights came on as I glanced down and saw two wrinkled twenties folded into my palm. I looked up quickly and saw his bearded grin in my direction as his truck backed up and then started down the road, going back in the direction that we had come from, the empty cans clanking together in the back. An arm stuck out of his window in a wave, and I lifted my arm in return. I stood there like that until I could no longer see the red lights on the road, arm poised in the air, fist clutched around forty dollars, and belly full of food. My hand slowly lowered, and I turned towards the dark quiet 'town.'

CHAPTER TEN

THE SUIT

I OPENED MY eyes at the sound of a coin being dropped into the paper cup that was sitting by my feet. In the second it took for my eyes to adjust to the day, the man who had donated the coin was already at the end of the block so the "thank you" that had been forming in my throat stayed put. I looked past the brown cardboard sign sitting between my outstretched legs and watched the shoes march past me on their way to work. This was the best time to be out. There were fewer competitors for the change in the pockets – as half of them were still passed out from whatever they drank or injected or smoked the night before. Most of the workers sauntering past me were still hopeful for the day. They still expected it to be fruitful and positive and were more than willing to put positive energy into the world by tossing their change down into my paper cup. Red heels clicked past my view. Then a pair of sandals. Who wears sandals to work in this city? I followed the line of the legs and saw a pair of shorts that were topped by a t-shirt and a normal looking face. Then I saw the tray with 4 coffees. Ah – delivery. I looked back down, making my best attempt to look contrite and hungry as people continued to chatter by.

A pair of fancy shoes stopped in front of me and turned. A dollar was pushed into the cup. My eyes followed up from her practical heels to a nice-looking grey suit with a plump body squeezed into it and further up to see the large face of a woman smiling at me, her eyes full of pity. She stood there hovering over me, waiting, hand poised over the cup where she had just made her donation. "Thank you and God bless you," I croaked. Her self-assured grin widened. She nodded at me before walking away.

I tried not to glare at her back. I should be thankful not angry at these people. They might give me their dollar or change to feel better about their own sad lives, but they still don't have to do it. And I benefit. Maybe I just woke up on the wrong side of the bed this morning. I chuckled to myself. The wrong side of the park bench. Does that count? I silently sent the woman a good thought as a thank you and tried to genuinely hope that her day would go well. Who was I kidding? I didn't really care. My ass hurt from sitting on the cement and my beard itched. I watched the feet walk past, the traffic slowing as more people made it to their grey cubical lives. The life I remembered like a distant dream.

Finally, the street was almost silent. I leaned forward and lifted the cup, knocking the cardboard sign flat against the ground and tipping the cup onto it. I sifted through the coins and dollar bills and pulled out the smooth grey rock that kept the cup from blowing away before rubbing it a few times and pushed it into my front pocket and counting the bills. Counted, folded and stuck in my pocket. Then the change. Twenty-two dollars and fifty-three cents in total. Not bad for a morning of sitting on cold concrete. I poured the coins back into cup and sat for a moment, trying to shake the funk that I woke up with. I had another dreamless night. Not a single dream since the night before dinner with Phil. Who would have thought that I would miss a mind-bending dream that ended with a jolt to the system? I did though. I missed it. I missed the peace it brought before the scream.

"Hiya Frank!" I instantly clutched my cup of change as a recognizable figure slid along the wall to sit right next to me.

"My name is not Frank" I mumbled at him.

"I know. But since ya won tell me or any of us what ya name is, I decided to make one up. Ya look like a Frank. Or what I think a Frank looks like. I 'ave never really met a Frank. So… Frank, what is your name?" He always talked too much.

I kept my hand over the top of my cup and closed my eyes as I leaned my head back against the brick wall.

"So, you still ain't gonna to tell me, huh? Well, you know… we've been talkin'." I had never seen him with anyone and never had any idea of what he meant when he said 'we.' "And we think that ya were in war. Or maybe you were a banker. Is that it Frank? Where you in a war and then became a banker? Then maybe you lost your mind and your money and that's how you ended up here with us." When I first found this fruitful corner, I saw him, sitting on the other side of the street from me, with his sign and his glass jar and talking at everyone that would take a moment to listen. I started to listen to his chatter, his voice loud enough to carry across the road and over the bustle of the footsteps. He would tell stories about his childhood and his motherless children at home and whatever else would be the flavor of the day. He saw me watching once and waved. I nodded back. He hadn't left me alone since then.

"So Frank, how'd ya make out today? I seen a few people drop something in your cup. Me? Oh yeah, I did pretty good. Made myself over twenty bucks. I might go get me a burger. Or a beer. Or maybe just beer. I don't know. Days like these I wish I hadn't quit gettin fried. Money in my pocket. Sun in the sky. Good day to get high. What do ya think Frank?" I didn't mind the chatter or really the fact that I never had to chime in. I did mind the fact that he always smelled like he had recently taken a piss on himself. But other than that, he was probably the nicest kid I had met out here.

"OK. See ya Frank." He jumped up and took off walking down the road. I never knew where he went after he left me each day. He shuffled down the sidewalk and I wondered how many years he had left in his short life.

I folded my legs under me and worked to stand, my left hand pushed against the brick wall to help me up. Once I was upright, I watched the small brick indentations fade from my palm before leaning over to pick up my sign and cup. I folded my sign and slid it into the plastic grocery bag that had been shoved into my back pocket. All squared away, I started walking towards the cheap burger chain on the corner. It had to be just about time for the lunch items to start being served from the menu. I was so focused on the glass front door of the restaurant that I almost tripped over the leg that was outstretched in the same exact way mine had been just a few moments earlier. I looked down into a dirty face snarling at me. Angry bright green eyes pierced out beneath dirty brown hair and the skin had loosened to rivets around her cheeks. She looked like a worn-out version of a woman I used to know. Or maybe that I had seen in a movie.

"Idiot" she mumbled at me. I rolled my eyes at her and tipped my cup into hers, the coins clanging against each other as they slid into their new home. Her scowl changed into a toothless grin, but it just made her lack of beauty more apparent, "God bless you, sir!" She said in a syrupy sweet voice.

"Yeah, yeah, whatever" I mumbled back at her, before pulling open the door to smell the flash frozen meat being grilled. I looked around at the few bodies sitting in the hard plastic booths. They all looked like me. Sad and alone and worn out from eating this shit every day. I had planned on using my cup change for my early lunch today, but my own self-hatred had gotten the best of me and the woman with the green eyes got my coins. I pulled the new cash out from my pocket and counted out five one-dollar bills and laid them on the counter.

"Two burgers, a small fry, and an iced tea." The scrawny teen behind the counter barely hid his disgust. Whether that was caused by me – although in this spot he should be used to the ragged coming in and I am better smelling than most – or in him with the job that he had to work. I never found out. He laid the cash into the register and poured some change into my outstretched hand without saying a word. I stood waiting for my order as I heard the click of heels come in through the door behind me. There was a whiff of sweet perfume and she stood so close behind me that I could almost feel the warmth of her breath. I didn't want to scare her by turning and staring so I scooted to the side and made room for her to order. And, selfishly, so I could sneak a peek at the woman who was ordering a burger at a fast-food place in the middle of the morning wearing her heels and her best perfume. I didn't know what I expected to see, but a picture started forming in my mind before I turned slightly.

THERE WAS NO one there. I shook my head. I swore I felt her standing there. I must be hungrier than I thought. My mind was trying to place where I've smelled that perfume before when someone shouted in my ear, "DUDE. Your food is ready."

I grabbed the sack and the cup, "Kid, you don't have to yell everything."

"Well maybe if you grabbed it the first hundred times I said it," he rolled his eyes and turned towards the fryer.

I grabbed a handful of napkins, more than I would need, and a straw for my tea and found myself sitting in a corner booth, watching the door as I ate. The few stragglers left. No one else entered. I sat for longer than most days, not sure of what I was waiting for. The smell of the perfume that hadn't been there still tickled my nose. My mind wandered as if in a fog. It must have been the lack of sleep. Eventually I was aware of the glaring coming from kid behind the counter. I glared back. The door opened with the signal of a bell and heels click against the floor and I slowly turned my head to the repeated scene. I held my breath as I took her in. The vision dashed. In place of what I had hoped, there stood the woman who had shoved a dollar into my cup earlier this same day. Followed closely by a handful of men in suits and women in blouses. Crap, how long had I been sitting here? I had never made it to the lunch rush before. I grabbed my empty cup and my grocery bag and made my way to the door. The crowd parted to let me pass and I heard their voices lower to hushed whispers. I kept my eyes on the floor as I pushed their stares. Pricks. If they could see me in my prime, they wouldn't be staring at me in horror or disgust. I made it out of the joint and onto the sidewalk just as I could hear someone say something behind me and they all started laughing. Laughing at me? What did I care? I didn't care what they thought. I had already been to hell and back. I stopped. Who was I kidding? I cared. The woman outside who still held the cup full of my change joined in the laughter, without knowing exactly what she was laughing at, just trying to bond in a moment to gain more cash. I hurried down the street and tried to ignore the sounds of laugher boiling up behind me and forget the smell of that perfume following me like a cloud.

I walked a few blocks, not needing to pay attention to the path. Turned right onto the quiet city street knowing what would be waiting for me as I turned the corner. "Hi Maria" I pulled two of the dollar bills from the pile in my pocket and laid it down on the rolling cart.

She smiled up at me, "Hey!" She always smiled at me. No fear or disgust in her eyes as she handed me a baggy filled with cut orange fruit and her rough sticky hand patted my arm as I inhaled the sweet scent of freshly cut mango. Every day she stood here and cut fruit after fruit to sell on the street. Not once had I seen her looked discouraged or lost. She seemed to have her life figured out more than the people in suits who passed her throughout the day. Much more than me.

I smiled, "thank you." I calmed at her smile and friendly pat, the storm that had been brewing in me since I woke up dulled to a distant rumble. I put my bag of fruit down into my grocery bag and continued my walk down the street.

HALF AN HOUR later, I was sitting on the soft green grass in a small park. My back against a rough tree as I hid from the sun that was just about to start disappearing behind the top of a tall building. I sucked on the thick fruit and inhaled the familiar smell as a drop of juice slowly escaped and ran down my chin into the rough fur that lived there. I wiped it away with one of the extra napkins I had taken from lunch and licked my fingers. My shoes and socks sat to my side and my toes stretched over the grass beneath my feet. I watched the people walking by and imagined what their lives were like when they weren't in this park. The woman with six dogs attached to her by small metal grips around her belt. What does she do when she's done walking stranger's dogs? Does she go home to her own dogs who waited to be walked? The older woman that is carrying around a small child. She must be his grandmother. Does she live with the family and work as their free nanny? Or does she go home to her own quiet house each night and sit in the silence each evening? Where are the people with their own kids and their own dogs? Who was I kidding; I didn't have a kid or a dog. How could I possibly know what it was like? I was alone and I always had been.

I finished my fruit and watched the afternoon sun disappear behind the building; the sky stayed bright as it would well into the evening but at least the shade had started to come. I pulled on my socks and laced up the shoes and pushed up from the ground again. Realizing I felt almost complacent. Maybe it was time to move on again. I was comfortable. I had sixty-eight dollars now shoved into my front pocket and another forty that stayed shoved in my shoe, untouched since Phil had snuck it into my palm. I looked around to make sure no one had their eyes on me, before ducking into the alley behind the apartment building next to the park. Slowly pushing open the heavy lid of the first dumpster to make sure it didn't slam against the side and draw unwanted attention. I put both hands on the dirty side and pulled myself up and into the hot space. It smelled of rotted food and dog shit. I pulled my shirt up to cover my nose and pawed through the bags that held potential treasures. After the first few bags, the smell started to make me dizzy. I gave up on door number one and hopped out closing the lid after me. Moving over to the second dumpster; I found the smell not nearly as paralyzing as I landed in between the black and white plastic bags. I opened the first bag and tossed it aside when I realized that it was full of strips of paper and a few empty soda cans. My eyes rolled at the people and their lack of recycling habits before laughing at my own priorities. The second bag proved fruitful with half of a loaf of bread with only a small spot of mold, a not so empty bottle of shampoo and a mostly full tube of toothpaste. Wasteful. I tossed these right next to the dumpster in the alley so that I could grab them when I was done. Bags three and four held nothing of value and as I was lifting a fifth bag to start searching, I saw a peak of orange fabric sticking out from two bags to my left. I spun around and lost my footing, landing hard on two bags that must have been full of glass. I groaned as the bruised soreness crept into my body. After I caught my breath, I leaned towards the fabric and wrapped my hand around the top of the large black bag dreading to see what was wrapped in orange. What was hiding in this dumpster? I pulled the bag up to reveal no orange fabric or anything else except for another bag. It must have been a reflection of light. I looked up at the sunless sky. Maybe not. I shrugged. It wasn't the first time I was seeing things.

I pulled open the bag that I held in my hand and found what I had originally been looking for. Sitting alone in the trash bag was a small duffel bag with a broken handle. I surveyed the rest of the bag and found the shoulder strap and zippers all intact and no holes in the fabric. I tossed it out of the dumpster so it would land next to the soon to be forgotten plastic grocery bag and climbed out after it. I was done for today. I stood for a moment in the alley, feeling the lumps beginning to form from my fall. Pushed in each one and felt a small stab of pain but nothing broken. I would hurt worse tomorrow. I grabbed the bag and slid the zipper open to shove my newly found things, my cup, and my sign into it and tossed the old plastic bag into the dumpster I had just leapt out of.

The shoulder strap was wrapped firmly around my back, and I cradled my new bag like a baby throughout the night. I slept a dark and restless sleep curled up on a wooden park bench. Jumping awake every time I heard a sound to make sure that my bag was still in my possession. Every time I woke, I would lay for a while listening to the rustling of the wind in the trees above me, the distant car, a couple whispering as they walked by, and my own voice talking around the fog in my head. The same as every night in this city, I waited in the dark for the morning to come again.

I OPENED MY eyes as the sky had just started to lighten and rolled my feet to the ground to slide up into a sitting position. My head turned and I looked down at the dirty shoes that had landed on the ground and saw the fabric at the top of the shoes move minimally as I tried to stretch my toes. I unwrapped the bag strap from my arm and rubbed the red mark that lined against the skin where the strap had stretched while I slept. The bumps from the night before were sore and pushing against the fabric on my lower back and my thighs. Deep breath in. Long sigh out. Stand and walk. Move.

The streets were quiet, only a late-night straggler or an early commuter, as I followed my daily steps to the business district. I looked up at the neon sign that said 'Open 24 hours' and pulled open the door to walk into the overly air-conditioned restaurant that sat under the bridge. A few people were placing their breakfast orders and a teen waited on them impatiently, holding his heavy weight up against the counter and not looking at me as I walked past him and towards the bathroom. I closed the door behind me and flipped the lock.

Doubtful anyone would come use this bathroom in the short time that I was here, but I didn't want to risk it. Walked over to the row of urinals against the wall and leaned my hand against the dirty tan false brick wall as I relieved myself. Then I turned to the row of sinks and put my hand on either side of the sink as I leaned close to the faded mirror and stared into my eyes. I looked tired. And dirty. Mostly just tired and worn out though. Drifting without purpose. Grease shone in my pores and my eyes were bloodshot. How long could I keep this up? Where was my answer? I shook my head and pulled the bottle of shampoo out of my bag. The blue top popped open and I had a whiff of the sweet clean smell that reminded me of another time. I turned the faucet on the right all the way, letting the cold spray splash around the bowl. Then the one on the left, slower and using my hand to determine the level of heat.

Once I had found a temperature between scalding and frigid, I tilted my head forward and used my hands to cup water onto the back of my head, letting it spill around and run down the tip of my nose. I grabbed the shampoo bottle and scrubbed. First my hair, then my short beard and face, and ending with my arms; letting the sweet-smelling shampoo wash the dirt down the drain. My shirt was wet with the runoff as I moved over the air dryer, sticking my head underneath it to dry off the long strands. Once it was dry enough, I moved back to the sink and grabbed the toothpaste out of my bag and used my newly clean finger to brush the layers off my teeth. I rinsed and smiled into the mirror. I still looked tired, but it was an improvement. Someone pushed against the door, and I heard a loud grunt followed immediately by the type of knocking that happens with the full fist and not just the knuckles. I pushed the toothpaste back into my bag and tossed the empty shampoo container in the trash before unlocking the door and pushing my way past the portly employee without making eye contact.

I worked down to my street corner and felt every sore spot as I lowered to the ground. Pulled the crumpled but legible sign out of my bag along with my newer paper cup from yesterday. I pulled my rock from my pocket making sure not to also pull out any dollar bills and tossed it in the cup after a few rubs with my thumb. It made a thick satisfying plop as it hit the bottom, securing the cup from the wind. I leaned my head against the wall and closed my eyes, waiting for the morning traffic to begin. The morning was quiet, and I started to drift into the fog.

TAP. TAP. TAP. I opened my eyes to see a grey pigeon standing close to me. One brown eye focused on my face as his beak tapped my little cardboard sign that was propped between my legs. I reached for my bag, and he lifted his head up to peer closer at me, quickly jerking his view to look between my face and hand. "It's OK buddy, I've got a treat." He must have understood me. This seemed to calm him down and he stood, just looking at my face and tapping his orange leather claw impatiently against my sign. I pulled out a piece of the remaining bread and broke off a small piece and tossed it forward in between my outstretched legs. He tilted his head to look at the offering and walked his determined fragmented walk to it. He stabbed at it with his beak, pulling a little piece off at a time. The whole time we kept eye contact, his small brown eye telling me his own story as he ate. The world slowed down around us, and his movement became less fragmented and more fluid as he continued to watch me and eat, standing between my outstretched legs. I could almost reach my hand out and touch him and I was sure he would let me. He lifted his head and stood frozen as if waiting for my touch. And then the world caught up to us and he launched into the air quickly as the noise of the morning rushed back into my ears. I watched his wings flap gracefully through the air and he was gone.

I sighed as I watched him go, thinking of the fact that I needed to follow him and fly. A voice interrupted my thoughts, "Holy shit! Is that you?"

I knew that voice. The man I used to be knew that voice. I slowly turned my upturned face from the empty sky where the bird had gone and towards the source of the voice and I struggled to keep the recognition out of my eyes as I stared at him blankly.

"Dude, you know everyone has been looking for you, we all just assumed you were dead," he crouched down, his grey suit crinkling where he bent.

I burrowed my brow at him and deepened my voice, "na man, I don' know ya." He squinted his eyes and leaned closer to my face. I turned my eyes down thinking for a moment that maybe he was trying to see what was in my soul. He looked unsure then determined.

"It IS you. I know that it's you. We've got to get you home." I thought back to the memories of this man in the suit, he was one of those people that was always helpful. Not because of some sense of misdirected pride or obligation, but he was genuinely nice. I felt bad that I was lying to him, but the man he was looking for was long gone and I did not know this person in front of me anymore.

I looked back up at him and prepped to say something to get him to go away when another familiar voice came from my right, "Hiya Frank!"

"No, I think you have it wrong. I know this man. His name is…"

"Oh, ya know Frank? He my best buddy, ain't ya Frank?"

"No, I'm very sorry but his name isn't Frank."

"Yeah. It is."

"No, young man. This is a friend of mine, and he obviously needs help. Now please go away."

"How could he be your friend. I ain't never heard of you and me and Frank; we've been friends for ten or sumthin years, ever since I came to this city"

My head went back and forth between the two fighting over my identity. My talkative friend in the lose jeans that smelled faintly of piss versus the well-intentioned man in a suit and smelling of shaving cream.

"Ain't that right, Frank?" I looked to my right blankly, not catching what had been said. "I said we been friends for years. Ain't that right, Frank?" I nodded and we both looked to the left at the man in the suit. I saw the disappointment enter his eyes. He looked at me, probing with his sad eyes, and finally looked down with uncertainty.

"I'm really sorry man, I just… I think I was just searching for someone else in you." His eyes stayed down as he put his hands against his knees and pushed back up. He walked on past us, and I watched his back all the way down the block. He stopped to turn and look back at me and I looked down quickly so that he didn't catch me watching him walk away and see the faint sadness reflected in my eyes.

"I knew it! You are hidin' from someone, Frank" my dirty friend whispered excitedly into my ear, his breath warming my neck.

"Yeah. I am." I started grabbing my belongings, shoving my rock into my pocket and the sign and cup went into the bag and I stood up. My friend stood up with less effort than me and faced me straight on as if blocking my path. I sighed, "Listen man, I have to go. I can't stay here anymore."

"Yeah. No shit, Frank." He leaned close, the smell of urine getting stronger and mixed with stale beer. He stared into my eyes. "But it don't matter what you runnin from. Someday you gotta face that shit, Frank." He stepped sideways to let me pass and patted me twice on the back as I walked away, his words repeating in my brain like an echo without end.

I made sure the man in the suit wasn't around the corner as I turned, and I started jogging. I needed to get out of here and fast. I think he believed us, but I couldn't wait around to see. I jogged towards a road that I knew would get me out of the town and maybe moving in the right direction again. Whatever 'right direction' that was. By the time that I made it to the diner, sweat was running in rivets down my face and back. I opened the door to the blast of cold air and the welcoming smell of bacon on the grill.

I recognized the woman behind the counter. My hand came up in a quick wave to pinky and I saw a slight sign of recognition in her eyes as she smiled back and gestured to the booth. It felt like a lifetime ago that I slid into this booth, the plastic squeaking audibly under me. This time I sat on the side that faced the door. As I drank my coffee and forked eggs and sausage into my mouth, I watched the door. Every time it swung open, the sound of the bell chiming, my heart rose and fell when I saw it was another stranger coming into the diner. I don't know why I thought he would come. Maybe I thought he could sense me here, in his diner, and show up for a conversation. I laughed at myself angrily. I was an idiot. I finished my lunch and pulled the forty dollars from my shoe. It was sweaty but this is what I had been holding onto it for. I pulled a twenty out and shoved it into my pocket with my other bills, leaving the other twenty sitting on the table and I left with one last half smile to pinky before leaving this city for good. I made it to the street and looked both ways. Right was the way I came and the way that Phil had went. Left was new territory with no idea what to expect. I turned left and the words continued to echo in my mind, "it don't matter what you runnin from. Someday you gotta face that shit."

CHAPTER ELEVEN

THE BEER

I STUCK MY thumb under the cold metal tab and popped open my second beer; the other four sat next to me on the rock, still held together by the plastic rings. The cool wind blew my growing hair around my face as I watched the water slowly churn in the river below me. I tipped the can up and the cool liquid trickled down my throat. The sounds of families riding their bikes came from the path behind me. I liked this hidden town along the river. It had a feeling of almost lazy friendliness that entered and calmed the recent storms in my mind. Early this afternoon, I decided that I had enough money to buy this six-pack and was already planning on doing so. But as I stood in line with my beer, a young couple in front of me offered to buy it. I turned them down and thanked them. But they insisted and smiled at me as they walked off hand in hand, without pity in their eyes. I thought about them as I sat on my rock. They had walked down towards this river from the store, and I followed, not sure if I wanted to say anything to them. I saw her curly hair blowing in the wind as they laughed and smiled at each other. They had started down the bike path and I decided to not interrupt their happy moment with my awkward thank you. So, instead I sat down on this rock and enjoyed my first cold beer and then opened the second, not wanting to get up yet.

My lower back leaned against the short rock behind me. It was more comfortable than it looked at first glance. I watched the birds dive gracefully for an afternoon snack beneath the waves and wondered where this river ended up. As I finished the second beer, a couple of young men climbed down into my sanctuary and glanced at me as they sat on a nearby rock. One of them pulled a slim joint from his pocket and lit the end, inhaling deeply before passing to his buddy. The smoke drifted over to me and reminded me of days from my past. I breathed the scent in deeply and when my eyes closed, I saw a woman laughing as we passed a joint between us. We talked about our dreams and goals and the life we had wanted together. I didn't recognize her. Was that my wife? I didn't remember her laughing like that. I opened my eyes and saw the second man pass it back before the first man leaned towards me with the joint in his outstretched hand and a friendly grin on his face. He must have seen the raw desire in my face as I watched them. I nodded in thanks and reached out my hand. I closed my eyes as I inhaled and let the smoke swirl in my mouth before I sucked it down into my lungs. It sat for a moment and then pushed back out so I could watch the white smoke fade away into the air. I passed it back over,

"Thanks... uh... you guys want a beer?" They both grinned at me and nodded. I pulled two of the cans out from their plastic rings and passed them over to them.

"Thanks," man one pushed his thick brown hair out of his eyes and smiled at me. I sat for a moment and then opened my third as they each enjoyed their first. They tried to pass the joint back to me, but I waved it away, my arm liquid from the first puff. They finished it off and the three of us sat and drank our beers in silence, watching the water work its way west. Or maybe south. I wasn't quite sure. I snuck a few glances at them and recognized the logo on their polo shirts from a sporting shop that I had seen in town.

"Hey," they both looked at me. "Does your store have cheap jackets?" I gestured to the logo on the brunette's shirt. He looked down, lost for a moment before the realization of what I was asking dawned in his eyes.

"Sure man," he grinned and pushed the hair from his eyes again. "We have a discount rack. Come in tomorrow after eleven, and I'll give you a deal. I'm Travis." He reached out his hand and I shook it in return and smiled.

"I will. Thanks." Then we all turned back to our internal thoughts and silently finished our beers in peace. They eventually stood and climbed up the small rock and back onto the path disappearing with a small wave in my direction, taking their empty cans with them. I looked back towards the water and sat holding my own empty beer can.

THERE WAS A small kayak working its way slowly up the river. The paddle hardly made any noise as it pushed its way in and out of the green water. The person in the small boat looked determined but happy. I looked down into the water and wondered what would happen if I fell in right now. Would the current carry me out to the ocean or would I just bump along the bottom of the river until I floated to the top? My empty body waiting to be found by a local stranger. Would it be Travis and his friend, telling everyone, "I think we shared a smoke and a beer with that guy?" They would pull me out and bury me in an unmarked grave and no one would mourn. I could fall in right now and sink into the cool green water, watching the bubbles float lazily out of my mouth as I sank to the bottom. I could see the fish floating lazily above me, lighted from the sun above them. I shook my head of the thought and leaned back against the rock. The buzz of the beer and pot washed over me. My muscles relaxed as I drifted into a nap with only the sound of the wind rustling through the trees.

Here I was again. In the grass of the dream that I knew. I smelled the sweet air and let it fill my lungs. The buzz from my waking state seemed to carry over into my sleep and I decided to just lay here for a minute; I didn't worry about the scream to come. I closed my eyes and breathed in and let my ears fill with thick silence. I hadn't visited in a while. But here I was now. The comfortable familiarity of it wrapped me like a warm blanket. Home. I opened my eyes and stood. My body felt young, and I didn't have to push myself into a standing position. I looked towards the town that I knew would be standing in the distance; silent and dark and so far, and I knew that I wouldn't be able to move before I even tried. But I was calmed. Something was different this time. I felt unstoppable. It was probably the buzz I still felt. I started walking. I didn't question that I could move this time. Instead, making my way lazily towards the town and it seemed only more natural as I got closer. I recognized the buildings as if I had always known the detail in their brick sides. The tall grass ended, and I was facing a street that looked like it was possibly the main street of this ghost town. I stood with the grass at my back and looked down at my feet. My clean shoes were standing in short, yellowed leaves and right in front of my toes the cement street started, boldly cut off from where I stood in a perfectly straightened edge. I felt a sharp pain in my back and reached my hand back to see what was causing it. I rubbed the spot but felt nothing there. I lifted my right foot to step onto the pavement and expected nothing but peace as I prepared to enter this town of my dream. The sharp pain in my back pushed again as the town started to darken. I said the words out loud in the moment that I was thinking them, "No. Not yet."

I OPENED MY eyes; the rock that was comfortable when I first sat down was now digging painfully into my back. I sat forward and rubbed where the rock had tried to puncture the skin. The buzz was completely gone and was replaced by hunger and a slight headache. It was almost dark out, but my spot was still lit by a streetlamp from the park behind me and the reflection of the moon against the river. The early night was loud with the sound of locusts shaking in the trees and I could hear a couple giggling to each other on the rocks to my left. I pushed myself up and pulled my bag over my shoulder before grabbing the empty plastic rings holding a single remaining warm beer. With both feet on the cement, I looked down at my dirty shoes and stared at them where they stood planted on the grey. I tried to recall the feeling that I woke up with, looking at my feet with a memory that was quickly fading from my mind and blending all the dreams into one. A bell chimed with a warning as a bike sped past and into the night. I watched the red reflector fade and started past the path and into the grass, cutting through to the welcoming town; lit up in the night. I walked on the cobbled street and listened to the laughter coming from the restaurant patios as friends and families enjoyed the evening weather while they ate and drank. The smell of bar food drifted into my nostrils and my stomach grumbled to remind me that I was hungry.

I walked towards a distant corner that held a neon pizza sign above a brick wall. A few slices of pizza and a nap in the park overnight and I hoped I would be able to shake this feeling that had interrupted my short-lived peace.

I STOPPED SUDDENLY, one foot still poised and hovering above the ground, as I heard a faint sound underneath the patio chatter. I slowly turned in a circle; people walking around me not noticing; and looked for the source of the weeping. I froze when I finally located it. In between two buildings sat a figure, hunched into a mound and shaking with sobs. I recognized it. It was the physical representation of a feeling deep down that I had found recently but kept trying to push back into its hidden spot. It was desperation. It was loneliness. I hesitated for a moment before slowly walking towards the figure and realizing that desperation and loneliness looked an awfully lot like a young woman. Her arms were freckled by the sun and full of bumps from the cold wind. Her shoes were old, and her legs were pulled up tight to her chest. Her messy hair was laid onto her arms that were folded over her knees and she shook with the cold and the tears. She didn't notice me as I walked to her, drawn inexplicably to the familiarity of her pain. I got closer and knelt in front of her and laid my hand on her arm. She tensed and looked up at me in fear. The bright eyes glared out at me, past the strands of hair and above the tear streaks in her dirty face. She must have been in her late-twenties or maybe younger if she had been treated poorly. We looked at each other, her green eyes changing from fearful to questioning and then understanding and the tears stopped flowing from her open eyes. She moved the arm that was under my hand just a bit to unfold her other arm and she placed her hand on top of mine. Then she rubbed her cheeks, trying to rub away the sticky streaks and I moved so that I was sitting cross-legged on the ground in front of her. She leaned forward into me, still curled like a child, and I wrapped my arms around her. She shifted and almost sat on my folded lap as I held her. I felt her hiccup a few times and then slowly stop shaking, the goosed flesh on her arms slowly disappearing under the warm embrace. A man walked by and glanced at us sitting there with curiosity in his eyes before he continued his walk down the path. I held her like the child I never had, and she sat folded into me like I was a protector.

We sat until the sky had fully darkened and I could feel her body relax even more. Her breath slowed and her head drifted against my chest. And she slept. My arm fell asleep, and I was sitting on a rock that was working its way to another pain. My hips ached and my back curved in a way that was no longer comfortable. My stomach grumbled and my mouth watered at the thought of warm pizza. Yet I sat without moving scared she would awake. She moved slightly in her sleep and made a soft noise but pushed deeper into my chest. I held her and watched more people walk past our hidden pain, never looking into the darkened alley way to see the two lonely strangers sitting here clutching at one another. I looked at her arms in the darkness and the freckles there reminded me of the freckles on my mother's arms as she would hold me. I remembered tracing the freckles with my small finger as she laughed down at me. Her music reverberating through my memory. I would look up at her and she would smile back at me. The smile never quite reaching her eyes, but she hid the pain behind her laugh quite well.

I was forced back to the present when the girl moved and made a noise before her green eyes looked up at me with sleep still heavy in them. She looked embarrassed as she slowly uncurled from my lap and scooted back against the wall, sheepishly grinning at me. I grinned back, trying to not let the worry or recognition of her pain show in my face. She leaned forward and patted my arm and I struggled to stand. I shook the sleep out of my leg and arm before reaching out my hand to help her stand, willing her to come with me and get some food. She shook her head and looked down at her folded hands that were sitting in her lap. I thought for a moment and pulled off my sweatshirt and leaned down, wrapping it around her. She didn't make a move to stop me. I pulled Phil's remaining twenty-dollar bill from my front pocket and pushed it at her. She shook her head again. I grabbed the last beer from the afternoon that seemed like years ago and sat it next to her with the twenty stuck underneath it so it wouldn't blow away. She continued to look down and I lifted my bag and turned to walk away when I felt a small hand intertwine with mine. I turned back to see her looking up at me. She squeezed my hand and nodded, as if she were releasing me from the responsibility of her pain. I nodded back. We were no longer smiling at each other. Replaced with a shared understanding between us. She let go and I walked out of the alley, refusing to look back at her.

I walked towards the pizza sign and stepped through the door that was propped open. I tried to replace the past few timeless hours with the enticing smell of peperoni. The guy behind the counter smiled at me and I tried to smile back.

"What can I getcha?"

I looked at the container with the last few slices that looked a little cold, "Can I get the two slices of pepperoni, the slice of cheese, and two cokes?"

"Pepsi OK?"

"Uh... yeah that's fine"

"That'll be eight fifty"

I pulled the cash out of my pocket. I had saved over a hundred dollars all in small bills even after Phil's twenty I had just given away. I gave him a ten, "keep the change."

"Thanks dude" he tossed three dollars into the tip jar next to the register and turned to get a box for my slices. The two cans of Pepsi, two paper plates and some napkins went into a plastic bag, and he handed it to me along with box with my slices. I walked out the door with a wave, knowing the direction I was headed.

I worked my way back to the alley way where she had sat, hoping to get another smile as I presented her with some pizza and a drink, and I turned the corner into the dark. Maybe I could ask her about her story. Maybe she would tell me. But there was no one waiting there. She was gone and so were the items I had left with her. I rushed out of the alley and looked both ways trying to glimpse her walking away on the cobblestone road. She was nowhere to be seen. Defeated, I worked my way back to the park by the river and tried to recognize her in each woman that walked past me. I sat hard on the grass and opened the pizza box and looked at the extra slice that I had bought to surprise her with.

Once I had finished off two of the pieces, saving the other for the girl I hoped to see again, I laid back in the dampening grass and folded my arms into my shirt to warm them in the cooling night wind. The stars were so bright that they shone like holes poked into the dark blanket of sky, even with the lamps still lighting the path in front of me and the town behind me. As I laid there, I saw one stray star fly above me. What was that my mom had taught me? I squeezed my eyes and tried to remember the words. I whispered them into the night, "star light star bright, first star I see tonight, I wish I may I wish I might, have the wish I wish tonight." I closed my eyes and silently wished for the girl to find her peace, not wanting to say my wish out loud so that it would snake into the air and disappear to nothingness. A childish gesture: one I hadn't done since I was small. I closed my eyes and tried to sleep.

FOR THE FIRST time since starting my lost journey, I dreamt of something other than the grass and the town and the piercing scream of a strange woman. I dreamt that I was small and sitting on her lap, my tiny finger slowly tracing the freckles along her arm, trying to connect the dots into something that would make sense. A Christmas tree! I laughed and showed her, looking up into her eyes as she laughed with me. She shook her dark hair and called me silly and asked what else I could find. I looked back down and traced along another line of freckles to make a firetruck. That was a hard one to find. Pleased with myself, I looked back up, but she was looking away from me. Her eyes focused on something in the distance and a frown on her face. I looked where her head was turned but I just couldn't find what she was looking at. I turned my face towards her again and reached up to pat her soft cheek. She turned her eyes towards me and smiled, "you know I love you, my sweet man?" She said in her soft voice. I stared at her eyes as I nodded and for a quick moment, I saw her eyes in a different way. They were motionless in her lifeless face as she lay in a hospital bed, surrounded by doctors. Dad shielded my eyes just as they started breathing into her mouth; trying to bring her back to us. I fell back into the moment where I sat on her lap and started crying at the sadness in her eyes. She smiled at me and wrapped her cool arms around me as I inhaled in her sweet perfume. She smelled like oranges and slightly like the syrup that had covered my pancakes at breakfast. I could feel her soft body shake with sobs as her tears sprinkled into my hair. She squeezed harder and then suddenly stopped crying as her eyes snapped open and stared into mine. She leaned forward to whisper into my ear, "It is time for you to wake up."

CHAPTER TWELVE

THE BIKE

MY FACE WAS wet from the rain falling from the dark sky. An involuntary groan fell from my mouth. It felt like I hadn't really slept at all. The pain from my dream still fresh in my mind and the pain in my body made worse by the cold wetness all around me. I could feel the water soaking through everything I wore. My arms still folded into my shirt and against my body, shivering to try to stay warm. If I could go back to sleep for just a short while maybe I wouldn't notice the rain and the cold, and this will disappear as just another bad memory. I squeezed my eyes tighter and tried to convince myself into a dreamless sleep. The persistent rain continued to drum against my curled body and soak into my uncovered hair. A crow in the branches above me shouted to another and the response come from further away. I was awake and there was nothing I could do about it. A new determination to dry off hit me fast. I opened my eyes and uncurled from my position, quickly launching myself off the ground as I snatched my bag and started a slow and jilted jog to the restaurant patios that lined the park. The wet pizza box and empty Pepsi cans were forgotten in the grass behind me. I jumped over the short decorative railing of the first patio and dropped my bag on a metal table under an ugly orange awning that boasted that this was the place for the 'very BEST tacos.' I shook my head and then my body to try to spray the water off me like Dog after a rain. It wasn't successful. I sat on one of the chairs and started to feel more of the soreness in my muscles from the night on the ground, the quick morning movements, and the clenching of the muscles against the cold damp. My legs pulled up towards my chest despite the wet jeans sticking to my legs; and my bare arms went back into my shirt to hug my skin. My whole body shivered against the cold, and I watched the water fall in drops from the awning until the morning started to lighten the sky. I tried to force myself back to sleep with the peaceful sound of rain falling above me and the early morning crows looking for their mates.

The cold rain was still coming down when I saw a couple walk past with their arms wrapped around each other trying to make it easier to share their small umbrella. A woman jogged past the other direction; head hidden from the rain by her bright visor. Then came a young man in a drenched polo shirt, not bothering to hide from the rain but still hunched against it.

In his hands were two small to-go coffee cups. I leaned forward on my cold seat and peered in the direction he came from trying to see if I could locate the source of the coffee. I couldn't see anything from my safety under the awning. Shit. Guess I would have to go out and chance it. I stood slowly, taking my time to pull my strap over my head and prepared to re-soak my almost dry shirt in the hopeful search for warmth. I hopped back over the railing, catching myself before I could slip on the water-soaked cobblestone beneath my feet. As I walked the direction that the man had come from; I saw a smiling woman with an umbrella covered with painted on rain drops, bright orange polka-dotted rain boots, and a large paper cup in her hand with a little face stamped into the side. I had to be getting close as I saw the steam floating out of the hole at the top of her plastic lid. I could almost smell it as she walked past me.

Picking up speed at the thought of holding a hot coffee cup in my hand. Then I saw it; the little house almost hidden behind a tree. There was a large sign that said 'OPEN' sitting right beneath the larger sign that said 'COFFEE.' The screen door creaked loudly as I pulled it open and stepped inside the warmth. The coffee shop was made up of multiple rooms, almost like it used to be a house before being turned into a coffee haven. I walked up to the quiet counter and the girl behind it smiled at me questioning with her green eyes. I halted. She almost… almost looked like the girl from last night. Only this one had her long hair pushed into dreadlocks and the freckles on her arms were partially covered up by an intricate tattoo of bright pink flowers. I had almost forgotten about her in the cold and rain filled morning. I'm not sure how I did since the reason why I was so cold was because she was wearing my sweatshirt. The girl in front of me stared at me waiting and I squeezed out, "large black coffee" she squinted her eyes at me, "please."

She smiled and turned her back to me, calling to me over her shoulder, "room?"

"I'm sorry?"

"Do ya want room for cream and sugar?"

"No. Full please."

She turned back around and sat the brimming black coffee in front of me, a little face of a woman stamped into the side. I wrapped my hands around the flimsy paper cup, and she laughed. I looked at her just as she asked, "Where is your jacket?"

"Uh… in my car" I lied, not wanting to shake the image that I am mere steps away from a normal life.

"Well, it is s'posed to rain most of the day, you'll prolly want to go for it soon. But stay here as long as you like. No limit on Wi-Fi." She smiled as she took the three dollars from my hand. The bell above the door chimed and she stuck all three of my dollars into a jar on the end of the counter before she turned to chat with a young man who just walked in. She pushed herself up on the counter with her small arms and leaned over far enough to give the man a kiss, then plopped back down to her side of the counter. I grabbed my cup and wondered into the room that I pictured as the previous living room of this coffee shop that used to be a home. There were two couches, a few chairs, a table covered in board games, a pile of books, and right in the back of it all was a fireplace that was filled with red and orange flames. I walked back and sunk into the armchair that was to the right of the fire and let the flames warm my body as I sipped on the coffee. The window next to me provided a view of the rain falling into river that flowed behind this sleepy town. The water was no longer lazily drifting along but raging angrily towards the ocean. There were birds playing in the grass, enjoying the rain.

I SIPPED UNTIL my last small amount of remaining coffee was cold and my clothes were dry and warm. At the counter, the girl was leaning forward and gazing towards the young man. The man was talking, and she looked completely enraptured with whatever was coming out of his mouth. He had on hiking boots beneath his cargo shorts and black hooded sweatshirt. There was a bright red logo that took up the full back of his sweatshirt. I could read it while his back was towards me as he leaned over this side of the counter finishing his story. There was a long guitar down the spine of the shirt and the words spelled out 'Slim and The Bear Band.' I hadn't heard of it before, must be a local band. She saw me staring at them and smiled around her boyfriend's head, so I stood up from my spot and worked my way over.

"Refill?" She asked as if she could read my mind... or at least my empty cup. I nodded and pulled out a few bills from my pocket. When she saw the money she grinned, "Nah, refills are free." I smiled back and nodded and turned to the young man. He was staring at me, a slight look of annoyance across his face for interrupting his conversation with the pretty young woman.

"What's the Slim and The Bear Band?"

The annoyance fell from his face as he looked at me, surprised, "You know who they are!" I shook my head. He grinned, pushing his hair out of his face, and fished an MP3 player out of the cargo pocket on his. He pushed a few buttons and put it on the counter, turning to her, "Hey babe, put this on and turn on the speakers in the living room."

She picked it up and looked at the screen before glancing up at me, a smile on her face, "Oh you'll like this one." I clutched my refill and made my way back to my warm seat to wait for the music to come on, not really knowing what to expect. A guitar strummed loudly above my head and a small amount of coffee splashed on my lap as I jumped.

I heard a shout from the counter, "SORRY!" before the music started back up quieter, the sound of the fingers against a guitar calming me.

People drivin' around in this local town, nothin' left to do.

And twenty miles away, people do the same, they're cruisin' with their crew.

The voice reminded me of something I heard in my childhood, and I looked to the counter to see both the man and her staring at me grinning.

Now many years ago, I was younger so I would do the same.

Now I got the pictures in my pocket, they don't remember my name.

He shot me a thumb up and looked like he had a question in his face. The music picked up,

All of these years and I still don't know who my friends are.

I grinned and shot a thumb up back at him.

Through all these fears and I don't know how I made it this far.

He clapped his hands together as if he had succeeded in something and they turned back to each other to continue their private conversation.

Invisible man, stranger in a strange land. Invisible man, this I know that I am.

The chorus went a few times and then a quick guitar solo.

I was dreaming, some thought I'd buy a gun and put it to my head.

And with a passing sigh, the world would wave goodbye and I'd be dead.

But there's something on the border there, on the corner, keeps me hangin' on.

Maybe the thought that you lose more than you gain when you play god.

I closed my eyes and sipped on my coffee; relaxing in the warmth of the continuing fire, the sound of the rain drops against the window and the magical voice of Slim… or The Bear… as he sang to me, the words mirroring my own life.

Eventually the music turned off and my coffee turned cold in the bottom of the cup. The sun outside had started to peak through the rain clouds, and it was time to go back outside and leave this moment. I stood and dropped the cup into the blue trash bin with the recycling logo above it. I didn't see the girl or her friend on my way out, and I pushed the screen door open, smelling the freshness that comes after a storm. The air had started to warm with the sun, but there was still a cool breeze. The water collected in puddles along the sides of the cobblestone street and the grass shone bright green in the sunlight. I could hear the water rushing down the river behind me and for a short moment, I again pictured being pulled down into its depths. I breathed in deeply, filling my lungs with the fresh air and it filled my body with hope and peace for the day. I took a long sigh out and tried to remove the funk that was still trying to rear its ugly head from last night. I remembered where I wanted to go. I adjusted the strap of my bag and started towards the sporting goods store. I stopped where I stood, in the middle of the sparkling street filled with kids jumping in puddles and couples holding hands and I tried not to turn my head towards the dark alley; scared of what I might see there. My body moved as if controlled by another person and it turned towards the dark alley, letting my eyes adjust to the blackness. Nothing. There was nothing there, lying on the ground, waiting for someone to find. Deep breath in. The air sat in my lungs. I turned and continued down the street, the weight returned to my shoulders and the darkness behind my eyes.

I PULLED OPEN the door and saw a half-dozen young men milling around in their orange polo shirts with the store logo stitched into the front breast pocket. I looked around for the familiar dark brown messy hair and the friendly tanned face, but all the guys looked about the same. All the similar version of the thirty-something surf or ski 'bum.' Tanned faces speckled with stubble. Bright eyes shining with excitement out from under their mops of unruly hair or knit caps. I saw one such man starting towards me but before I could wave him off, there was a pat on my back, "Hey man, good to see ya. Looking for a jacket, right?"

I turned, "That's right, Travis. Good memory." He laughed as if I had said something intentionally funny and led me to a rack in the corner.

"Everything on this rack is like fifty percent off or something. And I'll give you the family discount so that's like another fifteen or something of the new price. As a thanks for the beer." He grinned like we were close friends, sharing a secret. He sauntered away and I turned to rack. I wanted something that would keep me dry and warm but not too warm if I didn't need it. I pulled a green one from the hanger and pulled it on, looking at myself in the mirror that was leaned against the wall. It was nice and would work well but it would be too hot for a day like today. I put it back and pulled out a blue one. It was perfect. Exactly what I needed. I held up the sleeve and looked at the paper hanging from it and tried to do the math in my head. Even with the discounts it came to more than half of the money I had. I placed it back on its hanger and picked another. After looking at another six jackets, I was almost giving up hope and about to settle for the blue jacket, spending more money than I was comfortable with, when I saw a bright orange sleeve poking out from between two green coats. I pulled on the hanger and found the sleeve was attached to a reflective hiking windbreaker.

The outside was a dark orange with shiny silver reflector straps along the sleeves. There was a hidden hood that came out when needed and a detachable soft inner layer. I did the math three times to make sure I was right. If Travis was right with the discounts, this jacket would be about twenty dollars. I unzipped the two layers and pulled on just the soft grey layer, carrying the outer orange layer with me to the counter. Travis was standing there telling a young blonde man about his morning run in the rain. He turned to include me in the telling of the rest of his story as he rang up my purchase. "Ohhh Kay. That'll be eighteen dollars and twenty-three cents." He held out his palm and I handed him a twenty trying to look like I wasn't surprised at the price of this jacket. Just another dude buying discounted sports gear. Right. After he dropped the change and receipt into the palm of my hand, he leaned towards me, "Hey man, you wanna buy a bike?" The questioning surprise must have been obvious on my face, and he stood back with his hands up in front of him. "No. no. It's not what you think. At least I don't think it's what you think. One of my roommates met a chick and moved to California.

He left all his shit at my apartment and still owes me more than a month's rent. So, I'm selling his stuff. None of the assholes in this town would wanna buy his bike – they're all too picky."

I looked around at the outdoorsmen milling around this store, "yeah that doesn't surprise me." I turned back to him, "Thanks but I don't think I can afford to buy your bike."

"My roommates bike." Travis corrected me, "Just come look at it. I'll give you a good price." He turned and motioned at me to follow him towards the back door of the shop.

We stepped through the back door and into a dark storage room. "Watch your step." He called over his shoulder as he stepped over unorganized boxes of extra hats and backpacks. He pushed open another door and I shielded my eyes against the bright sun that shone through the open space. I followed him into the alley behind the store and saw a bike rack with a half-dozen nice and expensive looking bikes chained up... and one worn out bike with a basket rigged behind the seat. I looked at Travis as he stood, poised over the bike like Vanna White, as if that would make it more appealing. He put his hands down and sighed, "Ok man, to be totally honest, it's a piece of shit. It rides fine and has new tires, but the fourth gear sticks and you'll never be able to go off road with it. BUT" he looked back up, "for forty bucks, I'll throw in a repair kit." I looked at the bike and looked back at Travis. I prepped to tell him that I wasn't interested. That I didn't even know where I was going. What the hell would I do with a bike?

Instead, unexpected words came out of my mouth, "I'll give you twenty-five dollars."

He grinned and stuck out his hand, "Deal."

AN HOUR LATER, I was pedaling down a paved side road and away from the town. My bag was shoved down into the basket behind the seat of the bike as I rode in the middle of the pavement. The wind was blowing against my grey wool inner jacket as my arms made their way out and up into the air as I steadied the bike with my legs. My head lifted to the sky, and I flew down the road. There was a freedom that I hadn't felt in years as I floated towards my next destination.

CHAPTER THIRTEEN

THE STATION

MAN, I SURE missed that bike. Stranded somewhere behind me and buried under mounds of snow. It had taken me further than I would have ever gotten from just walking or the random ride from a stranger. I had felt free while riding. I could go where I wanted and when I wanted. My legs had just started getting used to the daily push of the pedals by the time the leaves had finished falling from the branches and the wind started blowing colder. I had zipped up the outer layer of my jacket and pulled the hood tight as I made it almost across another state on the power of my own legs. I eventually found a stocking cap and some thin fabric gloves. I bundled and rode against the rapidly freezing wind, not willing to give up my wheels, trying to make it south of the winter. Until one tire blew. Not for the first time. But this time I wasn't close to a town where I could repair it and I didn't have the right supplies to fix it on the road. I had to accept that the bike would stay where it was rusting until spring. I had turned back twice for it, thinking maybe I should find a way to fix it again. But the second time I turned back; I felt a small wet spot hit the bridge of my nose. I looked up just in time to see the white drifting slowly from the clouds above me.

THE HEAVY DOOR shut behind me as I stomped my shoes against the ground. Wet snow clung to my jeans making them sag against my legs and I pulled the thin gloves off my hands before turning back towards the outer door. I thought back to a time that I spent starving and sitting in the bitter snow thinking that I would die. My fingers ran down the wet glass and I stared into the thick white snow that was beating down from the sky. The flakes were so large, I could almost make out the shape of each one and I thought about the patterns I had cut from folded paper when I was small. Now looking at the real thing as it continued to pile against the door, I knew that it was deadly, just as it was beautiful. I stood mesmerized by the shapes of the freezing snow against the dark backdrop and considered my own mortality, picturing my corpse frozen beneath the snow next to my discarded bike. A figure came into view, running towards my door. He slowly got larger and larger and then he was tugging at the door in front of me. I stepped aside to let him in from the cold. He stomped his boots against the rug and nodded at me, his nose and cheeks bright red. The man pulled off his stocking cap and shook, covering the ground in white for a second before it disappeared into wet spots on the tile and rug. He walked past me and into the warmth of the station.

I turned to follow him and the blast of warmth coming from the vent above the inner door calmed my dangerous thoughts of the storm. I pulled my hat off and stuck it into my bag next to the damp gloves. People milled about the large open room, and no one seemed in a hurry to go anywhere. The sides of the room were held up with pillars of smooth marble. A room from the past but stuck in the present. I looked up at the electronic sign that showed delays and cancelations next to destination cities. The trains moving as slowly as the people in the threat of abandonment out in the cold. No one noticed me as I walked past them; just another guy taking shelter in here and waiting for a train. I worked my way to a side room where long wood benches sat in rows and found a spot to lean against the arm rest to wait for my clothes to dry. Luckily this discount jacket of mine kept the snow from wetting my layers underneath, but my jeans were completely damp all the way through. My socks and shoes were filled with melting snow, but I would need to wait to take them off and try to dry them until the crowd had cleared a little. I knew that if I looked like a squatter and not just a forgotten traveler then someone might ask me to leave, and I wasn't ready to die in the snow quite yet. The bench I was on had smoothed down from years of travelers. Made in a time when more people chose to sit and wait for a train. A younger couple sat on the bench next to me, quietly whispering to each other. I tried to listen to their conversation but could only catch a word here or there over the chatter of the people walking past the large open door to the main room.

A small child wondered into the room and his big brown eyes looked at me as he started his cowboy walk to my seat. He made it all the way to fall to his padded butt right in front of me. He looked up and smiled a wide grin showing me his two small teeth that were planted in his mouth. His dark brown eyes reflected my own face. I couldn't help but smile back at him in response. I made a little wave with two of the fingers on my right hand and he giggled before being picked up and carried away by an apologetic mother. Across from me was a man about my age lying on the bench. His backpack was pushed up against the side and being used as his pillow and his foot kicked a little while he slept. He must have been dreaming about something nice and his face split into a smile as he lay there with his eyes pressed closed. The couple got up and walked away holding hands. Her voice carried as she was whispering something in his ear about heading back home. I wondered where their home was. Were they trying to travel to get away from home or trying to get to it? I watched them walk out of the doorway and a uniformed man came into view as they walked out. He took a quick look at the people inhabiting of the room I was in. His eyes stayed on the dreaming man a bit longer than the rest of us, but he must not have seen anything of concern. He looked at me and nodded without a smile on his face. I must have checked out as well. Just a normal traveler. Not a 'leather' or a squatter. I nodded back and he turned to continue his rounds.

I pulled a granola bar out of my bag and munched on it wondering what the man was dreaming about. His foot kept twitching as I chewed and then washed it down with a swig of water from the bottle from my bag. I remember my father bringing me to a station like this when I was young. My small hand clutched in his as we found a space on a bench just like this one. We waited patiently for our train to take us somewhere. I don't remember where. I had sat on the old wooden bench and swung my short legs. He would check the board and double check his ticket and rub his hand up and down my back as we waited, comforting me. A few more people wandered into the room as I sat. An older man walking with the help of a stick sat heavily at the end of the bench behind me. A woman that looked upset with the world sat down next to the sleeping man's feet. She pulled a book out of her purse and stared at a page for a few minutes, checking her watch instead of remembering to pretend to read. The book went back into the bag, and she pulled out a ball of bright multicolored yarn and two long sticks. Glanced at her watch again before she sighed loud enough to be heard over the foot traffic walking by and started weaving the sticks in and out of the yarn to continue what looked to be a future scarf. Maybe it was a blanket. Maybe it was nothing but a way to keep her hands busy while she waited for her train. I watched the long metal needles click together while she wove; mesmerized by the pattern she was creating. I always wondered what it would be like to learn a skill like that. Something to keep my hands busy. I had thought of it for a short while years ago when I quit smoking. She checked her watch again and sighed again and then kept moving her hands in the deft motion. I scooted down on my bench a bit and shoved my duffel bag against the arm rest before curling up to mirror the dreaming man across from me. I laid and watched the long needles move back and forth, the yarn being wrapped around and then pulled through the existing pattern. Over and over the needles worked, and her scarf or blanket became a rainbow of bright colors floating across a blue sky.

I WAS BEING prodded in the arm with something hard, "You can't sleep here." I opened my eyes and saw a different man in a uniform standing above me, a plastic rod in his hand as he poked it at me. The other uniform must have forgotten to tell him that I checked out OK. I rubbed my eyes and sat up on the wood bench. Huh. I must have passed out for quite a while. The sleeping man was gone and so was the knitting woman. I craned my head behind me and saw that the elderly man with the walking stick had been replaced by a young family. I smiled at them, and they all stared at me, the young mom squeezed her handbag closer to her chest. "I said you can't sleep here." He poked me again, this time in the chest.

I looked back up at him, "Yeah, I got that. I'm just waiting out the storm."

He glanced at the family behind me and shrugged in their direction before leaning down closer to me, "listen friend, if you ain't waiting for a train, you can't sit here. There are a few places across the street that you can stay at for a decent price and a couple pubs up the road to grab a drink." He nodded at me and stood there as if waiting for me to get up so he could follow me to one of these places to stay. I wondered if he would follow me all the way there. I grabbed my bag and followed him out the door and into the main room as the sun shone through the large windows above us. My clothes weren't damp anymore and the overly heated room was almost uncomfortable. I unzipped my jacket and pulled it off so I could carry it in my hand as the uniformed man followed me into the opening. The marble shone against the sheets of morning light. I turned and nodded at him and lifted my hand in a little wave to let him know that I was walking out. He nodded but kept his glare on me for a moment before he turned back to his rounds, tapping his rod against his other hand. I looked around the large main room and saw that the trains must be running again as people rushed around me, no longer in a lazy holding pattern. A man with a briefcase pushed past with an annoyed look on his face. "Excuse me," I said in his direction, but he didn't seem to notice in his rush. I walked to the opposite corner of the room and tried to decide if I was safe to stand for a minute before braving the frigid weather outside. I didn't see the uniformed man anywhere and I stood, hidden in the corner, before I decided that it was probably safer to find another place to finish out the day before finding my next spot. I pushed through the first set of doors and saw the sun blasting through, the outer doors propped open to the outside elements. This wasn't right. I walked slowly through the crowd of people that were streaming in and was met with sun and warmth as I exited the station. The snow was completely gone, and the wind blew heat against my face.

I STEPPED INTO the bustling sidewalk and froze in my tracks when I saw a car roll by that looked almost exactly like one that I had owned years ago, still in pristine condition. Those were rare anymore. But then there was another. People walked around me as I turned slowly on the sidewalk and noticed the women wearing skirts and dresses that hung to just below their knees. Some in jeans that drastically widened at the bottoms. The men wore a mix that either mirrored the women's jeans or suits with jackets and hats. Underneath the blaze of the sun, I seemed to be the only person who was seeing the strangeness around me. I stopped turning and looked down at my own clothes and could see that I am alone in my crass hiker fashion. There must have been an event going on today and I missed the signs. No one seemed to be in a festive mood and the day seemed like a normal one. I stood motionless on the sidewalk and tried to make sense of the world that I was standing in. I must be dreaming. I fell asleep watching the knitting woman and no one woke me up. Was I dreaming? I didn't like this dream. Why is no one looking at me? I stood, the man out of time and place, alone in a crowd of strangers. Maybe these people couldn't really see me.

I clutched my bag tighter and started to back slowly towards the train station watching people as they continued to swerve around me. "UMPH" I ran right into a woman who was walking past me. I stopped. She stopped. She looked me up and down and continued walking down the road, giggling to her friend. "I'm sorry," I called to her back. She didn't look back. So, they could see me. And feel me. I watched where I was going and kept moving until my back was against the large tan stone bricks of the train station and slowly sunk to the ground, clutching my jacket and my bag. Wake up. Wake up. How could I wake up? I pinched my arm. Nothing. I pinched harder, enough that it left a mark in my skin when I let go, and I squeezed my eyes shut. I opened my eyes again and continued to see the people walking past, occasionally looking at me with pity or questions in their eyes. Why couldn't I wake up? This wasn't right. I closed my eyes. What was going on? I felt the warmth beating against my face and heard the chatter of the people walking past me on the uneven sidewalk. I pulled my limbs into my body and tried to hide into the corner of this dream world where no one could find me.

Something softly rested against my folded knee, and I kept my eyes shut so it would go away. A familiar smell drifted around me. I inhaled it as I started to calm. "Sir are you in trouble?" a soft voice asked me as I felt the hand push heavier onto my knee. I opened my eyes and my breath caught in my throat as I saw those eyes inches from my own face. Her nose was speckled with freckles and her hair blew around her face in the warm wind. The people that were rushing around behind her seemed to slow and their voices dimmed as I stared back at her. An angel lit from behind. She lifted her hand from my knee and moved it towards my face. I reacted out of instinct as I tried to move my head back away from her touch and she froze in alarm for a moment before placing it on my forehead. The cooling touch reminded me of something my mother used to do when I wasn't feeling well. She leaned back a little. "You don't feel warm. You don't look like you are feeling well though." She looked at me with a question on her soft face. Her face was almost familiar as if I had dreamed her before. Or that I'm dreaming of her right now and that's enough to force familiarity. She had to be no more than sixteen or seventeen.

CHAPTER FOURTEEN

THE TILE

I SEEMED TO find my voice somehow, "I'm OK. Just..." trying to figure out how to explain that she was in my dream right now, just a figment of my own imagination. She had to be though. There was no other explanation. That was why she reminds me of... someone else that I couldn't quite place. She waited for me to finish my sentence. "Lost..." I whispered to her.

She looked confused, "are you trying to get to somewhere?"

I hesitated, "uh... yeah. But I've... I've forgotten where I was going." I didn't know why I was saying this to her.

"How can I help you?" she asked me as if she really meant it. She had no idea what she was asking.

"I don't think you can help."

Her brows furrowed as she seemed to think about my answer. I should have told her that I was dreaming. That I needed to wake up. That I didn't know how to wake up. I knew her and I put her here. Into my dream. But I didn't know how I knew her or how I created her in my mind. This young girl. And I didn't know how to leave this world.

I opened my mouth to tell her this and was prepared for her to run away, when we were interrupted by a loud voice, "El, leave the man be, let's go!"

I saw the look of concern on her face take a different form. A flicker of fear in her eyes as she turned her head to look over her shoulder, her hair falling to hide her face from me. "Just a moment, please."

She started to turn back towards me when he came over and put out his hand to help her stand, "Eloise, we're going to be late. This man is not your problem." I looked up but couldn't see his face. He was lit by the sun behind him and became only a shadow, a demon, standing there trying to take my angel away. She pushed against my knee to help her stand. They turned to walk away as she looked apologetically over her shoulder at me, and he led her away. She gave a small smile and a wave before disappearing into the crowd. The crowd sped back up to normal and the noise was almost deafening compared to the quiet that she had brought with her. I thought I could see a peek of her dress as she disappeared from my dream. This was a dream. This had to be a dream.

I didn't see the people walking by. Everything was blurred by the moment of clarity that had just happened. If this was my dream, I could bring back the girl I had just met. She seemed so familiar. Where had I seen her before? I closed my eyes and tried to will her back to me. This was my dream after all. I felt a small touch at the side of my foot and opened my eyes, excitedly expecting to see her familiar eyes looking back at me. No one was kneeling there. I felt the touch again and looked down to see a small mouse nosing at the hem of my jeans. I adjusted my bag, and he ran along the wall away from me in fear. I unzipped the bag and pulled out a granola bar as my stomach growled. If this was a dream, why was I hungry? I pondered the thought as I chewed and saw the little grey furry nose reappear as the mouse started hesitantly walking back towards my seat. I broke off a small piece of oat and tossed it down next to my little friend. He slowly ran towards it and finally reached it to sniff at before he grabbed it and held it as he ate. He finished and I tossed him another before I finished my portion.

HOW LONG HAD I been sitting in the dream? The sun was setting, and the foot traffic was heavier as I stood, the mouse was still sitting by my bag as he cleaned his whiskers. He looked at me as I leaned against the cooling stone wall and tried to recognize any of the other faces that were walking past me. I tried to place the man who was walking towards the propped door of the train station. Nope, I didn't recognize anyone. My dream. Why don't I know anyone else that I created? I walked through the doors as part of the transit crowd and moved to the side once I entered the large room. It was no longer lit with sunlight and instead had dim lights glowing at the edges.

I looked towards the screens and notice that they weren't digital anymore but had little flaps for the destinations. Maybe I imagined the screens when I was dizzy with the cold storm the first time I entered. The trains showed that they were all still on time. I scanned the room and saw the uniformed man walking towards the other side of the large room. I looked to my left and could see a row of small doors and I rushed towards them. The first door was locked. I looked behind me and saw the uniform starting to turn in my direction, but the second door pushed open easily and I slid in before he saw me. There was a dim light over the single sink and a small toilet in the corner. I locked the door and peered into the mirror. I looked better than I thought I would. My hair was crazy from the storm now a distant memory, but the snow must have cleaned any dirt from my face. I took off my bag and tossed it in the corner before I sank to the floor next to it.

The floor was surprisingly clean for a train station bathroom. My feet pushed against the door as a second precaution, and I thought about where I was as my fingers lightly traced the grout that was pushed between the small white hexagon tiles on the floor. I could hear the rush of the travelers beyond the bathroom door, and it rattled once as someone tried the handle before moving on to the next open stall. My body slowly started to cool and relax. This must not have been a dream. If it was a dream, then why would I be tired? Just the fog that had been building in my brain since the storm had started. Who was I joking? The fog started well before that. Water slowly dripped from the faucet and soon I was lulled to sleep by the sound of the ongoing drip and the quieting sounds in the large open room of the train station. There were no dreams within my dream. Just calming darkness.

SOMEONE POUNDED ON the door with their full fist. "You can't sleep in there, buddy!" My eyes shot open, and I stared at the locked door. Again, someone yelled from the other side. "I'm going to unlock the door in ten minutes. You have that long to gather your shit, got it?" I heard footsteps walking away. I must have been asleep for a while as there was no longer any light shining through the little window. I looked down at my fingers and noticed that the tile was a darker grey than I originally thought. The light above the sink shone with a white tint and I could see the trash pushed behind the toilet. I stood up and saw that the sun was trying to peek through the window, but the window was covered in black paint with only a few scratches that let in the outside light. Huh. Must have slept way longer than I thought. All the way into the next morning. I looked at the mirror and saw a long crack running from one corner into another. The faucet turned on and cold water ran through my hands before being splashed against my face and rubbed into my tired eyes. I pulled the collected bathroom supplies out from my bag and got undressed, folding my clothes to sit on the yellowed toilet. I used my own soap to clean my body, drying off with the paper towels that were folded and sitting on the toilet tank. Washed and brushed my hair. As I was pulling my dry jeans back on over my legs, I heard the clink of keys being pushed into the lock on the other side of the door. I unlocked it and pulled it open, still undressed from the waist up. An overweight man in a blue uniform, one I hadn't seen before, stood on the other side with the key poised in the lock. I grinned at him, trying to appear friendly and non-confrontational. "Sorry man, I was just cleaning up. Long day of travel, ya know?" He looked at me and noticed the shirtless chest and looked past me at the supplies on the sink.

"Oh, that's fine. I know it was tough with all the trains stopped. We had an overdose in one of these bathrooms not too long ago, so I just have to check." He pulled the key from the lock, and I nodded at him. He held his hand on the door before I could close it, "Just don't take too long, cool?"

"Yeah, I'll be out of here in five minutes." He nodded and turned away, letting me shut and lock the door. I thought back to the warm day and the train traffic and shook my head. It was a dream. I knew that. I chided myself for the moments in the dream when I questioned the reality of the situation. I brushed my teeth and finished pulling on my warm clothes, knowing that I would have to prepare to go back out into the snow. The warmth of the dream gone. I put everything back into my bag and lifted it over my head so it could hang on my shoulder and turned to unlock the door. Hand frozen on the door lock, waiting to go back out. Why couldn't I shake this feeling that something wasn't right? What wasn't right? I had dreams before. A lot of them. This one was slowly fading in my memory to live with the others, but even as it was fading away, something wasn't right. What is it?

My hand fell from the lock before I turned it and I shifted so that I was looking back at the interior of the bathroom. How did I get here? I fell asleep on the bench in that other room. Then I had the dream where I went outside. There was the girl who I knew but didn't. That sweet smell that follows me. And I came back here and fell asleep. But that was all in the dream. So how did I wake up in this bathroom? The granola. I had bought a pack of six granola bars. I pulled my back over my head and dropped it on the dirty floor and kneeled beside it. I had eaten one granola bar the day before last. Then another yesterday morning before the snow hit hard. And another sitting on the bench in the train station. That means there should be three left. I pulled out the box that held my granola bars and opened it, pulling out the food wrapped in plastic. One. Two. My hand went back in for the third but there was nothing else in the box. This didn't make sense. I must have had another bar and forgotten about it. That had to be it. I put everything back and zipped back up my bag. I ran cold water again and splashed my face trying to make myself wake up further. There had to be an explanation. I placed both hands on either side of the sink and stared at myself. "Pull yourself together man, that wouldn't make any sense. It was a dream." I was trying to convince myself through the nonstop fog swirling through my brain.

A knock came from the other side of the door followed by a voice, "c'mon buddy, you promised you wouldn't stay in there. You gotta go." I pulled my bag back to my shoulder and looked at myself one more time before turning the lock on the door and walking back into my reality.

CHAPTER FIFTEEN

THE EXPLORER

MY FOOT SLIPPED on the wet rock, and I hit my elbow painfully as I landed heavily. "DAMMIT," I yelled out loudly in pain. There was no one around to hear me. I was pretty sure this hidden place got busy later in the day and later in the season. Right now, it was just me and the snow slowly melting into the frigid water that ran between the rocks below me. I pulled my bag off my shoulder and sat it on a large moss-covered stone before rolling the sleeve of my sweatshirt up on my arm so I could get a handle on the damage I just did. The skin around the elbow wasn't broken but I could feel a welt beginning to form. Another day. Another bruise. I pulled down the shirt sleeve and slid my jacket back on to cover my dry clothes from the spray of the water. The walls that stretched above me were covered in bright green moss and small clumps of untouched white snow. Above them the sky was blue with sunlight that was beginning to shine. Down where I was, the new sun couldn't quite reach me to warm my face. I looked down at the clear water where it rushed towards the path I came from as if it were trying to escape this mountain. I stuck the toe of my shoe down into the water and the cold water felt refreshing against my warm foot. These shoes were a good find. The old sneakers and four pairs of socks were stuck down into my duffel bag, and they had been temporarily replaced with a slightly too big pair of rubber bottom shoes that were made for hiking through water. I pulled my soft grey rock from the pocket of my jeans and rubbed it between my fingers as I watched the water flow in and out of the dumpster found shoe and waited to see if the sun would find me.

I stood carefully so that I wouldn't slip again and continued to work my way over the large rocks. My hands were helping me keep myself steady as I lightly touched each foot to the ground before committing to each step. Last thing I needed was a serious fall back here where no one would find me until later in the spring. I made it over the rocks and then saw my path was blocked by fallen trees that had been smashed in-between the nature made walls. I was determined to make it further and find the start of the running water, so I pulled and pushed my way to the top of the log dam. Careful footing, arms out for support, bag banging against my hip as it tried to push me over; I kept climbing. Finally, I stood at the top of the trees and looked back towards the path I came from. I felt

KASSIE J RUNYAN

accomplished. I felt powerful. If only for a moment. I could see the light peaking around the corner of one of the large rocks but could no longer hear the trains or cars over the running water beneath me. The walls seemed to go up even further here. I could see trees at the top, somehow finding their own footing on the rough surface for a while before they would eventually come crashing down to the bottom. A bird called in the distance, and I realized that I had found my own moment, untouched by the world of men or the empty hosts that called themselves such. There was no trash scattered along the sides of the water and no fence to keep me out. Trees grew above and lay where they fell, purely from their own weight against the winter waters. The air was crisp and clear. I stood on the apex of the dam, one leg bent to stand steady on a slightly higher log, and I put my fists on my hips so I could stand like the explorers that found this place before me. I felt like a man. Just for this second, I was not just a shell. There; just for this one small moment; I oversaw my own fate. I was an explorer. I closed my eyes and breathed in the pure air as I stood.

Eventually, I turned towards the hidden path that continued beyond my tree pile. The light back there had started to sneak through from the top of the gorge. The large rock walls curved, and I could only see sections of my path. The water widened and I would have to clutch the wall to get around the next bend unless I wanted to go for a cold swim. I didn't. I sat down on the log that I had been standing on and slowly worked my way down this side of the dam, crawling over and around the large fallen trees. I made it to the last large log and jumped off it to land firmly on a pile of small rocks. They had been worn down by the water being run over them for so long and were now little wet black pebbles that clanked together when I stepped on them. I stood, looking down at the rocks and seeing the familiarity as I pulled my own from my pocket. I leaned over and set my rock down on top of the darker ones before standing up and surveying the ground. It matched the other rocks with the only exception being that it was lighter grey and dull, where the other rocks were darkened and shined from the water around them. Interesting. I grabbed my rock before it was lost amongst its peers and stuck it deep down in my pocket where it belonged before walking back along the nature made path towards the curve of the wall.

I stopped long enough to roll up the bottoms of my pants all the way to my knees. I wasn't planning on wading in the water, but I had no idea what lay around this rock edge. I checked my bag and squeezed my body against the cold rock wall and slid around it to reach the other side not sure what I was expecting. The walls spread wide, and I was greeted by another opening that had been created by the years of water flow. I jumped over the water that ran next to my foot and landed solidly on another beach made of small dark grey pebbles. The water was quicker here, rushing over the larger rocks behind me. The snow here was almost completely melted and there were just small clumps of white stuck to the crevices in the stone. There were no more logs to block the water and it flowed freely past me. I could hear the water hitting the rocks beyond yet another curve. The water looked a little deeper there and the ledge for walking was completely gone. I could either lower into this frigid water to see the end of the path or turn back where I came from, work myself back over the logs and continue down the hiking path I had been on. I pulled my strap off over my head and let the bag fall behind me, the rocks making a muffled sound as it landed. Then I pulled my pants off over my shoes and folded them before setting them on top of my bag. I stood, in only my found underwear and water shoes from the bottom down. That should be enough.

I dipped the first foot down into the water and let it land heavily on one of the larger rocks before reacting to the freezing water that made it to my ankle. Shit that was cold. The second foot followed and soon I was walking in the direction the water was flowing from. The air around me darkened as the sun was blocked by more trees above and the narrowing rock walls. The water made it to my knees. Then to my thigh. It became harder to walk against the water as I waded it deeper, but I kept going, pushing for the small opening between the rocks. I was careful with my footing, not wanting to slip and get the dry layers under my jacket wet. I made it to the opening and looked back at my bag sitting in a spot of sunlight before moving forward. Determined.

My hand pushed against the wet rock beside me to help get around it and I dipped my sore elbow into the cool water. I looked back at where my hand sat, tan and worn, on top of dark grey rock with slick green moss and turned my head towards the back of the rock to see the source of the stream I was standing in. I walked further; mouth open in awe at my find. Water was jetting out of the wall that was rising high above me. I watched one stream as it shot out of the top and fell to the bottom to spray against the rocks beneath it. Standing there, watching the rush of water as it fell and splattered before joining the stream, I felt so small. I was nothing but a man against this nature that had existed for thousands of years, carving the crevice behind me, molding the rock into the shape that it needed to be. Maybe if I stood here long enough it would mold me into something else. Make me into what I needed to be. I moved closer to the crashing water and the air was cold as my legs came out of the stream a bit. My eyes closed and I felt my skin dampen from the spray. The chirp of the birds was completely drowned out by the flow of the water. It was just me and this powerful and beautiful force. My toes were numb. I looked down at my legs still standing in the water. I sighed, not wanting to leave this spot but knowing that I couldn't stay long. I looked back at the top of the falls wondering where the water came from. Maybe I should go find it. I turned and made my way back to the crevice opening and worked back to my bag. I used an older shirt to dry off and rub the feeling back into my cold legs before sliding my jeans back on. I filled up my water bottle with the cold stream water before working my way out of this gorge and back to the path along the highway that I came from.

I looked back at my hidden spot. How could I find the top? I put my hand against my forehead to block the sun and looked up at the mountain that I stood next to wondering if I could get to the top of this or how. Maybe if I just kept following this path. This seemed like an area with hikers. There had to be paths just about everywhere. I walked, uphill then downhill, left then right. Rubber shoes catching my steps. My legs had lost some of the soreness that had found me at the beginning part of this journey, and I kept moving. How could I ever get to the top like this? Finally, the path split into two. One continued along by the highway, but the other turned left towards the mountainside and inclined out of view. I turned left. I must have been hiking for more than an hour when the path split again. Both sides kept inclining but went in two different directions. The first one looked rougher with tree roots coming out each way and narrowed in-between the tall trees. The second looked smoother and wider. I stood at the intersection and looked down both paths trying to determine which one was best. As I looked toward the second path, I noticed a sign in the distance. I walked up the second path just to get a closer look. It was made of old wood and worn so badly I couldn't make out the wording. I reached out to push some of the nature off to see if I could make the carved letters readable. I squinted at it as if that would make it clearer. 'Ange'... maybe an I at the end, then a few shapes that didn't make letters and it ended with a 'k 1.2' and a small arrow that pointed up the smooth path. Well, something was at the end of this path, I might as well see what is there. I kept climbing up, surrounded heavier by tall thick trees; moss hiding the bark in spots. The dark path was made of tiny rocks that were almost sand combined with needles from the trees. The birds sang above me. The sun had risen to be straight overhead, but it was so blocked by the pine needles and branches of trees, that it only lit the path in random spots. It was almost as if there were small spotlights scattered and buried beneath the path to light my way.

A YOUNG COUPLE, maybe in their twenties, walked towards me. They were in matching shorts and hiking boots with small packs on their backs. They both wore stocking caps with the same symbol and there was a small dark lab that ran around their feet as they walked. As they neared, I focused my eyes on the path in front of me to not draw their attention and moved to the side to give them room to pass. The sounds of their footsteps grew louder and then the wriggling dark puppy ran into my view. He couldn't stay still, he was so excited, and his small paws kept stepping on my shoes. There was a bright orange bandana wrapped around his neck, his fashion accessory. He looked at me with his large brown happy eyes and I smiled down at him, leaning over to reach out my hand. Before I could pet his shaking body, he turned and lapped at my hand. I laughed down at him and crouched to get closer.

KASSIE J RUNYAN

"John!" I looked up startled at the interruption of my moment. The hiking girl stood there, smiling. "I am so sorry; we don't usually see people on this path, so we don't leash him." I sat crouched and frozen, with the dog licking my face now. She came closer and took ahold of his bandana, "John, stop licking the poor man" she laughed apologetically.

I felt that I could move again as the air left my lungs, "You said his name is John?"

The boy behind her laughed, "Yeah, weird name for a dog. I don't know, he just seemed like a John." They had to be teasing me.

"Oh ok" I responded, waiting for them to tell me that it was a joke. The three of us stood there for a moment, her trying to keep ahold of the dog to keep him from running to me again. Finally, the boy leaned over and picked up the dog, letting it squirm in his arms.

He looked back at me, "You going to the peak?"

"Uh... yeah." Oh. Those must have been the letters I couldn't read from the word that ended in 'k'.

She smiled again at me, "good day for it. We just came from there. Not a cloud in the sky."

"Uh... cool," I looked down at my feet for a moment before looking at the dog again. The couple smiled at each other with a hidden secret that must have been shared just between them.

She looked up at me, "Ok, happy hiking!" and they walked past me, her hand absent mindlessly patting the dog that was still attempting his crazy escape from her partners arms.

I smiled and lifted my hand as they walked past, "You too."

I kept walking on my path, not seeing another person. I should have asked them how much further it was. My body was almost warm under my layers and jacket, even while my face was still cold with the chill in the air. I could feel the blood pumping through my legs as I continued to walk at an uphill slant. It really couldn't be that much further. The path split again and to my left I saw the same type of path, with trees growing on each side and the overhang of the branches covering the path. To my right, I saw another sign and then a wall of light where the trees ended. I walked to the right and suddenly I was thrust into a new terrain. The trees were at my back and so was the soft path. I was standing on a large tan rock that jetted out of the hillside like it was put there specifically for this reason. It was long and almost flat as I walked out onto it further before noticing how high I had made it from the highway. I looked over the edge of my rock and could see the small cars moving down beneath me. Beyond that I could see a train track that ran through the rock. And then there was the river. A wide river that mirrored the mountains on the other side of the blue water. That couple was right, not a cloud in the sky. The sun shone against the bright blue and the sounds of the world seemed far away. I looked behind me and could see the rest of the mountain rising behind me, the trees hiding the paths that were meant to be explored.

I sat on the edge of the rock, my legs dangling over the world below me and zipped open my bag to pull out my water bottle. The liquid was still cool as it worked its way through my body, and I watched as a train flew west. It looked like a tiny toy, so far down below. I pulled my box of granola bars from my bag and counted them before pulling one out to quiet my rustling stomach. I had three left in this newest box. I made a mental note to remember three, not wanting to misplace one again. The sun warmed my jeans as I sat and I was alone in this world, high above the rest. Peacefulness filled me. Deep breath in. Long sigh out. Little trains and little cars and little lives moving silently below.

A CLICKING NOISE came from the rock behind me and interrupted my quite reflection. I turned my head to see a woman walking straight towards my spot, using a stick to help her navigate the rough rock steps. She got close before she looked up and froze, seeing me sitting there watching her move.

She smiled widely, "Oh company. Good." I nodded at her and turned back to watch the tiny world as she made her way over and sat down next to me with a soft grunt. She folded her legs out and let them swing next to mine. "Sure does takes things out of perspective, doesn't it?" She looked down at the movement below our spot and grinned.

"Yeah." Her eyes closed and I stole glances at her while she sat next to me, short legs hanging over the edge. She had on soft grey pants and a fleece jacket. Her grey hair was pulled into a braid that hung from the top of her head and there were deep lines in her face from years of laughter even though her face looked almost sad in this moment. She carried a little drawstring bag on her back that had a big E stitched on the front. Her eyes opened and I quickly looked back down the rock so that she wouldn't see that I had been staring at her. She pulled her little bag off her back and opened it to pull out a sandwich wrapped in plastic. My stomach growled and I hoped she didn't notice as I peered at her from the side. She didn't glance at me as she pulled the bread apart and reached towards me with half of it in her hand. I thought for a moment about letting her know that I wasn't hungry, but as I looked at her, I knew it wouldn't make a difference. So, I took the half a sandwich with a "Thank you" and took a bite.

I savored the smoothness of the bread and the crunch of the nuts buried in the sweet peanut butter. We ate in silence, each enjoying our lunch on this rock that we found. We finished eating and washed it down with swigs from our own water bottles before she turned to me. I waited for her to ask me about my story just like everyone that I have shared a meal with lately. I was prepared to tell her the lie that I could now parrot easily. But she didn't ask. Instead, she started talking and it was my turn to listen to someone else.

"I woke up this morning and thought, I need to go for a hike. To this spot. A spot that I haven't been for years. I don't know why this morning of all mornings. I thought I would come up here alone and think about my poor lonely life, eat my little sandwich, and go home to my quiet house. Yet here you are so I'm going to talk to you instead." She waited. I nodded. "My husband is dead. Shit. That sounds horrible saying it like that. But there is no other way to say it. Now there is no one left to talk to. He was always there, listening, arguing, laughing, and now he's just not. One day he was there, teasing me about my anger with... I don't even know now... then he wasn't there anymore. It doesn't make sense. Every day is quiet now. Every night is the same. Every morning is the same. I'm stuck here every day, knowing that my life is no longer complete. I have seen what I wanted to see. I have done what I have wanted to do. And I did it with him. Why would there be anything else now?" She paused, leaving her question floating into the air, not looking at me. She didn't want an answer. She just wanted to ask the question. "There is just emptiness now. I can't quite describe it. It's been over a year, but the emptiness hasn't left. I tried to do things at first, joined a widow's group. That was a depressing group of people. None of them made me want to talk. My sister came for a bit and stayed with me. I didn't want to talk to her. I never really liked her anyway. She was always just so. You know? I got a part time job, but that just made my days longer. So now I sit at home. I watch television with no one to talk to about the show. I go for walks and see people laughing and smiling and it makes me wonder, why I am still here. Why I was left here alone. It just doesn't seem fair, does it? You know, there's an old friend of mine, one I don't talk to anymore, and she hates her husband. But he's still there. Hell, he will probably out live us all, but she wouldn't miss him if he just up and left one day. Me on the other hand, I miss my husband. I miss my friend. It's nothing but a shell of a life that used to be."

She paused and we sat in silence for a moment. "We had a son once. But he's gone too. A long time before his father. I had thought that was pain. But this is worse. This is beyond pain. This is emptiness. Why does it feel this way?" This time, she turned to me, the question still on her face. I looked into her worn blue eyes and didn't know what to say. We both turned back towards the opening stretching before us. "I haven't told anyone this before. You know, I think that I knew that I would find you today. A quiet soul that mirrors my emptiness that would understand what I'm saying. You do understand, don't you?" She looked at me again and I nodded back at her in silence. I did understand. "I knew it as soon as I saw you sitting here. You were like me. Well then, why are you lonely?" I thought about how to respond. Telling her about the loveless marriage that had started promising and made me forget about the sadness, if only for a short time. But that was a lie. I got here so much earlier than that. I closed my eyes and let the words come, a croak at first and then clearer. They came before I even knew what they would be.

"MY MOTHER DIED when I was young. She had a cancer that had grown into her bones." The memories came flooding back, the sadness, the hospital rooms, the medical staff in our home, the final room where she lay dying. "She couldn't fight it and one day she was just gone. That didn't empty me though. I could have fought that. But then my dad gave up. About a year after she had left us, I came home from a friend's house. I had spent the night there, which was odd even to me at the time, since I never spent the night anywhere before or after my mother's death. I was dropped off by the friend's parent and the door was unlocked." I saw the feet hanging in the darkness of my closed eyelids. "I walked towards his office, knowing he would be there. He was usually in there. There he was. He was still swinging slightly but he was gone. I didn't know what to do, I was so small. I called 911 like I had been taught and they came. Someone sat with me while they lowered his body. There wasn't even a note. I will never know why he left his child alone in the world, to be raised by relatives I didn't even know. If he felt..." I took a breath, "emptiness or was just so alone after my mother died, that he didn't have another option. I would have understood. I just don't..." I felt her hand squeeze mine and I kept going, "Since then, I did everything I was supposed to do. I went to school. I went to college. I moved to a small town and watched it grow into a bigger town. I met my wife and loved her, so we got married. I starved my emptiness by trying to find things to fill it. Trying to do what I was supposed to do. But here I am. It came back. The emptiness came rushing back and here I am. Alone. I think maybe I was always broken. And now I am without a family, or a name, and I have no idea what I'm doing. I'm not doing the right thing, but I don't know what else to do or where else to go. I'm moving without reason. There must be something that just won't allow me to find my peace or a meaning to being here at all," my voice shook as I shared the thought that had been on my mind for years but never spoken out loud before this moment in front of this stranger who knew my pain.

"What is the point of me being here in this world if I don't really exist to begin with? You have an empty shell of a life now. But I think I might have always been an empty shell playing make believe at being a man. Always. There was never anything inside of me. There never will be." The tears ran down my face as I felt her move closer to me. I pictured the room, and sat underneath him on the dark grey carpet, watching the feet sway back and forth. And then I saw the town in the distance. The town from my dream. It was thrown into this memory by mistake. I opened my eyes, and she was right next to me, wet tracks running down her face as she nodded up at me. We both shook with our spoken words that we shared with kindred strangers on this rock that hovered above the world.

Slowly my tears stopped and dried, and she sat next to me. Our hands were intertwined and for a moment I felt that maybe I was supposed to be right here. The signs had pointed in this direction for a reason. The literal and physical signs. She needed to say what she needed to say, and it turned out I did too. We needed to say it to someone that felt a similar pain. It didn't make sense but here we were, watching the sun drift across the cloudless sky. Finally, she turned towards me and smiled.

"Well honey, it looks like we aren't alone in this world after all, huh?"

I smiled back; the emptiness seemed to recede just a fraction, "maybe not." She pulled her little hand from mine and flung her pack onto her back as she used her stick to help her stand back up on the rock.

She leaned down towards me until her face was inches away from mine, "Thank you for listening" and she gave me a cool kiss on the lips before walking towards the path she had come from. I watched her disappear into the trees and heard the clicking of her stick as she went back to her lonely house. Did that just happen? The fog swirled in my brain. Was she even real or just another dream? I shook my head and looked back down at the cars moving along beneath me. I could taste peanut butter stuck in between my teeth. I looked down at my hands. The hands that now looked and felt like mine. When did that happen? And I let them push myself to stand on the cliff. I spread my arms wide like I was going to swan dive into the world below and breathed in deeply. Then I turned and grabbed my bag before disappearing back into the trees. I made it back to the fork in the path and looked up the path without a sign. That would probably take me to the top of this mountain and to find the start of my waterfall, but I didn't feel the need to explore anymore today. I turned away from the path and walked down the mountain.

THE SUN WAS setting behind the trees by the time I made it to the start of a path that led to the highway. I ran across the road, missing the cars that were speeding along and forgetting to look at the beauty that surrounded them. Shells. I made it to the other side and looked back up at the mountain I had come from. I could see a small tan rock jetting out from the trees, lit by the setting sun, and smiled up at it before turning towards the train track. I could make a bed on the other side, right next to the river and follow the track in the morning. I heard a horn in the distance and watched as the train got closer and closer and as it finally rushed by me, I saw a car with an open side. Sitting there were two men with their legs dangling in the wind, riding the car. The train slowed, and I could see the detail in the men. One of them was wearing worn jeans and a bright orange jacket. He had a long dark beard that was specked with grey and a warn sun tanned face. His left hand was bandaged, and bag sat to the side of him. He lifted his arm in a wave and I lifted mine in return. I watched as the train disappeared, my arm still raised in a farewell at the stowaway explorer as he made his way west.

CHAPTER SIXTEEN

THE BUFFALO

THE SMALL BROWN birds soared above me in the blue sky, chasing each other and the bugs that buzzed around them. I watched them and envied the movement of their smooth wings as they flattened against their bodies to dip and dive towards the earth before expanding again and turning back towards the sun. The ground beneath me was still cool from the winter storms but the snow had all melted and dried. There was a quiet road to my left with only the occasional minivan driving by. It was a peaceful afternoon, and I enjoyed the company of only the birds and occasional worm making its way out of the ground and into the spring. The last few days had been filled with conversations shared with strangers in cars as they drove me south, then east, then west. Wherever they went, I went. Letting others determine my path. But I was out of lies for now and decided to walk down this quiet road instead of having to make mindless chatter with a driver. Finding this soft hill next to the road to take a quick nap before I continued climbing up into the rocks. I saw a sign that said there was a lake coming up soon and I was looking forward to a bath in the cold water after my nap.

I sat up and took a swig of my almost empty water bottle before I stood and pulled my heavy bag up over my head so that it would sit on my right shoulder. I needed to switch it up today to try to save my left shoulder from the weight. I kept collecting things that I thought would make my path just a little bit easier; new shoes and jeans, another box of granola bars, and enough toiletries to make me feel human whenever I could find fresh water. It made my bag heavier against my shoulders and it smacked against my back, but I wasn't comfortable giving my newly found items up... not just yet. I walked down my little grass covered hill towards the two-lane road and looked both ways to see no cars coming from either direction. The small road stretched to my left, straight and almost flat as it flowed down the hillside. To my right it started to bend as it worked its way up into the hill above. I could see the small sign in the distance that pointed towards the lake on top of the rocks. My body turned to the right, and I followed the dotted yellow line that led the way in the middle of the dark asphalt. The sun stretched into the sky as I walked. The birds chirped and soared, and I focused on my echoing footsteps as I worked my way up the road that stretched in front of me.

I heard a small sound behind me. It was almost as if there were someone following me. I could hear their soft steps echoing mine. I froze and the sound stopped. Slowly, I spun in a circle, expecting to see nothing but a ghost drifting away into the air. Another trick of my mind as it continued to make a world that was only ever there in the fog.

TEN PACES BEHIND me stood a beast. He was taller than me and wide across the front. His brown fur was dull and caked with dirt from the road and grass. There he stood, in his full glory, frozen as he was interrupted while trying to cross the road behind me. His large brown eye shone and reflected my face in the glassy brown surface. I could feel the heat coming from his large body and a cloud raised from his nose as he breathed heavily. I watched his breath and reminded myself to breathe again. Deep breath in. My leg started to cramp from the twisted position I stood in. I couldn't move, for fear he would see it as a threat and turn towards me, ready to attack. He breathed. The chirps around us disappeared and the orange sun warmed us on the road. My leg shook from a cramp, and we competed in the longest staring contest of my life. He lifted his hoof and kicked the ground twice before lazily finishing his way across the road and into the other side of the grass to continue down to the hill. I watched as the buffalo continued his solo trek away from me. Long sigh out. Once he was far enough away that he posed minimal threat, I turned and continued my path before I had been interrupted.

I was still climbing up and the path started to curve around the mountain when I heard another sound. A small motor approaching from behind. I moved to the side of the road with my back against a dark rock wall to give room for the motor bike that was quickly approaching, trying to make its ascent up into the mountain. It slowed and pulled to side in front of me and the rider pulled his helmet off after steadying his bike. He had black hair that was buzzed short against his head, and I could see three thin lines shaved into the side when he turned to look back at me. There were two small saddle bags that hung from the back seat. He grinned and I could see all his teeth shining white in his face.

"Are you headed to the lake?"

"Uh… yeah. You?" I had to shout back to make sure he heard me over the hum of his motor.

He nodded and his grin grew wider. "I work at the coffee shop on the rim. It's quite a hike. Betsy can hardly make it somedays." He patted his bike and looked back up at me, "So ya wanna ride?" I looked at 'Betsy.' I must have looked doubtful; when I looked back up towards the young man's face, he had a look of raw pride. "She might not look like much, but she'd get us there. It might just take an extra minute than normal." He sounded almost defiant.

"Of course. I bet she's a good bike. Uh… sure. Thanks."

"I only have the one helmet, but I've never gotten in a wreck, so you should be fine." He pushed his solo helmet back over his head as I swung a leg over the bake seat. My hands moved around looking for something to hold onto so I wouldn't have to embrace this small stranger. Finally, I found a small handle on either side of the seat and grabbed on. He shouted over his shoulder, "Here we go" and we were off. Slowly. We moved quicker than I would have walked, that's true. A little quicker. Betsy purred as we continued to incline and eventually the rocks on the side of the winding road gave away to tall trees. The road curved back and forth as we climbed the mountainside, and I watched the thick red trunks pass by. The trees continued to get thicker as we climbed. A small horn sounded behind us and a minivan passed before we reached one of the curves in the road. The passenger didn't look over but made a little wave with her hand as they passed. The back seat held small heads, and two eyes stared at my driver and me as we sat on Betsy, making our way up the hill. The van passed and the small head turned so the eyes could watch us from the back window as the van disappeared around the curve.

I turned back to the trees to watch them as we finished our purring climb up the mountain. Betsy slowed and I looked around the helmet of my driver to see a parking lot entrance to the right with a shop behind it. Betsy pulled into a spot, and I hopped off. My thighs burned and my legs were weak from just the short time on her. I shook my legs to try to steady them as the young man hopped off and pulled his helmet from his head. He was still grinning, "So better than walkin' huh?"

I laughed, "Yeah, you were right. Betsy got us up here in no time."

He nodded and rubbed a hand along the side of the bike, "Yeah, she's a good one."

I looked around at the empty parking lot with only one old van near the entrance, "Kind of a slow day?"

"Yeah, it's off season still. The gift shop doesn't open until noon on these days. Makes it nice for me."

"I bet." I followed as he started walking towards the building that was built to look like a rustic log cabin. The only give-away were the carved bears in Hawaiian shirts that guarded the entrance. I wonder if bears came around here like that buffalo. He pulled the door open, and I followed him in as he waved a greeting at a young woman; her hair swept under a scarf. She was folding shirts off to the side and gave a quick wave back before he walked over to a small counter with a coffee sign hanging over the top. He looked in a few of the large silver containers and looked back at me.

"If you want to hang around for a few, I'll get some coffee made."

"Sounds great."

I watched him for a moment as he wrestled to get a bag of coffee grounds from a higher shelf, and I turned back to the room. It was filled with shelves of things with logos on them. Shirts and jackets in one corner. Books about the area and random things like beer glasses and moccasins were organized in another corner. Overpriced vacation items. I used to have a collection of stuff like this, memorializing vacations. Before…

I wondered over to a shelf and saw a travel coffee mug with a photo of a lake on it. I turned it over and saw a sticker for $12.99 *including tax. It was one of those spill proof mugs that you could turn over and nothing would come out. I pulled thirteen dollars from my bag and walked over to the young girl that was still folding shirts. She was so focused on her task; she didn't notice me standing there. "Excuse me," She jumped as if I had startled her and looked up at me from her crouched spot on the floor. "I'd like to buy this." I showed her the mug in my hand and held out the cash to her. She sat for a moment as if she was trying to register what I was telling her. Then she took the cash from my hand and smiled as I nodded and walked away before she tried to respond to anything. I walked over to the coffee counter and put the mug on the wood surface. "Can you put the coffee in here?"

He turned and grabbed the mug, "perfect timing, just got done. You'll have to pay Karen for the mug."

"Already done." He looked over at the woman and I followed his glance to see Karen give a thumb up at his motion of the mug. I turned back to him, "How much do I owe ya?"

He laughed, "Nah man, don't worry about it, it's just a cup of coffee. Plus, you bought a mug."

I smiled as he handed me back my spill-proof coffee, "thanks man. And thanks for the ride." I turned to leave the little shop but stopped before I made it far from him and turned back towards him. He was already setting up for the rest of the day and filling a small metal container full of milk. "Hey," he looked up at me, "do you mind filling up my water bottle?" He grinned as he put down his container and held out his hands. As he filled my bottle from the small sink, I found myself looking at my hands for a moment, "So, are there a lot of buffalo in the area?"

He looked up, confused, "No. There haven't been wild bison around here for years."

"Are you sure? I saw one before you picked me up."

"You saw one? Then it for sure wasn't a bison. They don't really travel alone. Are you sure it wasn't something else? People are always mistaking things in the hills and trees." His grin had faded from his face as I shoved my newly filled bottle back into my bag.

I had been right next to it. Staring into its eye. "Yeah, I'm sure it was one buffalo... uh bison." He shrugged and I thanked him for the coffee and the ride on Betsy again before I headed out to the lake.

Somehow, I didn't see it when I had walked into the shop. Stretching out beyond the parking lot and the faux log cabin filled with logo gear. The trees sat on the ledge around the circle and the land bent before falling quickly into the bright blue water. It was larger than the lake I expected, and the water looked so clear that you could see the dirt and grass trying to hide beneath the surface. It was almost like someone took the bowl of land and dug out a hole in the middle to pour the water into. The smooth surface of the water mirrored the sky above and I could see the detail of each cloud in the reflection. I walked towards where the edge cut off and looked down into the water. It didn't look like there would be a good spot to bathe. I shrugged to no one in particular. I had bathed just a few days ago. Another few days wouldn't hurt. I could still stay here a bit. In the quiet. I worked my way down the edge and walked until I found a flat rock that was hidden from the parking lot and the shop.

There was a perfect spot for my spill-proof mug, and I sat it on the rock in a small nature made cup holder. Then I pulled off the duffel bag and let it fall to the rock before sitting. I sipped my coffee and watched the sun work its way back down into the trees. The sound of a few cars pulled up into the parking lot behind me, but my spot stayed secret, and I ate a granola bar once I finished my coffee. I watched the clouds slowly start to roll in and the blue water turn to grey as the day faded. I pulled myself up from my spot and stuck my new mug down in my bag before climbing out of my hiding spot and heading back to the parking lot. Betsy was gone and so were any other cars. I must have sat longer than I thought I did. I looked up at the clouds that were quickly turning dark. There was no way I could make it off this mountain before the rain started. I would have to find some place to hole up for the night until the man returned on Betsy, or I could walk down the mountain.

I TURNED TOWARDS the store and tried to find cover in the awning as the first heavy drops started to fall. There was nothing, no place to hide against the log exterior. The rain started falling quicker and I started to shiver against the cold drops. I looked up at the emptying clouds. This was going to be a big one. The clouds looked thick and heavy with rain, just waiting to be let loose. I walked quickly back to my hiding spot, trying to remember if I had seen an overhang from the rock that I had sat on. There was nothing. The rain was falling in a sheet now and I pushed the wet hair out of my eyes and tried to block the water so that I could see as I turned in a full circle looking for any kind of shelter. On the second spin, I saw it. Up where the land had started to bend and a little walk away, was a large grey rock that was propped up creating a man-sized cave beneath it. The rain was coming harder now, and it pushed against me as I walked. I pulled my hood over my head and pulled it tight to try to block the rain that was stabbing my face. I covered my eyes and tried to peer through my hands towards the shelter to see that I wasn't any closer. My pants were soaked with the cold rain and my jacket was working hard to try to keep the water out but wasn't successful. I didn't have the energy to pull the thin gloves from my bag and my fingers started to turn white in the cold downpour. I kept pushing forward, determined to make it to the shelter and start a small fire with the matches and maybe one of the magazines that was stored in my bag. I hoped they were still dry. I tried to remember if I had put them in the plastic bag, even when the sky was cloudless this morning. I looked again and finally it looked like I had worked closer to the shelter. I put my head down again and kept moving carefully towards the edge for the final straight shot.

I was getting close when my path was blocked by a fallen tree. I lifted my leg and put it on a branch, testing the weight before pulling the other leg up to follow. The sky lit with a rumble as a shot rang through the air. I jumped slightly at the unexpected sound and turned my head up just in time to see another flash as lightning stretch across the sky. The streak branched out and lit the clouds to reveal how they had grown in the dark rain. Crack! The thunder followed quickly and then was followed by another loud crack. Another shot of thunder? I hadn't seen another streak of lightning. I realized slowly that the last sound had come from below me instead of above as I felt the log give under my weight and started to tumble down the ridge. I launched towards the side of the incline and reached out my hands to find something to hold but they grasped nothing but dirt. The shelter was almost right above me before it disappeared, and I slid down towards the water that had been so beautiful just a few hours ago. The strap on my bag snapped and I was separated from it in the fall. I kept rolling and trying to grasp on to anything that would hold me in the dark storm. It felt like I was falling in slow motion. My hands kept closing on air. My breath caught in my chest as I was stopped by my leg. It hit against the rock before the rest of my body did and I could feel a small snap in my ankle before my brain registered that I had stopped moving. I lay there, trying to catch my breath, as the rain pelted down, and the lightning lit the sky again above me.

I whispered into the storm, "don't pass out… you can't pass out…" My already dark view started to fade out right before I whimpered, "I don't want to die." My own cry seemed to wake me, and I pushed myself up onto my elbows to try to figure out where I had landed. The clouds lit up the sky as another strike went through them and I could see that I hadn't fallen nearly as far as I thought I had. I could see the ridge just paces behind me and the top of my shelter sitting there waiting for me. The rock that had stopped my fall loomed in front of my crumpled body and I scooted close to it so that I could use it to help me stand. I pushed against it with wet worn hands and tried to balance on my right leg for a second before putting my left one on the ground. The one I had heard snap but didn't quite feel. A bolt shot from my left foot and up my leg as I screamed out in pain before falling back to the ground. Shit shit shit. There was no way I could stand on this foot. I sat back up and felt around the pained ankle to see if I could tell it was broken. There was no bone sticking out to where I could feel but the skin was hot beneath my touch, and I could feel it starting to swell. Maybe it was just a sprain. Few days and I would be right as rain. I grinned ruefully as I looked up at the rain that caused my careless fall. I looked back up the ridge and knew that I still needed to make it under some sort of cover. I couldn't lay here and just freeze to death. My arms stretched behind me, and my body followed, scooting backwards against the ground.

My body screamed in pain, and I had to stop after only six scoots. My face was wet, tears of desperation and pain mixed with the cold rain. My body was caked in mud and every movement shot pain from my leg that overcame the pain in the rest of my body. I looked over my shoulder and saw that I was a little bit closer to the ridge that registered as the top part of the land. I scooted faster, trying to get this done with. I could feel my hands being sliced by the hard rocks beneath them as they slipped over the tops, but I didn't stop. Faster. I couldn't see past the darkness and the water flowing from my eyes. Faster. I bumped my ankle and my breath caught again at the pain. I stopped and looked behind me again, waiting for a light in the cloud to show me how much further. Nothing lit up the sky. My body throbbed, not knowing how much further I had to pull myself, and I screamed. I had never heard that noise come out of me before. It was the sound of an animal, full of fear and hatred. The desperation and the loneliness I felt all came out in that scream directed at no one. Maybe I was screaming at my father, maybe the man I was, or maybe the man lying right here that was going to die in this silly storm. I reached my arms behind me again and kept scooting. Finally,

I felt a sharper incline and I used my right foot and my arms to pull myself backwards over it to see the shelter right above me. I scooted back a few more times until my back was against a rock and my legs were out of the rain. I made it. I did it. The world in front of me faded to a dull black.

CHAPTER SEVENTEEN

THE SMOKE

I WAS IN the field again. The sharp pain of the fall gone. But I was not completely healed like my previous dreams. My body was full of aches and soreness as I sat up. There was something else that was different. I couldn't quite figure it out. But while I was here, I might as well enjoy the heat. I lay back down in the golden grass and let the sun warm my cold body. I heard a noise but kept my eyes shut. What did I need to worry about here in my dream? The sound came closer but still I didn't worry. It was a sound I knew, the rustling through the grass, someone was walking towards me. Someone I knew. I felt the warmth of her body as she knelt to me. A soft press of her lips against my forehead. I opened my eyes slightly and saw a slight shimmer of orange from her sun dress. Her green eyes sat above the freckles on her nose and her hair fell around her, strategically curled to frame her round face that had yet to lose all the child fat in her cheeks. She must not have been older than thirty. Her eyes showed more years than that though. They shone as they looked at me, unblinking and unafraid. She had a small necklace around her neck that was made of shiny orange jewels. They looked delicate against her skin. I looked back into her eyes as she leaned over me, her arms sitting on either side of my body in the warm grass. Can I stay here? I thought the words but didn't say them out loud. She shook her head as if she could hear them anyway. I saw her mouth move but the words took a moment to catch up, almost as if she was talking to me from far away. The words were faded and echoed. "Not yet." I looked at her and thought, is this death? She shook her head again, "No." She must have seen the confusion on my face as she leaned closer to me, her eyes burrowing deep into my own, just as her voice aligned with her mouth and came in clear and loud, "Don't die."

The sun was shining through the clouds when I pushed myself out of my cave just a bit. The world was covered in water. Raindrops were falling off the trees and new little streams were flowing into the lake beneath me. I stared at one large drop of water that hung, lit by the sun, off a large green leaf. It slowly got heavier and then fell to the earth while the leaf swung from the weightlessness. I stuck my tongue to the roof of my mouth and took a couple of breaths trying to make enough saliva to gulp down. Damn, I was thirsty. I was obviously off any type of path and most likely a decent little trek to the gift shop and parking lot. It was still a bit too cold for normal hikers and it was the middle of the week. I think. I honestly wasn't sure. But that seemed right. I couldn't backwards scoot all the way to the fucking gift shop. I rolled up the pant leg to look at my left ankle. The swelling had started going down but had been replaced with the start of a large black bruise. I touched the area gently and ground my teeth against the pain, but I couldn't feel a spot that felt like broken bone. Maybe it really was just a bad sprain. I pulled myself up using my shelter to prop against, ignoring the pain in my hands for now, and tested putting a small amount of weight on the ankle.

Someone should have been able to find me from the volume of the scream that followed. Walking would not be an option. I sat against the rock to catch my breath before looking for my bag. The sun rose higher in the sky and the clouds started to clear away. What had become my hell last night now looked cheerful. Like a place to relax with the kids, not die alone in the mud. My spirits rose as I saw the corner of my bag sticking up just past the rim. I was lucky that the strap broke, and it didn't follow me all the way down. I lowered myself to the ground and turned so I could scoot towards my belongings, checking my direction as I went. I reached my bag and pulled it up to my side of the rim and while it was soaked, it seemed undamaged minus the ripped strap. I turned back towards the shelter and put the bag on my lap as I scooted back towards my dry cave.

MY EXTRA CLOTHES and the box that held my granola bars were soaked through. Luckily, I had thought ahead, and my matches and magazine and book were all still dry and tucked away into their plastic gallon bag. I pulled out a water bottle and took a long swig before turning it over and pouring a small amount onto my open palm, sucking the air through my teeth at the pain. The mud washed off and I could see deep ridges cut along my palm from the rocks. I switched hands and cleared off the other. Not as bad but not good. I pulled one of the old shirts from my bag and the pair of worn scissors I had found and hacked off two thin strips of wet fabric. Would have been better if it were dry but it would dry off soon enough. I wrapped my left hand first and followed with my right. My stomach growling the full time. I pulled the box of granola out and pulled out four granola bars. Was that right? I thought there were more. Dammit. I thought I had been counting but none had gone missing in a while, and I went lax. That wouldn't buy me much time. I tossed the mushy box out front of the cave to let it would dry in the sun and ate one bar before putting the other three back in the duffel. Then I pulled myself out of the shelter again and laid the wet clothes along the top of the rock. Someone might see them and come see who was in here. At the very least I might have some dry clothes in a few hours. Either way. I dug out a spot in the dry dirt in the middle of my tiny cave and crumbled up some magazine paper making a nice ball, just enough to warm a bit. I struck a match and watched the perfect flame for a second before lighting the paper on the outside of my horrible makeshift fire. The flame turned green as it burned through the paper and warmth touched my outstretched fingertips and my muddy face and I closed my eyes to revel in the fact that I just made fire. Almost immediately I started coughing. My eyes shot open, and I was met with dark black smoke that filled the inside of the shelter unable to escape fully through the door at the front. I tried breathing in and started wheezing, my body wracking with the coughs as I pulled myself out of the cave. My eyes burned and I closed them as I lay with only my top half outside of the cave, sucking in the fresh air. I should have known better; fast burning magazine paper and small enclosed space really didn't mix. I took a deep breath and coughed back out again. I took another breath, and this time could exhale a little easier. I kept my eyes closed as the tears from the smoke streamed down each side of my face and into my hair before hitting the ground. Through my closed eyes, I could see my own eyes reflected in the large brown eye of the buffalo. I had almost forgotten about him. He stood there, staring at me, daring me to move.

I opened my eyes and saw the black smoke flowing out into the sky above me. Maybe that would bring help. I watched the black turn to grey and drift away, the fire having quickly burned through the remaining magazine paper. My lungs started to feel almost normal as I sat up and looked at the burned pieces of ash that lay in the middle of the floor of my cavern. At least the fire didn't burn anything else. I pulled myself back into my cave and took another swig of water. I needed to get out of here. The sun stood in the middle of the sky. I must have already been here half a day. I knew I should rest. If no one came for me, I couldn't make it out of here for sure in just the remaining daylight. I lay down in the cave and closed my eyes, exhausted from the stress of the last two days and drifted into a dreamless sleep.

It was almost dark when I woke, the sun setting behind the trees. I could see few clouds in the sky as it gave off a pink hue that faded into blue. I checked the clothes above the rock and found they were dry and almost warm before pulling them into the cave and leaving my shelter. I scooted around like a lame dog, adding small sticks to my lap until I had enough that should work. I made it back to the front of the overhang and dug a spot in the dirt, laying some sticks along the bottom and then balancing the rest in a sort of teepee, just like I remembered from when I was a child. I pulled out the bag that contained the remaining magazine and my book that I found but hadn't read yet. My eyes moved back and forth between the two paper objects in my hand, and I knew I would never read this book. I sighed and pulled some pages from the back and front, trying to keep most of the story intact. The pages crumpled beneath my fist, and I place them under the branches before striking a match.

The first match blew out before I could touch it to the paper, and I counted the remaining matches. Five. I carefully leaned towards the small pyre and struck a second match, holding my breath as if that would keep it from going out. The paper caught and I gently blew at it to turn it into a small flame that eventually started burning my small hole in the ground. The fire danced and sang in front of my little home, and I let my hands warm for a moment before adding more branches. I leaned back against the rock to enjoy the moment, trying to ignore the throbbing pain coming from my left foot. I watched the sky change color with the lake reflecting. It really was a beautiful spot. I could only sit for a second. I had work to do. I pulled the duffel, repacked with clothes, over towards me at the entrance to the cave and pulled out the thick hospital socks and the pile of bandage straps I cut from my shirt. There was half a magazine worth of paper left. I pulled it apart so that I had two sections roughly the same and put one in my mouth to bite down on while I pulled one thick sock over my left foot. The pain shot through my leg, and I ground my teeth onto the magazine paper. Shaking with pain, I took the half magazine not in my closed mouth and slid it vertically down into the sock along my ankle, using the sock to hold it tight. I reluctantly took the other piece from my mouth and slid it down into my sock on the outside of my foot. Pushing both sides down to make sure that they were in securely, I tried to move my foot through the pain. My ankle still bent and screamed. I pulled on the second sock over the first to make sure to hold everything together and provide some extra padding and scooted back towards the flame to try to calm the pain by the burning fire before continuing. I pulled another granola from my bag and finished it in two bites, forgetting to savor one of my remaining bars. Once I had stopped shaking, I started working on my hands. I unwrapped the first one, the cloth sticking to my hands as the wounds had started to heal against the wet fabric. I groaned as I pulled at the skin and looked at the hand, swollen and the edges of the cuts white. The smell hit me like a ton of bricks as it became completely uncovered and I threw the dirty cloth out of the shelter. I poured a little water over it before covering it in a dry cut of cloth from the same shirt, and then followed suit with my right hand. I added the remaining branches to the dying fire and tried to enjoy my last few minutes with the warmth, preparing for what was going to come the next day. I watched the flame dim and was greeted with the dark night, stars reflecting against the clear water below me.

I WOKE UP shivering against the damp. Dew covered the ground and the remains of my fire. And me. The sky was dim as the sun was rising over the fog that blocked my view of the lake and would make it difficult to navigate through. I knew that I needed to head left from the entrance of my cave. I had two options. I could lay here and let myself die, no one finding me for weeks... or months. Slowly starving as I shivered into each night until I just didn't wake up. I saw my corpse lying there. Like the stories of the hikers lost all over the Pacific

Northwest that I used to read about. Or I could get up and move. I took a quick swig of water and put the bottle in my bag before zipping it up. I grabbed one of the last three shirt bandages, the long ones I had cut the previous day, and wrapped it through the side hooks of my duffel bag and tied each end into a knot, replacing the broken strap with a shorter grey makeshift strap. Then I grabbed the last two strips of fabric and tied them together to make a longer strip before pushing myself to a standing position against the rock, making sure to not step down on my left foot. I folded my leg up and wrapped the fabric around my shin and up onto my shoulder, tying a knot at the top to hold my leg off the ground. Last thing I needed was to accidentally hit it against a rock. I pulled my bag over my shoulder by my temporary strap and used my bandaged hands to help me navigate against trees as I hopped on my right foot towards the place that I knew I needed to go.

The fog sat heavy against the side of the hill, and I could only see a short distance ahead of me, but enough to keep against trees and rocks to help my one-legged path. I almost stumbled and found myself staring down at a single branch that had fallen into my path. I leaned down, balancing against a tree, and pulled up the branch. It came to my waist, and I grasped onto it with my left hand while still using my right hand to balance against anything I could find. I could go a little quicker and easier now, using the newfound walking stick as a replacement to my leg and ignoring the pain coming from my hand beneath the bandage as I grasped the top of the stick. The fog slowly rolled off my mountain and I could see the sun high in the sky as I continued to walk in the direction that I thought was right. I wanted to sit, to eat a granola bar and chug some water, but I had to be getting close. I had to keep going. My leg throbbed and my left hand shouted in pain. I kept moving. I saw the rock from what seemed like weeks ago, not just a few days. The one I had sat and drank coffee on. The one where I had looked at this beautiful lake and saw hope. It now brought hope to my mind again. I was close. I turned left and knew I was getting closer when I heard the purr of a familiar motor. I hobbled quicker and stepped out of the trees and onto the paved surface of the parking lot.

A different spot than the open space I had entered before, but I didn't care. I could see the faux cabin with its door propped open in the cool day and only one beat up van sitting close to the building. Then I saw Betsy sitting further out in the parking lot, having just pulled up, and getting off her was the most beautiful human I had ever seen. My eyes blurred as the tears bubbled in them and I could see his face running towards me. The vision on the outside of my view started to darken and he caught me as I fell into him as I mumbled, "there was one god-dammed buffalo."

CHAPTER EIGHTEEN

THE GROUP

I DRIFTED BACK into my body to the smell of bacon cooking on a griddle. I slowly opened my eyes and saw the sun coming through the slits in the blinds that covered the one window in this tiny apartment. I pushed myself up into a sitting position and tried to remember my dream. The warm grass. The town. Was there a house? My hands came up to rub the sleep out of my eyes and the rough healed skin on the inside of my palms brought me back to reality. I opened my right hand and stretched it, seeing the scars that still shone from my fingertips to my wrists. I opened my hand open further and watched the new skin bend over the bones.

"Phil, breakfast is almost ready." I looked over to see a white toothy grin looking in my direction. I nodded and pushed to my feet, favoring my left as I stood and turned to scoot my blanket and pillow to the side of the worn brown couch that had been my bed for weeks. The crutch was propped against the small coffee table, but I turned from it and hobbled towards the bar top that served as the table and sat heavily against it. He scooped scrambled eggs onto a paper plate and follow with two slices of bacon.

"I told you that you didn't have to make me breakfast every morning." I said it even though I didn't really mean it. I had never had someone make me breakfast every morning like this and I found that I woke craving it now each morning.

He filled his plate and perched on the stool next to mine. "And I told you, I like making breakfast. Besides, Alana said you would need to keep your strength up. How's the ankle this morning?"

"Good. I think I can try today without the crutch again. Just a little stiff." I shoved the eggs into my mouth to keep from answering another question.

"Mmmm. Cool. Take it slow." I looked at him out of the corner of my eyes while we ate. He was a good kid. How would I explain that it was time for me to leave again? It had been unspoken between us since he first brought me to this apartment. I was sure anyone else would be looking forward to it. But not him.

We finished our breakfast, and I tossed our plates into the trash bin before hobbling slowly towards the tiny bathroom. The bathroom was made up of white and grey tiles with bright white lights shining from above the mirror that stretched the full room. I looked at my face in the mirror. A little bit of stubble and tired eyes from the night of dream filled sleep but overall, I looked like an older version of the man I would see in the mirror from years before. Just with something extra that hadn't been there previously. I couldn't figure out what it was. I used the toilet and then started the spray of water from the shower head, letting it warm before taking off the shorts and t-shirt that I had slept in. I stepped under the spray and closed my eyes as the warm water ran over my face and trickled down my body.

I HAD WOKEN up on the brown couch that I now used as a bed. My mouth had been so dry that I could barely squeeze out "water" to the three blurry and worried faces hovering over me. One disappeared as the other two each grasped one of my arms and helped me sit, one of them pushing more pillows behind me for support. Everything hurt and I looked down at my hands to see them wrapped in thick bandages. My eyes followed up my left arm to see a tube sticking out of it and attached to a bag of clear liquid that was taped to a yard stick and stuck in the edge of the couch. My eyes slowly started to focus as a hand with a cup of water came into view and it was tipped slowly into my mouth. At first, I could barely swallow; the water came back up and down my chin. A hand wiped it away with a small towel before trying the water again. This time I could drink more of it, and I shook my head when I was done. The water cup disappeared, and I looked down to see one of the people down by my foot at the other end of the couch, checking on the ace bandage that was wrapped tightly around it. I didn't recognize her. She had bright blonde hair that was painted pink at the ends, and she turned to me and past me and smiled.

"Looking good Phil. He's healing nicely." She spoke to me and the two people still hovering at my shoulders. I looked up and recognized the man. His mouth split into a grin as he looked at me. The woman next to him had her hair pulled up into a blue scarf and nodded at all three of us before sitting in one of the stools that must have been put there to watch me sleep. I looked between all three of them trying to remember what had happened. I looked at the man I knew and had to focus to force the words from my mouth.

"Uh Phil? What's going on?"

He laughed. "No, my name is Kyle; do you remember me from before? I gave you a ride on Betsy up to the lake." I nodded so he would keep going. "A few days after you had left, I was pulling up for work and you were there, coming out of the woods. You looked like death and I didn't even recognize you because of the mud. You were in bad shape. I'm not sure what happened. Karen and I loaded you into her van and brought you to my apartment here. I assumed you weren't a hospital man 'cause of how you were traveling." I nodded again in agreement. "So, we called Alana," He pointed at the woman with pink hair, and she gave me a thumb up,

"She dropped out of medical school but now she's our unofficial vet slash doctor in these areas. I figured she would know what to do. So, she came and fixed you up and here you've been. You've come in and out a few times and we all had to hold you down to wrap your ankle but sounds like you're doing pretty good." He paused.

"How long?" I looked at the three of them.

"Have you been here? Two days. Karen and I, we've been covering for each other at the shop so one of us could stay here with Alana and you." Karen nodded and looked at Kyle, pointing at her watch. "Oh yeah, ok. You go and I'll be back tomorrow." She nodded again and got up, waving as she walked out of view. I heard a door open and close behind me and I assumed the silent Karen was gone. Alana took the open spot at the stool and Kyle moved back to join her on the other. She smiled with a row of perfect teeth. They must have a good dentist around here.

Her voice was almost a song as she spoke, "So, what happened out there?"

I took a second, wondering what they knew about me or what I shared while I had been in and out, "There was a storm that first night." They both nodded so I continued. "I couldn't find any shelter or get off the mountain by the time it hit. I was working towards shelter but fell and hurt my ankle and had to pull myself up to a rock." I shrugged as if that was the end of the story.

I looked back up at their faces, "but, how did you get back?"

"I bandaged up the best I could and just made my way out." My voice was raspy again and Kyle leaned forward to give me the water cup. I finished it and turned to them again, "Why do you think… uh… how do you know my name is Phil?"

Kyle spoke this time, "One of the times you were awake, I asked if you knew your name. You told us 'Phil'." I hesitated for just a moment before nodding, agreeing with the lie I knew was obvious and looking at the empty cup in my hands.

We sat and talked for a while before they let me go back to sleep. I lay there with my eyes closed and listened to them talk about how lucky I was, and I heard Alana ask him if he really thought I was who I said I was. He answered yes and then she asked him what he would do. I drifted off before I could hear the answer. I woke up the next morning to the smell of bacon cooking on the griddle. He brought a plate to my makeshift hospital bed. The tubing was gone from my arm and there was a crutch and a black oversized boot next to the couch, along with a bottle of pills without a label and some folded clothes. We spoke as we ate. He told me that he brought some extra clothes that wouldn't be missed from the shop and found me some other clothes from a box of Alana's ex-boyfriends that she brought over. He had also cleaned out my bag and the stuff in it, but he left some to throw out like the clothes I had been wearing. He knew I wasn't going anywhere and didn't want to announce my stay to anyone else. So, we came up with a plan. I could stay here for as long as I needed to, and as soon as I was able, I could come help him and Karen at the shop in return for the free room and board and care. I knew I was getting the better end of the deal and tried to argue it, but he wouldn't have any of it. He was maybe twenty years or more my junior and he was already a better man than I would ever be. That was five weeks ago, I think. Four weeks of working with him and Karen at the shop. Four weeks of looking at the lake that I almost died alone next to and now I spent that time with the three people who helped save me. Nights were filled with dinners sitting in one of their apartments, talking about nothing and everything. I was their old mysterious friend. The one that they never really knew. Karen had yet to say more than a dozen words to me, but the other two spoke enough between them that I rarely had to contribute. It was a peaceful existence.

THE WATER STARTED running cold, as I quickly lathered soap through my hair and around my body so I could shut the water off before it turned frigid. I got out and dried off with my small towel before putting on my pants that were just a tad too big, even with the full meals lately. They were good pants, could unzip to shorts right above the knee. Perfect for me. Then I pulled on a t-shirt made from bright blue cotton with big letters stretch across the front that said, 'I'd rather be at the lake'. Followed by the inner fleece layer of my own jacket. I looked in the mirror again before running my fingers through my wet hair to smooth it down. I looked like an old hiker that retired early after a rough life and decided to work at a shop next to a lake. Appropriate. I tossed my towel over the hook and hobbled back to the couch to wrap my ankle in the ace bandage, not sure if I still needed it. I was ready for a day of work.

Karen picked us up a few minutes later, and I climbed into the back of her beat up van. She hummed along to Cat Stevens as I looked out the window at the sunny scenery whipping past. The flowers were starting to bloom, and the days were warming with just the slightest mountain chill in the air. None of us really worked at the shop. We each did our little tasks, mine were now starting up the coffee and filling the containers with cream and milk, then folding shirts, while Kyle and Karen did everything else. I think Karen was the manager or owner, but I never asked, and they never said. Then we just sat around while waiting for people to drift in and out. I read most of the books that scattered the shelves of the shop before the human hurricane of a vacationing family would come in and then we would pick everything up again and put things back where they went, and then wait for the next group. After about six hours of this - we would clean up, lock up, and Karen would drive us back down the mountain and to wherever dinner was for the night. This night was at Alana's. Her new boyfriend joined us and sat awkwardly trying to work into the easily flowing conversation between Alana and Kyle. At some point, these kids needed to figure their relationship out. Karen watched everything in her silent way and at one point she grinned at me and winked. I had a feeling she knew everything I did and more. She was always watching. Dinner ended and the next two days followed the same pattern as all the days before. I could walk with just a slight limp from the stiffness of my ankle but very little pain. And at dinner on that third night, with just the four of us again, it was time.

I cleared my throat a few times and three pairs of eyes turned to me as the two voices stopped mid-conversation. "I want to thank you all for what you have done for me." They all nodded, but the smile left Kyle's face. "But I think... I know... it's time for me to go."

Alana looked between Kyle and Karen then back to me, "Where are you going to go?"

"Uh... I'm not sure, the same path I've been going I suppose." Everyone sat quietly and I felt the need to close the gap of quiet, "I really don't know, but I have been here too long. I need to keep moving. I need to keep looking for..." my voice drifted off. How could I explain this need to them? We hadn't talked about it, but they knew. Kyle and Alana sat, uncommonly quiet.

Karen was the one to speak. "I had a dream about you." Everyone looked towards her. "You were standing in front of a house. A small house in a street where all the houses matched. This house was different though. It was in a small town that was filled with people that knew you. There was a woman. She was waiting for you to find her. I think you need to go and find that town. That house. Once you do, you will know." She turned back to her plate and took another bite of her chicken as if she didn't just say something profound that chilled me to my core. We all watched her as she continued to finish her dinner. The house. I could picture it in my mind. I had seen it before. In a dream? I wasn't sure. We finished eating in silence. Alana gave me a hug and reminded me to be careful as we stood, ready to leave. Karen drove us back to Kyle's apartment in silence. The van stopped and instead of taking off with a wave as she did most nights, she hopped out of the driver's side and ran over to me, stopping inches from me. She put both hands on my face and touched her nose to mine. "Be careful out there, Phil. You may find what you are looking for. But it might not be what you were expecting." She turned and got back into her van and drove away into the night.

Kyle laughed uncomfortably, "Karen… uh… sometimes, you know." He turned towards the apartment and shrugged.

THE NEXT MORNING, I woke before the sun had broken into the sky and was showered and dressed before Kyle wondered into the kitchen where I was making bacon and eggs. He rubbed the sleep from his eyes as I poured him a cup of coffee and he sat on the stool on the other side of the counter from me. We ate in silence and once we were done, I tried to form the words. "Listen…"

He cut me off, "I may not understand all of this, your life and your path, but I accept it. It's just… yours." He got up abruptly from the stool and patted me on the back before heading back to the bathroom, closing the door behind him. I got up and tossed our plates into the trash before grabbing the bag I had packed the night before, full of newer clothes and my refilled water bottles. The strap now a colorful woven and sturdy strap that Karen had made. Full of bright orange and teal string with the name 'Phil' stitched into the thick material. I watched the bathroom door and waited for him to come out. He didn't. I went to the kitchen and grabbed his small notepad and a pen that he kept there and wrote.

Thank you again. I can never repay the kindness that you all have shown me but I hope that someday I can think of a way. I don't know what I believe in but if there is anything, I think I would believe that good things come to good people. And you are good people. I will always think of you as my friend and I hope that you do the same. Thank you.

P.S. If you are open to advice from an old lost soul like me, maybe it's time for you and Alana to give it a shot. Life is too short to wait for the next moment.

I left the pad and pen sitting on the barstool, took one last look at the closed bathroom door, and walked out into the cool morning.

I SPENT THE day riding in an old car full of three old women who spent the day singing along to the radio. They asked me my name and I had the normal response ready, "J."

"Oh, HEY JAY!" one of them chirped and they all giggled. I told them, "Wherever you are" when they asked where I was heading. They laughed and said they didn't have a clue. They were on "an adventure!" So, we followed the roads and I got further away from the spot that I called home for a short while. I pulled myself from their car late in the day, miles from where I started, and found a small park in a small town to call my own for the night. The car drove away, and I could hear their loud and out of tune voices singing through the open windows. I opened my bag and reached in for a granola bar when my hand found a box that I knew I hadn't packed. I unzipped my bag further and saw two clear plastic boxes. I pulled them out and examined them under the setting sun. The first one held bandages, matches, two twenties, paper and a pen, pain pills, and single use wet wipes. The second was full of snack foods: granola, nuts, chocolate. Kyle. He must have added these to my bag while I slept. I smiled and shook my head as I broke off a piece of chocolate and stuck it in my mouth to savor the taste as it melted against my tongue.

CHAPTER NINETEEN

THE TOWN

HERE I WAS again. It was starting to feel more real to me than the days I spent wondering the streets. Maybe this was my real life, and the other life was the dream. I sat up in the grass and the warm breeze brushed my face. The scream didn't pierce the silence much anymore, and I wasn't expecting it today. Today felt different. I stood and stretched my arms over my head and looked down to see my bag in the grass next to where I had just been laying. That was new. I didn't remember my bag with me before. I lifted it up over my shoulder, noticing the bright strap no longer had 'Phil' stitched into it, but rather the initials, 'J.D.' I spoke out loud to no one, "interesting." My voice sounded miles away. I somehow knew that I could make progress walking towards the town today and I took a few steps before the thought flittered across my mind again, "maybe this is my reality. Maybe I can make it something else."

I turned away from the town and started walking towards nothing. There was a group of mountains in the distance, and I shifted my stride towards those instead. Why did I always want to go to the town anyway? I had seen it so many times now and nothing special had yet to happen there besides the repeated echo of a past scream. Maybe I had it all wrong. Maybe the town wasn't the destination I should have focused on. I walked for what seemed like hours before stopping to take a break for a drink of water. The water from my bag was crisp and cool, almost like it had come straight from the waterfall months ago. When I was the fake me? Or the real me? I looked up at the sky in surprise when a lone bird floated over my head. It sang mid-air and I could feel its happiness as it swooped and danced through the cloudless sky. It was a bright red color and stood out against the blue. He dove low towards the grass then back up to the sun before soaring towards the town and disappearing from my view. I turned back towards the mountains and zipped my water bottle into place before starting to walk again.

The ground was soft beneath my feet, and I looked down to see the wrap missing from my ankle and my hiking shoes like new. I pushed through the grass in the silence without the singing bird and almost trampled on a lone flower. It was almost covered by the grass, and I bent to look closer at it. It had big flat green leaves down at the base and the flower stem was long and somehow held up three heavy looking flowers. They each had five flat petals that opened to a sixth smaller petal that seemed to support the center seeds. There were another three buds that had yet to form into flower. It was flawless and beautiful in a way that I had never seen before. I dropped my bag behind me and sat down so that I could spread my legs around either side of the pale orange flower, and I started pulling the grass away from it to let it breathe. It seemed to stretch towards the sky opening to the sun. I pulled out my water bottle full of cold water and poured just a little of it on the leaves of the flower to let it soak. I sat there, wondering how this perfect and beautiful flower grew all the way out here. What kind of flower was it anyway? I studied the flat petals and touched the thick leaves. The scream broke the silence and I jumped to a standing position, making sure not to trample my flower in the process.

THE SUN WAS rising into the sky above me, and my back was damp with the dew that had settled in the night. I had slept on the soft grass of a small park in what looked to be a suburban town. There were a few people wondering around early this morning, but no one seemed to be in any type of hurry. I sat for a few moments before my stomach started to rumble. Maybe this was a good morning for a full breakfast, now that I knew I really enjoy waking up to bacon and eggs. I took a drink of my water and stuck a twenty from the box down into my pocket, rubbing the smooth rock that it joined a few times with my thumb. Then I stood and walked towards a small strip of buildings that one couple had just gone towards. Follow the people, find the food. I watched as the man in front of me held open the door for the woman who was with him, and I could smell the food coming from the opening. He saw me there and motioned for me to walk through the door as he continued to hold it. I nodded thanks and walked into the dim faded restaurant to a sign that told me to seat myself. There were worn red booths with only a few people sitting scattered in them and I chose one that was further away from the current dinners. The booth creaked as I slid in before a large plastic menu was placed in front of me along with a white cup with coffee steam rising from it. I looked up but the waitress was already gone to the next booth. I looked back at the warm coffee and tried to ignore the faint pink lipstick that hadn't quite been washed off the side of the cup.

The booth was almost private, dark wood paneling stretched above the seats and above that were bright stained-glass windows to split each spot. I looked at the stained glass and studied the marble eye of the blue fish that took up most of the space. The photos hung on the wall next to me included photo that must have been taken years before. A man with a mustache stood on a fishing boat and grinned at the camera, a large fish with bulging eyes lay in his arms, all hung against the dark wood paneling that made up the full wall. I looked at the menu that had been stuck in front of me as I took a sip of the hot coffee and tried to avoid drinking from the same spot as the lipstick stain. Breakfast specials were plastered along the front, all included coffee and a cup of juice and ran around six dollars. Perfect.

"What can I get ya, darlin'?" I looked up to see a woman, younger than I had originally thought, standing there with a pen poised over a note pad and a large smile plastered to her face.

"Uh… I'll take a number three with orange juice"

"Howda' like those eggs?"

"Scrambled"

"Biscuit, Sourdough, or wheat?"

"Sourdough"

"And last question, I promise ya." She smiled. "Bacon or sausage or you can have some salmon for an extra five bucks."

"Just the bacon please."

She nodded and took my menu before turning away. I pulled my coffee cup closer and stared at the fish made of glass until a plate was slid in front of me. I tried to eat slowly as I lifted the eggs and bacon into my mouth. It tasted like 'home.' I almost licked the plate clean before turning to the toast. So many jam options on the table. I reached for the strawberry and spread it thick on the bread before taking a bite. She came over and made some comment about my appetite and we laughed together before I paid and walked out. Just a normal guy eating breakfast. The couple that had come in with me, still there and talking quietly in their private booth over the remains of their meals.

The sun was burning hot as I walked through the town, so I shoved my jacket into my bag to reveal the shirt that had been a 'gift' from the shop. It was a grey shirt that read, "The Lake is where the Heart is." I passed a hardware store and another store with paintings hung in the window. Then another with a bunch of craft materials and some fishing baubles. It reminded me of a place from my past. One of those small towns that maybe my dad had taken me to… I pictured the swinging feet and shook my head to rid myself of the thought. I rounded the corner past the shops and saw a tree that was like something I had never seen before, just a few blocks down. I walked towards it wondering what it was and by the time I made it so that I was standing beneath it; I found that it was one of six trees. I stood underneath two of them and looked up into the flowers that formed a pale pink canopy that blocked the sky. For a moment I was hidden from the world beneath their pink branches. I looked down at the ground reflecting the pink from the fallen flowers that had been trampled into the sidewalk below. The air smelled sweet like a dream that I could almost remember, and I reached out to touch one of the delicate flowers before turning towards the buildings again. There was an arch that stood out against the brick wall. Bright green ivy stretched over the top of the wall covering the red brick and there was a little sign next to the arch that announced that the 'secret garden' was open. I looked around but there was no one in sight so I walked towards the entry way and stepped under the arch.

CHAPTER TWENTY

THE GARDEN

THE INSIDE OF the brick wall was almost unseen beneath the ivy with plants and trees all around me. A small stone path wove towards the hidden parts of the large yard, and I started following it, holding my bag to make sure it didn't knock into any of the plants that were growing around me. The air was still, and I headed towards another pink tree that sat in the nearest corner. Next to it was a small bench and I swept some of the flowers off it before sitting beneath to look at the garden that had been hidden in this small town. I closed my eyes and drifted into a dreamless sleep as I sat in this found paradise.

"Excuse me." I opened my eyes and saw her standing there. A short woman with dark brown curly hair that was speckled with white. Her green eyes peered at me through her bright orange glasses as she smiled at me. Shit.

I sputtered, "I'm sorry. I just saw the open sign and wanted to see in here. I didn't mean to fall asleep."

Her smile widened, "Oh I don't care if you take a nap in here, but I'm thinking that since you found my garden, maybe you would like to help me."

Help her do what? "I'm not sure what I can help you with," I motioned at my bandaged foot.

Her laugh echoed through the leaves, "I'll show you." She motioned for me to leave my bag where it sat and held my hand as I stood. She came to my shoulder and her pale shirt was covered in so much dirt that I almost couldn't make out the pattern of pink flowers on it. Must have already been a busy morning. She held my hand and led me towards the opposite corner.

She saw me look back at my bag sitting on the bench "Your bag will be fine. No one hardly comes in here and if they do, I usually know them." I nodded and let her continue to lead me away. Another tree stretched in this far corner, but the pink flowers were replaced by broad green leaves and the branches were so thick that one held a swing. The swing was lopsided as one side of the rope was hanging down to the ground beneath it. She let go of my hand and turned to me, motioning at the swing, "first task; tie the swing back into the branch please." I obediently picked up the rope from the ground and looked up at the branch when I heard a sound behind me. I looked back to see her dragging a stool over to me, I assumed to stand on. I looked hesitantly at the rickety stool, but she smiled up at me, "It'll be fine. I'll hold it." And her little hands grasped each side of the stool. I awkwardly climbed up, rope in hand and favoring my left leg, and steadied myself against the branch. Her voice floated up, "tie that tight now." I tied the rope around the branch and hopped down from the stool, landing on my right foot. She grinned and sat on the swing, her small legs pumping just a little to get it to sway. "Perfect." I smiled back at her as I sat on the stool and watched her swinging back and forth, her feet swaying beneath her.

She jumped off it, spry for a woman her age, and motioned me to follow her towards a little shed next to the brick wall. Pulled it open to reveal more garden tools than should fit into that space. She rummaged around for a few moments before pulling out two pairs of gloves and a small shovel and I followed her down another stone path. We stopped next to a bare patch of dirt with some flowers sitting in little green plastic pots next to it. She sat down on the path, and I followed as she handed me one of the pairs of gloves. I pulled them on while she showed me how to pull the flowers by the stem and squeeze the green plastic container to pull the flower out without harming it and keeping the dirt and roots intact. I pulled the next flower out as she used the small shovel and started making small holes in the dirt. We worked like this for a while. She would dig a hole and I would pull the flower out and hand it to her. She would set it down into the ground and pile the dirt back around it, patting it down to fill in the space. We went through the dozen flowers that were saved for this spot before moving to the next spot. Once we were done with the two new flower patches, we filled a small container with water from a hose next to the shed and watered them. The whole time she talked to me about flowers and the earth. She showed me the plants and flowers that would continue to bloom each year and not die if they were taken care of and loved. We kept working, her chatting and me listening. I lifted a handful of dirt to my nose and breathed in. The smell filled my nose like nothing I had ever smelled before. It was warm. It smelled like life. I felt something move on my hand saw a little brown worm wiggle out of the dirt. It worked its way through my fingers and back down onto the newly planted flowers. I moved to pick it up, but she told me to let him be. He would help them grow.

Next, we worked our way over to a little pond that sat against the back wall, and she showed me how to pull the weeds from the rocks around it. She went away for a moment and returned with a small handful of pellets that she dropped into the water. We stood and watched as the white and orange fish swam lazily along the bottom before rising in the water and breaching the top to grab the food with their mouths. She bent over and stuck her hand in the water above one of the large fish to rub along the side of it while it swam. Looking over at me, "they like to be pet." I couldn't tell if she was being serious or trying to tease me. I stuck my hand in the cool water and a fish that was pure white bumped against my fingers. I laughed and pulled my hand out of the water. She laughed with me, a sweet sound in the quiet day, and we continued to watch the fish take turns eating and moving around under the bright green lily pads that floated at the top of the water.

SHE LED ME over to a small green table that sat in a corner and told me to wait. I leaned back in my metal chair covered in metal flowers and I looked up at the live leaves stretching above me. I was covered in earth, but I didn't feel dirty. The sun was high in the sky. I heard a clink and a shuffle behind me and turned around to see her balancing a tray carrying two plates and two glasses. She sighed as she placed it on our little table and motioned at me to eat from one of the plates. I took a deep gulp from the glass closest to me and the sweet tea flowed down my throat. A bite of my peanut butter and jelly sandwich and one of the apple slices, before I realized that she sat there watching me eat. I smiled at her and she smiled in return, "So, J, what's the scoop?"

I laughed "So, Trina, why do you think I have a scoop?" I responded.

"Well, I know that you aren't from around here because I haven't seen you before. I know you aren't here on vacation or work because you wouldn't have spent four hours helping me in my garden if you had any place else to be." Witty woman, this one.

"I really don't have a scoop on anything. You asked me to help, so I helped." I shrugged and watched her shrug in return, accepting that she wouldn't get more out of me. We finished our sandwiches and fruit as she told me about how she moved out here when she was younger, trying to escape a relationship. She never had any children but started this garden to welcome kids and families into her life.

She laughed, "Although I hate it when kids actually come in, they trample flowers and break my swing without so much as an apology from their parents." She called it her secret garden, tucked away from the world. I learned that she made money for her garden from selling flowers to shops in the town. She lived a quiet and peaceful life tucked away behind these walls. I finished my tea and chewed on the ice from the bottom of the glass while she talked.

"Well J, you had probably be going back to your non-storied life. But you'll want to clean up before you go." She got up and piled everything on the tray and took it away, before coming back with a small container with soapy water and a small towel. I kept missing the door she went and came from to get this stuff. She was like a fairy in her own garden. I wiped my arms and face with the cool water before drying off and standing to go find my bag. I thanked her and kissed her small hand, a gesture that I have never done before and probably will never do again, but it seemed right in the moment. I took a path that would lead me to the corner with the bench and my belongings. The table and Trina disappearing between the branches and leaves of the plants that surrounded it. The largest tree grew out of the middle of the garden, the path turning to avoid the roots that grew out of the ground. I turned with the grey stones stuck into the dirt and froze. There, poking out of the roots of the dark tree stood a flower that I recognized. Its soft orange flowers were open to the spots of sun that shone through the leaves of the tree above it and the thick green leaves spread down, hiding its tubular roots from the world. I dropped to ground next to it as I called out, "Trina!"

I heard her little footsteps coming up behind me and her hands clap as she exclaimed, "Oh J, you found Eloise!" I turned towards her and stared like she was speaking another language.

"Eloise?"

She laughed, "Yes. That's Eloise, my most favorite orchid." She came and knelt next to me, brushing some dirt way from the leaves of my flower. "I raise orchids and sell them, but this is my orchid. My Eloise." How did my flower end up here? Where did I see my flower before? I know I had just seen it, but I couldn't remember where. All I knew was that this is my flower.

"What is it?" I asked.

"It's an orchid. Derived from the Greek word 'orkhis'. They were named by an ancient Greek botanist who thought the roots," She motioned at the tubes sticking out beneath the leaves, "looked like male parts." She giggled. "Men, always thinking everything resembles their penis. They didn't even notice the flowers. The Greeks even thought that if the man ate the thick root tubes while his wife was pregnant, he could guarantee that she would give birth to a son. The things they did. But they did have one thing right." She looked at me and I waited for her to finish. "The orchid represents love." She smiled at me, and I smiled back at her, feeling a connection with her and our newly shared obsession with this little flower. I stood and helped her to her feet before shocking her and myself by giving her a quick hug before turning back towards my bag. I lifted my bag to lie on my shoulder and stepped through the arch of the secret garden and back out into the world where the sun was already starting to drift back down into the late afternoon.

I took one last deep breath beneath the pink trees that had marked the entrance and turned towards the street that I had come from this morning. Maybe I could still find a ride to hitch out of town before it was dark. I turned a corner back towards my breakfast restaurant when I heard a motor approaching from the road behind me. I turned towards it ready to stick my thumb out and get a ride, when I heard something small hit the window of the brown truck. The truck didn't slow and sped down the street while I stood looking at the tiny red body that lay in the middle of the road. I walked over slowly and could see the feathers on the breast rising and falling slowly. It was still alive. I slowly bent down so I wouldn't scare it and gently folded his wings in towards his body before lifting him into my cupped hands. I walked back to the side of the road and sat on the curb. Slowly trying to softly stroke his bright red feathers as his little black eye looked at me. That truck that had hit it was long gone. I couldn't tell if anything was broken on him, but when I stroked his wing, he gave a little noise. It might have broken his wing. Shit. I don't know what to do with a bird like this. How can I fix it? How can I save it? I leaned my face close and looked into his eye, "How can I save you?" He didn't answer. I held him, cupped in my hands, trying to sooth him. His breathing started to slow. He must be calming down. That's a good sign, right? I looked around me to see if there was anyone that could help me, but the street was empty. I couldn't move, I couldn't balance on my right foot well without jarring him and if he was hurt and I moved him, would that be worse? No one was there to answer me. "Help!" I called out to no one. He moved a bit in my hand from the shout of my voice. Bad idea. I didn't want to scare him. I was barely aware of the water running from my eyes as I watched him in my hand, stroking him softly with my thumb. "Come on buddy. You have to live. You can't die." His breathing slowed more as I looked into his eye. His small white eyelid closed to cover only half of his dark eye and his breathing stopped. "No no no no no no," I moaned as he lay unmoving in my hands. My whole body shook as I sat there holding his little body. I looked around again but there was no one there. His head fell to the side, and he lay there, lifeless. "Please please come back. Please live. Don't die. Don't die."

I cried into my cupped hands, begging him to hear me and listen to me.

I felt a small hand on my shoulder, "J, he's gone. There is nothing you can do." I shook with sobs and could feel the hand as it stayed there for support and tried to help me rise out of this moment that I had found myself in. This just wasn't right. Why was there nothing I can do? I thought it before I said it out loud, "Why is there nothing I can do? This just isn't fair. He was so happy." I wasn't sure if I was talking about the bird in my dream or the one now laying in my cupped hands.

I heard her behind me, "Sometimes death… and life… just aren't fair." I turned to look at Trina, my face and heart distraught. I froze. Behind me wasn't Trina. It was a woman I didn't quite recognize. She was there, her eyes were wet with unshed tears for me or for the little red body in my hands, I wasn't sure. Her small hand was on my shoulder, and she is wearing a soft orange dress. Her favorite color, I knew. The freckles on her nose were almost invisible in her round face. She looked sad as she talked to me, "Sometimes you can't save them. It's just time."

I held the little corpse in my hand as I stared up at the ghost from my dream, and I didn't realize what was coming out of my mouth before I said it, "El… Eloise?"

CHAPTER TWENTY-ONE

THE DODGE

THE SUN WAS rising into the sky above me and my back was damp with the dew that had settled in the night. I had slept on the soft grass of a small park in what looked to be a small town. There were a few people wondering around early this morning, but no one seemed to be in any type of a hurry. I sat for a few moments before my stomach started to rumble. I opened my bag and took a drink of my water before grabbing a granola bar out of the bag and zipping it back up. A big breakfast of eggs and bacon sounded amazing, but I tried to ignore the saliva that came into my mouth as I imagined it. The granola bar was enough, and I didn't feel like stopping in this little town for long. There was something… off about it. I couldn't quite put it into words. The wrapper went into a pocket of my bag, and I stuck my hand into my pants pocket, rubbing the smooth rock that lived there a few times with my thumb. Then I stood and walked towards a small strip of buildings that one couple had just gone towards. I watched them enter a little restaurant that looked like it probably served a pretty good breakfast but shook my head and kept walking towards the end of the block.

I got the corner and looked down the street at the pretty pink trees down at the end before turning back to the road I was standing on and continuing to walk past the shops. I walked past a small older woman in a faded orange top covered in dirt. She smiled at me. I smiled back. A motor came up behind me and I turned to stick my thumb out. The brown truck sped past, the driver not even glancing over at the upturned thumb. I turned back and kept walking up the street towards the end. The other side of the town held a small road with a faint line separating the two sides of traffic. There were a few cars in the distance, and I turned left to go a few paces past the main road of the small town before turning back and sticking out my arm.

I rode most of the day in a beat-up dodge with minimal air-conditioning. The two kids up front were polite and talkative. They were still up there, talking excitedly about their apartment that they had worked to get before the start of their first year of college so they could move early to start working over the summer and help offset their cost. The kid driving was talking almost non-stop while the passenger interjected here and there just to correct a piece of a story or add an explanation to an inside joke.

They had been friends since they were kids and had applied to and gotten into the same school across the country, trying to get as far away from home as fast as they could. They had been driving for two days broken up by moments of sleep along the side of the road. I had forgotten their names in the hours of chatter. In my head I named them Kid 1 and Kid 2. They both were lanky and long, their skin standing out against their bright collegiate shirts that they were wearing, a tribute to their drive to college town.

"I mean, we could've both been sucked into the shit around us, you know. But we were lucky. My brother, he was arrested at sixteen, and most of the other kids we grew up with didn't make it to graduation." Kid 1 said with a nod from Kid 2. "We were lucky. There were programs meant just for us, we had mentors and teachers that were worth a shit. We had one teacher, Mr. Johnson, he really focused on us together. Helped us both with our grades and even with recommendation letters to college so that we could get in. He helped us find jobs and save money and even helped me have a conversation with my mom about leaving." I watched his eyes in the rearview mirror as he spoke. They looked back and met mine for a second. "You actually remind me of him a lot." Kid 2 looked back at me and then laughed and nodded.

I grinned, "What, you kids think all of us old white guys look alike?" They both laughed and Kid 2 nodded again. I chuckled with them.

Kid 2 continued to look back at me for a moment before he spoke, "You seem quiet... but you listen. That's really what it is. Mr. Johnson was the first person who really listened to me. And now look at me. Off to college." He looked over at Kid 1, "both of us."

Kid 1 pipped in, "You know, it was Mr. Johnson who got us our summer jobs out there too. He called a friend and said if we could leave right after graduation, we could work all summer and make enough to cover some of our costs. I mean, we both got grants and Daryl got a partial scholarship, but it's just not enough."

Daryl turned back to me, "I know you said you would go as far as we were, but are you sure you want to make it all the way? We won't get there until tomorrow night, but we'll stop for sleep tonight at some point if you don't mind sleeping in this car." I looked at the duffel back sitting on my lap as I was squished into the leftover space next to their bags full of clothes. They had pushed things aside as much as possible, but the space was still cramped.

I looked back at him, "Yeah, I'm good with the full ride."

He grinned and looked back at his friend again, "Then how about a food break?" Kid 1 (now just Kid) nodded in agreement, and we all turned back to the road, watching for a place to stop.

WE TURNED OFF the small highway to a sign promoting food. Kid found a spot to park his small car, smothered in between two pickup trucks and I pulled two twenties out of my bag before pushing it down on the floor beneath the seat I had been sitting. We squeezed out of our seats and started walking towards the restaurant. A grown man with the scratch of a beard and worn vacation clothing and two clean cut lanky black kids. I'm sure anyone who would see us walking towards this lit stop in the dark would wonder our story and how we fit together. Kid and Daryl were jumping around like they hadn't been driving for over two days and laughed as they playfully hit at each other. I followed closely behind, laughing at their excitement. I knew they must be tired of the drive and life in general, but it didn't show as they lunged at each other, laughing in the night. Daryl put his arm over the shoulder of Kid and looked back to me with a grin on his face. I looked at the restaurant. Beneath the lights that promoted food and beer, were a few windows that were covered so that you couldn't see what lay inside and I had moment of hesitation before pulling open the heavy door. The stench of cigarette smoke and the sound of country music hit me like a blast.

We walked in; my eyes didn't need to adjust to the dim interior after coming in from the dark night outside. There were a few people perched at the bar, but the rest mingled around different spots throughout. One by one, the men turned to look at me, nothing registering on their faces, before the eyes changed just a small amount seeing the boys following me inside. I turned to the boys, grins still plastered on both of their faces and turned back to the room. No one was looking at us. I must have imagined it. We found three empty chairs at the bar top and the bar tender walked over to us, wiping his hands against his old jeans. His rough hair was white, and he looked pissed off at no one particularly. Or maybe everyone. He stopped in front of our trio and looked at each one of us, before his face broke into an unexpected smile.

"Hey boys. You're s'posed to have a good football team next year" he pointed at the shirt of Daryl sitting next to me.

The boys grinned back, and Kid chimed in, "Yeah. It's going to be great." I realized that I had been holding my breath and it came out in a long sigh of relief. I don't know what had worried me.

"So, what can I getcha? We have food served for another hour and if y'all boys are under 21, you have to leave the bar after an hour anyway, so it works out." We ordered three burgers, three Pepsis, and three coffees. Just to help us stay awake as we drove. The talk got louder behind us as we ate the burgers. It tasted like any recently thawed hamburger meat should taste, but the Pepsi went down like sweet water. As we ate, we talked to each other at a yell to be heard three barstools apart, over the chatter behind us. The bartender kept walking by to keep serving the men cheap beer and would wink at us as he went back and forth, obviously proud of the boys with the good football team.

I took the last bite of my burger and a gulp of soda to wash it down and continued my train of thought, "But how could you have never seen the Star Wars movies? They are such a classic."

Kid laughed, "No man, I told you, I saw Star Wars, I just still don't get why the dude went so evil and killed all those kids."

"No no no no. Not the new movies, the old ones. With Luke and Leia. Harrison Ford?"

"Who? The old guy? I don't get how you guys all think he's so badass. He's like my grandad's age."

"Ok, fair enough. But if you saw him in the original movies, you would see him as the badass he is. Please tell me you saw the Indiana Jones movies."

"That movie with the aliens?"

I smacked my hand against my forehead in mock frustration. Kids these days. "No. Just no. Temple of Doom? Raiders of the Lost Ark?"

"Those sound like horrible movies. Completely lame."

"How can a movie named 'Temple of Doom' possibly sound lame? There is a temple full of doom!"

Daryl laughed and sipped his coffee.

"Ok ok. I'm going to make you boys a list of movies that you must promise me you'll watch while you're at college. They will open your eyes."

Kid laughed, "deal."

The bartender had stopped being pulled in either direction and was listening to us with a grin on his face, before grabbing an orange box out of his shirt pocket and pulling a cigarette from it. I motioned at him, "Hey man, could I get one of those?" He tossed me one and I stuck it in my mouth as he lit the end before snapping his lighter shut. I breathed in and let the smoke fill my lungs. I hadn't smoked in weeks. Maybe months. But sitting in this shitty bar in the middle of nowhere, debating the validity of classic movies, it just seemed so normal that I wanted to do something else that seemed normal from my past. I blew out and watched the white smoke billow out in front of me before noticing Kid and Daryl both staring at me.

Daryl yelled over the crowd, "You know those things will kill you." Shit. I forgot about that whole thing about setting an example. I moved to snuff out the lit end when I saw a big hand land on the shoulder of Kid.

We swung around at the same time to see a large man standing there, glaring at the three of us. He had scruff on his chin that mirrored mine but wasn't quite so steady on his feet. I put the cigarette out in the ashtray on the bar and slowly turned the rest of my body to prepare for the threat that stood there. Kid grinned at the big man as Daryl scanned the room for other trouble, or maybe help. I perched to the edge of my stool and deepened my voice, "Hey brother, anything we can help you with?"

He didn't even turn to look at me but focused on the thin boy that was sitting directly in front of him, "You drivin' that shitty dodge out there?"

I looked at Kid as he smiled, "Most likely, unless there is more than one shitty dodge out there." The warning flags of when to use sarcasm haven't found him in his young age yet.

"You dented the door of my truck, boy." His fat hand still on Kid's shoulder.

"The hell I did." My young friend looked incredulous. I knew he was telling the truth as we had all squeezed out of the car doors at the same time, watching that they didn't hit the large trucks that bookended the small car.

"You did. Joe saw ya. What are you going to do about it, boy?" He took his hand off the shoulder and took a step back as he was met by another friend standing behind him, nodding.

"I don't know what 'Joe' saw, but our doors didn't hit anything," I interjected as I slowly stood and tried to move my body in front of Kid just a small amount.

I heard a voice come from behind the bar, "Now Carl, you know you always be dentin' up your truck. These boys just came for some food not trouble. Go back to your game."

Carl turned his glare behind the bar, "Stay outta it, Mike." I looked back to see Mike put his hands up in a surrender, the smile gone from his face. I turned back to Carl, moving more so that I was standing completely in front of Kid as I heard him start to talk.

"Listen fuc…" I cut him off by putting my hand towards him to motion to not say anything.

I looked into Carl's eyes, "Listen Carl, we don't want any trouble. I'm real sorry about your door, but I was with these boys when they got out of their car and they really didn't dent anything. They are just driving to school. It's gonna have a real good football team this year." I had one hand still facing Kid and one towards Carl as a sign of peace, as more patrons stopped what they were doing to watch. A few more men stood facing us, likely on Carl's side of the argument. Shit. This wasn't good. I looked back at Mike to see him looking down at the floor, his friendliness gone. I turned my head slowly back towards the boys and tried to communicate with my eyes, telling them to keep their mouths shut. I turned back to Carl to see the men backing him even closer. "Listen Carl, let us just pay for our meal and we'll get out of here. I'm sure we can exchange information and if you still think we dented your door then we can work it out later."

Carl glared at me, "Whatcha doing riding with them boys? You into that sort of thing? Huh, faggot?" He laughed and turned to his friends like he had just made a funny joke. They laughed back. He turned back to me, "Well faggot, how much money you got on you? We'll just take that now and call it even and let you go back to your little black boys." I could feel Kid starting to stand behind me and I put a hand on his shoulder and pushed to get him to sit back on his stool.

"Yeah Carl, that's funny. Unfortunately, we only have enough money for dinner. So, how about we exchange our information and then we'll be on our way." It was almost slow motion, but not enough for me to move out of the way. I saw Carl's meaty fist barrel towards my ribs right before I felt the impact and I doubled over in pain, trying to catch my breath. Pain shot through my side as another blow landed. There was a low, "get out of there" right before I heard something slam against the bar. I was still trying to catch my breath as I straightened back up, two pairs of lanky arms helping me on each side, and I got a glimpse of Mike behind the bar with a bat as he yelled at the crowd.

"Now y'all know the rules. No fighting here or I'm callin' the police. And I'm pretty sure that'd be your second strike there, Carl."

Kid was on my right and Daryl on my left as he said in my ear, "Let's get out of here before they start again." We hobbled to the front door and pushed out into the night. I looked back and saw a scene frozen in time. Carl glaring at us with two buddies on each side. Mike behind the counter armed with a baseball bat. Everyone else still sitting or standing, watching us leave. We quickly got to the car and looked back to see if anyone was following us out. The door stayed shut. Kid left my side to unlock the car as Daryl slowly let me lower to the gravel and lean against the shitty dodge. My mid-section screamed in pain, and I was still trying to catch my breath as I looked up into the eyes that hovered next to me. He was pushing on me a little and asking if something hurt but I couldn't quite focus on what he was asking.

He suddenly jumped up and I watched him step in front of Kid who was walking around the back of the car, "What are you doing, Trey?"

Trey had a small knife in his hand and was looking at the truck parked next to us, "I'm going to slash that fucking red neck's tires." I worked to focus on his face and saw a raw desperation in it. His eyes were wet, and he held the knife like he hadn't really used it before. Daryl held up his hands in the same way that I had held them up to the assholes in the bar.

"You can't do that. It's not worth it. They aren't worth it." The crazy need fell from Trey's face, and he folded the knife and put it in his pocket, his head dropping in defeat. Daryl put his arms around his friend, and they stood there for a moment as I pushed myself up to my feet with the help of the bumper. I stood there, holding my stomach, trying to will the pain away, as they turned to look at me. In unison, they walked to me and put their arms around me and the three of us embraced, united in our fear of the unknown and the hatred of what lay within that bar. We separated and silently got into the car, making sure to not dent the truck next to us, Daryl sliding into the driver's seat this time.

We pulled out of the lot, the door to the bar still closed to hide the hate from the rest of the world, and Trey switched on the music. It was a song I had never heard before but the boys both mouthed the words and I slowly drifted off to a dreamless sleep.

I WOKE UP with a start, the bruising pain radiating from my stomach to the rest of my body. My neck was sore from the odd position pushed up against their bags of clothing in the tiny back seat. The car was silent, and we were no longer moving down the road. The night around us was pitch black as I listened to the boys breathing heavily while they slept in the front seat. I muffled my groan as I leaned forward to check on them. Both pairs of eyes were heavily closed against the night but the young man in the passenger seat twitched slightly as he dreamed. They were both so different in personality and looks, but still connected by their past and their relationship. Daryl seemed to be the one with a clearer head on his shoulders and his face reflected that. He looked almost peaceful as he slept, and his left hand was holding his head tilted at an angle. Trey had put on a sweatshirt and was curled up more, almost hiding in his sleep. His face was pinched, and his hand was lying over the top of his short hair like a hat.

He mumbled something, and I leaned back in my seat so that I didn't trespass on his dream. I wanted to stand and stretch, but I feared waking them by opening a door. So, I sat silently in my uncomfortable position and thought about my own young years. They both seemed to have figured out something that I wasn't even close to when I was that age. Or even now.

After my parents were gone, I stayed with my uncle for a while. He wasn't a bad guy. He just didn't really give a shit. I knew I had to make it on my own, just like the sleeping kids in the front of this car. I got good grades and made it into a state school. I thought back to days of working and studying and trying to unsuccessfully relate to the other kids that I was around. Trying to not show the emptiness that was inside me as I watched family come to visit my roommate. I thought about the day that I met the girl that would eventually become the wife to a man she never would really know. It seemed like a dream, that life. There was nothing of me back in those memories anymore. I watched the pieces float through my mind like a show that I had no attachment to. She had come to me in desperation, and I had helped her. We became fast friends then lovers. The first time we had sex it was like I wasn't completely alone for a moment, and I clung to that like she was a lifeboat in the ocean. But did I ever actually let her in? I never was fully myself around her. It wasn't fair to her. I had used her. The man I was had used her. I shook my head to clear the thoughts of her smile that had eventually faded away from my mind and I came back to the reality that is here and now, in the back of this car in some state I wasn't even sure of. The soreness of my body reminded me of what happened tonight and what would continue to happen to me if I didn't find something to continue living for or make the decision to stop living altogether. And the threat that would continue to follow these boys for their whole lives. I closed my eyes, a tear rolling down my cheek and falling from my chin before I drifted to sleep again.

CHAPTER TWENTY-TWO

THE ARREST

"WAKE UP"

A soft voice whispered in my ear, and I could feel her soft lips press to my cheek. I lifted my hand to shield my eyes from the bright sun coming through the car window before opening them. The sun went away, and my eyes widened to focus on the light that was now shining in the passenger side of the car as something tapped against the window. I could see the outline of a gun and I sat up straight, remembering the fight from the night before.

I could hear the boys in the front of the car start to move and Daryl asked no one in particular, "What is it?" I shook my head as the passenger door opened and I could hear a voice come from the darkness outside.

"You can't sleep here, whatcha boys think y'all are doin?" I was still trying to place what was going on when my door opened, and a hand appeared to motion to get out of the car. I pushed out and stumbled on the wet gravel before catching myself and following the officer to the back of the car. I was standing in a spotlight that was made from the headlights of the police car that was parked behind us and I stood looking at the silhouette of the two officers while Trey and Daryl joined me. A light was shined in my face, and I lifted my hand to block the light.

"I asked you, whatcha boys doing out here at this time of night?" I looked at the two boys next to me, eyes still full of sleep from getting woken up mid-dream and turned back to the officers.

"Sorry sir, just getting these two to college so they can start work before classes start up. We'd been driving quite a long time and needed some sleep. Didn't know that we couldn't sleep here." I saw one officer nod at the other and the second one went around to the driver's side of the car and opened the back door. I turned back to the first officer, "Is there something that we did wrong?"

He shined his light back at me, "We'll we heard that there were two black boys that started a fight at a bar a bit back the road and that y'all left without payin'."

Trey moved beside me like he had finally just woken up, "What the f…"

Daryl jumped in, "We didn't start any fight, sir. There was a fight started. But it wasn't our fight. We did leave without paying though. I have some money in the car to pay for it."

"Bullshit. You just stay right there."

I motioned at the boys to stay quiet, "Excuse me, officer. But what he said was right. There was a fight but it was only started and instigated by a guy named Carl. The bartender can back that up. I have money in my pocket for the food; can I reach in and grab it?"

"Just keep your hands where I can see them. All y'all. You," he shined at me again, "what are you doin' riding in a car with these thugs?"

I looked at the boys, "I'm just trying to get home and they picked me up yesterday. They are good boys just trying to get to school."

"Did I ask you about their history?"

"No, I..."

"Shut your mouth. Did you know that hitchhiking is illegal here? I could arrest all three of you right now."

We heard a noise, and all turned to the car where the second officer was tossing a bag of clothes out the gravel and ripping open a second bag, searching for something.

Trey moved towards the car, "Hey asshole! Those are my clothes." The second officer turned towards us, his right hand down on his gun holster as he flipped the strap open.

"Stay back!"

Trey moved back and put his hands up, "What the fuck is going on. There's nothing but clothes and books."

"Yeah right," the officer turned back to the car and ripped open the last plastic bag, spilling the clothes on the ground.

I turned back to the first officer, "Hey, you know this isn't right. There is no reason for you to be searching this car or holding us right now."

"I said shut up. You thugs started a fight and lying to us about what you all are doing out here right now."

"We aren't sir. We really…" Daryl was interrupted by the officer.

"Stop going through their shit, we got enough to take them in." The second officer stepped through the pile of clothes on the side of the road and walked back over to us. Officer one put away his flashlight and I could see their faces in the lightening morning sky. The second officer looked familiar, but it took a moment before I recognized him as one of Carl's backers at the bar, I think the one he called 'Joe'. Shit.

The first officer walked towards the boys and motioned at Trey, "turn around and put your hands on the car."

"Fuck no. I haven't done anything."

"We got you on the fight in the bar, stealing food without payin', pickin' up a hitchhiker, and now resistin' arrest. Now turn around. Don't make me ask you again, boy."

I took a step forward, "You can't arrest us. You have nothing to hold us on."

"Stay where you are or we'll arrest you too, asshole. We might not have anything to hold them on, but at least we'll get them off the street for a night." I could see his face reddening.

"What fucking street? They are trying to get to college you idiot."

"I said stay where you are." I stopped and put my hands back up, trying to work this out in my head.

"We ain't gonna arrest you. You didn't start the fight. But you best be moving on before I pull you in for hitchhiking." I stood there frozen watching as Trey stood his ground, his eyes shining with anger and for a second, I thought he might charge at the cop. I should step in. I should fight for him. How? The cop and Trey stared at each other. One fat hand holding handcuffs propped open: the other twitched above the gun in his holster, threatening. Shit. There wasn't a sound in the morning sky. Finally, the kid sighed, defeated again, and turned to put his hands behind his back. The cop looked almost relieved for a second before the triumph rushing over his face like he just won some sort of battle over the unarmed and harmless kid in front of him.

Daryl looked at me, aged years in just a few moments. "We'll take care of it. Just go." I shook my head. How could I let this happen? I looked up and down the road, trying to will a car to come along and save us. No one came. I looked at the second officer again as he stood there with a grin on his face and his right hand resting on his gun. I stood, numbed, as they handcuffed Daryl and led them towards the cruiser. One of the cops pushed Trey a bit as he paused and looked back at me. He turned and followed his friend into the back seat of the car. But I had caught the shine of the tears running down his face before disappearing into the back seat of the patrol car. I didn't move as they rolled past me with both boys in the back seat, not looking at me. I read the name of the town on the side of the car before it sped away. Knowing there was nothing I could do to make a difference in their fate.

Bullshit, I thought to myself. I went back to the car and packed up the clothes that were strewn on the gravel and put them back into the back seat. I dug around the front of the car looking for some sliver of help, but there was nothing. The cops had taken the keys. I pulled my duffel back from the back seat and locked the car from the inside before closing it up. I looked down the road towards the way the cruiser had gone and started following it on foot, towards the rising sun. The sky shone in shades of pink and orange and a red bird flew overhead, completely oblivious to the shit still going on in the world below her.

BY THE TIME I made it to the town where the boys should be, the sun was high in the sky, and it beat down on me. Sweat ran down my legs and my arms and I tied a bandana around my head to try to keep it from running into my eyes. I found the police station in the middle of town, the name matching the one that had been on the side of the police car that had stolen my young friends. I heard to the bell chime innocently above the door as I pulled it open. There was a small woman behind the counter, and she looked at me like I walked in three heads.

"What... uh... how can I help you?" I looked around the bright clean station but there wasn't any sign of the boys or the officers who had taken them.

"Yeah, I'm looking for two boys that I think were brought here last night, by an officer that I think was named 'Joe'."

She didn't bother to hide the surprise before opening her mouth, "Oh honey, they're gone. They were brought in, but we couldn't hold them, and someone took them back out to their car just a bit ago. It was just a tactic that the guys sometimes use to scare them straight, ya know?"

I looked back at her, my surprise mirroring hers, "Jesus, those boys didn't need to be scared straight, their lives already did that. They are headed to college. What is this backwards fucking town? You people are..." I let the words fade as I turned and pushed out of the station before she could issue a reply. I walked down a block and sat heavily on the step of a building, my body giving into the pain that I ignored while on my mission to find them. They would be long gone by now, thinking that I had left them to their fate. Back on the road again towards their bright future full of fight and struggle. And I was alone again.

I found another small town before the sun set, not wanting to spend the night in the town that arrested innocent kids but aware that each town was probably identical. As I held my bruised body close and my sweat dripped into the grass, I fell into a hot sleep trying to escape my pain and emptiness. The pain did fade away and I felt the sweat dry from my body as the cool sun shone on me in the place I drifted to when I slept. I opened my eyes, craving the peacefulness that this place brought, and I sat up, ready to explore. As I rose, I saw that I was not alone in this dream. The two boys sat with me. Their names coming back to me again as I spent my night talking under the sun to Trey and Daryl. There was hope in our conversation and I cried as I embraced them and said goodbye, before I opened my eyes back to the rain clouds that hung above me in the hot morning in a small nameless town that my body was in. The dream with the boys and the conversation faded away quickly as I realized that I had no companion in this lonely world. I stood painfully and grabbed my duffel bag before continuing done the road, looking left and right to try to decide which direction to go today.

CHAPTER TWENTY-THREE

THE SHOWER

I REALIZED WHY people hate summer in the city. The hot sun shone down harder than ever; magnified as it reflected against the glass of the buildings above me. I sat on a hot cement bench that I was pretty sure was meant to be art but became a seat over the years. Now it was stained different colors from misuse and had turned a mix of grey and brown. My legs spread with my duffel bag down between my feet, and my head lay on my folded arms trying to hide from the sun above me. There was no escape, but I wasn't ready to go inside quite yet. I could hear people shuffle in and out of the building behind me, talking of where they were going to go this afternoon or gossiping about someone they both knew. People walked past me on the sidewalk in front of the building and I picked up some of their conversation as well, which always seemed to dim as they passed the building with the bench. It must have a reputation. I hadn't completely decided yet if I would go inside or not. It seemed hot for this time of year already, maybe a little early for this heaviness of heat. Scenes ran behind my closed eyes as I drowned in the talk around me and procrastinated on my decision.

The boy's eyes as they were being driven away in a police cruiser in the faded morning light. The smile of a dead man's wife. The feet of a father swaying back and forth well above the floor they should have been standing on. The silence in his mother's dead eyes. The warm grass swaying beneath my fingers. The town that I could almost explore. An orange dress blowing as she walked down the street. A bird dying in my hands. A hand tapping the keys on a laptop in a dull grey office. The laughter of Phil as he sat across from me at a diner. The conversation of three friends gathered around a dinner table. Watching lightning run across the sky above me as I lay in pain, pelted by a storm. My own eye reflected in the large brown eye of a buffalo as it stood there daring me to move. Lying in a field as a teenager and feeling as lost and alone as I do now. That teenager staring at the night sky trying to decide if he should just end it. Dog laying in the clearing by a house, watching me leave him behind. The thoughts drifted in and out like pictures in a book, sometimes it unfolded in front of me like I was living it right now.

Sometimes I was watching the man I was relive it and I could see his expressions with each memory. I paused the show when my stomach groaned painfully. It had been over a day since I had eaten anything. My granola stash and my cash gone. The cash from my pocket had been spent along the way, and the little remaining cash in my duffel bag had gone missing from underneath me. Literally. I had been sleeping, hugging my bag to my body as I curled over it, but when I woke up in the morning, the cash was gone along with some Band-Aids, my recently found book, and a pair of socks. I didn't have it in me to ask people for money. Whatever drive had been remaining had been beaten out in that bar weeks ago. I could smell myself as I sat on the step. My clothes and body were covered in sweat and dirt and piss. My hair stunk as it lay around my head. My beard was coming in again and it smelled too. It was too much. I would die as I sat here, my own smell not giving me away for days. I listened to the footsteps as they walked past. Back and forth. Right and left. Stop. Right in front of me. I opened my eyes and lost my string of self-hating thoughts and pulled my head up over my arm to see a uniform standing there. I immediately prepared to back up and put my hands up to show I wasn't a threat, fear immediately erasing all other thoughts. He took off his hat and kneeled so that his head was even with mine.

"How are you doing today?" I looked behind me. Was he talking to me?

There was no one sitting behind me, so I turned back to him, "Uh…" my voice was cracked and dry. I coughed to clear it, "just fine… and… uh… how're you doing, sir?"

He smiled, "I'm doing good too." He reached towards me, and I froze, waiting for a blow. But in his outstretched hand was a bottle of water, still mostly full. I looked from the water to his face as he said, "I think you might get more use of this than me." I reached out and tentatively took the bottle from him, barely being able to control my shaking hands as I tipped the water into my mouth. I drank half the bottle and then looked at him still kneeling in front of me. What did he want?

"Uh… thanks," I mumbled at him.

"No problem, bud. It's a hot one today. I think they said record. You may want to find a place to duck inside soon." He pointed at the building behind me before getting up and walking away with a little wave, fitting his hat back on top of his head. I took another drink and finished off the bottle, making up my mind to go inside.

I pulled the clear glass door open and walked to the large counter. There were two older women working behind it, both pecking away at their keyboards and neither looked up at me as I neared them. They sat behind a clear Plexiglas window that separated them from the rest of the room and there was a man about my age, leaning over the back of one of them, looking at her screen. He wore a slightly wrinkled button-down shirt and grew an impressive brown mustache on his thin face.

"Excuse me?" All three of them looked up and then the two women looked back at each other before the woman farthest away continued her typing with the man looking back at her screen. The woman closer to me had kind eyes and a smile on her soft face. She didn't look disgusted or fearful of me and it made me curious what else she saw working in this place.

"Yes honey, how can I help you?" I could hear her clearly through the glass that separated us.

"I uh... I'm looking for a place to stay tonight."

"Well, our doors don't open until four and that's about," she looked down at her wristwatch, "three hours from now. Have you stayed with us before?" I shook my head so she would continue. "No worries honey. Well, have you stayed in any shelter in this area before?" I noticed a slight accent in her words as I shook my head again. "Ok then. Well, we are pretty standard when it comes to long-term shelters, but we pride ourselves on our cleanliness and privacy. Are you aware of any bugs or infection on you?" The man looked in my direction and I shook my head again. "Ok then, you will want to get in the line to my left for the newcomers that are still in trial for short-term stay." She motioned to the rope over to the right of me. "Once we open up for beds, you'll come back up to this counter and give me your state ID or other identification and fill out a few small pieces of paper and then we'll get you sorted into the line for showers. Then you'll get some food and an introduction before headed to bed. You can take your wallet with you into the sleeping room, but not your bag. Since you are here early, you'll get a bunk, but in the future if you get in late, you might get assigned a mat in the cafeteria. If you get here too late, you may not get a spot at all unless you are approved as a long-term resident. Tonight, is chili for dinner. I know, not the best for a hot day like today, but it warms the soul. We have a small reading room with books that you can read while you are here, in between meal and lights out. And you can stay for up to two weeks before we need to verify you are still looking for a job. If you get a job in that time, we can handle your deposits and open an account for you, and we can take your sleeping and meal charge out of that after your first two weeks. It's minimal but our goal is to prepare you for a transition out and into full-time housing of your own. You have to make an effort to stay here, and we will make an effort for you as well." I stood there trying to figure out everything she just said and thinking maybe I should just starve outside rather than in here.

"Um, I'm sorry ma'am, I don't have an ID."

"Any ID? How about social or arrest records?"

"No, how can I get it?" She looked over at the other woman who had stopped typing and the man straightened as they both looked over at us. The woman shrugged and turned back to her screen.

"Well, we have some office staff that may be able to help you, but they won't be back until tomorrow. If you don't have an ID, we can just have you fill out the forms for tonight and we can go from there in the morning. Does that sound fine?" I nodded. She motioned to the little rope that separated out a part of the room with a small sign that read, 'line starts here' and I moved to stand behind it and prepared to wait out the next three hours.

I sat on the ground and crossed my legs and waited, watching the little clock that hung on the painted brick wall over the desk, when I saw the man walk over and say a few words to the woman who helped me. Her head popped over the counter and she looked down at me sitting on the floor and shook her head.

"Come back here please, honey." They both stood there waiting for me. They were going to kick me out into the heat before I even got to eat or anything. I knew it. I walked slowly back to the separation, trying to delay the inevitable. "You know, we don't normally do this, so don't spread the word but would you like to take a shower before getting back in line? Then you can skip the shower time before meal and maybe sit in the reading room for a minute or perhaps go to the chapel." A long sigh escaped my lips, and I couldn't stop the tears from filling my eyes. She looked like a little round angel. I nodded and she smiled. The other woman still typing away and shaking her head, but with a slight smile on her face as the man and woman in front of me both smiled. The woman in front of me put a form on the counter with a pen and slid it under a little opening on the counter. "My name is Anne, and this here is Jeremy."

"J" I responded with my standard name lie. I turned to the paper and lifted the pen to fill out the paper that might save me today.

First Name: J.

Last Name: I thought about this one longer than I should have *Philips*

Home State: Massachusetts

Birthdate: June 28, 1966

ID: TBD

Known Health Risks: N/A

I handed the form back and she looked down at it, checking each line. She smiled back at me, "Happy late birthday, J!" I looked back at her. Did I really miss my birthday already again? It was funny how I forgot about something like that. "Do you have clean clothing and bathroom items?" I shook my head and she looked back at Jeremy. "Okie dokie then, Jeremy here can take you to the bathroom and clothing lockers on your way to the shower." She slid five small rectangles that were each the size of a stamp through the opening. "If you need more clothing while you are here, take the orange stamp to the clothing locker when we are officially open. The three blue ones are for dinner tonight and then breakfast and a sack lunch tomorrow. You'll want to put these someplace safe like your wallet. The green one is for your bunk. Tomorrow, you'll need to take off after breakfast and chapel or skills block. You'll be able to job hunt and do what you need to do, and if you come back to us at night, we'll give you three more stamps for food and another for a bunk. Sound good?" I nodded and closed my eyes for a moment, searching for words that wouldn't come. I opened my eyes, and she was looking at me, "You're welcome," She smiled. I nodded and waited for Jeremy to come out from behind the counter through a small, locked door before following him.

We walked down a hallway towards a room at the end. The room opened into what must be the sleeping room. There were rows of bunk beds with no sheets or pillows, and it smelled slightly better than I did. I followed Jeremy to the end of the row, and he opened a locked door with one of the keys from his bracelet full of them that hung on his wrist. He turned to me,

"So, what do you need in terms of clothing?" His voice was deeper than I expected out his thin frame and his mustache moved dramatically as he spoke. I looked at him as he looked me up and down, "I'm going to guess just about the whole shebang, huh?" I looked down at my clothing.

"Is there someplace I can wash my clothes?"

He shook his head, "Unfortunately not, we can't wash all of the clothes that come in on everyone. We have laundry volunteers, but they won't pick up until Friday." I nodded like I knew what day this was. "You could probably rinse them while you shower and then wring them out. But for now," He turned towards the closet and started pulling out items and putting them on the floor between us, "a shirt, sport shorts, jeans, socks, underwear." He rummaged around a bit more, "I'm afraid I don't have a sweatshirt in here, we didn't get a lot of cold wear in our last donation." He looked at me as I stared at the clothing sitting on the tan tiled floor.

"This is perfect. I have a sweatshirt and a jacket that aren't bad." I gathered up the clothes and waited for him to lock the door behind him before we walked out into the dim hallway again. He stopped and found another key on his wrist before unlocking a closet in the hallway.

He pulled more items and laid them on top of my clothes pile that I held to my chest, "shampoo, soap, shaving cream, and razor?" He looked at me with a question in his eyes. I nodded. "Toothpaste, toothbrush, and I think that is about it." He made a move to close the door before I stopped him.

"Uh I don't suppose you have any scissors?" He looked at me and squinted his eyes.

"What do you need scissors for, J?" It took me a second to recognize his meaning. Questioning, I looked down at the razor in my arms and noticed it was a rubber single blade. Difficult to do much damage.

"Oh no, just... well... I want to cut my hair and my beard is almost too long to be able to get at with just a razor." He looked at me for another moment and I started to feel uncomfortable. He opened the door again and pulled out a pair of small craft sheers.

"But these you have to return to Anne up front after your shower, deal?" I nodded earnestly. He pushed open a swinging door next to us, after locking back up the closet and I was presented with a shower area just like the ones that made every high school student dread gym class. Only this one belonged to just me at this very moment. Jeremy turned to me, "OK J, you can shave at one of the sinks, brush your teeth, and shower, but you have to promise me that you will come back out and get back into line once you are done, deal?"

I nodded and tried to think of the words but all that came out was, "Why?"

He picked up my dirty hand and held it between his thin two clean ones and looked at me, "Listen, no matter what you believe in, everyone needs to feel that someone is watching out for them at some point in their life. And I feel like this may be a time in yours that you need to remember that. I was alone once, on the street. Someone watched out for me. Someone trusted me. Like I'm trusting you." He let go of my hands and turned to head back down the hallway, leaving me standing there in the door jam.

I LOOKED INTO the bright white bathroom that was meant to shower twenty men at a time and took my new supplies to the sink near me before leaning forward to see myself in the pane of metal that served as a mirror. Shit. This might be up there with the worst I had ever looked in my life. My beard had grown in a bit uneven and there were patches of white now mixed into the brown fur. My hair was knotted in pieces around my head and hung in greasy clumps trying to frame my brown face. My face looked thin and was covered in dirt with streaks running on it from the sweat, maybe tears, I wasn't sure. Is this what I had become? So quickly I had fallen back into a man that I didn't recognize. He had changed so much while I hadn't been looking. Fallen so quickly.

I dropped my duffel bag right there and laid my new clothes on top of it, before turning to my bathroom gifts. I grasped some of my knotted hair in my hand before using the small shears to cut it a finger length away from my scalp. I continued until I had made it all the way around my head, before starting on the beard. Getting it down to a rough stubble and I pulled out the shaving cream and lathered it on my face and neck. It masked the smell of my body beneath it as I slowly started shaving away the remains of the fur on my chin. I looked in the mirror again. Not bad for what I had to work with. I gathered the hair from the sink and dumped it in the metal trash before I peeled off the shirt I had been wearing and ran it under the sink, rubbing at it with the bar of soap from my donated toiletries, before wringing it out and draping it over the wood bench behind me. I followed with my hiking pants, and then my underwear. I pulled my clothes from my bag. My jacket was still in good condition and so was my sweatshirt. My other pair of underwear and the two pairs of socks followed a wash and hang, and I stood in front of the makeshift mirror looking at my dirty naked body. I grabbed my soap and shampoo and stepped under one of the spouts that lined the edges of the shower stall. I turned the handle, and nothing happened. Shit. All this prep work and I wouldn't even get a shower. I tried another and after a moment, the water started shooting from the faucet. I let it heat up before standing beneath the full blast and letting it run over me.

I watched the water circle the drain until it had turned from black to brown to clear, and then I scrubbed. And scrubbed. Images ran through my mind, and I washed my body vigorously as if that would make them go away. The eyes of the boys as they were being led away. I rubbed my eyes. The look from a dead man's wife. I scrubbed my arms. The bird dying in my hands. Scrubbed my legs. Finally, I turned off the water, knowing that I had been in here for too long. I grabbed one of the rough folded towels from the pile that was on the wooden bench and dried off, checking my damp clothes that were still drying on the bench. I slid into the new to me underwear and followed with the sport shorts and the new t-shirt before putting back on my water shoes. I took a few minutes for each piece of still damp clothing to dry them under the hand air dryer along the side of the room before sticking them back down into my bag. I put the remainder of the bathroom items in my bag and headed out of the blinding bathroom and back into the dim hallway.

I headed back the way that Jeremy had walked and slid the scissors through the slot under the Plexiglas before going back to claim my place, still at the head of the line. There was no sign of Jeremy, but both women looked over at me and smiled.

"Well, now. Look at you. You look like a different man there, honey." I smiled back, feeling that maybe a small amount of the torment washed away down the drain along with the dirt.

"Thank you again for the shower, ma'am." Anne held up her finger to her lips and made a shush sound before turning back to her screen and continuing her typing. The door opened behind me, and two short older men walked in and waved at the front desk. They were both carrying small bags and wearing more layers than should be allowed in the heat outside.

One of them yelled, "I'm on day six Anne girl! Still this line?" He motioned towards me as Anne smiled and nodded back at him. They both came and stood in line behind me. The man who had yelled his entry stood close to me and I tried to ignore him and his partner while patiently waiting for the line to officially open. Something tapped my arm. I pretended I didn't feel it; I wanted to be left alone to stew in my shit for a few minutes more. A few more people wondered in and got into my line or the one that mirrored us along the opposite wall. Something tapped my arm again and I turned to see both men looking at me. "Yes?" The first man grinned, showing off the spaces in his mouth that had lost teeth.

"Hi there, friend! How ya been?"

I shook my head at him, "I'm sorry, but I haven't seen you before." I turned back to wait and heard the door behind us, announcing more people joining the lines.

Something tapped my arm again and I turned back to the grin, "Nah. I don't forget a face, do I Dick?" he questioned the man standing behind him.

Dick responded, "He never forgets a face."

The first man looked back at me, "Or a name. I never forget a face or a name." He paused and looked down at his feet before looking back at me, "What's your name again?" I knew I wasn't going to get out of this one, so I gave in. Might be best to repay the kindness that the people behind the counter had given me.

"My name is J." At this point one would think that I had said it enough that it would feel like the truth. But it didn't.

He smiled, "Oh yeah. Well J, I don't think I've met ya before." I barked a laugh before I even knew what I was doing. The man jumped back a step like I had slapped him.

"I'm sorry; I told you we hadn't met."

He looked down at his feet, "I wasn't trying to be funny."

I tapped his shoulder and he looked back at me, "What's your name?"

He still looked a little sullen, but he answered me, "Herman."

I stuck out my hand, "Nice to meet ya Herman."

He looked at my hand like there might be something attached to it, waiting to bite him, before he finally reached out and clasped it, shaking it strongly, the grin returning to his face. "Nice to meet ya, Jay-boy!"

I shook the hand of the man behind him, "And nice to meet ya, Dick." Dick grinned and shook my hand too.

Anne stood up in the front, still hidden behind the false safety of the Plexiglas, "30 minutes, everyone. Make sure you have your ID ready to go so we can get in quickly and get to the showers. Due to the heat, we'll be setting up some extra mats in the cafeteria tonight so everyone should get a bed."

Something tapped at my shoulder again, "You gonna shower?"

"Nope, I showered earlier today."

"Eh, Dick and I need a shower. It's too hot out there today, isn't it Dick?"

"Sure is. Too hot out there today." Dick agreed.

I nodded, "I might find the reading room before meal. But I hope the meal is soon. I'm starved."

Dick reached into the pocket of his bag and reached towards me with something clasped in his palm. I opened my hand under his, and he dropped a hot snickers bar into it, the wrapper still shut tight. I looked at him, "Are you sure?"

Dick nodded, "Oh yeah, we ate a half dozen of those suckers today." And Herman nodded in agreement. I opened the wrapper and ate the full candy bar in three bites, trying not to choke on the melted chocolate as it squeezed down my throat. The two men watched me, grinning. I shoved the wrapper into the side pocket of my bag and licked the melted chocolate off my freshly washed fingers.

"Thank you." They just grinned before starting up a conversation about someone they both knew, wondering if he was going to make it back in time to get a bed or a matt. I turned back to my own mind. Like a shot, the normalcy of the moment was gone and replaced again by the guilt that I had been trying to push down inside me. I turned back to interrupt their conversation, "Can I give you something for it?" They both looked at me. "For the candy bar?" I clarified. They shook their heads in unison before starting back up their conversation; this time about a shelter in another part of town that they heard got a bad case of bedbugs. I turned back forward again and waited uncomfortably, thinking of the itch that just started in my hair.

Anne got up again and shouted towards the back of the room, "Guys, in or out, leave the door closed and the line can start outside again." I looked back to see that both lines reached past the doors and into the heat outside. Finally, both women waved to the first person in their respective lines, and I stepped up to the desk. "Ok J, you are already checked in and have your stamps. Now you have two full weeks that you can stay here, another 13 days. Since you don't need the shower, you can head straight to the reading room, the chapel, or to the bunk room. But remember, if you are going to the bunk room, you'll have to lock up your belongings first, but you might get a better bunk. Dinner call starts at six with lights out at ten. You'll want to get to the cafeteria right at six if you don't want to wait though. Ok?" She smiled at me. I nodded and thought of the words I could say to show my thanks, but still nothing seemed quite right, and the words caught in my throat. She looked past me at Herman, "Ok, next" as she waved me behind her. I noticed a sign I hadn't seen before pointing towards cafeteria, sleep room, shower, and finally the reading room. I went in the direction of the reading room, looking behind me to see people rushing towards the showers.

CHAPTER TWENTY-FOUR

THE LIBRARIAN

THE DOOR WAS propped open with a small wooden triangle and there was a fan on the other side of the room. It was about the size of a large bedroom, with a few chairs scattered around and short shelves, filled with books, lining the walls. There were two small windows and an older man sat in an armchair reading a book. He looked up as I entered, then looked at his wrist.

"Is it really that time already?" He looked at me. I looked back at him. He wore pleated tan pants with a button-down shirt. There were two pens sticking out of his shirt pocket. He pushed his glasses up on his nose and his thin white hair was cut short against his temples. He must have been nearing eighty, but it took no effort for him to rise from the comfortable looking char. "Well then, I'm the librarian here." He used his fingers to make air quotes around the word 'librarian.'

"Have you been in here before?" I shook my head and he motioned to the room. "This is my library. While you are here you can check-out a book. Meaning that you can read it and hold it for your stay here, but it isn't allowed to leave this room. You can read between meal and lights out, but you'll have to come back and visit me again tomorrow morning to keep reading. We don't get a lot of people in here. Mostly they sit in the cafeteria and play games or talk. Do you know what kind of book you are looking for?" I shook my head. "Ah the strong silent type huh?" He winked before looking me up and down and holding up one finger as if to shush the words that I wasn't saying. "I think I have just the book for you." He turned and walked along the wall of books, stopping every bit to read a title and shake his head, before shouting a small "found it!' and pulling one book from the shelf.

He motioned for me to take a seat, and I sank into the chair. It felt like I could never get up again, the chair was so soft beneath me. He walked over and stood in front of me. "Now this is a book that found its way here by donation, much like most of our books. But this is a special one. If you are searching, which it looks like you are, this might be the book you've been searching for." His eyes almost twinkled as he handed me the book. The cover was dark and plain; the title stood out in stark white letters, *The Life and Death of Eloise*. I looked up at him and he was standing there motioning for me to open the first page. Eloise? Why did that name sound so familiar? I opened to the first page of the book and started reading.

Chapter 1 – The Death

I died today.

I froze and looked back up to see that the librarian had turned away from me and was getting ready to settle himself back down into his chair. I looked back down at my page.

I found myself slowly falling back to the earth, my body feeling weightless as it floated down and down, stopping with a light thud as I entered the body that was laying on the bed. I kept my eyes shut and watched the black turned to red as the daylight hit the closed eyelids. How long could I delay the day that was going to come? Deep breath in. Long sigh out. I smelled the sheets as I breathed in again, a mix of fabric softener and morning musk and the color grey.

I shut the book. This seemed all so familiar. I opened it again.

The color grey... It floated around in my head trying to make sense of how to describe how a color smelled. It smelled like the dust that had built layers on a counter for more than a year. The path down an old gravel road.

I closed the book again and turned it slowly so that I could see the back cover. There she stood in front of a house that I could be mistaken for any house. She stared back at me, timeless in the black and white photo. And even though the picture didn't show the color of her eyes or dress, I knew they had been green and orange, in that order. I stared into the eyes of the photo and dropped the book on the couch next to me before standing abruptly, grabbing my bag and walking out of the room. I looked back to see the librarian watching me from his chair with a questioning look in his eyes.

A LINE WAS starting to form next to the door for the cafeteria, so I joined it. The large man in front of me turned to glare at me for a moment before staring at my bag just long enough to make me uncomfortable, "Whatcha got in that bag?"

I held the handle tighter, "just my clothes and the bathroom stuff they gave me here."

He kept staring at it as if he could see through the fabric, "looks a little heavy." He turned back to face forward in line before I could respond, not that I knew how I would respond. The line kept building up behind me and I could see a freshly washed Herman and Dick further back. The door opened and my stomach growled audibly when the smell of food hit my nose. The line moved and I followed at a slower pace, trying to place inches between me and the towering man with the interest in my bag. The cafeteria was set up with rows of folded tables and metal folding chairs. There was a long counter with a few people in hairnets standing behind large containers filled with food. I followed the line and was handed a tray that was then stacked with a bowl of chili, a plate of salad mix, a roll, and one paper cup with milk and one with water. I grabbed some plastic utensils and then looked around the room. The big man watched me as I found a table on the opposite side of the room from him, and the benches around us slowly filled up. I took a bite of the chili and tried to remember to chew before swallowing. It was the best tasting chili I ever had in my life. I was scooping another big spoonful in my mouth when Herman plopped down in front of me and Dick to my right. "How ya going there, friend?"

I smiled, my mouth full of chili and swallowed before responding, "Doin' good here Herman. How are you?"

"Doin' good. What did you say your name was again?"

I made sure not to laugh this time, "J. Just J." He nodded and they both started eating while the noise grew around us as more men continued to join. A plate was placed to my left and I looked at the man who was sitting there. He focused on his food and didn't turn to look at me, so I turned back to my plate.

I jumped as a hand slapped my back and turned to see Jeremy standing behind me with a hairnet to cover the hair on his head, his mustache out for all to see. "Hey there J, you clean up nice. I see you've met my friends, Herman and Dick. You boys treating J here nice?" They both nodded their mouths full of chili beans. "Ok good." He turned back to me. "Once you're done eating here, I'd like to talk to you for a moment. Can you come grab me from the food line?" I nodded and took a bite of the stale bread that was left on my plate. He walked away. I wondered what he wanted. Maybe I wasn't supposed to have my bag with me. Maybe they were going to tell me to leave. But at this point I was fed and showered, and I could make another day. Hell, I could make another month. I could see the big man on the other side of the hall still watching me through the crowd of people. Maybe it would be safer out there than in here.

I finished my meal and shot a wave at the two men that I had eaten with as I picked up my tray, leaving my space for someone else to join, and went back to find Jeremy. I waved at him, and he said something in the ear of the woman that he stood next to. She looked up at me and nodded. Shit. Was there anyway that they knew me from my past life? I wracked my brain trying to place them, but I came up blank. He took off his hairnet and tossed it into the trash as I followed him out into the hallway. We walked past a line of men still waiting their turn for a meal and he shook a few hands and patted a few backs on our way out, calling everyone he passed by name. I looked back over my shoulder and could still see the eyes of the big man following my bag out the door. We made it past the line before Jeremy turned to look at me and I stopped, waiting to see what would happen.

"So, J, I've been thinking. I heard that you went into the library before meal." So that's what this was about.

"Shit. Yeah. Sorry was I not supposed to do that?"

He smiled, "No, it's not that. It's just that Ray, the librarian, doesn't get a lot of visitors in there so when it happens, it sticks out. Are you a big reader?" I nodded slowly, not quite sure where this was going. "Ok good. Well, we are working on a reading program, to try to teach some of our mid and longer-term residents to read and get them closer to finding a skill. That's a lot for one man to take on, along with organizing and checking the books that come in from donation, and everything else. He's wanted an assistant for a while. I'm sure you are looking for a job during the day, but in the meantime, we thought we would ask if you might like to work here a couple days a week. I know you don't have an ID, so we might be able to pay you some in cash and some in trade. And you could still be first in line each night you're working. Now, you'll still have to check-in with everyone else and start showering at night after check-in. Would you be OK with that?"

I nodded again, slowly. I hadn't even said a word to the librarian. "Ok great. I have to double check with some of the other staff here and make sure that there aren't any issues or questions. But I can let you know tomorrow if that works. Introduction and service is tonight at nine and I'll…" He was cut off by a loud clang in the cafeteria behind me. I turned around and we could see a man punch another one in the room past the doorway. Jeremy started running towards the cafeteria as I stood there, wondering which direction I should go. A large man was holding another and they burst through the cafeteria door followed by Jeremy, who was talking at their backs. The man being pushed through the hallway was the same large man who had been eyeing my bag and he tried to lunge at me when he saw me. I jumped back so I was flat against the wall as I heard Jeremy say, "Jesus, Chris. How many times do I have to kick you out this month? No fighting…" The big man was held back from me by another man with a nametag, and the voices drifted away as they continued towards the front of the building. Well, there's one threat gone. I looked back towards the cafeteria and then turned back towards the reading room.

The librarian still sat in his chair with a book on his lap. The book that I had been reading was still lying where I had left it. He glanced up at me, "So that wasn't the book that you had been looking for, huh?" I shook my head and he tossed me his book. I caught it and looked down at it as he said, "Then let's switch." I leaned over and picked up the book I had been reading and tossed it to him before taking a seat and opening my new book. One that held less questions and was full of the adventure of a young teenage couple lost in the woods and trying to find their way out. I made it about a third of the way through before I was interrupted by his voice, "Better get headed back to the cafeteria for service and introduction." I nodded and handed him my book which he sat on top of a small pile of books next to his chair. There was a little sign propped in front of them that spelled out, 'books checked out, find another.' I nodded at him and turned to leave the room. He shouted after me, "See you tomorrow."

I turned and looked at him for a moment, "Yeah. I'll see you tomorrow." He looked back down and started reading again but I could see the small smile form on his lips before I headed back towards the cafeteria.

There were a few small tables still set up with some groups of men circled around a game of Chutes and Ladders and a few games of Checkers. Everyone else was sitting in the folded chairs or along the floors and talking in groups. A few scattered on the outer walls lost in thought. I sat against the wall close, but not too close, to a man that was mumbling under his breath. I watched him out of the corner of my eye as he clasped his right hand with his left, trying to control the shaking that his right hand was doing. I pulled my bag close to my chest and closed my eyes. Seeing the pictures float beyond them in the darkness. They had faded a bit. The details not so sharp. But they were still there, and I went through them one by one, searching for the lost bits. My torment was interrupted by a loud voice coming from the middle of the room. I opened my eyes to see Jeremy and a few other people standing there, "Good evening, everyone."

THE ROOM CHORUSED the response around me, "Good evening."

"It's a hot one out there tonight. We will do the normal – first group that got checked in got a bunk stamp, but we will do the mats in here tonight to try to get everyone out of the heat." People nodded around me and a few clapped. "Now, I'm sure many of you heard, there have been rumors of a bug outbreak at Sister Cross. I can't confirm or deny this, but we haven't seen any carry over here yet, and if we are all diligent, we should stay that way. Now onto the new business, I see some newcomers here tonight. Let's say welcome."

The room spoke up again with a loud "Welcome" and someone coughed in the corner.

"Yeah, guys. That was pretty weak, but I'll let it slide tonight. So, we're going to skip our normal introductions tonight for a special treat. We've got a few visitors tonight. They are here from a local recruiting office and are here to give some tips for you all as you spend your days searching for a job. Which I'm sure you are all diligently doing, right?" A few people laughed. "Once they are done, we will end tonight with our prayer and then off to get a full night sleep out of the heat. Tomorrow is supposed to be a little bit cooler, so here's to hoping." He motioned at the woman who was standing next to him. The same one that had been in the food line with him. Her bright red hair stood out now that it wasn't hidden beneath a hairnet. She didn't look scared or intimidated being surrounded by men in a room that smelled like burnt chili and body odor. At least she joined the group after showers had been completed and the stink of a hot day had been washed off.

I ignored her words as they started and closed my eyes again, letting my head rest against the wall. I watched the movement behind my eyelids, playing like the movie reel that I couldn't get rid of. No dreams lately, just this, over and over each day and each night, burrowing deep into my soul. Something cool touched my hand and I opened my eyes slowly to see another hand sitting in mine. It was frail and shaking but it clasped my hand firmly. I looked over to see the man next to me had scooted so that he was mere inches away, and he stared at me with a worried expression in his bright eyes, while he still mumbled under his breath. I couldn't look away. I could hear the woman talking in the middle of the room but couldn't make out what she was saying. His blue eyes stared into mine; the mumbling unintelligible, the shaking hand vibrating my own and I couldn't move when he leaned forward and placed his forehead against mine. He smelled like toothpaste and shampoo and just a little bit like onion. We sat there, shaking together, and his eyes bore into mine, so close that if I closed my eyes, my eyelashes would kiss his face. His white beard tickled my own chin. He moved his left hand and placed it on the back of my head, patted my head twice, removed his shaking hand from mine, and scooted back to his original spot on the wall.

What the hell was that? I realized I had stopped breathing. I looked over at the room but realized that no one had paid any attention to what was going on in our little corner. I looked back at him, but he was sitting there like before, almost like he hadn't moved from that spot at all. I leaned my head back again and closed my eyes. They shot open again at what I had seen, and I slowly closed them wanting to see more. There was the grass and orange hazy sun and a bird flying overhead. Not a memory. But like I was there, dreaming it in real-time. I opened my eyes again and looked back at the man. Nothing. He was sitting there lost in his own mind and minding his own business. Everyone around me bowed their heads and I followed suit, letting the new images coming to my mind rather than listening to the prayer, but following the rest of the room as they spoke in unison, "Amen."

I lost sight of the man before I could ask him anything, as people shuffled out of the room. I grabbed my bag and dug for my green stamp and waited in line outside of the bunk room that I had passed through before. This time, there was a young man at the door. He reached for my bag, and I instinctively backed up. "Don't worry; you'll get it back in the morning. We lock them up away from the beds at night for safety." I pulled my bag over my head and handed it to him, and he handed me a little coin, like a poker chip only with a number on the front. He stood there looking impatient. "Do you have your bed stamp?"

"Oh yeah, sorry" I handed him my stamp and he handed me a flat sheet, a blanket, and a pillow.

"Keep moving, lights out in twenty." I shuffled into the room to see men quickly making beds before sitting on them and talking to the men in the beds beside them. Some immediately covered themselves in their blankets and put their pillows over their heads. I walked to a section where there was an open bunk and looked down at the stain that was permanently fixed to the fabric. I looked around and saw a few empty ones on the other side of the room, but more than a few people eyeing the mattress next to where I stood. I quickly made the bed and sat down on the washed sheet, rolling over to my side as I pulled the thin grey fabric around me. "Lights out in five," I heard by the door, and I closed my eyes, waiting for the lights to turn dark and the voices to subside. Eventually, the night was silent except for an occasional snore or other bodily noise throughout the hall. Someone talked in their sleep, but the fans helped drown out the noise. I kept my eyes squeezed shut and drifted into the first dreamless sleep I experienced in days, not haunted from the ghosts of my past.

"I K...K... NOW" I looked over at the man that was bent over his book, the librarian hovering over his shoulder.

The librarian pointed at the page, "Remember, if there is a k and then a n, the k is silent. Know."

The man nodded like a good student and continued, "I know not w... hat to call this, no... nor will I ur... urge that it is a secret, over... rooling decree," He looked up at the librarian, proud of himself and the librarian nodded so he continued, "that hur.. hurries us on to be the... shit."

The librarian looked down and said the next word for him, "instruments."

"be the instruments of our own... dee... struck... tion," he spelled it out slowly. "even though it be before us, and that we rush up...on it with our eyes open."

The librarian nodded with a smile, "Great. That's just great. Want to keep going? There's another twenty minutes before intro." The student nodded proudly at his newfound skill, and his finger moved to the next paragraph.

I turned back to the third box of books that we got today from a group of teenagers. Donated from their school, they said. I pulled out the book on top and thumbed through it, looking for missing pages or damage, before writing the title and date on my notepad and adding it to the pile behind me, waiting for a home on one of the shelves in the room. I had reorganized the room one day so that the books were grouped by genre to make it easier to find a book that someone might like but may not know the name or author. Rather common around here. The man continued to read out loud behind me and his words blended in the background as I focused on the task at hand. Once I had finished getting the books out of the box, only four had to be discarded in the 'free to take' pile due to damage, I turned to the shelves and started finding spaces for the books.

I looked at the last two down in my hands, not quite knowing what genre they should fall into when the librarian interrupted my thought, "Hey J, time to go." I looked over and saw that the reading lesson had been completed, and the man was carefully putting his book back in the checked-out pile, handling it like it was a treasured possession that was easily broken.

I nodded and handed the two remaining books to the librarian, "I'm not sure about these two."

"No problem, I'll handle it." He took a bill from his pocket and handed it to me, "Thanks for your help again today." I stuffed the bill down in my own pocket, next to the other bills that I had acquired and the smooth rock that never left that spot. "Ok, I don't think we have any donations, or anything planned for tomorrow. Maybe it's time for you to go explore the city and get out of this dank building for a day." I nodded again and opened my mouth to say something.

But I stopped and shrugged instead. "Ok then boys, I'll see you both tomorrow evening for a read." he dismissed us with a wave on his hand. I looked back to see him sink slowly into his own chair. No book appeared next to him, but his hand rose to remove his glasses before rubbing his eyes. He came in here every day. Never taking a break from us. He had to be tired.

I followed the new reader down the hall and into the bustling cafeteria. The same thing every night. Some playing games, some sitting around talking, and some on their own. I recognized maybe a third of the faces. The ones I didn't recognize might have been here before; I just wasn't paying attention. I don't know why I looked tonight. I walked over to my normal spot against the wall and slid down it so that my ass landed firmly on the floor. I looked to my left, expecting to see the old man talking to himself as he was every night. He hadn't looked at me since the first night, but I watched him. Same spot each night and I dreaded and hoped for a moment to speak to him. Tonight, in his place, there was a group of young men whispering excitedly. One of the young men looked over and saw me looking at them, with a question on my face. "What the fuck do you want, old man?" The rest of them looked over and a few of them laughed. I turned back to look at the center of the room, hoping that they would just ignore me now that I looked away.

They went back to their own muffled conversation, and I focused on Jeremy, walking around and chatting with people as he worked his way to his normal spot in the center of the room. He waved and everyone stopped chatting and turned to him waiting for his words to start. Tonight, was a talk about some new people, staying safe, some job opportunities, and the end prayer. I tuned it all out but stared at him, pretending to listen to the words. "Amen," I mumbled in unison before jumping up and walking quickly down the hall to get a better spot in the line that was forming next to the bunk room. They already had my bag tucked away per our agreement and I nodded at the kid that managed the bunks as he handed me my bedding in exchange for my daily stamp. I found the spot that I liked best, a top bunk in a back corner of the room, where I could lay at night with my back against a wall.

My bed made, I took off my sandals and held onto them as I slid between the sheet and the blanket and watched the room prepare for bed. I could see Herman across the room, chatting to an Asian man with a goatee that wasn't quite grown in full across his chin and instead hung in strands to his chest. A few days ago, I asked Herman where Dick was. The smile had disappeared from his face as he informed me that Dick hadn't met him at their normal meeting spot the day before and he hadn't seen him since. He said it happened sometimes. I avoided Herman after that. It was a selfish move on my part, but I wasn't here to make friends or find someone new to add to my nightmares that started showing back up each night. Stay quiet. Don't make connections. Survive the nightmare.

CHAPTER TWENTY-FIVE

THE TENT

I SAW THE group of young men that had sat next to me at introduction; they were bunked close together and still chatting amongst themselves. They kept looking at the kid handing out the blankets and the pile of possessions behind him, waiting to be locked up. Shit. I should probably say something. Stay quiet, I reminded myself. Instead, I decided to stay awake so I could keep an eye on them. Not that I knew what I would be able to do if they started trouble. I pulled my blanket up further around my face so only my eyes peaked out and I continued to watch their huddle until a shout announced, "lights off." The kid with the bedding was gone and the bags were locked up out of sight for the night. The huddle of men slowly got into their beds and one of them looked around, lingering on my corner for just a second, before climbing into his bunk. The lights went out and everything plummeted into black. My eyes slowly adjusted to the darkness, and I kept them open, waiting for any movement. I could hear someone coughing in the middle of the room, and whispering going on from another direction, but nothing moved. I would stay awake all night just to make sure that everything stayed just as it should be.

I woke with the lights coming on the next morning and shot up on my cot, hearing a groan coming from the cot beneath me. I wondered how long I had managed to stay awake and looked over at the bunks that held the threat. They were slowly waking up individually and getting shoes and shirts back on, stretching in the morning. I jumped out of my own cot and pulled the sheets off, while watching them each doing the same. I gathered my dirty bedding and slipped on my sandals, nodding at the man on my bottom bunk. He was still sitting there, trying to rub the sleep out of his eyes when I walked to the door and tossed my bedding into the large hamper before walking down the hall towards the cafeteria; the rows of tables were set back up for breakfast and this morning was oatmeal with thawed blueberries folded into it. A cup of juice and a cup of thin black coffee and I was ready to go see what else existed in this city that I had only glimpsed at before. I rubbed my chin that had been freshly shaven yesterday and felt the small prick of hair trying to grow back in already.

I ate breakfast in silence before walking out the door, exchanging one of my stamps for a paper bag on my way out of the cafeteria. I walked down the hall and gave my little round casino coin to the morning kid so he would let me walk into the room full of bags. I had to dig around a bit to find the duffel bag that held the little bits of my current life and as I pulled it out, I thought about the day that lay before me. I walked down the hall, against the crowd waiting to get their possessions, to work my way into the reading room. The librarian was already there, looking at a few books on the shelf. He turned as I came in and smiled his recognition.

"Mind if I leave my bag in here today?" He nodded and I took out my water shoes to replace the thong sandals that that I wore inside the building, before taking some of the cash out of my pocket and pushing it into a folded pair of socks down at the bottom of my duffel bag, looking over my shoulder to make sure the librarian wasn't watching. Not that I was worried he would steal from me, but why even give him the option. I grabbed a plastic grocery bag out of my duffel and put my sack lunch down inside it to carry it around my wrist. I tossed the duffel bag on the floor behind a chair and waved as I walked out.

"See you tonight, J," Ray called out behind me, but I didn't look back to see him as I left. I was swept out the front door of the building by the trickle of men that were taking their daily trek back out into the world. I looked at the bench that was no longer art, where I had sat and tried to close my eyes to the world, only to be met by the visions of the people who I had wanted to forget. It felt like I was walking away from my home.

Even though within that building the men that thought they knew me, knew nothing about my life or my past. Only what I had chosen to tell them. I was homeless, had been for a while, and I had been laid off from my job and my wife left me. Almost all lies. I felt ashamed. Some of the men I had met in that building, including Jeremy, had rough lives and didn't choose to end up on the street. But I had. It was my own choices that brought me here. I shook the thought from my head and walked up the street towards nothing that I really knew.

I SPENT THE morning talking to a few people that I saw on the street, ones that I recognized from the shelter. I sat for a few minutes as they held their signs and cups and reminded me of when I had done the same. They did this every day while they told the shelter they were searching for a job. It wasn't really questioned if they had money and didn't cause any trouble. One man told me that no place would hire him even with the promise of fair hires. He had a criminal record the length of his arm, he said, before quickly assuring me that he didn't do any of that shit anymore. I didn't ask him what crimes were listed on it even though I could tell that he wanted me to. I didn't want to ask for money, I had money back at the shelter. I didn't want to look for a job, I wouldn't be here long enough to make it worthwhile anyway, plus I had no identification and couldn't give someone my social without an investigation that could end with me being found. I didn't know if anyone was even still searching for me… or if they ever did at all. But I couldn't risk it. The city wasn't big enough for me to fully find something new that I hadn't seen in any of the other cities that I had been in. Instead, I just walked slowly in circles around it, not knowing what to do with my day while watching the hot sun work its way across the sky.

I wanted to find central air. I looked up at the blinding sun and shielded my eyes from its heat before looking around me. I saw a building across the street that had a large sign spouting a new exhibit with pictures of muscle and bone. I walked up the white stone steps towards the large wooden brown doors and pulled one open to a blast of frigid air. A man stood there in a uniform with a flashlight tied to his belt instead of a gun. He looked at me doubtfully. "Uh, do you have a bag?" I nodded and showed him my plastic bag still full of my sandwich, chips, apple and a bottle of water before he stepped aside and motioned to the desk behind him with a ticket sign above it. I moved over to the desk and a young woman with a small diamond stuck in the side of her nose, looked up from her phone; a smile already plastered on her face.

The smile disappeared quickly as she saw me standing in front of her, "What can I help you with?" her eyes flickered to the security man who was still posted at the door.

"I'd like a ticket, please. How much?"

"Uh… well if you are a member," I shook my head. "Ok then, it's twenty-two for the exhibit. An extra five if you want the audio tour." She held up a little machine that looked almost like an old walkie-talkie.

"Twenty-two dollars?" I had the money, but I was in shock at how much they could ask of me to just go inside and look at figures frozen in time.

She nodded, "listen, maybe this isn't the place for you." She said it quietly, like that would make it less insulting. I looked down at my clean clothes and knew that the stubble was minimal on my clean face. What could she see that made me different than anyone else that walked into this building? She smiled at something just past me and I looked behind me, seeing a young family waiting for the solo woman working the ticket line today. They were standing there quiet, but I saw the man's eyes flicker towards me. He stood with his body positioned slightly in front of his young family, like he was prepared to protect them. From me. I could feel my face flush as the anger bubbled up inside. I looked clean; I smelled clean; I had money in my pocket. What could possibly make me any different from the other people inside of this building? My eyes stung unexpectedly as I spun towards the door and walked hurriedly out, barely hearing the woman behind me apologizing to the young family, "sometimes we just get people off the street trying to cool off." I sped past the inefficient security guard and down the clean stairs. I made it to just around the corner of the white stone building, to where the man with the flashlight couldn't see me, before I stopped.

I doubled over in pain as a loud cry burst between my lips. A cry I didn't plan and one that surprised me. It was full of suffering as the images of disappointment and loneliness started flashing past my eyes, as if they were sped up by a fast forward button, and now included a young family looking at me in fear. I screamed, trying to release the pain that I had been hiding from behind the walls of the shelter. The pain that had released the numbness that had lived in me for so long. I stood back up and opened my eyes to see people scattered around the sidewalk, all motionless and staring at me, none moving towards me to try to help me. A moment frozen in time. I had seen this moment before. No one moving. Had that been a dream? This wasn't. They all turned and started walking on their original paths, just shifted a little so they could walk in a wider circle around me, whispering about the man they just saw lose it on the side of the museum.

I stood up straight and wiped at my face, surprised when my hands came away wet. I rubbed my hands against my clean pants and started walking as if there was nothing abnormal about my momentary lapse into the darkness that lived within me. I looked up to see that the sun had started to hide behind one building and sky now shone orange.

I TURNED THE corner and saw a figure sitting against a wall. I knew that figure. I walked quicker to him, ready to ask this unnamed peer where he had been the night before. I slowed as I stood right in front of him, seeing brown speckled through his beard and his hair, instead of the shine of pure white I was used to seeing. His bright blue eyes looked at me curiously and I noticed his hand wasn't shaking.

"I'm sorry, I thought you were someone I knew," I said as I looked down at this man that looked so much like someone else.

He shook his head as he looked up at me, "No son, I don't think we've met before." I kneeled, focusing on his face. His face had fewer wrinkles than the man who had stared into my eyes. The man I watched each night. He stared back at me, his eyes looking just the same as the ones I would remember forever.

"Have I seen you at the shelter?" I asked.

He looked confused, "What shelter?" The voice sure and steady. It couldn't be him. But it was him. It wasn't him; he just looked much the same. I turned so my back leaned against the wall and put my legs out in front of me.

"I don't know," I put my hands over my face, "I just don't even fucking know." I heard him laugh and I looked over at him, startled by the sound.

He looked back at me, the eyes I knew out of the face I didn't as he said, "I haven't known anything for a while either." We sat in silence, watching the legs of the people walk past us. The sun lowered further in the sky as the shadows made by the buildings grew longer, until our spot was completed shaded.

"So, you need a place to stay tonight?"

Shit.

I looked up at the sky and realized that it was probably after check-in time, "Yeah, I think I do." He nodded and stood, pushing himself up against the wall and motioned at me to follow him, before turning and walking slowly down the sidewalk. I followed in silence as we turned right, and then left. The city in the darkening sky looked different than I remembered. Smaller. Lights were off in the store fronts already and there were flimsy gates covering the windows and doors. I had my plastic bag, still full of my uneaten lunch wrapped around my wrist as we walked. I continued to follow him as he crawled through an opening in a small fence, warning bells not quite reaching my ears. Behind the gate were two large boxes that were fashioned together to make one giant box.

They were covered with plastic and made up a space large enough for two grown men to lay or sit comfortably in. The man pulled a lighter from his pocket and held the flame in the torn entry of his home, motioning at me to look inside. There was a pile of clothing folded neatly against one side. Most of the space was filled with two comforters and pillows at the end. There were cans of food stacked against the wall next to the clothing pile. He turned back to me as I stood from my viewing position, "You can stay here with me tonight. No one ever finds me. But you can't tell anyone that I'm here.

Sound good?" I nodded in agreement. He stuck out his hand towards me, "Everyone calls me Vern."

I shook his hand, "Everyone calls me J." It wasn't even a lie anymore. Everyone who I had met did call me J. He turned from me and made a small clicking noise with his tongue. I looked towards the dim area around us to see what he was calling out into the opening and jumped back a little when a small figure bounded out of a bush. My eyes focused and I made out a ball of fluff, not much bigger than a pigeon. He leaned down and scratched at the cat's neck before lifting it into his arms.

"This is Bird. She's my little runt, aren't you Bird?" He smiled as he spoke to her, and she wriggled in his arms.

I reached out to pet her soft paw, "nice to meet you Bird." Her little teeth found my finger and playfully bit at my knuckle as I laughed. Such a different sound coming from my body than the one from earlier on this same day.

The three of us sat and made a meal from my packed shelter lunch combined with a few cans of food from the stash that Vern had in his makeshift home. We spoke and fed Bird and laughed as she ran around trying to catch a moth that was drawn to a lantern Vern had pulled out and lit. As we ate, Vern explained what had led to him being here on his own, never asking me to share my own story. Some of his story made sense and some I attributed to being out here too long and possibly losing a bit of reality along the way. He told me how he grew up in a smaller town and got married young. He started going to school but he wasn't smart enough to make it, and he decided to start farming. His young wife was happy and made him happy, even though they had to deal with the loss of three babies before they were even born. They were trying to make a home, when he enlisted in the army, living up to his expected duties. He described the horrors of war in detail that made my struggles seem mundane. His story would slip between the happiness of loving his young wife after a day of hard work and the excruciating detail of watching his friends die right next to him and the screams that he hears in the night.

"When I got back, nothing was the same. I was different; and she became scared. She had a right to be afraid of me. I wasn't right. We had to sell the farm. I couldn't keep a job. I wasn't the husband she knew anymore." He drifted off and in the dim light from the lantern; I could see his right hand start to shake. He saw me looking at it and flexed his fingers, "yeah. It does that occasionally." I looked back up at his face, seeing the blue eyes looking at mine before he continued. He ended up alone, people thought he was crazy, but he felt better when he was outside. Safer. He couldn't quite explain it, but he tried to describe it as a feeling of security without constraint. He had been beaten and suffered starvation and had been a drunk for months at a time. But now he was convinced he had it figured out. He liked this spot and would stay with Bird until someone made them move, and then they would start again.

As we lay, huddled under his makeshift roof in the dark, I could hear him mumbling in his sleep. I faced the wall towards his supplies; my back was to him as he slept behind me, huddled against the other side of the large box. I couldn't quite make out what he was saying as he was visited by the demons of his past. Bird jumped in and around us throughout the night, chasing her own dreams, as I drifted off into a dreamless sleep.

A CAR HORN blasted me awake. Sunlight was drifting through the door and lit the inside of the hut I had slept in. The memories of where I was and our conversations from the previous night, slowly coming back to my mind as my eyes tried to focus on my surroundings. The hut looked different in the hazy morning light. I couldn't see the cans that I thought had been there the night before and the clothes were strewn along the side of the cardboard wall, instead of folded. My mind started whispering a slight warning. I sat up to see the dirt covered blanket I had slept on. It was dirtier than I had thought it was in the darkness of the night before and there was a smell I didn't remember as I had drifted off to sleep. A musk. Bird was gone, out into the day, and I turned towards my friend. I stopped. Something wasn't right. I could see his stark white hair sticking out from the blanket that covered him. I reached over and tried to shake him awake but his stiff body didn't budge. Slowly, I reached my hand up towards the top of the blanket and folded it down. The dull blue lifeless eyes looked at me out of the face of an old man with white hair. The same man that had been mumbling to himself in the shelter as I watched him each night. I jumped back, shaking the wall that was his home. I turned and crawled out as quickly as I could manage without toppling the old and worn-down cardboard. I made it to the bush that Bird had bounded out of, before throwing up next to it. I heaved until there was nothing left in my stomach, crouched on all fours in the dirt. I looked down at the pile of vomit to see the corn mixed in from the can of food that I had eaten, and I turned my head towards where we had left the cans the previous night, but there was no sign of them. I crawled towards the branch that had been our bench and rummaged around the trash that I didn't remember, begging to find the can of corn that had to be there, my mind trying to find something that made sense. There were no cans. A raccoon. A raccoon had to have taken the cans. Or maybe a rat. My plastic bag with the paper inside it was still there, mixed in with the trash that must have blown in during the windless night. I clicked my tongue and waited for Bird to come bounding from some hidden spot. There was no movement around me and I stood, my body sore from the retching.

"Bird, come here Bird." I called quietly, trying to not bring attention from beyond the fence. Bird didn't show up. I closed my eyes and saw Dog laying there, his head on his paws, as I walked away from him and left him on his own. "Bird!" I said louder. Nothing. I walked slowly back towards the dirty cardboard home that had a bright blue tarp covering the top. My head lowered as I looked back into what was contained. His wrinkled face was frozen in time. Still there, motionless and recognizable. Not as the man I spent the night listening to, but as the man who had stared at me with his hand shaking in mine. What the hell was going on? Did I dream what had happened last night? How did I get here? Shit. Shit. Shit. What does someone do when they find a homeless man dead in a box? I tried to dust off the clothes I was wearing and wipe the dirt from my face, before crawling through the opening in the fence; it was still where I knew it would be.

Almost my whole body was through the hole and onto the sidewalk, my right foot still on the other side of the fence when I was interrupted, "Hey, where are you coming from, you can't be here." I looked up to see a uniformed man standing above me, looking more concerned than angry. I silently thanked nothing but the air, before finishing my crawl and standing before him.

"Sir, you have to help me. My… uh… friend lives here. I woke up this morning and he's dead. I don't know what to do."

His face didn't hide the shock well, "You must be mistaken. No one lives here."

"I am not mistaken. I was just with him. He's dead."

He leaned closer to me and looked in my eyes, "You drunk?" I shook my head. "You high on sumthin'?" I shook it again. He leaned back, "Ok then, let's take a look." I felt the relief run through my tensed muscles and I turned back to the hole in the fence. I squatted down, prepared to crawl back through to the other side, but only my head made it before I realized that there was nothing there beyond the fence. I froze for a moment before pushing the rest of my body through. I could hear the officer pushing through behind me, knowing that he would be proven right at any moment. As I stood in the small clearing, surrounded by bushes, I could see the pile of trash on the ground and my pile of vomit still over in the corner. I stood where the shelter had just been, complete with a dead body hidden within it. I turned in a full circle waiting for the officer to tell me that this had all been some kind of prank. He stood there watching me, dust on the knees of his uniform, waiting for me to show him where the body was. No sound would come as I faced the officer, confusion running through my body.

He waited, as I finally found my voice, "I swear, he was just here. I don't understand. I was here and he was here."

He held up a hand to get me to stop, "listen son, there are shelters around here. They can help you clean up and help you find a job. But I'm tellin' ya. No one has been back here in quite a while. We find homeless here and there dead of starvation or some other reason, but I can't help you if there isn't even a body."

I turned in a circle again, "You find homeless dead a lot?" He nodded as I faced him. He looked regretful but not like it kept him awake at night. I couldn't make sense of what was going on around me and I turned again before swinging the full rage caused by my confusion towards him, "then why don't you help them?" I shouted at him before running towards the opening and pushing through the fence, just beyond his grasp.

I ran through the city towards the building I hoped was still there. I made it to the art turned bench but didn't pause for a breath before running up the stairs and yanking on the door. It didn't budge, locked for the day. I cupped my hands around my face and peered into the building to see Jeremy standing behind the desk. I pounded on the glass to get his attention and he walked towards the door, pulling on a key from his bracelet of keys, and unlocked the door to let me in. "J, where have you been? We were worried about you." I walked into the cool air and leaned over, my hands finding a place on my knees as I tried to catch the breath that I had lost while running down the street. He waited, a hand on my back, until I stood back up.

"I don't know. I don't know. There was... something happened." I looked at him, trying to implore him to tell me what was going on, but he just looked back, confused. He led me behind the Plexiglas and had me sit in the chair that Anne normally sat in as I tried to calm down enough to explain what had happened. He knelt next to me, his hand trying to comfort me by resting on my knee.

"What happened?"

I looked at him and the tears started running down my face. "I don't know. There was a man and he's dead. But he wasn't the same man that he was before he died. I don't know what the fuck is going on." Jeremy nodded like what I was saying made sense. It didn't. I knew that. My tears slowed and I wiped my face with a tissue that he handed me as he waited. "There is a man who is here most nights. I saw him the first night I was here. He didn't talk to me but he... I connected with him." Jeremy nodded. "His name was Vern." Jeremy turned and pushed a button to bring Anne's screen to life and started punching away as I sat, dazed by the past twenty-four hours.

He looked over his shoulder at me, "I don't know a Vern that stays here. Are you sure that was his name?"

I nodded and gave him more information, knowing that Jeremy seemed to remember almost everyone that walked through his shelter, "He was old and had white hair and a white beard and blue eyes. He mumbled to himself and his hand shook. Do you know who I'm talking about?"

Jeremy turned from the computer and leaned back by me again, looking into my eyes. "Are you sure?" I nodded and his brows came together in concern, "I remember him. He hasn't been here for over a year though if we are talking about the same person. I don't remember his name but I'm sure we've got his information saved."

I stared back at him and started mumbling, "I don't know. I don't understand."

"Listen, do you want to get cleaned up and maybe get some rest, and then we can talk again?" I nodded and stood, waiting for Jeremy to open the door so I could exit the safety behind the Plexiglas. He nodded at me and told me that I could stay through the day and told me to come back after I had rested a bit, but I was only half listening. I made it to where the hall split and looked towards the bunk room and the showers, before I turned left towards the reading room. I knew that the librarian would be sitting in his chair before I walked through the door.

He jumped up when he saw me, "thank God. We were worried about…" He drifted off when he saw my face. We stood, looking at each other, before he nodded and reached behind the chair to grab my bag for me. I looked down and noticed that the zipper was open just a small amount and I could see the peak of pages of a book pushed down into the bag. I looked back at Ray, and he smiled at me before he stuck his hand towards me. I grabbed it and he pulled me in close to him, clapping me on my back, and whispered in my ear, "be safe out there."

I walked out of the room, not looking back. Knowing he would be standing there watching me go, before sinking back down in his normal spot and reaching for his book. I walked past the Plexiglas window, and I could hear Jeremy shout behind me, but his words drowned out as I pulled open the door that he had unlocked for me earlier; and I walked back out into the heat. I turned right and started walking out of the city. My books added weight to the bag I carried. My mind was racing with confusion, trying to make sense out of what had happened to me in the past days and weeks. My heart was heavy and when I blinked, the visions of my past flashed through the darkness, now joined by the dead blue eyes.

CHAPTER TWENTY-SIX

THE LIGHTNING BUG

I PULLED MY jacket from my bag; replacing it with the wrapper from the sandwich I had just finished eating. I had spent most of the day sweating in the hot sun as I walked on the road that led me to this spot. There had been few cars throughout the day, and one had pulled over. A navy SUV with a young couple in it. I saw them go past me, her legs up so that her feet rested on the dash, with a book held close to her face. They had slowed and pulled over just in front of me. A tall man got out and I froze before he called back to me and asked if I needed a lift. I said no and thanked him. He had leaned back into the car for a moment, I think talking to the woman and when he reemerged, he had a few things in his hands. I walked closer and saw that his hands held a sandwich in a plastic bag, a few orange cracker packets, and a diet coke. I thanked him and complemented his shoes, noticing that we wore matching black Velcro sandals, and we grinned for a moment before he gave me a wave and got back into the car to continue his drive up this dusty road. I shoved the sandwich and crackers into my bag to save for later but popped the top of the silver can right away. I took a long chug of the sweet cold drink while I watched their car disappear.

It took another couple of hours before I found the spot I sat in now. The land was flat here, with the mountains further than I could make today, but I was determined to walk it. I was trying to wear myself out enough each day, that my nights would be dreamless, and I could avoid being haunted by eyes. It hadn't worked so far, and I spent my nights rolling in the grass, moaning as I was visited by their greens, blues, browns, and blacks; my reflection showing in each one.

I had been walking towards the setting sun when I heard a whistle come just for me. It came from right of the road and I looked in the direction, trying to find the source. There was no fence separating the grass from the road as I quickly walked towards the invisible person who had whistled me over. I walked further and further off the road, looking back just once to see no cars as far as I could see in this piece of flat land. I looked forward again and realized that I had been walking towards a field that was covered in tall tan wild grass. It looked familiar, like something I had seen as a child... or maybe in a dream. I was drawn to it and as I got closer, I realized that the grass smelled sweet as it cooked in the sunlight. Deep breath in. Long sigh out. I was barely aware that the hot wind had died down and the sun disappeared completely behind the mountains as I sat down in a small clearing and pulled my bag from my shoulder, dropping it next to me.

Forgetting about the draw of the whistle that had brought me here. I leaned back, using my bag as a lumpy pillow, and looked at the sky. It was orange in the setting sun, with the grass around me making it seem like the sky was just there in that one spot: just for me. The sounds were cut off from the outside, and I lay alone in the world. My stomach had growled, reminding me that even in this sense of peacefulness I had found for a moment, I still needed to eat. I had eaten a packet of the fake cheese and peanut butter crackers that didn't really taste like cheese… or peanut butter. And then the sandwich, which did taste like peanut butter. I drank half a bottle of water, noting that I only had one and half full bottles left and counted four granola bars and two oranges in my bag. Adding the other packet of crackers to the mix, which should be enough to get me close to the mountains. I counted the cash stuck down in my rolled socks and it came to one-hundred and forty-two dollars remaining. Enough to stock back up and get me well over the mountains and to the other side, even if I needed to eat indoors. Hell, maybe I could splurge and get a cheap motel room for a night soon; take a real shower and sleep in a bed for a night. I knew I could find something for fewer than forty bucks if I didn't mind the smells. I laughed at my inside joke as I smelled the stink of sweat coming off my own body. The wind had picked up and the grass blew around my hidden spot; it cooled the last drop of sweat that was trying to work its way down my short hair and into the short beard on my chin.

And that is where you found me. But that comes later, doesn't it?

I pulled on my jacket to cover my arms from the slight wind that came, bringing a small amount of desired coolness with it. I yanked at the Velcro that held my sandals and pulled them off my feet, laying them nicely in the grass beside me. My toes stretched and I examined them in the darkening sky. They were rough and sore but had now grown to protect themselves with an extra layer of thick hard skin. Blisters barely formed on my feet anymore, but the widest part of the bottom of my foot hurt as I pushed against it. I rubbed my right foot first, trying to work the soreness out of the bottom to prepare it for a long day tomorrow. Then I followed with my left. Both feet pushed out in front of me in the flattened grass and I wriggled my toes again, to stretch out the muscles. Not bad. I followed with a quick stretch to reach my toes, and then a twist to loosen up my back and arms. My bones cracked as I turned and loosened my spine. Surprisingly nothing was incredibly painful, even my busted rib had dulled to a random ache that rarely happened anymore. My body was just sore, but nothing that I wasn't used to at this point. I lay back down, stomach and body as comfortable as they could be. My head against the full duffel bag and looked into the sky again. It had faded into a deepening blue and was slowly darkening the world around me. I could still feel and smell the grass, but I could barely see their outline in the dark night. Then I saw the light. A bright light just above me and I strained my eyes to focus on the star before it disappeared. Startled, I sat up and looked closer at the sky to see other stars appearing and disappearing quickly. Not stars, I realized. Lightning bugs. I didn't think I had really seen one since I was a kid. I must not have been paying attention. I lay back down and watched them light up in the grass, my mind drifting to one of the few good memories I still had of my father.

WE WERE SITTING on the front step of our home, waving as cars pulled away. We had been wearing suits and my tie was squeezing my throat, so I pulled on it, until it gave away, the buckle shining bright in my little hand. The yard was freshly mowed and smelled like hot grass and then I saw the first one. A little light shining, and I looked up at my dad pointing my finger in the direction of the mysterious light to make sure that he saw it too. His eyes had shone down at me before we both turned back to the grass just in time to see another. And another. Dad ran into the house, but I stayed on the step, mesmerized by the light show that played out in front of our dark yard. He came back out and had one of mom's little jars that she had used to hold jam. He had told me that if I could catch any of them, that I could put them in this little jar and take them inside, to use as a night light tonight. I squealed at the thought and jumped up running after the little lights. He showed me how to wait until the light went out and to focus to see the dark shadow of the body and to follow that to catch loosely in my hands before dropping it into the jar to join the others he was catching. "And don't accidently squish them." Then they wouldn't light up anymore. Unless you managed to squish it while it was already lit... which became a game of accidental discovery.

We ran around the yard catching them and filling the jar with more than a dozen, letting the jar become its own natural 'cold light' he had called it. We laughed and found some more before he resumed his spot on the step, holding my light jar as I tried, unsuccessfully, to catch a few more to add. I heard him talking behind me as I was watching in the dark for a light to give away another's position. At the time I didn't know what he was saying but the words came back to me in this moment, "they only live long enough to breed." I had looked back at his strange voice and saw him sitting on the dark step. A shadow with only a small amount of light coming from the jar between his palms. I walked towards him slowly and he saw me coming. He grabbed my shirt and pulled me to him, weeping as he squeezed me in his arms, the little bugs lighting their little breeding calls against the glass between us.

I FELL BACK into this moment as seamlessly as I had left it for the past and sat back up, knowing what I wanted to do.

That memory was the one time that I had caught one of these little bulbs and I wanted to replace it with a new memory. I pulled my half empty water bottle from my bag, swallowing the rest of it, knowing I would now have to find a stream for water tomorrow. I shook it upside down, making sure that all the water was gone from the inside of the plastic and screwed the lid back on only a little so that it would open easier. I stood slowly in my spot and watched, hunched over in the darkness, ready to pounce. There was a small light from the grass to my right and I pounced at it, my hands closing on nothing but air. I followed suit five times, staying close to my bag so I didn't lose my bed in the dark night. I could hear my dad's voice in the darkness, "you have to wait and show patience. Once the light goes out watch for the shadow and that's where you catch them." I stopped moving and let the grass blow against my face.

A light showed next to me, and I focused when the light went out, watching the little black body continue to move in the night with his little wings. I closed my hands loosely over him and transferred him to one hand so I could pull the water bottle from my pants, where I had stuck it for easy access. I held it in the crook of my arm and opened the top, dropping the little body into the plastic. I put the cap back on a little and watched the plastic to see if it worked. It lit from within, and I grinned like the child who had first tried this years ago. The rest were easier catches, now that I knew how to do this. I would have them serve as a night light for the evening, their lights timing with the chirping of the crickets and the breath of the wind. And in the morning, I would open the top and let them return to their normal lives, to carry out their business of making more little bugs. Once my bottle was filled with more than a dozen of the little lights, I lay back down and watched the others light the sky under the stars and the bright moon that had appeared while I was enthralled with my hunt. The bottle sat next to my head, and I turned in the grass to watch the lights shine on and off like they were controlled by a mischievous child who could reach the light switch. I tried to keep my eyes open as I watched them, not wanting to miss a moment of their company. But my body was sore, and my eyes were tired, and eventually the exhaustion took over and I drifted into a sleep, unburdened by my demons for this one night.

I WOKE AS the morning started shining in the sky, turning it a hazy orange as the sun rose against the fog that lay above me. The plastic bottle was still next to my head, and no longer lit by the bugs within it. They had lost their romance in the daylight and now just looked like little black beetles walking along the sides of the plastic. I pushed myself up and rubbed the sleep out of my eyes before grabbing the plastic bottle and twisting off the white cap, I watched them crawl towards the opening one by one, and disappear into the grass around me, a small flurry of small black wings. The bottle still held a few stubborn guys and I turned it, smacking the bottom to get the remaining ones to fall out into the ground before they opened their tired wings and followed the others. I sat, alone again, watching the fog move above my hidden spot, when I heard it. Someone was moving towards me. Fast. I hunched into a standing position, trying to hide beneath the cover of grass but prepare for a predator. I saw a flash of brown hair just before a body slammed into me with a grunt. I fell backwards, tripped over my bag, and landed firmly on my ass; with a child landing on top of me.

No. Not a child. A woman. A young woman but definitely a woman. She lifted her head from my chest, and I saw her face was wet with tears that did little to mask the red mark that was deepening on her cheek. Her green eyes looked startled, and she quickly jumped off me and scooted to the edge of my little clearing with her legs and arms pulled against her small body. Her legs were covered in navy pants, and her orange top blew around her small arms. Arms covered in bruises. I slowly sat up; my hands held in front of me, as if that would convince her that I wouldn't hurt her and scooted so that my back was against the opposite side of the clearing. She looked at me, her eyes shone with hatred that I didn't deserve as her messy hair blew around her face.

I froze for a moment before speaking in a low voice, trying to calm her, "do… do I know you?" Her face looked like one I had seen before. She glared at me and shook her head quickly. I noticed that there were no shoes on her feet that were covered in scratches, and there was a bright stream of red blood starting to show. There was a small gold bracelet wrapped around her wrist, but other than that, she wore no jewelry. I looked back up at her face, her eyes watching me, the red mark becoming darker with each moment. "Listen lady, I'm not going to hurt you." She looked like she didn't believe me. Someone whistled in the distance, and her head whipped from right to left as squeezed her legs closer to her body. "Is someone looking for you?" Her eyes softened just a bit and her head slowly tilted up and down once. Ok, so this was going to be how we communicate. I could do this. "Do you want them to find you?" She shook her head quickly, her eyes starting to fill with tears again. Ok. "Would you like to hide here with me? I can protect you." I could almost feel my chest blowing out with masculinity. She looked doubtful but nodded, the tears slowing. "Are you hungry?" She nodded again. I moved towards my bag, and she backed up into the grass so that it wrapped her. I stopped and put my hand up again, "I'm just getting you a snack, it's ok. I promise." She watched me as I pulled the crackers from it, holding them towards her. She looked at the orange package and back at me before crawling towards me and grabbing the package from my hand.

Her eyes drifted from me, back to the plastic in her hand and her legs folded beneath her as she mumbled, "what odd packaging."

I laughed and she looked at me startled, "Sorry, it's just I was surprised that was the first thing that you would say to me." She glared at me again and I wondered how someone with so much anger had found themselves running from a threat. She opened the package and pulled out a cracker sandwich, sniffing it suspiciously before taking a small bite. It must have been better than she was expecting, because she ate the rest of it quickly in one bite, shoving it into her mouth and chewing. Her eyes closed for a moment, and I could study the freckles that lived beneath the red mark and the tear-streaked cheeks. She opened her eyes as she grabbed another cracker and noticed me watching her. Her hand raised and she pushed her hair from her face before eating a third cracker, watching me the whole time with honest distrust in her eyes. She couldn't have been more than twenty-five. Her mouth was full of the fourth cracker when she spoke again, orange crumbles falling from her mouth, "water?" I nodded and reached into the bag again, pulling out the last bottle of water I had and handing it to her. She looked curiously at the bottle before sniffing the opening and taking a sip. Then a large swallow. Her animalistic tendencies towards food contrasting with her clean outfit.

She finished her crackers and studied the empty plastic before turning back to me, "what kind of cookies are these? They are so good."

"I have no idea. But I feel like I've seen them in every station."

She looked at me again, "You must not be from around here then?"

"Honestly, I have no idea where here is. I've been… uh… traveling and I think maybe I'm in…" I shook my head. "no. I'm not from around here." She nodded before handing me back the package that had held the crackers and took another swig of water. She handed the bottle back to me and watched me take a drink.

"Well, thank you, but I should be headed back." She seemed calmer and spoke with clarity but the marks on her body and the way she had entered my clearing made me worried for this stranger.

"Are you sure? What… who are you running from?" She shook her head but made no move to stand. I took a deep breath. The air tasted sweet like the grass that surrounded us and my stomach growled, alerting me that I wanted to eat too. I pulled the two oranges from my bag and rolled one along the bent grass. She picked it up and peeled it as I did the same. I took a bite of the sweet fruit, and the juice ran down into my beard. I was trying to rub it away as I heard a small, surprising sound and looked up to see her trying to muffle a laugh at my attempt. I grinned back and she immediately stopped smiling. We finished our oranges in silence and shared another drink of water. Shit. It's almost gone. At least she had to run from somewhere, I could pick up another bottle once I knew she was OK and on her way. She sat with the orange peel in her hands and seemed to be lost in some moment. "Excuse me," her green eyes found me again, "but you don't seem like someone who would be running. Who are you running from?"

She shook her head again, and a long sigh came from her, her body shaking from its pressure. Her voice started, small under her breath, and I had to lean in to hear it.

"It was my fault. I said I wanted to go the city with some friends. But, you know, he thinks the only people in cities are whores and hippies. It was just the wrong thing to say. He thinks I'm already into that stuff and that I'm just going to get worse. But... I'm not." She looked up at me as if I could understand what she was saying, but before I could ask any questions she spoke again, "So he said no. I questioned. I shouldn't question. He called me a spoiled whore like my mother and he..." she drifted off as she motioned towards the side of her face was shining bright red. "I shouldn't have said anything." There were so many things I could have said. I should have said right at that moment. After the moment all of them came to mind such as, 'how dare he' 'you didn't deserve it' 'what the fuck'... the list went on.

I was angry, but for some reason the only thing that came out of my mouth was, "What city?" She looked at me like I had sprouted two heads and opened her mouth to respond, when the whistle came again.

She dropped the rind that still sat in her hand and started to stand, "listen, I've got to go. He'll just keep looking for me and the longer it goes..." she drifted off as she looked down at her feet. It was as if she had just noticed that she wasn't wearing and shoes. I reached towards her hand, but she pulled it back as if I was made of fire. She looked at me again,

"I'll be fine. I promise. Thank you for your… kindness." She turned and started jogging in the direction of the whistle and disappeared into the grass. I sat frozen in place, trying to decide if I should follow or just stay out of the way. She obviously didn't want my help. But maybe she just didn't know well enough to know she needed help. I knew I was going to follow her. To save her. To keep her safe. I started to stand when I heard the whistle again and my legs gave out, my body falling back to the earth and my head landing smoothly on my duffel bag.

I WOKE AS the morning started shining in the sky, turning it a hazy orange as the sun rose against the fog that lay above me. The plastic bottle still next to my head, no longer lit by the bugs within it. They had lost their romance in the daylight, looking like little black beetles lying in a still pile in the bottom of the bottle. Must be daytime sleepers. I pushed myself up and rubbed the sleep out of my eyes, trying to pull back the dream that was slipping away. Was there a woman in it? I remembered green eyes and tried to focus on them, but they faded into the dark along with the rest of it. I grabbed the plastic bottle and twisted off the white cap, waiting for the bugs to crawl towards the opening. They didn't move. I was instantly transported back to my room as a child, sitting and sobbing by the side of my bed, holding the glass jar full of little black corpses. Dad standing there in the doorway mumbling something about, "Shit. Forgot to poke a hole in the. They suffocated." I was shot back to the present and I could feel the sorrow of my childhood building up behind my eyes as I clasped the little plastic filled with death that I had caused. Ending their lives. I should have kept them safe. Tears fell from my face as I dug my fingers into the morning damp ground next to me and made a small grave just large enough to fit a water bottle. I laid the plastic casket down into the earth and covered it, like I had done with the jar as a child.

I sat, alone again, watching the fog move above my hidden spot, when I heard it. Something was moving towards me. I stood quickly when I saw the source of the movement. He froze when he saw me, grass still hanging from his mouth. I held my breath as we stared at each other, and I studied his frozen frame. The brown fur looked soft against his skin, and I could see his muscles tense. His eyes shone brown just beneath the soft, fur covered antlers that were short enough to prove that he was still a young deer. His side was speckled with soft white spots and his eye blinked at me. I breathed out into the fog, and he turned and bounded away from me through the grass, his white tail being the last thing that I saw. I breathed again and sat back down already missing the beauty that had stood in front of me for just a moment and almost forgetting the newly dug grave next to me.

My stomach growled and I reached into my bag to pull out an orange and the packet of brightly colored crackers. Nothing. I dug in deeper, but my hand didn't close on either. I pulled my duffel back up onto my lap and pulled every possession I owned out to lay on the ground next to me. There were no oranges in it, or crackers. Just granola. Shit. I swore I saw them in there last night. I think. My mind was full of the same fog that hovered over my head. I grabbed a granola bar and my bottle of water, which was almost empty. It must have leaked in the night. Well, there was a town close to here. I wasn't quite sure how I knew that, but I did. I drank the last of my water and ate my granola bar, before packing up all my belongings and strapping my shoes back on my feet. I tossed my bag over my shoulder and stood in my little clearing and looked in all directions. I knew the road laid behind me, and the mountains were to my left. I couldn't see a hint of a town straight ahead where I thought I must have seen it in the night. I was standing alone in the grass. I knew there was a town there. Trusting my own mind, I started walking in that direction. I had to find something to fill my water bottle and purchase a second to replace the one that lay buried behind me. I needed some more food too, if I was going to make it into the mountains the next day.

CHAPTER TWENTY-SEVEN

THE FISH

THE SUN WAS almost overhead as I unzipped my jacket and pulled it off at the sleeves before folding it into my bag. I hadn't found the town yet and my throat was already dry In the quickly warming day. I was regretting my decision for walking away from the safety of the road where I might have stumbled onto a gas station or had the opportunity to stick out my thumb for a quick ride. I kept moving the same direction, knowing that it was too late to turn back. Focused on my sandaled feet to keep moving, one in front of the other. I didn't want to break and eat another granola bar, knowing it wouldn't do much to saturate my hunger and would just dry my throat further. So, I kept moving.

The sound of water rushing over rocks suddenly rushed to my ears. I ran towards it, tripping in the grass in my hurried excitement to quench my thirst. I fell out of the grass into an opening where the ground covering was cut short to create a view of the perfect stream, filled with rushing water. I dropped the bag where I stood and crawled towards the water, sinking my hands beneath the cool surface, and lifting them to my face as I swallowed handful after handful. I almost choked on it; I tried to drink it so quickly. Once my throat stopped burning, I lay there, my hands floating in the cool, watching my distorted reflection down below me. It almost looked like it was my body, laying there beneath the water's surface, lifeless eyes looking up at the sky. We stared at each other.

"Excuse me." I jumped up so that I was standing on my feet and looked at my reflection. Did he say that? Someone coughed behind me.

He sat there in a folding chair, just feet from me. I hadn't noticed him when I was rushing towards the water, focused on only one thing. He was sitting in an orange folding chair. Like one that people pack with them when they're going camping. He was wearing a pair of khaki shorts and worn leather loafers. His shirt said, 'I'd rather be fishing' and the irony wasn't lost on me since one hand was holding a fishing rod, its string dangling in front of him as he was poised frozen mid-air as he had prepped to drop it into the shallow water. He had a worn baseball cap on his head; his brown hair was sticking out from beneath it and his eyes crinkled as he smiled at me. But he couldn't have been much older than me. Maybe just ten years. "You mind? You're scaring the fish."

I looked back at the water that I had just drunk from and saw a few small bodies skirting beneath the surface, "uh… sorry about that." I backed up towards my bag and picked it up by the handle, not quite knowing where to turn.

He flung the rod back and forth in a swift movement, letting the hook drop into the water, before he called over his shoulder in my direction, "Well, are you going to take a seat over here or not?" I looked behind me, expecting to see someone walking out of the grass. There was only me. I walked over to where he sat and dropped my bag, squatting to sit in the mowed grass next to it. I watched him pull on the rod a few times, before he peered at me from beneath his cap. "I'm going to take a moment to not ask you what you are doing on my property, but instead I'm going to ask you one very important question." I waited, wondering what could possibly be more important than finding someone trespassing on your land. "Do you like to fish?" My eyes widened and I breathed out.

"Honestly…." he waited for my answer, "I've never been fishing."

"Never been fishing. Where have you been, living under a rock?" The statement brought something to my mind almost like a memory when it was interrupted by him again, "Would you like to try your hand at it? I've had a spot of luck today." He motioned to a small bucket on his other side, and I stood to see what he was pointing at. I could see two shiny bodies beneath the surface, with lines of pink against their dark brown tops.

"What do you do with them?"

He laughed loudly, "Well, I eat them. I don't enjoy the killing, but I thank them for their delicious meat, and I cook them. I don't keep them if I don't need to." He looked at me again as he bobbed the line in the water, "If you can help me catch another two around that size, we can make a pretty good lunch to share." I nodded and he stood from his chair motioning for me to take his place. He handed me the rod and showed me where to put my hand and how to hold my finger over the line, "now just wait for something to tug at it, and then start pulling the line in. You've got to pull it hard to catch them right, otherwise they'll escape the hook. Simple?" I nodded like I knew what he was telling me even though I wasn't quite sure. He moved close to the side of the water and reached to a rope that was tied up to a rock along the side and pulled something out of the water, when I felt a tug on the rod in my hand.

I yanked up quickly and started trying to pull the thin cord towards me, something fighting me the whole way. I could hear the man drop something into the water near me and suddenly he was by my side, shouting, "You got it, son. Pull him in." The pressure lessoned as the hook reached the surface and game out with a long body attached to the end. The man took the rod and pulled the fish towards us and showed me how to remove the fish from the hook, "If you can snag it like that," he showed me the hook clean through a hole in the fish's lip, "that's better. No pain coming off the hook. Why torture them, right?" I nodded in agreement and looked down at the fish for a moment before he was tossed into the bucket with the other two. I had eaten fish plenty of times, but I had never experienced pulling them out of the water and seeing them still alive. I wasn't sure how I felt about it. But I was hungry and the shock of the company next to me made me want to stay. The man went back to the rope he had dropped back into the water and started his task of pulling something out again. I recognized the cans of beer that lay within the basket. He grabbed two and brought them over as I moved to sit next to the chair again. I grabbed the beer as he offered it; kept cool from sitting in the water that ran in front of us.

I turned to him, "So you live here?"

He smiled, "well, near here. I own this land, but no one lives on it anymore. I just come out here occasionally to fish and sometimes I bring my camper and make a weekend of it. But less and less these days." I nodded like I could relate and took a drink of the cold beer, letting its dark liquid fall down my throat and attempt to quell some of the hunger. He looked at me again, "Oh shit. I guess if we're going to be sharing a meal, I should probably introduce myself. My name is Dean."

I swallowed another drink of beer before replying with an almost truth, "Nice to meet you. My name is J."

"So, J, what brings you to my property?" He said it casually as he sat down his beer into one of the cup holders on his chair and cast the line back out into the water. Where to start? What to share?

"I'm just traveling through. I found the grass patch back there and it was a good place to sleep, but I wondered the wrong direction from the road this morning and made it here." I shrugged and could see one of his eyebrows raise beneath his cap. I knew he could tell that I was leaving out some important parts. I shrugged again, "I don't know, honestly. I'm just searching." He nodded and looked back towards his rod.

Dean reeled in another fish before he directed me to hike up to his truck, trusting the trespassing man that he just met enough to take the keys with him. I was instructed to get the small bundle of wood, lighter fluid, potatoes, a second knife, and a small grate. It took two trips and when I came back the second time, he was leaning over the first fish that he pulled from the bucket. It lay on a makeshift cutting table; his hands covered in bright orange gloves. "Come over here J, I'll show you how to cut and cook these guys so that you can do it the next time when you are on your own now that you are a fishing pro." I dropped off the second trip of items and put his keys in the cup holder of his chair before turning back to him, dreading the moment I wasn't prepared for. I stood next to him as he picked up a small wooden object that looked like a club, "Now son, the first thing we do is we have to kill the little guy. I like to do it in the most humane way, so he doesn't suffer." He brought the club down against the fish's head, right below the eyes and the fish lay lifeless on the board. "This causes his brain to die with no pain, or so they say." Then he picked up a knife and pushed the dull side of the knife against the side of the fish, scraping away the scales until his skin was almost smooth. He flipped the knife around and used the sharp side to cut the fish just behind his head and slice along his back until he reached the tail. "Make sure you don't cut the backbone." He flipped it over and did the same thing along its belly. He then pushed the knife in at the flat part of the skin and slid it, holding the skin so that it pulled from the bone beneath and then sliced at the tail so that it separated. He did the same with the other side and put both filets to the side before dropping the remainder into a plastic bag that he had unfolded. "Ok then, your turn." I shook my head as he pulled a second fish from the barrel.

He glanced at me, and I stopped shaking my head. He peeled off his gloves and handed to me. I followed the motions he had just shown me, moving much slower and sloppier than he had done. But I did it. I looked down at the lifeless eye of the fish as I put him into the bag with the other bones. Dean patted my back, "I know it's not a fun task, but now you can do that, and it might just save you some day." He held out his hands for the gloves back, "I'll finish them up and you can go chop some potatoes." I nodded and walked back over to the pile of items I had brought down from his truck.

THE FISH WERE one of the best things I had eaten in my life. They had cooked over the flame from the fire, held up on tinfoil that covered the grate, and were joined by the cut potatoes that had browned fully. Before we had eaten, Dean had lowered his head and closed his eyes. I followed suit, expecting a prayer like the days I had spent in the shelter, but the words that came from his mouth were different, "Thank you fish for feeding us today." I opened my eyes to see him smiling at me again, his eyes crinkled at the edges. He was fucking with me. I laughed and repeated, "Thanks fish," as my mouth watered from the smell of the fire cooked me. We washed it down with another beer, and then sat and had yet another beer as we watched the fire go out and talked about nothing of importance. He told me stories about his parents, gone long ago, and his kids that were grown and moved away. We talked about his dogs, current and past and he laughed as he spoke about them. I shared my story about Dog, and he listened silently, sipping on his beer as I told him how Dog and I came to meet so long ago.

"No shit? You found a dead body?"

I nodded and kept my mouth shut about the other dead bodies that I may or may not have found. The sun was starting its path back towards the west when we picked up the trash and carried it to his truck.

"Can I talk you into coming and spending a few nights at my home? It's not much but I'm guessing better than the ground." I shook my head and thanked him. "Ok, well you can stay on this property as long as you want. I can leave some of that extra firewood for you and help yourself to the last few beers."

We walked back down to the riverbank to pick up the last of his stuff and I stopped and turned towards him, "Thank you Dean. Not just for the kindness but the lesson and this moment. I don't know how to say what it means." I wasn't aware of where the words came from, and I could feel the heat rise in my cheeks.

The grin left his face and he nodded solemnly before wrapping me in a hug. He hesitated and then let go before he picked up his chair and his board and I leaned down to grab the folded fishing rod and his small bag of tools when he looked back at me, "Nah, you leave that there. It's yours now." I opened my mouth to say something. Argue with him or thank him. I wasn't sure. He nodded at me, and I knew there was nothing to say. He turned and I watched him, silently, as he walked back up the hill towards his truck, not looking back once. I looked down at the folded rod and small tackle box that held hooks and the tools I would need to cut and cook a fish. The remaining potatoes lying on the ground next to them and I sat next to the embers of the fire. I leaned back so that I could lie on the grassy bank, my stomach full and my hope lifted, and I watched the sun move down further into the sky.

CHAPTER TWENTY-EIGHT

THE GAME

I LOOKED UP at the canopy of bright green leaves above me. It was astonishing how tall the trees grew with no leaves until the very top, forming a perfect umbrella from the sun. I felt a small movement next to my foot and looked down to see a tiny brown bird fluttering in the dirt beside me. He would freeze for only a second before thrusting his small belly into the dirt and flapping his wings excitedly, tossing dirt up over his body and onto my sandals. I tilted my head and continued to watch him do this a few more times, only to see him be joined by another small brown bird. The second bird watched the first before digging his tiny foot into the dirt and then spreading his wings and doing his own little manic dance. I laughed and the birds stood up straight to look at me before opening their wings and speeding to one of the tall trees around me. I looked around at my secluded and shaded spot in the morning sun. There were a few early risers on the edges, but I was tucked away and watched them like I was not part of their world, hidden and invisible in the shade. I had a small cup of coffee in a paper cup that had a mermaid on the side, and I sipped it in peace.

The morning air was cool even though I could feel the humidity of the summer beginning to prick my skin. The trees around me were planted in rows and the dirt beneath them had red chairs scattered about for the random coffee drinker like myself. I sat in one and it was made for comfortable lounging, molded so that the plastic looked like wood with small creases in the arm rest. I pulled a cigarette from the pack I had purchased for an occasional smoke in places just like this. A moment to feel like the man I might have been. I lit the end and inhaled, letting the smoke fill my lungs before I puffed out so that I could watch the smoke disappear through the trees. I pulled a book from my bag, one of the three that the librarian had given me, noticing that the only one left after this one had a photo of a woman on the back. A woman I could almost recognize in her black and white photo, maybe in her thirties, standing in front of a house that looked almost like every other house. I had given away the first book after I had finished reading it and would never read that last one, so I only had an option in the one I held in my hand. I finished my cigarette and put the flame out in the last bit of coffee that had remained in my cup, before opening my book to the first page.

The old ram stands looking down over rockslides, stupidly triumphant. I blink. I stare in horror. "Scat!" I hiss. "Go back to your cave, go back to your cowshed-whatever." He cocks his head like an elderly, slow-witted king, considers the angles, decides to ignore me. I stamp. I hammer the ground with my fists.

I focused on my book, only pausing every few moments to look at the world around me as it started to come to life. A couple pushing a young child in a stroller. A young man walking his dog; letting it pounce towards the dirt bathing birds, as if he might ever be able to catch one. Another solo soul like myself. Her light brown hair blowing in the breeze before she trapped it behind her ear as she sank in a red chair not too far from my own. She opened her laptop and pecked away at her keyboard, only stopping for an occasional sip of her own large coffee with a green mermaid on the side. My ass started to numb from the originally comfortable chair, and I marked my spot in my new book before putting it away down into my bag. I tossed my ash filled coffee cup into the metal trash bin on my way out of this little haven that had belonged to just me and the birds for a short while.

I WAS WARMED by the sun as I walked through the clean streets of this city. Shocked that I wasn't greeted by more trash on the sidewalks like I had been used to in some of the other cities. It was quiet and the only sounds came from the few cars that drove by and the birds in the air. I walked past few people and realized that their eyes never met mine, even accidentally. I stopped and looked down at my feet. Was I here? Maybe this wasn't real. Was I back in a dream? It seemed too perfect of a moment in time, in a place that seemed too quiet. Someone bumped into my shoulder, and I looked up to see a woman with jet black hair looking at me for just a moment.

She smiled at me, "Sorry about that, wasn't paying attention." I smiled back and she continued her way. I must be real. Or maybe I made up that interaction to try to talk myself into it being real. I turned a full circle and could see her disappearing around a corner. My right foot lifted, and I brought It down hard on the pavement, hearing thc ccho it made around me. If I was making this up in my head, would I choose to make the air so humid? Probably not. I turned and kept walking the direction I had been moving and found myself on a small walking bridge that worked its way over a narrow river. Above me the bridge stretched into a white arch towards the sky; the slender white poles that lead to the arch almost made it look like the skeleton of a long dead beast. Beneath me the dark grey water tumbled and turned, fighting to move down the river. I stepped my right foot up onto a small piece of metal that made up the bridge and clasped the handrail with both of my hands. If this were a dream, I could plunge down into the turbulent water and come out unscathed. I leaned over and looked down, realizing I could see nothing beneath the surface. I leaned just a little further. This wasn't real, right? Just a little further. A car honked and I looked up across the water towards the somewhat matching bridge that was made for cars rather than pedestrians. I saw a small orange VW speeding across the bridge. It was one of those old cars, one that anyone rarely sees anymore, and it was just far enough away that I couldn't quite tell the difference between orange paint and orange rust. I wondered what they had been honking at as there were no other cars on their bridge. I took one last look down at the water and turned to walk back to the quiet and almost deserted city.

I spent the day walking through every nook and cranny of the small downtown, watching the city slowly come to life around lunch time. I was hungry, but not hungry enough to spend money on lunch so I opted for a piece of fruit and a granola bar from my bag; both purchased yesterday to restore my stash. I found space on a comfortable wooden bench in front of a row of brick shops that were still closed to the public, even in the early afternoon sun. As I opened my bag, I made sure to be careful not to disturb the folded-up fishing rod, the hook carefully hidden away in the small box of items at the bottom, and I found the snacks I was looking for. I ate and watched the few people parking and walking around me and the occasional bird strutting past before being scared by an oncoming pedestrian and fluttering into the air for a moment.

More and more people started walking by and I realized that they were all wearing the same blue and red. I finished my late lunch before letting my curiosity finally get the best of me and asking one of the young men walking past, "Excuse me?" He stopped and looked at me, a silver can of beer paused on the way to his mouth. "Where are you all going?"

"To the game," he looked like I had just asked something ridiculous so I didn't ask a follow-up question that would have been useful, such as, 'which game?' or 'what sport?' Instead, something inside of me decided that it seemed like the right idea to pick up my duffel bag and merge into the crowd of people heading to the game. Because if this is really my own dream, that game would be baseball. Even though I hadn't been to a baseball game since I was a young boy, I suddenly had a desire to watch a game.

I worked my way to my seat and tried to not smack my bag against the people that I slid past, apologizing as I sidestepped past them. I found my seat and sat down in the small red plastic chair, using my legs to try to push the seat down as my hands were full. An ice-cold beer in a plastic cup in one hand; a hotdog in the other. My seat bottom finally gave way and I sat, hitting the man next to me with the bag that was slung over my shoulder, "Sorry."

He grinned over at me, his white goatee moving as he spoke, "No worries, man, hope you got something good in that bag." He laughed at his own unspoken joke as I pushed my cup into the plastic blue cup holder by my foot, spilling a small amount of the liquid on the cement. I pulled my bag over my shoulder and shoved it under my seat next to the random pieces of popcorn that must have been forgotten from a previous game. My hand lifted the hotdog to my mouth; the smell of onions and mustard reaching my nose just before I took a bite. I savored each bite as I watched the action play out on the field. It didn't take long before I learned which was the team we were rooting for and I would shout a little cheer with the crowd, my mouth full and the words coming out a jumbled mess. I washed down the last bit of the hotdog with a slurp of the beer, now not so cold from the onslaught of the sun above us. I was close to the field, which was pretty good considering that it only cost me ten bucks for my ticket at the small ticket counter that I had found at the front of the curved brick stadium.

I took another drink of my beer and sat it down into its spot as I watched the game. I was never what someone would consider a 'sports person' and wasn't fully sure about what was playing out in front of me, but when the goateed man next to me cheered or clapped or shouted a "Damn!" I followed suit. He was sporting a shirt that matched the jerseys that the men wore on the field so I knew he must know what was going on with his team. "Our" boys were spread throughout the green and I watched closely. The man in the center made a few movements and communicated with the man in black that was crouched behind the opposing teammate that stood ready to hit the ball. He turned sideways and turned the ball a few times in his hand, staring down the line he wanted to throw, lifted his leg and circled his arm in a perfect seamless motion, before the ball left his hand at a speed that would be hard for anyone to see coming. Whoosh. It went right past the man with the bat as he swung and missed for the second time and I clapped with the man sitting next to me, mirroring his intense stare at the mound. A third ball whizzed past the man with the bat and the boys on our team started running in towards their dugout. The man next to me cheered and I cheered. There was a moment of strange comradery as we sat there watching his team win in the afternoon. Both of us in single tickets and enjoying this game for completely different reasons. He held a bag towards me, and I pulled a small handful of peanuts, still in their shells, from the bag and I thanked him. I cracked the shells and pulled out the nuts from within, dropping the remains to the cement beneath me, the same way he was doing. I stared into the field of green as the game continued.

I WAS SMALL, not quite sure how old, and I sat in the safety between my parents. There was a small box squeezed into my hands that were covered in a sticky and sweet substance. I looked to my right and there she was. Beautiful brown hair that curled slightly around her face. Her eyes laughing as she watched the players on the field. She looked thinner than I remembered, and she sat delicately even in the uncomfortable wood chair. I looked up to my left and saw him there. Not laughing. Glancing at the field and then back at her, worry in his eyes. Why was he worried? This was a fun day. I looked back down at the box that sat clasped in my hands and reached down into it, pulling out little popcorn pieces covered in thick brown caramel. I shoved the pieces into my mouth, dropping a few smaller pieces down the front of my shirt.

"Dammit, son. You're making a mess."

I looked up, fearful that he was angry with me.

"Oh, leave him alone. We're celebrating." Her voice sounded like music as I looked up to see her scowling at him for a moment before her face broke into a grin again. "My little mess," she winked at me, and I tried to wink back. My eyes never worked quite the way I wanted them to, so I ended up blinking back, convinced it was close enough. People around us cheered and jumped from their seats and she turned back to the field, jumping up with them. Her hands widened and prepared to start clapping as her face suddenly went slack and her body folded. It was as if the world slowed around us as she fell into the man next to her, before crumpling to the ground. I stood from my seat as she was falling, the box spilling from my hands and onto the ground. And then he was there; pushing me behind him and out of the way as he knelt to her, screaming her name repeatedly. I could see his shoes tucked under his legs, the bottoms of them facing me. Then for a flash I saw his feet, in those same shoes, swaying in the air.

THE GOATEE MAN nudged me, "Hey man, you ok? You look white as a sheet."

"Yeah yeah, sorry was just in my own mind for a second."

He looked at me for a moment, the judgement clear in his eyes. I nodded and the judgement was gone, replaced by a smile and a shrug of his shoulders.

"Time to get up and stretch," He motioned towards the small screen at the other end of the field. 'Our' team was up by 3 and we were just entering the bottom of the seventh, something I had just learned to say. I followed him as he stood and made some stretching movements with his arms before we sat back into our seats and I lifted my beer cup, still a third full. I tipped it into my mouth and finished the last of the warm liquid, staring at the bottom of the plastic cup with a small triangle stamped into the bottom, before putting it back in the cup holder. I tried to keep focus on the last bit of the game, cheering when I was supposed to and booing when it seemed to call for it, but the thrill had gone and was replaced with an exhaustion brought on by the heat of the day and the demons that I had almost forgotten. The crowd cheered and everyone stood to their feet. I followed and prepared to grab my bag to make a quick exit when the man turned to me, "You are staying for the fireworks?"

"Uh… wasn't planning on it. Should I?"

"Oh yeah. They're good ones. You might as well stick it out. Besides you won't be able to get your car out of the lot for a bit anyway."

I nodded. Let him think that I had paid the ten bucks to park my non-existent car in a parking lot alongside his. We sat and waited, watching everyone settle back into their seats to wait for the light show with us. He asked if I wanted to grab a beer at a bar next door after this, giving him a few more minutes before he had to go home. He said it like it was a joke, but I wasn't completely sure. I paused. He said it would be his treat. I nodded. Why not, I wasn't going to get out of this town tonight anyway. The sky continued to darken and then the lights in the stadium when dark.

The roar of the conversations all around us dimmed and everyone turned their faces to the sky waiting for the burst that would come. The first one shot towards the dark sky, exploding in a ball of white sparks and the people around me sighed in unison, "oooooo." The next one came and made a shape that almost looked like a red heart in the sky, "ahhhhh." I almost laughed at the audible appreciation for something so simply made of spark and explosion. But with the next one, a giant circle made of orange, that made me feel like I rushed through space for just a moment, I found my mouth opening as I joined in. Explosion after explosion shook the ground beneath our chairs and for a moment, I forgot the world around me. It was me and the dark sky, the sparks shooting through it just for me. My eyes wouldn't blink just to make sure

I didn't miss one shot through the dark, and the world fell away with the childlike awe of the power above my head. There were a series of explosions, and the sky was lit with all imaginable colors and shapes, exploding at once like a symphony of light. The last one fizzled towards the earth and left a path of smoke in the sky as the lights turned back on in the stadium, bringing me back to the reality of the moment. The stadium that looked so perfect when I first walked in, now looked tired and washed out. Like me. I grabbed my bag from beneath my seat, dusting off the shells of peanuts and popcorn remnants before slinging it back over my shoulder, and I followed the man with the white goatee out into the crowd of people working their way towards the entrance.

He yelled towards me over the noise of the crowd, "I've got to take a piss. Meet you right here?" he motioned towards a wall that stood empty next to a dark ATM machine. I nodded and worked through the crowd to get to that spot on the brick wall. I watched him slowly go up the line of men waiting to use the bathroom and once he disappeared from sight I walked into the crowd and through the front gate of the stadium. He was a nice guy and I felt bad about leaving him there, wondering where I had gone to when he came out of the bathroom. I wondered if he would wait for me or look for me, or just shrug his shoulders and head out to the bar on his own. I just needed to get away from the heat of the crowd that had surrounded me, bumping into me on all sides. I followed a small line of people as they all walked towards their cars. The crowd getting smaller as a family, or couple would break off into one direction. Lost a large group of six adults and five children, all laughing and piling into a giant van. Soon it was just me on the lonely dark sidewalk in the quiet and clean downtown.

A TRAIN HORN pierced the air close to where I walked and I turned towards the sound, remembering a moment from a while ago, seeing men riding the train towards a new destination. I knew I had somehow made it east even though I had wanted to go west. The detriment of riding with people where I told them I didn't care or know where I was headed. I made it to a small fence and worked my way through, seeing rows and rows of tracks with some large trains stretching out in front of me. I started walking towards them, wondering how easy it would be to get up on one.

My feet stumbled over the tracks in front of me and I heard a noise to my right. I turned to see a white pickup truck with a light fixed to the top, running on a small road that ran past the tracks almost parallel with where I was walking. It was close enough that I could almost see every detail of the man behind the wheel, a badge attached to the left arm of his sleeve as his elbow poked out of the open window. Shit. I wasn't sure who or what he was, but I was instantly struck by the fact that I could not let him see me. I jumped to the ground and flattened myself in the gravel rocks that lay between the tracks. Waiting until I could hear the crunch from his tires moving away from me, but towards the trains where I wanted to go. I crouched up and could see the red lights from the back of his truck shine brighter as he pushed on the break. His arm extending from the window with something in his hand a suddenly a beam of light shot from his arm, down between two of the trains. He shone the flashlight around for a bit before moving forward again and I walked slowly, hunched close to the ground, towards the closest train. I walked the length of it, not seeing any place where I would be safe to sit for a ride and I moved to the second train in. There was a wide-open door with a small metal ladder hanging next to the door. A spot meant just for me. I peered inside but the corners were pitch black and nothing shone in the darkness. I held my breath and waited, listening for something from the darkness within, but nothing came. I was far enough away from the small road and the end of the train that I didn't hear the tires as they made another loop. The flashlight shone close to me and in a panic, I threw myself into the opening, letting caution take a back seat to the fear of being caught in the beam of light. I lay on the hard surface for a moment before succumbing to the pure exhaustion that raced through my bones and closing my eyes to the darkness around me.

SOMEONE WAS YANKING on my bag, trying to separate it from my body. My eyes shot open, and I sat up, my back sore from falling asleep on the hard floor. There was a small amount of morning light pushing through the still open door of the train car and it shone on the faces of the two men that were in front of me. The one that was kneeling next to me was young, couldn't even be in his twenties yet. His face was dirty and as his mouth turned into a grin, I noticed his most prominent teeth already missing.

He had a grip on the strap of my bag and was trying to pull it off me. Even with me waking up, he didn't let go, backed by the man standing behind him. The man was the scarier of the two. His head shined in the dim sunlight and his eyes looked cold. In his left hand, perched a knife. Not a small pocketknife. More like the length of the one I had in my bag for cutting open fish, only this one was thicker and looked like it had been used; I was sure it wasn't on fish. I glanced behind me and saw the world flying past us as we were speeding over the flat and open land. I turned back to the men, seeing that the grinning youth was still pulling at my bag and the bald man had stepped closer to me. I could feel the train slowing and looked again, allowing just a moment where I could see the front of the train as it curved around a bend. I pushed towards the young man without the teeth, knocking him off his feet and he dropped his hold on my bag as the older man lunged towards me. I pulled my bag into my arms and rolled out of the door, barely seeing the knife slash at the spot I had just been before I dropped out and onto the ground. I yelled out as I rolled through the grass, trying to not let my head hit. I could feel the skin scrape off my uncovered arm as I continued to slide at the speed of the train; and something twisted in my hand as I clutched the bag. I screamed out in pain and started to slow enough to stop my descent. I rolled onto my back, my arms opening to the ground beneath me, and I wriggled the fingers of my left hand; the hand I thought I felt snap, but I felt no pain. I lifted the hand into view and when I saw the finger that used to hold a wedding ring; the bone shining through the opening as it stood cocked at an odd position in the middle, my vision dimmed to black. 'I should have gone for a beer,' I thought just before I passed out.

CHAPTER TWENTY-NINE

THE SONG

I WALKED THROUGH the neon lit store that contained everything that any person might possibly need in their life. I had counted just over seventy dollars, still in my sock, before putting forty of it down into the pocket of my hiking pants to sit with my rock. Each item was priced out carefully before adding it to the small basket that balanced in my right hand. I looked down at the contents of my basket; new water bottle, pain pills, medical tape, snacks (a package of nuts and a package of those little orange crackers), underwear, two t-shirts. I think that was about it. I turned into the aisle that had office supplies and saw the last thing on my list. Tape. To fix the fishing rod that had broken in my fall from the train. The sign that showed the cheaper price had nothing on the shelf above it. Shit. I looked at the branded version and saw it was an additional two dollars. I picked it up and held it in my bandaged left hand for a moment before putting it back on the shelf. Maybe the tape I bought for my finger would work on the broken rod as well. I turned and walked towards the extraordinary long line of people waiting to check out.

As I stood there, a small child peeked around the legs of her mother to stare up at me. I smiled down at her and she smiled back. We all moved up in line. She pointed at my hand, "Ouch." I nodded as her mother turned to see what her daughter had found. The woman took in everything that I was a man with a short beard and buzzed short hair, probably a bit of dirt on his face even though he had just washed it yesterday, scabs along his right arm, left hand bandaged to the wrist, dirty shirt with a few holes, and halfway decent hiking pants. She turned her daughter around and they moved up even though the line before her hadn't moved. I sniffed my armpit, trying to not let anyone see as I did it. I still smelled like soap from my bath in a river last night. That was something.

I made it up to the front of the line and put my items on the counter. I looked past the girl as she rung me up and saw the shining red pack of cigarettes, lined up behind her. Not on the list. I handed over both twenties and received my change before walking out into the cloudy afternoon. Tilted my head up towards the sky as the clouds rolled around above me, threatening of the storm to come. I walked around the side of the new tan building that held everything and past the rows of employee cars that were parked at the back before stepping over the curb and into the grass that still lay behind the store, space just waiting to be developed. I knew exactly where I was going. To the stream that I had bathed in the previous evening. I had found a space behind a row of incomplete houses that looked like they were going to be the first piece of a nice neighborhood in this previously untouched land. Soon the trees would be cut to make a better view of the stream, and children would run down from their large homes to splash about in the summer. But for the time being this piece of land belonged only to me. I had left my bag there as a claim for my little home; the next few days I would try to gain back some of the energy I had recently lost. I found my spot, hidden beneath a large old tree and sat my plastic bag down next to my duffel bag. I could hear the thunder rolling though the sky and pulled a folded tarp from my bag along with a few pieces of rope. Using the branches of the tree above me, I awkwardly used one hand and half of the other to pull and yank until the tarp created a shelter large enough for one person and waited to see if the rain would start.

The clouds continued to churn above me, but nothing fell from the sky. I pulled everything from my duffel and lay them on the ground around me, choosing what needed to be discarded and what I could keep or would be replaced with the new items from my shopping trip. I pulled the shirt that I was wearing up and over my head and cut it into strips before putting it back into my bag, expecting that would come in handy at some point. I tugged one of the new shirts over my head, making sure not to hit my bandaged hand. It was tighter than I would have liked but it would stretch out. I looked down at myself and smoothed the cotton down. Dark grey to hide the dirt that would soon be there. Next, I surveyed my fishing rod. Two of the folded pieces had snapped while the bag had tumbled beneath me. I had yelled at the men in the train, even though they would never hear it, when I pulled the mangled mess from my bag and mourned its loss before picking it back up and deciding that I would fix it. I opened the box of tape that was meant for muscle and bones and used my teeth to rip a small amount.

The one-handed fix looked like a mess, but it had to hold. The tape wound tightly around the two splintered pieces in a way that prevented them from moving. I pieced the rod together and strung the clear line through the small holes like Dean had taught me. Tying a small hook to the end of the line, I followed it with a small piece of gummy candy that had been stuck down into my bag, chewing on another as I worked with limited fingers. Finally done, I looked at my work and felt proud. I had found enough sticks the previous night to make a small fire and my mouth watered thinking of the warm fish filling my stomach. I could see a few small fish swimming beneath the clear surface, and I tried to aim the hook towards them as I awkwardly flung the rod back and then forward, my line looking less like the arch it was supposed to and more like a child's throw. It landed close to the fish, and they scattered from it rather than moving towards it. I pulled a few times, trying to draw their attention to the gummy candy that floated just beneath the water's surface, and pulled a few times more when I saw two of the little guys turn and slowly swim back towards it, expecting food. One moved so that he was right on top of the hook, and I yanked. Too early. The fish sped away. I pulled the line in and tried again, this time aiming a little further from the fish to drive them towards the treat instead of scaring them.

I stayed patient, focusing on the fish and the line floating in the water, waiting for it to feel a pull. Too long. I pulled it back out and swung it back into the clear water of the stream; my cast feeling less awkward and almost close to a natural movement. The line held in the water for a moment, and I waited for nothing to happen, prepared to pull it out again. Something tugged on my right hand. Surprised, I yanked the rod into the air and staggered to a standing position as I tried to fight the catch to the surface. It was more of a fighter than I had experienced when I was fishing with Dean, and I could see its large body splash within the clear water. A yelp came out of my mouth and the excitement raced through my body. I pulled and fought with the fish, willing it towards me as I could almost imagine the hot filet cooking over the fire. I pulled harder. Snap. Shit. I looked at the small piece of rod still in my hand with a strand of white medical tape hanging from the end. Before I could react and try to grab the line, there was a much smaller snap and I fell to the ground behind me in the release of pressure. My left hand reached out behind me out of instinct. I screamed out as the ground met my broken hand, only partially healed, and tears streamed down my face at the pain and the instant devastation of the loss of fish. I watched as the other half of the rod floated down the stream, possibly still attached to the fish that won another day of life.

"SHIT" I screamed towards the rolling clouds, and I threw the last piece of the busted rod into the stream to follow its other half. I reached into my pocket with my right hand and found what I was looking for before I knew what I wanted to do. My hand closed around the smooth rock that I had called my good luck charm. I took it out of my pocket and looked at it for only a moment, before chucking it into the water after the rod, yelling as I watched it sink beneath the surface. It took about five minutes to get the top off the container that held the pain pills and then another five to get the water open and drink them down. I held my left hand towards my chest and waited for the thundering pain to subside long enough for me to recheck the damage and maybe soak it in the cold water. As I rocked back and forth, clutching my hand like it was a small child, a sound started coming from my mouth that made me freeze for a moment before I continued my rocking. I let the noise continue to push past my closed lips, humming a song that came from a past that I didn't quite remember. I didn't know where the tune came from, but it seemed natural coming out of someplace deep within my soul, trying to comfort myself as I continued to rock, the tears spilling down into my cradled arm.

My head was pounding as the clouds continued to roll overhead. I stared into the small fire before me; watching the flame jump and fall as the small sticks spewed sparks into the sky. I could hear the water still churning in front of me, full of uneaten fish, almost as if it were teasing me with its rumble. I pulled the tape from my left hand slowly, squeezing my teeth together so that I could focus as the tape yanked on my fingers. The last bit came clear, pulling the small stick that had held it straight as well as a small amount of scab with it and I swore at the tape. Trying to convince myself that it would make me feel better. I looked down at the finger and tried to see the damage against the flickering light of the fire. It was swollen but the skin hadn't broken back open in the fall. The finger had turned bright red again but the skin down into my palm remained a dark purple. I tried to move it a small amount but that only sent a shock of pain back up into my shoulder. Rolling over to my knees, I crawled towards the rushing water and slowly lowered my left hand into the cold letting it splash against my arm. I could still feel the heat throbbing off it as I pulled it back up towards my face. Good enough. I crawled back towards my setup by the fire to dry it off before using a new stick and my new tape to set it back into place. I finished and laid back into the ground so that my head was just covered by the tarp that made up my shelter for the night. The humming started vibrating through my dry lips again as my eyes fell, giving into the full painful exhaustion of the moment.

I sat on her lap, yet again, her soft brown hair flowing down around me as she watched me trace the freckles along her arm looking for a shape that wasn't there. I started to cry at my own lack of skill to be able to make exactly what I wanted, and she leaned down to whisper in my ear, "What it is my little angel?" I pointed my left hand towards her arm, barely noticing that my little third finger wouldn't bend at all and was bent backwards in a weird angle.

Instead, I focused on trying to tell her what the priority at this precise moment was, "I ca… ca… can't make a house."

"A house? What kind of house?"

"I wa… want to make a small hou..house. Like the one in my dr…dr…dreams." I closed my eyes and pictured a small orange house at the end of a street; in a small town; a town that was surrounded by grass. I knew that I was looking for that house when my eyes closed and when they were open, I wanted to see it in her freckles. I looked around the stark white room. It was always just me and her in this room. He never liked to come. There was a rhythmic beep coming from the machine in the corner.

"It's Ok my boy; don't you worry about that house. Would you like me to sing you a song?" I nodded my head and snuggled into her, smelling her clean scent that just barely masked the smell of coming death. She started humming a song that I didn't remember but still seemed so recognizable at the same time. And then her soft magical voice sang to me as I clung to her.

Hold thy way, 'my bonny bairn,

Hold thy way up on my arm,

Hold thy way, thou soon may learn

To say Dad, so canny.

I wish thy daddy may be well,

He's long in coming from the keel,

Though his black face be like the de'il.

I like a kiss from Johnny."

I snuggled closer and closed my eyes, trying to picture her face above me… or was that another face that I was trying to see? I wasn't sure. The face was a blur; all I could see were the green eyes. Were her eyes supposed to be green? I thought maybe they were supposed to be grey.

Thou really has thy daddy's chin,

Thou art like him, leg and wing,

And I, with pleasure, can thee sing,

Since thou belongs my Johnny.

Johnny is a clever lad,

Last night he fuddled all he had,

This morn he wasn't very bad,

He looked as blithe as any."

A sound pierced through the white room, a long and sorrowful howl. My head jumped up to see where it was coming from before her hand reached up and patted my head, motioning me to return to where I had just been. I lay back down and closed my eyes again as her voice continued.

Though thou's the first, thou's not the last,

I mean to have my bairne fast,

And when this happy time is past

I still will love my Johnny.

For his hair's brown and so is thine,

Thine eyes are grey, and so are mine,

Thy nose is tapered off so fine,

Thou's like thy daddy Johnny."

This time the howl was replaced with high-pitched yips. I woke up to the complete lack of light. The fire had gone out and the night had deepened to a pitched black as I slept. The pain in my hand had lessoned to a dull throbbing that pounded up through my forearm, but it was manageable. I scooted towards where I knew my bag would be and dug around until I found the bottle of pain pills. Propped it in the crook of my left arm and I took the top off before reaching into the bottle and grabbing three pills. I held them tight in my fist so I wouldn't lose them in the darkness, before putting the container back into the bag and reaching around with two fingers, looking for what I wanted to wash them down with. Finally, I felt it, my one warm can of beer left. I pulled it out and held it firmly between my folded legs as I searched blindly for the tab and pulled, smelling the aroma and hearing the satisfying fizz. I tossed the pills into my mouth and let them tumble down my throat with a chug of beer when light flashed across the sky, lighting the clouds above me and my sad campsite below for just a second. I looked hesitantly at the sky but could see nothing above me. I took another drink of beer and reached back into my bag for a cracker packet. I ate and drank as the pain pills slowly started to work at the throbbing in my arm.

Something howled right next to me, and I jumped, spilling my beer. Shit. I froze, waiting to see if there would be another sound. Nothing. I slowly reached around, trying to find my turned can. When my hand finally located it, it had been spilled completely, watering the ground beneath it with the beer I had hoped to drink to numb my mind and my pain. Something yipped and growled to my left and I jumped again before remembering to freeze. The yip was joined by a few other howls and some growls which sounded like they were all around me. I reached forward and found the strap of my bag before pulling it to my chest and working my way backwards until I was sure that I was under the flimsy shelter of my tarp. My back hit the tree behind me, and I stopped, clutching my bag and waiting for the noises to stop. Were they getting closer? I couldn't tell. It sounded like there were dozens of them, just waiting for me to go to sleep. They were all around me as they continued to make noise in the night. The night lit up again as lighting raced across the clouds and I tried to look for any dark figures hunting me in the night. It turned back to darkness before I could make out the shadows that surrounded me, but I was convinced that they were getting closer.

The song came back to my lips. The song that I was convinced I had never heard before tonight. I sang it low under my breath, letting it protect me, as I sat through the darkness of the night, too scared to close my eyes and see demons of my past instead of the approaching real ones. My low song was only interrupted by the sounds of animals around me, ready to pounce, and the occasional streak of light across the sky.

Thy canny dowp is fat and round,

And like thy dad, thou's plump and sound,

Thou's worth to me a thousand pound,

Thou's althogether bonny.

When daddy's drunk, he'll take his knife

And threaten sore to take my life,

Who wouldn't be a keelman's wife,

To have a man like johnny.

CHAPTER THIRTY

THE JUMPER

I OPENED MY eyes just before I realized how much my body ached from falling asleep sitting upright against the tree. The bag had fallen to my side in the night and spilled its contents along the ground. My left hand that hid beneath the white bandage tape throbbed in pain as I looked around my small makeshift campsite. I was looking for any sight of the animals that I heard around me in the night, but everything was as it should be. The empty beer can lay on its side in the dirt next to the pile of ashes that were all that remained of my small fire. The tarp lifted and fell above my head, being pushed by the lazy wind. Every bone in my body cracked and every muscle groaned as I stood and stretched in the warming morning air. The clouds had gone away in the night and taken the last bit of their late summer cover. I bent down and rummaged through the items that had fallen out of my bag before finding the bottle of pills. I took three and washed them down with the water that remained in my bottle, while looking at the stream churning in front of me. My shirt came off over my head, moving gingerly around my left hand so not to hit it and cause more pain. My stomach grumbled painfully, and I rubbed my naked belly with my right hand. It felt strange; I looked down to see the thin skin stretched over my ribs. When had I gotten so thin? I thought back to the times I had stood in front of a mirror lately and suddenly realized that I had been growing thin this whole time, sometimes it was just ignored by the consistent shock of seeing my own face. Just now, touching my stomach and feeling my hip bones and ribs sticking out, I realized just how much smaller I had become. That wasn't a good sign. I sat and grabbed two of the five remaining packets of crackers and ate them all, ignoring the fact that they were increasing my thirst and I had no water in the bottle to wash them down in this exact moment. When I was done, I slid off my shoes and stood to awkwardly undo my jeans with my one working hand. Something in my pocket hit against my leg as I tried to slide the pants off and I froze for a second before I finished removing then and reaching my right hand down into the pocket.

My fingers closed on something round and smooth and instantly recognizable by touch. I closed my eyes and could picture it sinking into the water yesterday, before I pulled the soft grey rock from my pocket. My pants dropped to the ground, and I stood, staring at the rock that I had thrown, now sitting back in my hand like it had never left. I looked towards the water and back at my hand. It was still there, heavy and constant, just as it should be. I kneeled and stuck it back into the pocket of the crumpled pants that lay in the dirt before searching for my soap and small towel in the pile that had fallen from my bag. I walked toward the stream and dropped my towel on the ground as I stepped into the frigid water and just kept walking, making sure that I kept my footing against the slippery rocks along the bottom. One foot in front of the other. The cold made my breath catch in my throat, but I refused to stop moving forward, deeper into the stream. I focused my breath.

Deep breath in. Long sigh out. I walked until I stood in the middle of the stream, the water rushing around my hips as it reflected against the sun above me. I sank down and let the waters cool me, trying to wake me up from this strange dream that had no end. Was this real? Sitting here in cold water; my body attempting to starve itself; before getting back up and continuing to wander from place to place, sprinkled with all kinds of people that never quite fit together. Or maybe they fit together too well. Was that a coincidence? Maybe this was the dream, and my body was back in my warm and overly comfortable bed that smelled oddly of the color grey. The wife that I didn't know… that didn't know me, taking a shower down the hall. Was she ever down the hall at all? Maybe she did know me. I saw her eyes smiling at me. Grey. No. Green.

They were green. Or perhaps that field next to that town. That was real. The rest made up. I looked down at my arms floating in the water; the loosened tape making a pattern beneath the sparkling surface. Maybe I should test the reality of this world. Put my head beneath the water and let it all fade away as my thin body slowly swelled as it washed down the shallow water and stuck to the rocks beneath me. Instead, I lifted the bar of soap and one handedly scrubbed away the dirt and the soreness. And the pain.

EVERYTHING WAS SHAKEN off and packed neatly back into my bag, both water bottles refilled from the stream. My body was cleaned off and in fresh underwear, socks, and a shirt. My hiking pants had gotten a good cleaning in the stream and were already dry by the time I packed up; the bottom part of the pants unzipped so that they made shorts in the potentially warm day. I had replaced the sandals on my feet with sneakers; ones that I had found that fit perfectly. Someone had thrown them out for the simple reason that a shoelace was broken. It had cost me a dollar to replace. I needed these shoes and my clean socks on today; I knew where I was going and what that meant. I had left a small pile of trash; adding a human element to this piece of nature that would soon be filled with families and homes, assuming that it would probably be washed away by the time anyone else found and used this spot. If not, it would just be discarded as another pile of old trash left from a previous inhabitant of the world. The old underwear and bandages; the beer can and wrappers; they all sat in a nice pile under the tree. Maybe they really would stay there until discovered to prove that this spot was previously claimed by a grown man that enjoyed beer and wore cheap grey boxers. Maybe not.

My bag was full enough without adding to it with that garbage and I didn't think much more about leaving it there. I swung the bag over my shoulder and started walking towards the large store with the neon lights. And beyond that would be my transportation out of this town. I walked towards the large beams that would soon make houses. They still had long grass growing all around the clean tan wood, no driveways or yards yet, just a dirt path for the trucks to bring workers and supplies. A road that would soon be a paved as the families drove their minivans and SUVs towards this up-and-coming neighborhood, looking for a place to raise their happy family. I stood and looked at the row of squares, all in different levels of completeness.

I could picture the houses all done, different shades of grey and tan. Beautiful homes with brick along the fronts and garages large enough to fit both cars as well as all the kid toys that were reserved for outside play and even all the yard supplies. Sunny days like today, the neighborhood would be filled with dads outside pushing their mowers to fill the air with the sweet smell of freshly cut grass. Moms kneeling over their pretty flowers with gloves on their hands, turning their heads to look over their shoulder at the kids running through the sprinklers in the freshly mowed lawn or swinging on the clean swing sets and pumping their little legs to get higher and higher towards the sky. Everyone laughing and happy. Finishing the day with a nice dinner on the back porch, grandma and grandpa coming over; hugging everyone as they arrived just in time to eat a delicious meal. Maybe a splurge with a beer or a mixed drink as the sun sets over the stream they could see in the distance. I wondered if I would have been happy in that life. Would I have been the doting father, taking a break from mowing to push my daughter on the swing? Her brown curls flowing behind her and her green eyes sparkling as she giggled. I shook my head to clear the images. Instead seeing the stark-naked wood down the street with the dirt yards and dirt roads. The sun shining through the empty houses as I realized that this is what my life looks like. The empty shells of homes with no laughter or love. Maybe someday I could be like one of these future houses, filled with joy. Maybe if life had been different. Maybe if I had been different. I turned from the row and continued towards the store. And beyond that to where the train tracks stretched. The empty houses and hopeful dreams forgotten behind me as I walked away.

I HAD TO be more cautious this time as I walked through the rows of trains. Bright daylight didn't leave much room for hiding in the shadows and I could be caught at any moment. I hunched down low as I heard voices coming from the other side of the car that I was standing next to. I held my breath and waited for them to fade away followed by the crunch of their work boots against the gravel. I stood back up so that I could peer into the empty car with an open door. It held shadows and curled into one of the far shadows I saw a sleeping man. He was small and seemed unthreatening in his sleep, but I hesitated to climb up and into the car, picturing the bald man with a knife. I stood at the door, my head and shoulders reflected in the shadow on the floor. A loud horn sounded once. And again. And the train that I stood next to as I hesitated, started vibrating before it slowly creeped forward. No time to wait any longer, I pulled myself up into the car and pushed my body so that I was sitting with my back pressed against the wall next to the open door, waiting to see if the sleeping man would wake up. The train picked up speed, blasting its horn three more times as I peered sideways at the scenery that was picking up speed outside the door and we left the train yard and continued west towards the open air.

I watched the sleeping man, wondering if he was so drugged or drunk that the rough rocking of the train didn't wake him. Then I wondered if I jumped into a train car with a man who was already dead and couldn't be woken. I peered further into the shadow that he slept in and thought I could see his chest rise and fall even against the bumping motion of his body against the bottom of the train car. Just sleeping then. I let go of my bag and set it on the hard floor next to me so that I could pull a bottle of water from it and take a drink, still not taking my eyes off the sleeping man. I then reached into the bag and felt around until I found the skinny book I was looking for. I pulled it from the bag and looked at the cover for a moment before opening to the page I had folded to mark my spot. I turned just a bit so that I could both keep an eye out for movement coming from the corner of the sleeping man and to see the words of the page that were lit up from the sun coming through the cracked door.

I am mad with joy. –At least I think it's joy. Strangers have come, and it's a whole new game. I kiss the ice on the frozen creeks. I press my ear to it, honoring the water that rattles below, for by water they came: the icebergs parted as if gently pushed back by enormous hands, and the ship sailed through, sea-eager, foamy-necked, white sails riding the swan-road, flying like a bird!

A sound came from the shadowed corner where the man slept as the trained rattled forward. My head shot from my book, and I looked in his direction to see that the sound came from his still sleeping mouth. I assumed it was a moan in his sleep as he dreamt of the horrors that he has seen in his travels that brought him to this point. There was no other sign that he was waking up from his sleep and I turned my eyes back to my page. Hoping to finish it in the little time I expected to have before he woke up.

I could feel them coming as I lay in the dark of my cave. I stirred, baffled by the strange sensation, squinting to the dark corners to learn the cause. It drew me as the minds of the dragons once did. It's coming! I said. More clearly than ever I heard the muffled footsteps on the dome of the world.

I looked up as I heard a noise from his corner again expecting to see him still moaning in his sleep; my book dropped, losing my spot on the page as it folded closed. He was awake. He was sitting in the dark corner; back pushed up against the opposite wall from where I was sitting. I could see his eyes wide with fear and reflecting the light that came from the doorway of the train car. His legs were pulled up against his chest; his arms wrapped around them holding them tight and in his right hand was a stick. The stick was held towards me like he would try to poke me with it if I came close to him; even though we both knew it would do little damage.

He looked like a frightened and wild animal; shaking in his spot where he was forced into a corner and threatened. I slowly moved my hand towards my book and slid it away from the wind of the door. My thought to save a book with only a few pages left to read should have been a minor priority in hindsight, but in the moment, it made sense. Then I lifted both of my hands, palms facing the young man with the wild eyes, and I tried to focus on him to see what else I noticed. His shorts were covered in so much dirt that I could barely see what color they had started as. His shirt had some small holes throughout and had prominent brown stains spotted through it. Blood? His hair was cut to just above his ears but stuck out at uneven angles, matted and dirty. The stubble on his chin was coming in uneven and had patches of white even though his face looked hopefully youthful under the layer of mud. His eyes were swollen with sleep and dehydration and his mouth was slack under his wide eyes. He had no shoes on his feet and they looked like they were caked with mud. He had a small bag with him was so overfilled that the seams were about to burst. "I'm not going to hurt you."

"Bullshit" it came out jumbled in the voice of a scared young man.

"It's not bullshit. I don't want any trouble. I just am trying to ride in peace."

"That's what everyone says."

This wasn't working. I understood. "What would you do to me if I did want trouble? Try to poke me with that stick? It would break as soon as it hit my skin and you are much smaller than me. Really, if I wanted to hurt you, I would have done it while you slept."

His eyes looked down at the stick that shook in his hand, and it lowered to his side. "I don't have anything worth stealing." He glanced towards his bag.

"No shit. And again – if I had wanted to steal from you, I could have done it while you slept." He stared at me, trying to take me in and decide. Finally, he nodded and seemed to relax just a small amount. I nodded at him and put my hands back down and placed them in my lap. "My name is… J."

He squinted at me again, "You don't look like a 'Jay'. Is that your real name?" I shook my head assuming that he would know to let it go.

He did. "My name is Tylor."

I smiled, "Is that your real name?" He shook his head and smiled the smallest smile back at me.

I put my book down into my bag and looked back at him still huddled into the corner of safety. "So, Tylor. Are you hungry?" I was thinking that I could pop open the can of nuts that lay unopen in my bag and share them with him to get him to loosen up a bit and become less of a threat. To my surprise he shook his head. "You aren't hungry?" He shook his head again and then stretched his legs out in front of him. He pulled the drawstring on his small bag, lifted it up, and turned it upside down. I looked at the pile that had spilled out of the now empty bag. Packages of snack foods; beef jerky, snack cakes, chips, cheese, and more.

He looked back at me, "Are *you* hungry?" I nodded, my mouth watering as I spied a sausage and cheese combo packet. He leaned in my direction, pushing the pile so that it sat closer to the middle between us, before grabbing a few things from the pile and quickly scooting back flush against the opposite side. I was finished with the sausage and cheese and halfway through a snack cake when I finally thought to ask him where he had gotten all this food. He looked embarrassed and mumbled something that I couldn't understand. I decided to let it go, knowing that I probably didn't want to know. Or care. I noticed that there was nothing else in his bag so I rolled him one of my water bottles and he drank half of it before I reminded him that it would probably have to last him, since we didn't know when or where this train would stop. There was a decent chance we could continue even past the stops as they happened. But there was also a decent chance that we couldn't.

ONCE WE HAD eaten what we could, he wrapped his arms around his pile of goodies and pulled it back close to him before putting it all back down into his bag and pulling the drawstring tight. The empty wrappers were pushed out the door to fly away. I noticed that it seemed only about half full now and my stomach felt almost miserable with the amount of sugar and salt I had just eaten. I leaned back against my side of the car again as I could feel it start to slow. I stood and walked to the side of the car that he was on. I could see him watching me as he tried not to turn his head, still distrustful of the man who shared his space. I sat down and leaned against the side of the car, my front in line with the open door as the world slowed to a crawl while we passed through a town.

Small houses and small shops, all covered with brick. A flashing red sign went past the door as the chime that warned cars of our coming faded into the distance. The train picked up speed again and the wind blew back in through the open door and our window to the world became a blur of green and brown. I could hear the horn of our own distant first car as it blasted its goodbye to the small town.

"I haven't had a home in a long time." I nodded to his answer, as if I knew what he was talking about. I did, but not in the same way. I had asked him when he had left his home. "But that doesn't matter. I've been here," he made a sweeping motion with his arms as if to represent the great expanse of the world, "since I was about fourteen." I must have shown some surprise, the afternoon sun lighting my face and he could see the expression. "It's really not a big deal. It's just…. It is what it is. It's what I know." I nodded at him again. Trying to urge him to keep going and to share more about his life. Curious about his dirty clothes and his bag that only contained gas station junk food. I didn't want to come right out and ask him about all of that. I could tell that his trust of me was extremely limited, not that I was surprised by that.

He had moved so that he lay on the floor of the car again, this time a bit further out from the wall. Showing that he had started to trust me a little in the few hours we had spent talking. I had told him about my story… as much as I was willing to share. I told him about the worst parts of it, trying to gain some of his trust in the form of connected moments of shit in this life. He hadn't said anything as I told him about the real moments. The moments that I thought were real at least. I didn't share why I had left my home in the first place. How could he possibly relate to me if he knew that I had a safe life that I chose to leave for the certain path of a terrible life? I knew he wouldn't. So now I asked him questions, trying to get the answers I was looking for.

"Why did you leave?"

His hands played as they rested on his stomach and he stared at the roof of our moving room, "My dad... uh... well... he was a complete asshole. He lost his job when I was younger and couldn't find another. So, he picked up a hobby. Which was drinking too much and beating the shit out of my mom. I know... the same shitty story of almost every teen that makes it out on the street." I waited for him to continue. "My mom left eventually, and she left me there. Not really giving a shit what would happen after she left. When she wasn't there to beat on, he turned to me, and I became his new hobby. One night I hit back. I was fourteen but he was drunk, and I hit him... hard...and uh... he fell." He was still looking at the roof, making it obvious that he didn't want to look at me while he spoke. "He hit his head and blood started coming out and I took off. Not sure what ever happened to him. Maybe he lived. Maybe he didn't." He shrugged awkwardly and looked over at me, "Your dad hit you too?" I shook my head but as I blinked, an image came to my mind. I closed my eyes again, watching the moments that I knew couldn't be real because I couldn't remember ever seeing them before. But as they were happening, I wondered if maybe they had happened in real life. I saw a hand. His hand. Coming towards me and felt the pain on my cheek as it made contact. Falling to the floor and looking up at him, tears streaming out of my eyes. He stood over me, his face distorted with anger and hatred and pain. The tears flowing down his face to match mine. His hands were balled into giant fists, and he was yelling down at me. What was he saying? It was muffled like he was yelling under water. I stopped crying and tried to focus on his lips. What was it? The words slowly came into focus,

"Your fault. All your fault. If you weren't here, she would have told me. I would have saved her. It's your fault," the spit flew from his mouth with the last word, "bastard."

Who was he talking about? Who would have told him? How could it be my fault that someone didn't tell him something? He turned and stumbled away.

"Hey J, man, you ok?" I opened my eyes to see my arms in front of my face, blocking it from the one blow of a man who had been long dead.

"Uh… yeah." I lowered my arms and saw him propped up against one elbow. I motioned towards him to show that I was ready for him to keep talking. I rubbed the fur that was growing in on my chin and waited to see if he would start up. He shrugged and leaned his back against the bottom of the train again before jumping back to his stories. It seemed like he needed to be able to talk to someone and as he continued, he slowly started to open up.

"The beatings from him though… the asshole… were nothing compared to the shit out here. I wish I would have known that. Seven or eight years I've been out here. I think you might be all right man, but the people like you… it's just not that often. There was a man… I was…" he closed his eyes, and I could see his body shiver from the thought playing out in his mind, but he kept going, "I was sleeping in a place, a park. It was before I was on here. I got comfortable. I stopped paying attention. One night, this man with a knife… he attacked me. I would have been bad enough that he took the things that I had collected or even that he beat me up and left me there. But the worst part…" a sob came from his mouth, and I worried and hoped that he would stop his story as his eyes pushed tighter. He didn't, "the worst part… was when he…he... he just took everything from me, and I laid there hoping that I would die." He stopped and I was hoping that he wouldn't start back up again. "Then I had this dream. I was still laying there… in the dirt… in pain… blood and dirt. And I had this dream. A woman was standing there in the setting sun, and she told me to get my ass up. So, I woke up and I got up. My shoes, my bag, everything gone. I could barely see out of my eye. I walked into a gas station where I watched until the kid behind the counter went to the bathroom. I walked in, grabbed some food and a bag, and then walked to this train… and here I am. Still wishing I were dead. And then you showed up." He opened his eyes and tilted his head to look at me. "I don't want to talk anymore." He turned his head back towards the sky and put his arms over his face.

I stood silently and walked towards the door to sit down and cross my legs under me, watching the world fly by in front of me and letting the wind hit my face. I thought about what he had just told me and realized that nothing in my life was even near the shit that he had gone through. I felt horrible. How would he ever make it? How had I even made it this far? It didn't make sense. I looked out at the grass flying by and felt a pain heavier than I had felt before. Not for my own recently recovered memories or my own life or even the life I left behind. But for the boy, who lay in the car behind me, trying to sleep without nightmares that were scarier than anything I could ever fear to dream of.

I looked down and could see the smear of the small tan rocks flying past as the train picked up speed. I moaned into to wind, trying to release the pain. It wouldn't go. I felt like a shell of emptiness again, filled only with hate for the world. Ignoring the images flashing in front of me of the good moments; of Phil, and the kids around the dinner table, playing catch with Dog, the women of the past smiling and laughing. Only focusing on the fists, and the hate; the scowls and the yells; the lost eyes of all I had left behind. The pain filled me until that's all I could see. Shaded red behind my eyes. I looked at the rocks and slowly leaned forward, letting my body topple down towards them. I could see in slow motion as my body rolled back towards the train, the metal circles spinning over the shiny silver track; the wood beams keeping them from the rocks below. I could hear the kid yell from the train car as it sped away and I was swept up under the wheels, the world and pain going instantly black. Hours later, men stood around the pieces of my body that remained and the blood that had splattered the once tan rocks, making their jagged edges look like small knives. They all stood there, shaking their heads at the tragedy 'that shouldn't have been' and wondering who I was.

One of them spoke up, "It must have been an accident." They all nodded.

Another said, "Another jumper making a mistake." They all nodded again.

A third said "Another suicide. What a way to go."

Again, they all nodded solemnly. All agreeing with one mind that it was one of those options. There would be no funeral, no grave marker. No one would come to claim the last pieces of my body because no one ever even knew who I was.

THE TRAIN HORN blasted, and I could feel the train start to slow as we neared another town. I opened my eyes and leaned back from the edge of the car a little before looking out at the dimming sky. We crossed a road with a line of cars waiting for the train to pass and I looked back to see a young boy in the backseat of a car, staring at me with wide eyes.

Probably trying to figure out what a man was doing on the train. Or how we could join me. He might tell his mother, and she'll laugh it off, only half hearing him. The train sped up and I pushed back into the car to grab my book from my bag. Maybe I could finish it before it got too dark to read. I glanced at the sky. I still had a few hours.

I made it to the last page.

Standing baffled, quaking with fear, three feet from the edge of a nightmare cliff, I find myself, incredibly, moving toward it. I look down, down, into the bottomless blackness, feeling the dark power moving in my life an ocean current, some monster inside me, deep sea wonder, dread night monarch astir in his cave, moving me slowly to my voluntary tumble into death. Again sight clears. I am slick with blood. I discover I no longer feel pain. Animals gather around me, enemies of old, to watch me die. I give them what I hope will appear a sheepish smile. My heart booms terror.

"What are you reading?" I looked over at him where he was still lying down but turned towards me in to watch me read. I closed the book and passed it to him. He read the back cover, and then opened to the first page, his mouth moving as he read the words silently.

He handed it back towards me, but I waved him away, "Do you want to read it? I'm done." He looked down at the book in his hands and nodded, looking back at me curiously.

"Do you read a lot?" I shrugged and he opened the book again and started to read. I turned back towards the open door and watched the sun get closer to the ground as the world sped past.

Tylor joined me after a bit, closing the book and shoving it into his small bag with his pre-packaged food. We ate some more sausage and snack cakes as we sat and watched the sky start to darken. We had entered another world. One that felt so familiar like I had been here before. The train moved slower as it kept curving through the rocks and mountains and the wind was low enough that we could hang our legs from the car as we watched the world pass us by. He was close enough that I could smell the stink coming from his body and clothes. I thought for a second about the items that were in my bag before turning towards him, trying to figure out how to word my next statement.

"You know, I have been collecting so much shit lately that my bag is so fucking heavy." He looked at me, a blank stare behind his eyes. I continued, "So, I was thinking... If you would like, I have a clean shirt and some other things too." I saw him shiver in the quickly cooling air coming and added, "And a sweatshirt."

He shook his head. "No man, I don't accept charity."

"Really?" I sounded incredulous, "you don't take charity, but you steal from a store. Do you see what might be fucked up with that sort of reasoning?" I smiled to lessen the blow of my words. He smiled back, a bit sheepishly. "Just take the stuff." He looked at me, longer than necessary, and nodded in thanks. I scooted back into the car and pulled a few things from my bag. My other new shirt and underwear, the sandals, the sports shorts from the shelter, and my sweatshirt. I handed them to him, and he stood and nodded at me before taking them and walking to his previous sleeping corner. He looked at me and I turned back to my bag, giving him an unspoken understanding that I wasn't going to look, giving him some privacy to change. I pulled out my orange jacket and slid it on to help hide my shivering arms from the cool wind before taking off my hiking pants turned shorts and replacing them with the worn out, but warm, jeans that were stuffed into the bottom of my bag. I moved back to the door, my lighter bag by my side and hung my legs through the opening again. I looked up and could see a waterfall in the mountains beyond the trees as the train rolled past. There was noise behind me as he changed, and I kept my eyes on the wonder of the world around me.

There was a small road running parallel with the train and I could see a few cars working their way down it. The road curved along the mountain with us for a moment before it started to climb; stone railings keeping any cars from swerving off the road and into the train tracks below. I seemed to know that there was a river behind me that ran the same path of the train, even though I couldn't see it through the wall of the train car. He finished changing and came to sit next to me. I looked over and he had almost a smile on his face as he smoothed down his sweatshirt. Still barefoot as he hung his legs out the open door next to mine; my bag in between us. I wondered if I could convince him to get off when I did and get him to a place to clean off. I bet he would feel better when he was cleaned up more, I tried to convince myself that that there was nothing selfish in my action. But all I could see were the young college kids as they were being driven away in the police car. I wanted redemption and I wanted companionship. Now I knew what he had gone through before getting on his train, the mud that was caked into his hair was more understandable and made him look sad rather than just dirty. I turned back towards the open air, and we watched as the sky darkened so that we could barely see the mountains that had loomed above us. I could almost make out a large tan rock that jutted from the mountain at a funny angle, almost making a seat for one to sit on – high above the world. The train slowed as it prepared to bank around a corner and its horn blasted into the darkening sky. As we started to slow, I saw a small walking path that led up to the train.

There on this path stood a man. A man that looked almost familiar. His shaggy brown hair blew from the wind that the train created. He wore an orange jacket and had a bag slung over his should. My eyes met his as I felt a wave of sadness wash over me. For him and for myself, knowing that he had no idea what was still going to come his way over the coming months. The coming years. He had no idea what lie ahead of him. I raised my hand to him and watched him return the wave, his hand frozen in the air as he faded from view.

CHAPTER THIRTY-ONE

THE SPIDER

I PULLED MY jacket against my body, trying to hold the heat in against the cold wind. The afternoon sun was hidden by the clouds that stretched across the sky. They were moving quickly, coming in from the ocean and towards the mountains that stretched behind me. I sat on a fallen tree that had been smoothed by the waves and the storms. I looked down at my feet that were pushing their way into the hardened sand and lifted one to watch the sand fall and join the others. The tide was starting to come back in, but it had gone so far out that I could see the ocean floor in the distance. The smooth black stones shining through the dark wet sand. Seabirds playing down where the waves had been and digging for bugs. They didn't mind the cold winds. Maybe I could be like them some day. I closed my eyes and pictured myself flying through the clouds to find the sun beyond the storm and playing in the sand without noticing the cold wetness underneath. I stretched my long white wings into the air and took off, looking back just once to see the shivering old man sitting alone on a log. I opened my eyes and looked back down at my feet, realizing I hadn't felt warm in days. I wanted to be warm. I stood, my back and legs moaning from sitting too long and grabbed my light bag before walking towards the path that led off the beach.

There was a parking lot, empty in the chilly fall weather. Past it was a brown building with windows in the front. It looked almost like a walkup malt shop that I remembered as a child, but I saw a sign that mentioned something about camping spots for hikers and bikers. I reasoned that I could count as a hiker. I walked to the window and smiled at the man behind the glass. I wondered what I looked like in this moment. Knowing it couldn't be good. I had watched the ocean waves more than once and thought about cleaning off in their crisp salty depths. But each time I was cut short by the freezing chill of the water and the image of being carried out to sea. The voice of death was coming more and more lately but I wasn't ready for that moment. Not quite. I worried that if the freezing water washed over me, it would become too easy to just let my muscles relax in the cold and float away. The window squeaked as a man slid it open. He had white hair peeking from beneath his green ball cap and a polo shirt with a park logo on the breast. He must have been older than me but the only thing that really showed his age was the color of his hair. His face looked younger and happier. Relaxed in this booth next to the ocean and beneath the cover of giant trees.

"I saw..." my voice came out rough and I realized that it had been over a day since I had last said a word out loud. I cleared my throat and tried again, "I saw a sign about hiker camp spots?" He nodded and I tell he was taking me in and deciding my value.

"Yeah. It is five dollars for the night, and you can use the showers and bathrooms. It's a shared spot but it's mostly emptied this time of year. I think we've just got one group back there now. You can set up your tent anywhere in the grass within the group spot." I could see him glancing at my duffel bag. We both knew there wasn't a tent in there.

"I don't have a tent." He nodded. We both knew that already.

"Not great to hike without a tent but I get it. Out in the wild, right?"

"Uh... yeah"

"Well, it's supposed to storm tonight. You may want a tent." He nodded as if he was agreeing with his own statement.

"That's great man. But I just don't have one."

He waved his hand, "Yeah. But I do. We have a whole pile of stuff that people can take from. It's all stuff that other people left here on purpose or forgot. Either way, you can help yourself. I think I have two or three small tents. We check them before adding them to the pile so they should all be in working order." He motioned at me to walk around to the side of the windowed hut and slid the glass window closed. I stood for a moment before walking around the corner to see him already there with a door propped open. I followed him into the hut and over to a pile in the corner. There was a giant box made of wood that had things tossed into it. "Dig around and grab anything you might need. If you don't need it after your time here, then just drop it back off after. Otherwise, you can take it with you. When you are done let me know and we'll finish getting you checked in." He turned back towards the windows up front and spun on his stool for a moment before opening the window again to a person standing there. I listened to the man check into a spot with a hookup as I pulled items from the large box.

MY DUFFEL BAG was almost empty before I walked into this building but now it was starting to be filled with a towel, a blanket and a small pillow, some shampoo, a lighter (tested and worked), a new container of toothpaste that wasn't even opened, and even a sweatshirt that had a hood and a picture of lake inside of a crater. The lake almost looked familiar. Like I had seen it in a dream. I zipped back up my bag, having to push down everything down into it to get it to close. Then I looked at the three small tents lined up in front of me. They all seemed small. One was held together with a large sturdy rubber band. The other two were zipped neatly into bags with carrying cases. I looked at them all, each boasting small size and assumed easy assembly. I would never get this thing back into a carrying case that was made for a first time use only. I grabbed the one with the rubber band and motioned at the man by the window, sitting in his swivel stool and watching me. He nodded and I put the remaining items back into the large box before walking out the door and swinging it closed behind me.

I walked around the corner and back to the open window and realizing that it was still frigid outside. I finished the check-in process, as he acknowledged my lack of identification with understanding once I handed him cash and made sure to let him see that I had more just in case I decided to stay for more than one night. He pointed towards the path for the hikers and bikers. I walked on the gravel in the quiet and almost empty campground. The sound of the waves roaring distantly from the direction of the ocean. The wind rushing through the trees above me only overcome by the occasional screech of a crow hidden among the branches.

THE SHOWER STALL was warm. Heated by nothing but the light that hung high up against the white ceiling and the steam coming from the water. It was a private room with a lock. The floor on the outer section was dirty with tracked in mud and I sat on a small bench, still fully clothed, letting myself warm up while the hot stream sprayed behind the shower wall. It had been running for about five minutes and I got up to turn it off. There had been a row of doors, all open, for private shower stalls and I knew that no one would care that I was still in here. No one was even here to notice. The steam floated around the small room as I sat back on the little wood bench. My new tent and my full duffel bag sat next to me. I wanted to take a shower, but I was dreading the moment that I would stand naked and turn off the hot water to the cool air again, so I waited. The steam disappeared and I sat with my eyes closed procrastinating for just a moment more. Finally, I stood and pulled some of the new items from my bag before peeling off my clothes and stepping into the shower portion of the small, tiled room.

Barefoot against the ground and the water on the floor of the shower had already started to cool. I turned the water back on and waited for the stream to run hot. Almost scalding. Almost enough to cook my skin. Then I stepped under it to see if it was hot enough to wash away the days of chilled bones and quiet pain. It wasn't. But it was hot enough to make me feel my skin prick under the spray. I scrubbed the dirt away and brushed my teeth while I let the water run down my body. I leaned my head back and the water combed through my hair and my eyes drifted shut. I could feel each stream of water as they ran down different parts of my body. One flowed from the back of my neck, slowly tracing all the way down my back and over my ass and down my thigh before drifting away and falling off into the puddle water trying to circle the drain beneath my feet.

The water shot cold, and I jumped back, shocked to the present by the sudden change in temperature. I held my hand under the spray as it shifted back into warm water. A glitch of a campsite bathroom, I'm sure. I hesitated before moving back under the water, preparing for it to change again without warning. Just enough time to get warm again. Just warm enough to possibly last me through the night and the expected storm. At least I now had a tent to replace the tarp that had ripped in the last storm, and a blanket. That was new.

I turned the knobs and tried not to be disappointed by my own decision as I watched the last of the water trickle from the spout and drift away towards the drain below. I shivered against the air as it quickly cooled. I reached around the smooth partition wall to grab my new towel and quickly dried off before wrapping it around me and sitting on the bench. Waiting just a moment before finding my clothes to slide into. Clean-ish underwear and socks, jeans, shirt, sweatshirt with a lake, and jacket. Check. I laced my shoes and then chose to continue to sit on the bench for a bit longer before heading to the lonely camp site and attempting to put up this tent. I could only hope that all the pieces are there since I was sure the shack with the windows was closed now for the night. I shut my eyes against the florescent light and leaned back against the damp wall tile. Deep breath in. Long sigh out. I could have sat for hours, eyes closed, resting and hiding from the beautiful outdoors. Something told me to open my eyes and I listened. They opened just in time to see a slight movement coming from the top of my bag. My breath held as I slowly turned my head to see what was attempting to interrupt my privacy. It sat, frozen on my bag, right next to my arm. I held my breath as I stared into his eyes. His legs bent almost lazily like he was just hanging out with me waiting in the heat. His small face was turned up at me and his mouth opened. I think it opened. Either way, I stared at him, and he stared at me. Each of us waiting for the other to make the first move.

"What's up dude?" Did I say that? No, I didn't say that. My breath came out in a rush.

I leaned closer to the small brown spider, "Did you just say something?"

I could see my reflection shining in all his eyes, "Yeah dude. I said, 'what's up?'" I closed my eyes and lifted my left hand to rub them. I must have fallen asleep. I opened them again to see him still sitting and waiting for my answer. Ok then.

I opened my mouth, "Well, where should I start?" Turned out I knew where to start. I started from the beginning. There were tears throughout. Tears I didn't know I still had in me. I told him all about the loneliness and the pain. I told him about everyone that I had lost over time and about Dog. I told him about the buffalo and about the dead man. I left out the times that I had sprayed my house for spiders. But besides that, I told him everything about my life. I even told him about her. All about her. I told him everything up until the moment here; sitting in this shower talking to this spider when I don't even remember knowing that spiders can speak.

"I don't want to go outside. When I go outside, then the next part is real again. The cold and the lonely sleep under another cloudy night. I wanted to get away from the monotony that made my own life unrecognizable. I needed to feel something. To do something. But now the pain is monotonous. The lack of talking, the outdoor sleeping, the loss of everyone after just meeting. It is monotonous and I'm fucking scared that I can't even deal with either of the options in my own life. Does that make sense?" I cried and looked back down at him to see him still sitting on my bag, tilting his head as if he were listening to me the whole time. My ass hurt from sitting on the hard wood bench for the last hour and the room had turned cold. I lifted my right hand and the spider jumped and ran over my bag towards the other side. I saw him creeping down the wall towards the tiled corner as I unlocked the door and pulled it open. Treating me with a blast of cool air in the darkening evening. I knew the spider hadn't spoken to me… right? Spiders cannot talk. I know that. I knew that. But I had to admit I felt better. It might have been the hot shower. It might have been the one-way conversation.

I WALKED TOWARDS the path that the ranger had pointed out and headed towards the spot for hikers and bikers. There was no one on the way even though the campground was large. I expected there to be no one in the shared spot, forgetting that the ranger had mentioned another group. As I rounded a corner of bushes and trees, I saw them. I group in their twenties. Three guys and two girls all sitting around a fire and laughing together as they all shared one joke. I nodded at them and found a spot of grass that sat apart from their tents, making sure they knew that I wanted to sit over here on my own. I shrugged my bag off over my shoulder so that it fell to the soft grass and then pulled the rubber band off the pile of sticks and plastic that made up my hopeful tent. I laid out all the supplies in the dim light and looked at them. Shit. Now what? I should have grabbed one of the tents that were still in a bag with a paper of directions. While I stood there trying to figure out what to do, I heard footsteps coming up behind me and I swung to face the threat. There stood two of the young men that had been sitting around the fire. One of them motioned towards the pieces of the tent that lay on the ground.

"Need some help? That's a pretty old one but I used to have one like it."

The relief must have shown openly on my face since they didn't wait for me to answer before picking up the pieces. They became my teachers, showing me what they were doing and why as they did it, giving me direction and having me help them as they worked. In less than twenty minutes I had shelter. I real shelter with a little door and a tiny mesh covered window and everything. It was the nicest tent I had ever seen, even if it would be tight fit for me and my bag. But it was mine. We slid the accompanying tarp over the top to keep out the rain that hadn't yet started. Then I tossed my bag into it and followed the two men back to their campfire, accepting the offer of warmth and food with a faint hope that this time would be different. That this time there would be no pain. It was just a fire. Just a meal. And I was hungry. Besides the spider had given me hope.

The two helpers introduced their three friends, names I quickly forgot due to the number of them and the determination that I wouldn't see them again after this one evening. I introduced myself with my fake name that had become almost real, J. The sky above the trees was black and the fire stood out in the night. One of the women got up from her chair and sat one of the men's laps to free a chair for me and someone else handed me a metal stick that had two prongs holding a hotdog at the end and a paper plate with a bun. I watched the meat as I held it over the fire, and it turned darker and split under the heat. The flames danced around the fire pit, turning orange and red with blue when one looked close to the wood. Every few seconds a shot would ring out and something would crack in the fire and sparks would fly. Everyone would laugh as they scooted away then immediately back towards its warmth. The meat finished cooking, and it warmed my stomach before I chased it down with a can of cool beer.

I listened to their stories and laughed with them as they laughed. It was easy and relaxing. They talked about their hiking trip. Two weeks in. Three weeks to go. All with sabbaticals from their respective jobs and not a care in the world for a few weeks. They asked if I wanted to hike a little with them and in the magic of the moment, I forgot my new rule and I agreed. We made plans to meet in the morning for a quick breakfast before heading south. I let them know that I could repay their offers of food and they waved it off, one of them telling me that they had bought more than they wanted to carry. He said I could buy the beer in two days, and we would be even. I mentally counted my cash that was in my bag before nodding. Cringing at the thought of how little was left but not wanting to disappoint this small group of friends.

I watched the fire, dancing lower and slower to a new song. It was a lazy movement and the heat had become less aggressive. I pulled my hat down over my ears and was mesmerized by the flicker of the flame. I heard a guitar strum and looked up, surprised by the sound. One of the men who had helped put up my tent was holding a small guitar that was made from a small cigar box holding only three strings. He strummed it a few times and turned the knobs before picking up a tune, the song on the tip of my tongue. The woman next to him started singing when he did. I looked back at the fire and noticed that it was dancing to the same rhythm as their soulful voices. I watched the movement, only surprised for a moment at the way it moved, it's arms swaying to the beat, before being lulled into its warm flame as they sang.

You belong among the wildflowers

You belong in a boat out at sea

Sail away, kill off the hours

You belong somewhere you feel free

Run away, find you a love

Go away somewhere all bright and new

The rest of the group joined in, and I looked at them smiling and singing around the dancing campfire. As if we were in a movie about friendship and free love made years ago. I sang with them, letting my own voice carry away my final reservations about joining them for the coming days.

THE NEXT MORNING, I woke to the sound of rain falling onto my tent and for a moment I felt almost free. Like a wildflower. For only a moment. Where did that come from? Shit. Why did I agree to go hiking with them? I didn't even know where they were going. This was a stupid fucking idea. The magic from the night before had disappeared in the cool morning air. My stomach growled and I remembered the other promise.

Breakfast. What the hell. I decided to hike with them for just a little bit and got up to grab my bag and head for the bathroom. The drizzly morning seemed brighter after I brushed my teeth and washed up. Seeing myself in the dirty and dented mirror and realizing that I didn't look nearly as bad as I felt. I walked back towards the campsite. Head covered in my hat and the orange hood from my jacket over that. Dry and warm… kind of. Enough. I pulled my tent apart and tried to shake it almost dry before wrapping it inside the tarp and the rubber band and joining my new friends.

Their tents were torn down and they were in the process of cooking oatmeal over a camp stove. It smelled amazing. Someone handed me a paper cup filled with hot coffee and I sat back into the folding chair from the night before and sipped the brown delicious liquid. I saw one of the men looking at my duffel bag and my tent pile sitting next to it and for a moment I felt embarrassed. I gave a false perception of my hiking tendencies the night before. I tried not to look at him as he said something under his breath to one of the other men and one of the women. I knew it. This was a horrible idea. They were deciding the best way to ask me not to join them. They were hikers with heavy packs full of crap I didn't have, and they were still able to carry it. Me, I was winded after years of this shit and still thought my duffel bag was heavy. I looked down at my coffee and pretended to ignore them, waiting for the inevitable. I heard them shuffling around, packing up, talking amongst themselves and I stayed eyes down, trying to delay the moment where I would grab my bag and walk away. Knowing they would be watching me with a mix of pity and scorn in their unforgiving eyes as they whispered, "we should have known better than to invite an old man to hike with us." Why was this bothering me. I didn't even want to go. Right?

"Hey J?" I looked up and prepared to stand. One of the men stood in front of me. I think it was the one that could play the tiny guitar. He had an empty backpack in his hands, like the ones they had all packed up and were sitting in a pile behind us. "So, we figured it might be hard to carry around the duffel bag and the tent, but all of our bags were pretty light so we combined our shit, and you can have this bag if you want. It's old but it might be easier to carry and should fit the tent."

He held it towards me with an expression that tore the anger out of me. I wanted to say, "Nah man, I don't take charity." But that would be a lie. I was proud but not that proud and after the thought of getting denied time hiking with this group, I realized that I did want to join them. I thanked them all for the bag and pushed my duffel down inside it along with the tent. After breakfast and a quick pick up of the site and trash, we finished tying chairs and the small guitar to the bags and walked away through the damp morning, the crows yelling at us from above.

The new pack made everything seem lighter, even with the new additions. It was almost easy. Almost. We walked high up into the hills. The drizzle continuing, making every step more and more dangerous as we climbed. The mood was light though and we joked and sang as we walked. Eventually we made it to the top of a cliff, and all stood looking towards the ocean at what one of the men claimed to be the best view of the hike. We laughed together at the wall of fog that made this view about as spectacular as a plain white wall. We talked about what we imagined lay beyond the mist as we sat on the rock and ate granola bars.

"I can see a pirate ship!"

"No no no that's not a pirate ship. That is a Viking ship for sure. I'm pretty sure I see Thor."

I laughed like I knew what they were talking about and chimed in, "I swear I just saw something move in the water. Do you think the Loch Ness monster could make it this far?"

They all laughed, "On sabbatical!" one of the women cheered and we lifted our water bottles to the monster's extended vacation. Successful for him as he was more than used to this wind and rain, coming from Scotland and all. It was a moment of complete normalcy that had rarely existed in my life and even though I couldn't remember their names and they didn't know mine, we laughed as if we had known each other for years. I could do this. I could stay here with them; finish their three more weeks' vacation. Then what? Hang out with them when they all got done at their respective jobs each day. Go to dinner at their homes? I knew that would never be a reality. I stopped laughing and retreated into the darkness of my own mind, letting them continue the game without me.

They finished and we all stood. Pulling our packs back onto our backs as I followed them down the path towards the beach. A few hours to the sand. We walked single file as the path got narrower and narrower. Their voices carrying back to me, trying to include me but eventually giving up. I looked at the thick trees as the fog was slowly left behind. It was beautiful. Giant trees lifting high above my head, brown and green and shiny from the mist. The sun was attempting to peek through the clouds above the treetops and provide even more brilliance to the two-tone color that surrounded me. We continued our decline, slowing in areas that were exceptionally narrow or hard to walk due to the slick ground beneath our feet. My companions were all well prepared with their hiking boots, but my shoes weren't quite ready for this angle in the rain. They continued to move quicker than me, quiet in their concentration as they marched downhill. I didn't call out; knowing that there was only one path, and I would catch them at the beach.

I heard a noise and looked to my left.

There. Something behind the trees. I stopped moving and peered towards the shadows filled with green and brown. There it was again. A flash of orange fabric, running between the trees. That couldn't be safe. What is that? A Hunter? I looked back at my group to shout and see if they saw it. They were gone. They must have been walking faster than I had thought. I would still catch them at the beach. That just didn't make sense. How could they have moved so quickly? I started to walk towards the direction they had disappeared and heard another sound, this time to my right. I swung around and there she was.

A woman that I knew. I don't know where I had seen her before, but I had. She was standing in the distance and between two trees. Her hair and dress weren't wet from the rain, and she didn't shiver against the cold wind. She stared back at me. I knew that I was her focus even so far away that I could barely see her eyes. We stood gazing at each other in the darkness of the trees. Deep breath in. She darted behind a tree and before I knew what I was doing, my breath shot out in a gust as I was sliding through the slick rocks and tree roots towards where she had disappeared. I stopped and looked for a flicker of orange to make sure I was still headed in the right direction. There! I started moving again. Slowing only when I realized I no longer saw her. Where did she go? I made it to the tree she had been behind but there was nothing. I turned in a circle. Nothing. Dammit. I'm seeing things. Again. Shit. I should have known. Why would she be here? Where had I seen her before? I made her up in my mind. That's why she seemed so familiar. I turned and started walking back towards the path, trying to ignore the cold and the soreness that flowed through my bones as I had rushed down into the wet land. I climbed a rock and jumped onto where path should be. Wait.

Where was the path? This is where it was. I was sure of it. I turned again. Twice. But the path was gone.

CHAPTER THIRTY-TWO

THE STUMBLE

I LOOKED UP at the trees. So tall. They stretched towards the blue sky. I continued to stay silent, waiting for the rustle. There it was. I could hear it in the distance, sneaking up on me. Closer and closer until the long branches above me caught the breeze and moved in the wind, rocking back and forth like the would just topple over if they kept going. They stopped moving and the rustle stopped. I waited for it to come again, trying unsuccessfully to stay warm against the cold wind. What else did I have to do in these dammed woods? I spent days chasing a figment of my imagination, lost to the world. I ate everything I had, drank everything I had, couldn't even fucking sleep anymore. Had no desire to walk again at all, not even to chase an orange dress that didn't exist. I knew it was a thing that my mind invented to torture me and make me run around getting more lost. But every moment that I saw it, I forgot that. I ran. Every fucking time. My body ached and I sat in the folding chair that I accidently stole from the young group of hikers. It had been tied to my pack. I wondered if they were curious what had ever happened to me. Had they turned back to look for me? I had never heard a voice calling out for "J," so I assumed not. I could hear the wind coming towards me again and ignored the pains in my stomach to watch the trees shake above me. Hoping that one of them might fall on top of me and end this shit. Soon enough I would be a dead man, still sitting here in this chair. Found years from now by some adventurous hiker that wondered off the trail. My dry lips cracked as I smiled at the thought of his face as he stumbled on a corpse in a discount jacket. There was a noise to my left and I slowly rotated my head to see her standing there, watching me, willing me to jump up and chase after her again. I shrugged in her direction and turned my head back towards the canopy of trees, waiting for another gust of wind. Screw her.

I slept without moving from my chair. Through another night filled with the stars that lived above me. Sometimes I could see them. I had tried to set up the tent at first but gave up quickly. I couldn't remember how the pieces fit together and my hands were numb. There was never a good spot to set it up anyways. The trees continued to sway without falling and they would block one star and then another. When I slept, she was in my dream. I could never be sure it was the same woman. During the days she ran from me in the trees. At night she ran from me in the warm grass. Every night was the same thing. Every day was too. Accompanied only by a memory. I was young and would get confused at school when my mother would show up in the middle of class and watch me through the open door. A year after she died. A memory I had forgotten. Until now. She would stand as I cried and screamed, and teachers would tell me that it wasn't true. That she was a figment of my imagination. A coping mechanism. But I knew what I saw. I knew she was there. Just like the woman in orange is here with me now.

This time when I slept and saw her peeking through the grass, I didn't chase her. Just like the waking day before. Or maybe this is when I'm awake and the trees are when I'm asleep. I shook my head at her. Refusing to run towards her anymore. The soreness and exhaustion and starvation had carried over from one dream to the next and I stood there staring at her as she stared back at me. She is the same. I think. Or is she me? I blinked and when my eyes opened, she was no longer standing there. I blinked again. Still nothing. I turned in a circle. Nothing. I sank to the soft warm ground too tired to cry. But I wanted to. I closed my eyes and tried to make the tears come. To release the pain that lived within me. The physical and the mental. I thought of the hospital and the hanging feet and the eyes changing green to brown to blue to grey. I thought of my wedding day where I was smiling and laughing. A sound came from behind me, but I couldn't find the energy to open my eyes and turn towards the noise. Warm breath hit my ear as soft words whispered, "It's not your time either. Wake up. Get up. Now."

MY EYES OPENED to the sun rising above the fog. I could hear crows shouting at me from a distance. Each call piercing through the pain in my head. I shielded my eyes from the backlit fog and tried to ignore the staggering agony that raced through my body as I tried to push up from the chair. My right arm pressed harder against the flimsy arm rest and the chair toppled over, taking me with it. I hit the moss-covered ground hard, and everything screamed. No sound came from me though, the shout stayed lazily silent within my throat. I rolled onto my back and watched the fog drifting around the trees, sending them swaying in the wind. The back of my pants was wet; I think I pissed myself in the night. I pushed into a sitting position wondering if I would ever have the energy to stand up or if I should just give into my own body and lay back down and let the moss grow over my dying body. It would be easy to do that. That's what I'm gonna do. I started to recline back into the padded ground, waiting for it to engulf me like a comforter. The coldness started to disappear from my bones even though I continued to shake uncontrollably. A hand appeared in front of my open eyes, replacing the view of increasingly blurry trees.

I know that hand. I stopped leaning back. It was large and worn. I looked past the hand as the face started to come into focus and saw the open grin hiding behind the large beard. I clasped the hand and let him pull me to my feet, feeling his strength in his pull.

"Hey thanks Phil."

Wait I didn't say that out loud. That was just in my head. Did he hear me? He nodded. Ok this could work. Less energy spent talking. Damn, I always knew he was special.

What are you doing out here? I asked with my thoughts.

He picked up my bag and answered using his voice, "I knew you could use some company, J." I nodded. He swung my pack around so that it rested easily on his back and we both looked at the broken chair.

I shrugged, *Leave it?*

"Yeah. Let's leave that. You shouldn't need it anyway and this pack already feels like a ton of rocks." He grinned at me and held out his arm to support me as we walked. I leaned into him and watched my feet as we started making our way through the rocks. The cold loosening her grip.

So really, Phil. How did you find me?

"I've been following you. Figured you didn't really need my help until now. You couldn't just stay on the ground like that. You would have died."

Maybe it's my time to die.

"That's bullshit and you know it."

Maybe.

"Are you still having those dreams?"

I think so. They've changed but they are still there. You?

"Almost every night. You're in most of them now though"

Well, I'm glad you think about me so much I've moved into your subconscious.

He laughed. The sound was familiar and heavenly. He smelled like hamburgers, and I tried to not let him hear that unintended thought of food. "I'm sorry brother. I don't have any food for you. We've just got to keep going and then we can get a big juicy burger and a coke. Ok?" I nodded.

How's everything going at the farm?

"Going great. We had a new calf a few weeks back and she's doing amazing. The crops were good this year too."

That's great. I'm happy to hear it.

"I got a new truck too. Nice one. I'll take you around in it when we get back to the road."

How far are we from the road?

"I can't tell you for sure. You wondered pretty far off track."

I saw a woman. I followed her. I'm sure she wanted me to, but I don't know if she was real.

"Most women aren't real." He laughed and I looked up from my feet for a moment so that I could see his large grin.

A welcome site. Looking beyond him into the trees. I could see her again, watching us as we walked. Phil followed my gaze into the trees, but I knew he wouldn't see her, so I looked back down to concentrate on my steps. Fearing I would slip at any moment. My legs felt heavy, and every step took an extraordinary amount of effort to lift the foot and place it back down. I hoped the road wasn't too far away.

There was a shift in the man next to me and I glanced over to see that he was no longer holding me up. Instead, there was a smaller woman wearing grey hiking pants under a fleece jacket. Her grey hair was pulled into a braid at the top of her head, and it tumbled down her back, to sit on top of my hiking pack that she carried. I started to fall back away from her in horror and she braced her feet and held onto my arm, refusing to let me fall.

"Careful there now. If you fall, I probably can't lift you back up." I stood back up letting her weight steady me.

Who are you? Oh wait. She couldn't read my mind like Phil.

She answered, "You don't remember?" I looked at her face, tracing the laugh lines with my eyes and she smiled at me, the smile not reaching her sad eyes.

I know you.

"Well, I would hope so. I had thought we shared a profound moment... but maybe that was just me." I felt guilty not remembering her like she seemed to remember me. Then

I saw her smile and realized that she was teasing me. The realization hit me quickly and the recognition clicked into place.

How are you doing?

"Still lonely. How are you?"

Still lonely too. Have you made it out of your house recently?

"Yeah. I got a job. It's in a small garden at a town close to me. Sweet lady runs it, and we spend all day planting and talking. Not about death. But about growth." We had started walking again. She carried my pack and my arm around her small shoulders.

Good. That's really good. Still hiking?

"Not so much. I went out once recently and met a nice man on a rock. But that's about all I've had time for. I see you've been hiking more."

I laughed, *if you can call getting lost in the woods and dying 'hiking' then yes.* The laugh sounded strange. A solo sound in the quiet rustle of the trees around us.

"So, how's that jacket treating you, dude?" I looked over to see a young man with a stocking cap and a jacket that both spouted the same sporting store logo. His long hair was pushed to the side under his cap so that his brown eyes could see me and the wilderness around us.

Travis, right? He nodded. *I love this jacket. It's the perfect thing to die in.*

He looked shocked for just a moment before grinning. "Nah, dude. This isn't going to be what you die in. That's a long way out." He looked around us as we kept walking, "Man this place sure is freaking gorgeous."

I nodded; *it really is.* My foot caught on a rock, and I almost stumbled to the ground, Travis catching me before I hit.

"Watch it dude. You don't want to face plant out here. I don't think I could carry you all the way back to the road."

Do you know where the road is?

"Nah. I know you've just left your path. Time to find it again, right?"

Yeah man. Time to find it. Hey, you know that bike you sold me?

"Oh man, I forgot about that. I told you it was a decent bike, right?"

It was. I was sad to lose it. But it got me pretty far. Thank you.

"Glad to hear it."

I need a break, Travis. I need to sit for a moment.

"Five minutes. That's all I can give you, dude. Then you have to keep going." I nodded and he helped me down to the ground on a rock made seat that was barely protruding in the path we made.

Thanks Travis.

He licked my face in response. Big brown eyes were shining out of a sweet brown face. I wrapped my arms around the warm wriggling body. Dog. My friend. He licked my face until it was clean and then he climbed into my lap. I held him and pushed my face into his fur, breathing in the warm dog smell that I missed. I slowed my breathing until it matched his and closed my eyes. Letting my body rest against his. I heard a noise in front of me and opened my eyes to see her. Still watching me from the woods.

The words came as a yell, *what do you want?!* She stepped behind a tree. Dog jumped from my lap and ran towards where she had disappeared. *Dog!* He ran behind a tree and was gone. *Dog?*

Replaced by a lanky young black man wearing a collegiate sweatshirt. I watched as he walked towards me. The fear I had last seen in his eyes was replaced by a kindness. He reached me and extended his hand. After he lifted me to my feet, he picked up the pack that was sitting next to me and slung it on his back.

"Come on man" We started walking. "So, I watched all of the Indiana Jones movies. You were right. They were pretty badass."

Told you.

"Yeah yeah."

Have you started school?

"Yeah. It's been great. I've got a job and it pays pretty well. My classes are harder than I was expecting but they're alright."

That's great. I'm glad to hear it.

"I met a girl too. She's perfect." I looked up and could almost see a blush to his cheeks.

Good. Be good to her.

"I will." I looked back down at my feet.

Listen. I'm sorry that I left you guys like that. I tried to find you…

He waved me off, "Nah man. Don't worry about it. It wasn't your fault." I kept watching my feet move over the ground. One foot then the other.

But really, I shouldn't have left.

"It was your time to leave Phil. You were on a journey." I looked over at Karen, her hair swept up under one of her colorful scarves.

Hey Karen. You know my name isn't really Phil, don't you?

"I always knew what your name really was. But it's not my place to share a man's name. That's your decision. For when you are ready."

I nodded. *How's everyone doing?*

"Good. But I'm not here to talk about them. What are you doing out here?"

My feet kept moving over the rocks and tree branches. *If I knew maybe I wouldn't be here.*

"Nah, I think you would still be here. But why are you here?"

I have no idea. I don't even know where I am.

"Not where. Why? Why are you here trying to die? You're smarter than this. This is off your path."

Please Karen. What is my path? You seem to know it. Tell me.

I could feel her shake her head, "Only you know what it is. I can't tell you that."

Dammit Karen. All of this is my fault. All of it. The fact that I'm dying in these woods. The fact that I left my life. That everyone since has left me. Or did I leave them? I don't know. I think everyone has always left me. It's my fault.

"It's not your fault, son. I know I told you it was. I blamed you. But you and I are the same man. It was me that I blamed. That's why I left you. It wasn't your fault." I lifted my head and saw my pack and my body being carried by him. The man that abandoned me. The man that towered over me when I was too small to defend myself. The man that loved and hated my mother so much that he could barely contain it. I felt the hatred boil up within me, but I was as defenseless now in my starvation as I had been as a child.

Fuck you.

"You have every right to hate me. I was troubled and I couldn't control what I said. What I did. There is no excuse."

Fuck you.

"Listen to me. Please son." I continued to let him help me only because I had no other choice.

Fuck. You.

"Please. You and I are the same. I see it in you as I watch you. You have the same affliction that I did. You need to stop blaming everything... everyone else for the darkness within you. For what has happened to you."

Likc you did?

"No. that is what I'm trying to tell you. I did it wrong. I did it so wrong. I don't think your mother ever knew the pull she had on me and when I was angry it was because I missed her so much. She lied to me about being sick. I couldn't have saved her. I know that now. But I didn't then. I blamed you but it wasn't your fault. Please forgive me. Forgive yourself."

That's a good one.

"Don't you remember anything good about me?" I closed my eyes and saw his feet swinging above the ground. The image replaced by his laughter as he danced me around the room. Replaced again by the lighting bugs and then the morning after. Pulling me out of the hospital room as the machines announced death.

It doesn't matter.

"It does matter. Remember those moments. Think of the good. Don't go out like me. You need to live. This isn't your time. Here." He motioned at a fallen tree. "Let's sit a moment so you can rest and then we'll keep moving." I let him help me to the ground and closed my eyes so that I didn't have to see him there, watching me. I heard a noise and peeked out, eyes widening when I saw two piercing blue eyes looking back at me. Inches from my face. Stark white hair covered his head, and he didn't say a word as he leaned closer so that our foreheads kissed. The eyes never left mine and I could see the reflection of my own green eyes in his light blue ones. I blinked and he was gone. Standing there, further from me was a young girl. She saw me looking at her and giggled, waving her little hand at me. I watched as she started skipping around in a circle, sending up clouds of dirt from the ground.

Be careful. The rocks are slick.

She giggled and stooped down to look at something in the dirt. When she stood, her fist was clutched around something, and she walked over to me with her hand held out. I could see a small round grey rock in it. Smoothed by years of natural weather rubbing the edges down. My hand instinctively reached into my pocket for my own matching rock. It wasn't there. It must have fallen out of my pocket. I looked back at the rock that now sat in a wrinkled hand and I grabbed it. My rock. I rubbed it twice and stuck it back into my pocket where it belonged before looking at the hand that gave it to me.

It was still extended waiting for me to grab it and get back to my feet. I let him pull me up and once my pack was fully on his back, we started walking.

"We are almost there, Jay. Almost there. Have you decided?"

What are you talking about?

"You'll have to make your decision. Soon. Have you read the book I gave you?"

Which one?

"You know which one"

I did. *No. Not yet. She's still there, in my pack.*

"That's unfortunate. The other two I gave you were for entertainment only. That was the one you needed to read."

I'll read it. I promise. What decision am I'm making? Can you give me a clue? The librarian shrugged his shoulders under my arm.

Well hopefully I make the right one then

"You will my beautiful boy. You know the right decision to make." Her voice was soft and lyrical. I didn't look up. Scared that she wouldn't disappear as soon as I saw her. We didn't say more words. We didn't need to. She hummed to me as we kept moving forward, my left finger coming up and tracing the lines the freckles made on her arm as she supported me. I watched my feet moving, one after another.

And then I saw one step onto pavement. I looked up and was shocked to see a small path. To the left it inclined into the trees. The right led to some steps and was clear of trees. I was standing alone. My pack on my back and feeling like it weighed more than the world. I was weak with nothing to lean against, but I was close and could keep moving forward. I walked towards the right and towards the stairs that must lead to a road. My vision was blurred, and I was scared to lose my footing, so I kept my eyes down, focused on my right foot and then my left foot. Down the stairs. Down more stairs. Man, I must have been high up in that mountain. I could hear the wind and another noise I couldn't recognize beyond my focus on my feet. How many steps. There was a railing and I leaned on it, continuing to work my way down.

MY FOOT DIDN'T hit a road. It hit a rock. What is this? I took another step, seeing that the other large rocks that were shining with bright green moss. This couldn't be safe. I stepped over one of the rocks and my foot landed in a puddle of water. I looked forward. The sun was shining so brightly, and my vision was foggy, but I could see more rocks in front of me, jutting out of the ground. There was no path. No road. I had made it onto a cliff. The ocean shined beyond my viewpoint, and I sank to sit on a wet rock. Leaving my foot sitting in the water, barely registering that it was cold. I didn't make it anywhere. There was no road. I was going to die here. There was no way I could make it back up those steps and to the path. Why didn't I go up? I should have gone up. I sat and closed my eyes, images flashing behind them. The pain quickly shifting to acceptance that my life would end on this cliff. At least it would end with a beautiful view of the ocean.

I opened my eyes again to squint against the sun, hoping for a final beautiful view to burn into my mind as I drifted away. There she was. She was standing at the edge of the cliff. Above the water. The spray from the waves hitting the side but not fazing her. Even in this cold day. Her brown curls blew around her face as she watched me, and her orange dress flowed around her like a cape. I pushed myself up so that I was standing and could see her more clearly. She turned away from me and towards the water.

And she jumped into the violent ocean beneath her.

NO.

I didn't realize I was running or that I could even run in my weakened state. She was gone but I ran towards where she had just been a second ago. I hit my arms and my legs against the rocks as I lunged over them, sliding on the moss. My pack smacked against my back and knocked me forward and back as I awkwardly moved towards the edge. I made it almost to the spot where she had jumped, and the green moss gave way. My foot slipped. I fell to my back and slid down towards the edge of the cliff. It was as if I were in slow motion as I fell, seeing the waves coming towards me prepared to throw my body against the cliff.

I couldn't see a sign of her orange dress beneath me as I fell, but I knew she was gone. My descent was violently stopped as pain shot through my shoulders and my side hit the rock. A grunt came from my mouth as I stopped moving and looked up to see a strap of my pack caught against the rock above me, holding me from my instant death. I could easily lift my arms and fall from its embrace, into the water below. I looked down and saw a wave smash just below me with a clap that sounded like thunder. Could I lift just one arm and grab the pack before my arm slipped out of the constraint? Could I lift both arms and slip into the waves below and join the woman in the orange dress? It would be easy. It would be quick. *It's not my time.* I don't want to die. I'm not ready. Or maybe I am ready?

For the first time in days a voice came from my throat as I yelled, barely carrying over the thunder below me, "NOOOOOOOO!"

CHAPTER THIRTY-THREE

THE TOWN

A HEAD EMERGED above my hanging pack. "Dad?" I whispered. It got closer and there was a tug where the pack held me from falling. The man came into focus, and I realize I didn't recognize him. It was a painful process as he was joined by another stranger, and they pulled me up towards safety. We laid on the rocks looking up at the sky. Seagulls flew over our heads as the cloudless sky sparkled blue.

"You sure are lucky." I shook my head against the rocks. Playing dumb seemed like the only optional answer. "Well, as soon as we saw you fall, my wife ran up to find a phone. Are you hurt?" I didn't know. I felt pain all over my body and my vision kept changing from blurry to clear. "Ok man. We will wait with you here until someone comes. Was anyone with you?" I shook my head again. Should I tell them about the woman that jumped? Did she jump? I opened my mouth, but nothing came out but a croak. "Need some water?" I nodded and realized that the second man was still, helping me sit and working to prop me against a rock. The first man pulled a bottle from his small pack, a tiny version of the one that had saved my life. I took a large swallow from the bottle and immediately threw it up on myself. I could see the two men sharing a look as I tried another smaller drink of water, and I didn't care what their look meant. This time the water stayed down, and my throat started to clear.

The voice was rough and foreign as it left my mouth, "Did you see me fall?" Both men nodded so I continued. "Did you see a woman jump?"

They shared a look again and the first man spoke, "No. Were you with someone? Did someone else fall?" He looked over his shoulder.

The second man spoke, "I was right down here. I didn't see anyone else. Just you."

I shook my head, "There was no one. Just me." I knew it was the truth as I said it.

Soon I was surrounded by new strangers in red jackets. The original saviors were gone, headed about their own lives. The new strangers talked amongst themselves as they checked my body up and down before making sure it was safe to get me up those steps. It was an awkward and long process of being straddled between two men as they carried me. I should have gone up the path. If I would have gone up, I would have found a parking lot and then a road. There was a hut with snacks and coffee in the parking lot. Did I still have money? I think I did but I didn't know where it might be in my pack. Where was my pack? The strangers had it. They sat me in a warm seat in a large ambulance and asked me questions I couldn't answer even if I wanted to. *How long had I been out here? Where was I going? What was my name? When had I last eaten?*

I looked down at the soup that was in my hands and was confused. Where had that come from? I lifted the spoon to my mouth. Even in my starvation, this soup tasted like shit. I noticed a tube poking through a vein in my arm. How did that get there? *Where are you from? Do you have any identification? Were you hiking with anyone?* I could hear them talking as one of them said, "I wonder if this is the man those kids had reported as missing." Another nodded. Am I that man? What kids would have reported me as missing? Someone took the soup out of my hands before it fell and I laid back, the darkness coming in around me.

MY EYES OPENED to the sunlight peeking through the tiny mesh window of my tent. I didn't want to get up. I could tell from the dampness inside the tent walls that it was cold out there today. Maybe that was it. The sign I was waiting for that it was time to leave. I felt something poking my side from within the sleeping bag and grasped the hard paper rectangle shape to pull it out just far enough so that I could make out the back cover. I still hadn't read more than a page of the book, even with my previous promise. But I fell asleep watching her face and paying attention to the sentence that said where she lived. Eloise. I was procrastinating and I knew that it was time to stop. I knew where I was headed. But to stop procrastinating, I had to first get out of bed. I moaned as I sat up, my head hitting the top of my tiny tent and sending a stream of tiny freezing droplets onto my pack and head, one running down my neck. Dammit. I pushed the book down into my pack and grabbed a granola bar and bottle of water. I should eat before I entered the cold morning. Starvation still fresh in my mind. I ate quickly and pulled on my jacket awkwardly before crawling out of the sleeping bag and the tent. I stood and stretched in the empty patch of grass that held campers in the summer and fall. The grass crunched under my feet as I walked around my little site and packed up my tiny tent. I didn't push it down into my pack with my duffel this morning, since the outside was still wet. Instead, I held it in my gloved hand as I worked my way down the silent gravel road towards the check-in booth. My breath showing in bright white clouds before fading into the sky.

I pulled open the door on the side of the booth and was hit with a wall of warm air. Thankful that Rick was in today. He blasted the small floor heaters as soon as he made it in each morning. I knew he would be sitting in the small chair in the corner, his laptop open on his lap as he watched for storms and visitors that were scheduled today. As each day, he sat in shorts and a t-shirt, even with the cold air outside. I had a sneaking suspicion that he turned the heat up so high for me, not for him. I took off my stocking cap and replaced it with a cap that matched his. A green hat with the park logo on the front of it and the words "volunteer" stitched into the back. I nodded at him and motioned towards the small file cabinet that had a coffee pot and paper cups sitting on top of it. I poured myself a cup of the coffee that he made too strong, even for me, and breathed in the familiar smell. Then I propped on the stool next to the glass closed window and swiveled back to look at him. "So, what's the plan today boss?"

He looked up from his laptop, "We only have two check-ins. Coming in early for the festival. Both are in cabins so we'll have to make sure those are good to go. Let's get the path to the water cleaned up too. Should be a quick job though since you cleared it last weekend. If we have time, let's clean up the other cabins too. We'll have a lot of check-ins tomorrow and Friday. I think those are booked solid, even a few camp spots." I nodded, taking it all in.

"Which cabins?"

"A14 and A16. Finish your coffee first, and get back here for lunch. I've got enough left-over Chinese food to feed an army." We had a small fridge and a microwave; both were used on almost a daily basis with Rick's leftovers. I couldn't imagine a man would naturally order so much food each night just to have three more meals worth left over each day. But he did. After my accident, it had been unspoken and decided by a handful of people in this small town to watch out for me. They had tried to coax a response out of me on who I was or where I came from and finally gave up, allowing me to continue to live amongst them as a victim of something they would never know.

They were polite but kept their distance. I don't know what ever happened to my hospital bills. I didn't ask. I worked here, I slept here. I made a little cash by helping Rick out and got free lunch, usually that carried into dinner, each night and coffee each morning. I took a hot shower each night before bed and the visions were gone. I didn't see the woman in the orange dress or anyone else from my past, ghost or breathing. I had stopped dreaming completely, maybe from the exhaustion each day. Maybe not. I still spent fifteen minutes each night chatting with my spider friend who lived in the shower stall. Doing my best to keep him alive even during cleaning times. Sometimes he chatted back. And I fell asleep each night looking at the photo on the back of my unread book and reading the name of the town. The flashlight that I had taken from the box of forgotten camping supplies, lighting up her black and white face.

I FINISHED MY coffee and grabbed the cabin keys before pulling a green windbreaker over my own orange jacket and making my way back into the cold day. There was no wind in the morning, just cold stillness. The path was quiet, and I could see a squirrel running to the trees. Something large was hanging from his mouth. Prepping for the winter that was sure to come any day. I found the right cabin and took the steps two at a time before unlocking the door. I think this one had been habited just a week before. It was shocking how quickly things reverted to normal here. I turned the heater on to start warming the cold inside but left the door open so that I could sweep the dust out. There were cobwebs already made into homes but none of them were built for my spider. I still captured the ones I could and put them outside before wrecking their homes with my broom that had been hanging on a hook at the wall. Sweep the walls, make sure there's nothing sticky or dirty lying around, sweep the floors and push all the dirt back out into the wilderness around the cabin. I turned the heat down a bit but left it on so the inhabitants would walk into something warmer than the outdoors after checking in. The door pulled closed, and I locked it behind me. Onto the next cabin and I followed each step as I had in the first. This time I sat in front of the heater for a few extra minutes to warm up before heading back outside towards the shed that kept supplies. I grabbed a few things before turning towards the path that led to the beach from the campground.

The path reminded me of the one I had hiked on once. I shook the image from my mind and started pulling a few wild weeds. I brushed the cobwebs from the path and appreciated the fact that I had done the heavy lifting on clearing this a few days before when the day was warmer. I made it all the way to where the path met a small, paved walkway and followed it. I had time before lunch. I walked under a large stone bridge and pushed myself up onto the ledge that held the road apart from the rock beneath it. The wind blew harder out here, and I could feel it sting my cheeks and my nose as I watched the grey waves hit against the sand in front of me. Clouds were drifting in, and I assumed the cold air would turn the rain to snow before the day was over. I watched the water, mesmerized by the churning nature of it. I had a new respect for it since the day it had tried to kill me. The day I had wanted to let it.

My stomach growled and I jumped from my spot and worked my way back down the path towards the heated building with Chinese food waiting for me. There was a small suburban parked in front of it and I could see a young man at the open window. Our first of two check-ins for the day. He was early but with the limited demand, we would be fine. I saw Rick behind the window as he looked at me, the question of the clean cabin clearly on his stubble covered face. I gave him thumbs up and he smiled before handing the man the keys to his cabin. I put the path supplies back in the shed before stepping into the check-in office and hearing the microwave already heating up our left-over lunch.

My mouth watered at the smell of the food, and I could barely let it cool before piling rice and overheated chicken into my mouth. I opened my lips wide and tried to breath in some air to cool it while Rick laughed. We talked about the upcoming festival and the storms coming in as we ate. He asked if I would finally let him buy me a beer tonight and I shook my head, like every other time he asked. He asked if I wanted to sleep one night in one of the cabins instead of my tiny shitty tent. Again, I shook my head. We ate until we could eat no more food and there was still half of a container left of chicken and broth. He put the lid back on and stuck it back in the fridge reminding me to eat it before I left so that there was room in the fridge tomorrow. I went back into the cold and completed cleaning out the other cabins before taking a hot shower. I knew Rick would be gone once I got out and that was good. That was what I wanted. I went back to the check in building and unlocked the door. Noticing the heaters were all turned off and the lights were out. I heated up the rest of the Chinese food and ate that thinking about the path that would get me to a train. I knew where to go now but I wondered if any of the trains that were currently stopped would be running again before anyone in this town realized I was gone. I should leave a note. What would I say? I had left so many notes by now. I threw the plastic container in the trash and pulled my duffel from my pack. I kept everything that I had collected but left the tent and the now empty pack in the large wood box that held the other forgotten and donated supplies. I grabbed a notepad and a pen and sat on the swivel stool staring at the paper. Outside it was started to get dark. I needed to hurry. I stared at the white paper. And scribbled.

I'm out. Thanks.

That should do it. I'm really done with long notes. I stood and pulled my stocking cap over my head before slinging my duffel bag over my shoulder and pulling the locked door closed behind me.

I SAT ON the train as it sped through the morning. Two pairs of pants on my legs, two pairs of socks under my shoes, three shirts under my jacket, and wrapped up in my sleeping bag. Fucking winter. The freezing wind whipped in through the open door and I sat on the opposite side so I could see wilderness fly by without having to be in the direct path of the breeze as we sped east towards my destination. I knew where I was going without quite knowing how I was going to get there. The train was the first step. Get to a town and then I could hitchhike from there. My car was lonely, and I had nothing to keep me busy, especially as my hands hid within the sleeping bag trying to stay warm. I shivered. And closed my eyes. Maybe if I could sleep, I could warm up, and the ride would go faster. There were no dreams while I slept. No images or visions of friends, real or not, dead or alive. I was alone and slept like the dead. The rocking of the cold train car lulling my mind into the darkness.

The train had stopped. Shit. I tried to jump up and found myself falling onto my side, still wrapped in my sleeping bag. I pulled myself from it, coming out like an ungraceful butterfly emerging from its cocoon. What an ugly butterfly I would make. I rolled the bag up into my arms and slung my duffel bag over my shoulder. It was lucky no one had found me yet. I walked towards the door and was smacked in the face with the blast of cold air from the outside. I peeked around the door. We weren't stopped at a train yard. We were just stopped next to a field of brown grass, dead in the winter. I couldn't see anyone walking around and I slid from the train car and knelt by it, keeping an eye out as I pushed my sleeping bag down into my duffel and zipped it shut. I jumped to my feet as the train horn blasted and started slowly picking up speed. I took a step back and the grass crunched beneath my feet as I watched the train move away from me and continue its solo trek east. The last car sped past, and I saw what had been hiding behind it. What I hoped would be hiding behind it. There was a small town sitting in the middle of this dead cold field. It looked almost identical to one I had been in before, but I couldn't quite remember when. I adjusted my bag and walked towards it, hoping beyond hope that there would be an open restaurant.

I walked through the street that housed rows of shops. All closed. The sky was already darkening above me. I must have been asleep for hours on that damn train. There was a small park and two benches. Where were all the people? I laughed at my own stupidity. They were all home staying warm in this cold winter night. Of course. Where I should be. I pulled my sleeping bag out and wrapped it around me before sitting on one of the benches. I pulled a package of orange peanut butter crackers from my bag, too cold to even see what I had left tucked away with my cash. In the morning I could figure out how much money I had left and how much farther I had to go. I didn't know what I would do when I finally made it to the town from the back cover of that book but that was a worry for the future. I just knew that was where I was heading. I lay down on the bench and pulled the sleeping bag up so that it covered my face from the cold wind. And I slept. Another dreamless dark sleep as I shivered through the night.

SOMETHING WAS MAKING a tapping noise. I pulled the cloth from my face so that only my eyes were exposed to the frigid air and looked for the source of the sound. Sitting at the end of my bench was a bright red bird. Tapping away at the armrest. My private little morning alarm clock. I moved slowly, wanting to sit but not wanting to scare the bird. He stopped tapping and tilted his head to watch me as I yawned a puff of white into the air around me. The sun was rising, and the sky was orange in the morning light. The bird continued his tap tap tap and I watched him as I slowly unraveled from my blanket and grabbed for another bar or cracker pack in my bag. My hand felt nothing. Shit.

I knew I was close to being out. I felt each corner of the bag but found nothing that felt like food wrapped in plastic. I should have bought more before I left. I apologized to the impatient red bird that I had no food to share with him and as if he understood me, he spread his wings and flew off to find another friend. I packed up my stuff and went in search of breakfast. It must be early, I realized as I walked by shops and restaurants all still closed to the morning light. My stomach growled painfully, and I smelled something delicious. I couldn't find the source. Nothing was open. I kept walking towards the smell, using my nose to figure out where it was coming from, and I turned a corner to see it. A dumpster. Shit. The smell was overpowering. It smelled like someone had baked a pie and made bacon all at the same time, and then threw it away into this dumpster. The heat of the freshly made food made even stronger by the cold air. I lifted the lid and couldn't see anything that even remotely looked like food, but the smell became stronger as I leaned my head inside. Well, what could it hurt? If there was nothing in there, I would just have to wait until one of the shops or restaurants opened.

But if there was and it tasted anything like it smelled, it may be the best meal of my life. I dropped my bag to the ground and pulled my body into the dumpster. Nothing in the first bag. Or the second. I started reaching for the third back and heard a slight cough above me. I turned my head slowly towards the figure standing there, peering at me in this dumpster. The snow had started to fall just this moment and thick, soft flakes were falling around her. I could see nothing but green eyes shining from under her hood and over the orange scarf that wrapped around her face, protecting her from the cold. She mumbled something that I couldn't understand.

"I can't hear you."

The eyes smiled and she lifted her hands to the scarf that covered her face. As she pushed the orange fabric down to uncover her mouth, I could see the freckles displayed prominently on her small nose.

"I said, is there something I can help you with?" I shook my head slowly frozen in recognition. She looked at me with a question on her face before she said it out loud, "I'm sorry, have we met?" I stared back at her, knowing her without knowing her.

"Eloise?"

CHAPTER THIRTY-FOUR

THE FUNERAL

SHE WAS REAL. I stared at her laughing in the booth across from me. The laugh I knew and that of a stranger all at the same time. How could she be sitting here laughing when I was sure that she was a figment of my imagination? She was wearing an oversized orange sweater, pushed up so that the sleeves didn't fall into her plate. I tried not to stare at the brown hair that fell around her shoulders. She wasn't as young as I had thought she was when I first saw her. But the way her face lit up when she spoke, and the summer freckles still sprawled across her nose, both gave her a youthful air that made her seem almost like a child. I hadn't told her how I knew her name and she hadn't asked. Instead, we came to this diner that looked like almost every diner I had sat in before. A plump waitress knew her by name and only gave me a funny look, knowing damn well I didn't belong here with this happy woman who sat across from me. I tried to ignore the small silver band that sat on her left ring finger and announced the world that she already belonged to another. I looked at the biggest freckle on her nose and followed it up into her bright green eyes. She was looking at me, questioning. Shit. What had she said? I nodded, embarrassed to admit that I hadn't been listening.

She laughed again, "really? You really like liver and onions? I've never met another soul alive who likes that."

Oh, that's what she asked me. "Uh, yeah. Sure." She laughed again at a joke I didn't make.

"So, J was it?" I nodded and she squeezed her eyes at me, obviously not believing me, "Yeah ok. So, J, are you sure we haven't met before?" I shook my head again. "I'm going to ask it," She pointed her little finger at me and leaned closer as if she could see right into my soul, "How did you know my name was Eloise?"

Shit. I knew this was going to come. I looked down at my own hands that were wrapped around a coffee mug. The coffee inside it had cooled while I watched her laugh and tell me stories about her life. I took a sip. Man, this coffee tasted even worse when it was cold. I must have made a face. She laughed, "Yeah, the coffee isn't the tastiest here but it's still the best place in town. You should try their burgers." I looked up to see that she that her question still hung between us, so bright that I could almost read it in the sky like smoke above her head *How did you know my name was Eloise?*

"To be completely honest, I've never met you. But I think I know you," I looked back down at my shitty coffee, "I don't know why or how but I feel like you've been in my thoughts before. Sitting there, wearing an orange dress and talking to me. And when I saw your face, I just knew your name. I know this doesn't make any sense. I know this is beyond creepy. I just don't know how else to explain it." I stopped talking and waited for her response. None came. I watched the film on the top of my coffee swirl in a circle. Still no response. I looked up at her and expected to see a look of disgust or terror sitting across her pretty face. There was only shock. "Listen…" I started but she put her hand up to stop me before I could continue. I waited for her to tell me to fuck off and leave her alone.

"I used to have an orange dress. It was my favorite thing. It was the dress I wore when I met my husband." It was her turn to look down at her hands, spinning her ring with the finger and thumb of her opposite hand, "Not that he would remember now." She looked up at me, "Orange is my favorite color. I tend to wear it almost every day." Like that explained anything that I just said. I didn't know how to respond.

"Why would your husband not remember your dress?"

She looked back up at me. Ok. Wrong question. But she started talking. The laughter was gone from her face, and I stayed quiet. Making sure to listen to each detail as she explained it. In a soft voice, she told me how they had met when she was just nineteen. He had moved here after college, following a job. They were happy. Laughing all the time. Living their own happy life, just the two of them. Then came the miscarriage. Then another. But they were still happy. Then came... she had stopped talking. I waved over the waitress and asked for a new cup of coffee, trying to give Eloise the time she needed to keep going. She didn't. She flew over a part where I was listening and jumped to telling me about her husband's new job. One that took a decent commute each way and each day. One where he worked long hours into the night as he slowly disappeared from her life, distancing himself mentally as well as physically. I asked her why he would do that, and she just shrugged, her shoulders barely moved under her large sweater. I asked about her job, "Oh, I uh... I don't work much anymore." She looked sad and stopped talking so I let it go and sipped my hot coffee, letting the liquid burn my tongue. She looked back up at me, smiling again. This time the smile didn't quiet reach her eyes and she suddenly looked older. "So, J, how long are you in town for?" Oh yeah. That. We hadn't gotten to that yet.

"I'm just passing through. I'm looking for someone, some place actually. But I just figured I'd stop here for a while." Trying to lighten the mood, "So Eloise," matching her tone, "what is there to do in this town?"

"First, please stop calling me Eloise. I feel like people only do that when they're mad at me. Call me Elle. Secondly, I can't really tell you about much to do. There's this diner and some shops. Just down the street we have rows of houses and the highway past that. There's a Walmart and a shopping mall. And the large industrial park with all the new office buildings is about a thirty-minute drive. We don't really have anything that is different than any other town. But the park is nice if you don't mind the snow." She laughed again.

"Do you mind the snow?"

"Me? I love the snow. There's not enough today but they say we are supposed to get so much tomorrow that we could build a snowman the size of a Buick." Her face lit at the thought.

"We could build it."

She looked at me, trying to figure out if I was being serious in my offer or not. She grinned and her head moved up and down. I moved my head up and down to mirror hers and she stuck her hand towards me. I clasped it and she shook it firmly. Up and down. Twice.

"It's a date then. Tomorrow. Lunch here and a snowman?"

"It's a date."

She looked down at the small watch was clasped on her small wrist. "Shit!" She grabbed her purse and started rummaging through it. "Shit shit shit. I must go. I have an appointment and then promised to meet my husband for dinner after."

I held up my hand, "I've got this." She looked at me in shock, we both knew that she had found me rummaging through a garbage can just a few hours before and she slowly shook her head. "Seriously. I've got the coffee and pie. You can get lunch tomorrow. Deal?" She laughed and nodded and grabbed her coat, sliding out of the booth as she did.

She shot me a smile as she clumsily put on her layers of oversized clothing, "See you tomorrow, J." And she was gone. Out the door, the bell chiming behind me.

"See you tomorrow, Elle." I whispered to only the shadow she left behind.

I WALKED THROUGH the mall, carrying my jacket as I passed the overzealous heaters. A group of kids ran past me, playing tag in the middle of the walkway. It was pretty busy for the afternoon. Maybe it was close to the holidays. The air smelled like coffee and dust. An odd smell to have while you are walking past window fronts filled to the brim with random baubles and trinkets. Mannequins lined the storefronts, poised in ways that didn't look comfortable for a living human being. Each one was maybe half the size of a real person. That's what makes the clothes look good, I guess. I was walking past each window, noticing the items in them with as much interest as I could muster. It was just a place to walk away from the snow that was still falling outside.

Something sparkled and I turned towards the window that it came from, everything went dark around the edges as I focused on this one thing. It hung on the neck of one of the skinny mannequins. A small gold chain that had a scattering of orange flowers. I could picture it now, hanging on the neck of my new friend. Her favorite color was orange. I wondered how much it would cost and if I had enough money in my bag to cover the cost. I could picture me handing it to her tomorrow at lunch, her face lighting up as she opened the box. I would spend all the money I had left for that necklace.

I hesitated, staring at the dyed orange jewels and I missed my opportunity. I saw hands unclasping it and pulling it from the slender plastic neck. My mouth hung open at my close encounter. I had almost had it. I stood for another moment watching the back of the man at the counter as he paid for my necklace and I walked to the door of the shop, not knowing what I would say as he walked past me. Maybe I could buy it from him. Yes. I would offer to buy it from him. I bent down and opened my bag, rummaging for all the cash that I still had in there and started counting it out. I stood cash in hand, as he walked out the door and turned away from me. My mouth opened but nothing came out. I knew him. Didn't I? He seemed so familiar; the clothes, the neatly cut hair, the rotund belly barely showing through his heavy jacket, the way he walked. How did I know him? He seemed like someone I had met before. I stood there, next to the store, cash in hand, as he walked away from me with my necklace safely tucked in the bag that swung from his hand. His gold ring shined brightly on his left hand. Who was he? I couldn't place him, but I couldn't chase him down, what if he knew me and recognized me as the man I was from my life before? Is that where I knew him? Maybe I had worked with him years ago? I shook my head and headed into the store, hoping beyond hope that they had another necklace just like that one. They didn't.

"WHAT ARE YOU doing? You can't sleep here!" Something poked my side. Hard. I sat up and saw that the lights in the windows were out and a security guard stood over me as he kicked my side. Asshole. I stood quickly and ran towards the door to go out into the world. The mall had become full of whispers. I pushed the handle of the door for it to open and was punched in the face with a gust of freezing wind. At least the snow had stopped. I forced my way out into and slowly worked back to the park. Still exhausted and not sure of the time, I wrapped up in the sleeping bag and sat down on the bench, making sure that none of my skin was showing in the cold. Sleep, I told myself. Sleep and tomorrow you'll see her again.

TAP TAP TAP. I felt it on the outside of my sleeping bag and slowly raised my head so that my eyes peaked out from the top. There was my little red bird, poking at me again. The snow had covered me in the night and the sun was blinding. It was cold but the wind had died down. I moved my hand, and the bird lifted his wings and flew to the tree in front of me. Obviously annoyed that I wasn't food. It was too cold to move. I didn't have the energy to go find food but knew that a large juicy burger was coming at lunch, so maybe I would just sit here, bundled against the cold, and wait for noon. I heard a door open to my right and turned so I could glance at the little store front. A man was opening the door to two women dressed in black. As I watched, more people came. All dressed in black. My plan to stay in this spot vanished as I found myself standing and stepping through the snow towards the propped door. I picked up some snow as I walked and scrubbed it on my face to be a little more presentable. The door gave way to the heat blasting from the inside.

There were coats lined along the wall, each hanging from a hook. I hung mine after shaking off my hat and gloves and pushing them into the pockets. I lay my duffel bag down beneath my coat and walked towards the voices. I walked into the large wood room to faces hidden in their own grief. A man shook my hand as I walked in. He asked me how I knew the deceased. I lied and said we knew each other years ago. It seemed to suffice. A few people shot me odd looks, shock registering across their faces as they took in my dirty sweatshirt and my snow-soaked jeans. I didn't care. I sat in the back and watched as more people filtered in, shaking hands or hugging the man who stood up front. He must be the spouse. Or the son. I couldn't see inside the casket from here, but I looked at the photo next to it. I didn't recognize the face, but they looked sad in the photo, like they knew this would be the one used after their death. The man broke down and sat, I could see his head shaking as he sobbed into them. Eventually the service started. Everyone bowed their heads. I followed suit. When I looked up again halfway through the prayer so that I could watch the mourners, I now recognized the photo. She had died too young. I remembered sitting up front as they read poems about my mother and my father sobbed into his hands. My little legs swinging since they didn't quite reach the floor. I looked down at my legs now and could see the floor had faded away and my long legs swung as they had in my memory.

My shoes were shiny and too tight. I looked back up to see if anyone else was confused and could see my father's face in the photo at the front. Now I was alone in my row. Many people cried but not like the funeral before. His photo was somber; just as he was in life. It looked full of pain. It must have been taken after she had died. I looked behind me to see if the man who had greeted people noticed the changing room. His head was still bowed in prayer. I looked back towards the photo and my mouth dropped. All the breath was rushing out of my lungs as I felt dizzy. I was looking at a photo of myself. The room was empty, and the casket was gone, replaced by an urn. What the hell was going on? I could hear a few sniffles and started to stand to yell at the room, I'm not dead. I'm right the fuck here. Flesh and bone. The ground came to meet me, and my feet touched the soft carpet as I started to stand. Something hit me like a punch to the stomach. The casket had returned. The room was filled in with people I knew. People I recognized. From where? I looked at the photo. That wasn't me. That was her. The woman I met yesterday. I shot from my seat and ran past the greeter, still frozen in his moment of prayer. I grabbed my stuff and was putting on my jacket as I pushed back out into the cold. The sun was high in the sky. It had to be close to lunch, right?

THE BELL CHIMED and I looked towards the door, expectantly. It was another stranger. I was through my fourth cup of coffee. I saw the waitress float by, "Excuse me, what time is it?"

She looked down at her watch, "two pm." Well shit. That can't be right.

I've been stood up.

I left a five-dollar bill on the table and gathered my things. She stood me up. I was almost to the door when I decided, with one last hope, to turn to the waitress, "You know that woman I was in here with yesterday?" I saw an expression I had grown to recognize. Full of concern and a hint of fear.

"I didn't work yesterday."

"Yes, you did. You waited on me. Me and a woman in an orange sweater."

She shook her head, "No. I'm sorry. You must have me confused. I had yesterday off."

I reached out and grabbed her arm, "You're fucking with me, right? Why? I was in here yesterday. You waited on me and a woman. Her name was Eloise. You knew her."

Her eyes widened as she stuttered, "Well... Yes... I kn... knew Eloise. But I'm not telling a lie. I wasn't in here yesterday." She turned around her, looking for someone to help. Crap. Why did I grab her arm?

I let go quickly and muttered, "I'm sorry." As I ran out the door. What is going on? She was here yesterday. I was here yesterday. And today she's not here and that waitress must be lying. Or maybe someone that looked like her worked yesterday. I should have asked. There was no going back in there now though. Should I go back? No. I turned down the street. And I turned around again. The white reflection of the sun melting the snow made me feel dizzy. I should walk back towards the mall maybe. I turned. No, the dumpster where I saw her before. I turned again. I stopped and put my head into my hands. What is going on? The white. It's so white. I tried to close my eyes, but it was even brighter behind my eyelids. I tore my hat off. I was sweating even in this cold. Should I go right? No. I should go... Maybe the park. I stepped off the curb, almost falling against the thick snow. Something hit my side and the brightness went away.

DAMMIT. A HOSPITAL again. How many times would I be stuck with these fucking needles? The inside of the room was bright. Orange scattered around trying to make it seem cheerful. The doctor had come and gone, and I should be able to leave any minute. I waited like the dutiful patient for the nurse to come take the thing out of my arm. They hadn't asked for my ID yet. I didn't offer. I was still dressed in the clothes I had been driven here in. The truck had barely bumped me; they were driving so slow in the snow. They think I passed out from the shock. Let's go with that. My legs dangled over the edge of the bed and for a second my sneakers flashed to shiny black dress shoes then back to sneakers. I need to get out of here. Out of this town. Something was… is…The nurse came back in. Friendly enough woman. She pulled the needle out of my arm and gave me a cotton ball to hold on it while she wrapped some tape around my elbow. She smiled and patted my knee. I liked her. She would make someone feel OK when they came into this stark white and burnt orange room. She helped me stand and I assured I didn't need help. I grabbed my duffel bag only barely registering that they still hadn't asked for my identification or insurance information. I followed her to the hallway, prepared to say my goodbye before they realized their mistake. She turned to me, a friendly smile on her face, "Ok then. Are you ready to see Elle?"

The shock must have shown on my face. How could it not? She didn't change her look as she registered my shock. What did I say while I was passed out? What could I say now? I nodded and followed her silently down the hall. She walked to the third door on the left and motioned for me to enter. There she was. The sweet and happy lady. She had tubes running out of her and a machine in the corner that beeped consistently. I walked to her side, the nurse gone, letting me have my privacy. I looked down and clasped her small hand. Her eyes twitched but didn't open and one word came to mind while I looked down at her. Cancer.

She was so thin, and I could see the veins against her paper skin. I had seen it before. In my mother. Why didn't she tell me about it when we spoke yesterday? Why should she, she barely even knew me. How did she look so different today? She had deteriorated so quickly. I glanced around the room to see that she must be loved. There were flowers and stuffed animals and balloons that shouted an extremely inappropriate 'Get Well Soon.' Where was her husband? I could see no sign of him but a blanket and pillow on the couch that sat under the window. He would probably be back soon. Beep. I looked up at the monitor to see the faded spikes that rose and fell, reminding me that she was still alive. At least for now. I had seen this before too. I remember that it does that. Rises and falls. And then it stops rising and just creates a never-ending line. I looked back down at her face, it looked older as she lay there, sleeping or dying... maybe both.

I wanted to see her green eyes sparkle again but if I woke her up how could I ever explain how I had found her? If her husband walked in, how could I ever explain who I was and what I was doing here? There was no explanation to my relationship with her. The way that I knew who she was without ever meeting her. The way that I knew that I had seen her before... maybe in my dreams. I placed her hand back down at her side, making sure to not disturb the needle that was pushed into the back of her hand. I leaned down and brushed my lips against her soft forehead. She smelled sweet. Almost like syrup. I knew she would never hear me as I whispered into her sleeping face, "thank you for finding me." I turned and quickly walked out of the room before anyone would see me and remember that I didn't belong here. I walked through the white hallway, keeping my head down towards the ground, trying not to draw attention. I walked down the stairs towards the door marked exit, pushing into the cold. The snow almost made the day seem innocent. I felt empty and hollow as I walked towards the interstate and stuck my thumb out, waiting for a car to stop. None did so I started walking along the edge of the interstate. I felt like everything that had started to grow within me for the last three years had just died all over again. I was a shell of a dead man who was long gone. Deep breath in. Long sigh out. Right foot forward; followed by the left. I walked away from the town and away from the dying woman that I shouldn't know.

CHAPTER THIRTY-FIVE

THE HELLO

I COULDN'T SLEEP. I lay hidden in the snow next to the small unused road. No cars had stopped to pick me up while I had been on the interstate, and I figured I might have more luck on a side road. But no one stopped to pick me up here either, because no one was driving by. I would try again tomorrow when people weren't trying to get home from work and perhaps more likely to stop for a stranger. Maybe. I listened to the wind blowing through the empty field and the faint hum from a bug. Poor bug. Stuck outside in this unforgiving night just like me.

I closed my eyes and told myself to sleep. Trying to convince my body to warm and relax. Even the top of my head was covered by the fleece lining of the sleeping bag. When I realized I wouldn't fall asleep anytime soon, I opened my eyes again. Not sure why I thought I would see anything but the darkness of my shelter and in that darkness, I saw her. Watching me from a distance; laughing at something I said, chatting with me over coffee; disappearing as she slowly died. Alone in a hospital room. I closed my eyes against the images. But they continued to play in the darkness that lived behind my eyelids. I couldn't escape them. I couldn't escape her.

I tried to think about something else. Anything else. Nothing came. I tried to see the blue eyes, the brown eyes, the things that haunted my prior days. Remove the images of her; ones from our one day together and ones that I knew had never happened; and replace them with the nightmares I recognized. The past images of all my mistakes. My mind didn't listen to my pleas. I could feel the inside of the sleeping bag dampen from the heat of my breath as I struggled to slow the exhale. Dammit. If I could sleep, I wouldn't give a shit about the fleece becoming damp. As I lay here awake though; I cared. Finally, I gave up and pushed the thick fabric from my head. "Ugh," I sat up, still constrained by the blanket roll from the waist down. There was no moon in the sky above me. The stars all covered by clouds and hidden from my view. It made the night even darker. But as my body slowly emerged, I realized that the winter must have started to break.

I walked away from the little road and through the melting snow in the grass to get to a lit parking lot. There were no cars, but the bright lights created circles on the ground, evenly spaced in the dark and as I walked through each spotlight, I felt naked. My neck tickled as if someone was out there watching me. I stopped in my next break from light and turned, trying to spot my stalker. No one was there. It must be two or three in the morning. I shook my head, laughing at my own paranoia. There was no one here watching me. I continued walking towards the road that I assumed would get me closer to a town as the air continued to warm. I walked parallel with a strip mall and could see only the small red lights of their security systems. Everyone long gone for the evening.

But then, pushed back into the corner next to one of the stores was a crumpled-up man. Dead? I didn't think so. But I was curious. I walked closer to him, bracing myself to run away if I needed to. He moved a little in his sleep and I froze. He's alive at least. I couldn't see his face, his body curled away from me; only showing me his back. I don't know why I stood there watching this stranger as he slept. It didn't feel voyeuristic. It felt natural. I watched as his back lifted with each heavy breath he took. The line of his sweatshirt moving up and down as he continued to dream. I was startled back to reality by the simple movement of him shivering. I was just thinking how the night felt warmer, but he didn't seem to be dressed for the chill left hanging in the air. He shivered again and cried out in his sleep. I unzipped my bag; slowly to not make any noise or wake the sleeping man; and pulled my sleeping bag from the inside. It was still warm from my own heat as I gently laid it over him, making sure to not let it drop. I stopped for one moment when I saw the small gold band that lived on his ring finger and wondered if anyone was missing him. I stood for another minute before turning and continuing through the parking lot.

THE SNOW WAS completely gone by the time the sun started to rise. It shone behind the clouds that covered the sky, turning it a deep orange color in the morning. There was almost a haze that fell to the earth as I started towards the center of town and the row of shops, hoping there would be a decent diner. I could use a cup of coffee after my sleepless night. I walked to the door of the diner that I found, wondering why I felt like I had seen it before. True they all looked just about the same, but this was more than just vague familiarity. I looked at the window and the dark seats within. I could see her sitting there across from me in the booth. Slowly I turned, not knowing why I didn't see this before. My eyes froze on the park across from the diner. The one with the comfortable bench that I had spent more than one night sleeping on. I turned to my right and could see the sign of the funeral home down a block. The one where I saw myself being forgotten as I was turned to dust. Shit.

"Hey!" I slowly turned to my left to see the waitress that I had now seen three days in a row, bouncing towards me. Only a light jacket covered her uniform, like there wasn't a blizzard just the day before. I braced for her confrontation, knowing that I had yelled at her yesterday. But there was no fear or anger on her face; just a big wide smile and she trustingly turned her back to me as she unlocked the door to the diner. She talked to me over her shoulder as she worked the lock, "You're here early. You'll have to give me a few minutes to set up and then want your usual?" My mouth hung open. Who did she think I was? Yesterday she had cowered from me and today she wants to make me bacon and eggs or whatever "my usual" is. She continued to toy with the door, almost used to how long it took to get the lock to click open. I walked away. I knew where I was. Again. So, I knew where I had to go. The reason I couldn't sleep last night.

I heard a noise and looked up from the familiar path. Above me were two red birds, climbing and soaring as they chased each other through the foggy morning. Enjoying the newly found warmth of the spring. Was it spring already? That didn't seem right. But I looked around me and realized it was true. Flowers were already starting to poke through the cold ground and work their way to the sky. The grass was turning green. I continued walking, not to be distracted by the day around me; and straight through the glass door with the white cross painted on it. I walked past the people waiting to be seen and up to the large desk that sat in the middle of the room. A young woman smiled up at me, practiced and true in her caring.

"How may I help you?"

"I need to know how to get to a room upstairs. I was there yesterday but I... uh... took a different path out. A woman is there. Her first name is Eloise."

The nurse sat waiting for me to finish. When she realized that I had said all that I was prepared to say, she shook her head, "Do you have a last name?"

"No."

"How about which ward she is?"

"Listen. I know this sounds crazy, but I don't know anything except her name is Eloise and she's dying of cancer. I came back for her. Do you understand?"

"I think I know the answer to this, but are you family?"

"Don't you think I would know her last name if I were her family?"

She was starting to look annoyed. Annoyed people don't help you. "Listen, I'm sorry. I don't mean to be rude. I'm desperate. She's... she's my friend. I have to see her again before she dies. There is something I missed. Please, can you just see if you can find her?"

Her face softened and she turned her eyes to the screen and started tapping away. "I'm sorry. I'm not finding anyone named Eloise that is checked in long-term care. Did she possibly check in under a different first name or maybe that not her real name?"

"That's her real name." I laid my hands on the counter and could feel my shoulders sag in defeat.

"You can go upstairs to floor three. If she's here, that's likely the floor she would be on. Check with the desk just to the right after you get off the elevator." She waved towards a bank of elevators behind her, and I shouted my thanks as I ran to them. My foot tapped against the tile as I waited impatiently for one to open and almost knocked over the poor woman trying to get off the elevator as I was trying to get on it. Mumbled apology. The doors slid closed, and I was alone for a moment. What was I doing here? I looked at my reflection in the silver elevator door. This was stupid. What would I say if her husband was in there? Or any other friends or family. What did I come back for? I said goodbye. Yesterday. Why am I...?

THE DOORS OPENED and I stepped into the hallway that I knew. I walked right past the front desk, no longer needing directions. I turned right. Then left. Three more doors. One. Two. Three. I turned into the room, hesitating only for a short moment, and I looked towards her as she lay in the stark white hospital bed. Expecting her orange quilt that she loved, to be pulled up to her chin to keep her frail body warm. Except, that's not Elle. I moved closer to the bed. That is not Elle. It's a man. A large man with a big beard that somehow still looks amazing under the machine that was giving him breath. I watching his thick midsection rise and fall as his body was forced breath. I stepped back and looked down the hall. This is the right room. I know it. I moved close to the bed again, waiting for someone to tell me that this has all been an elaborate joke. There was nothing but the sounds of the machines that echoed in this room that I thought was hers. I stepped closer and looked down as his closed eyes and his bearded round face. I knew him but I barely recognized him without the grin that stretched ear to ear. I could hear his booming laugh echoing through the hallway.

Without thinking, I reached out my hand and felt the warmth of his thick fingers below mine. The tears ran from my face as I looked at him, not understanding what was going on around me. Why was she not here? Why was he? This didn't make any sense. I leaned down close to his face and whispered my goodbye, "I'm sorry, brother," and turned to leave the room, rubbing the dampness from my face. I stood for a moment in the warm hallway before a woman in scrubs walked by, "excuse me?"

She turned towards me, "yes?"

"The woman that was in this room. Do you know where she went?"

The nurse looked confused, "Are you sure you have the right room? This man has been in there for a while. This is the long-term care wing."

I looked back and could see him still lying in the bed, unmoving, "Yes it was this room. She was here yesterday."

She shook her head, "You must have the wrong room; there was no woman in this room yesterday. What's her name? If she's in this wing, then I can point you to her."

"Eloise, but everyone calls her Elle."

She shook her head. "You must have the wrong wing. There is no one here by that name and hasn't been since I've been here. Going on two years."

"No this is the right spot. You must just not have noticed here. She was only in here for a day."

"Then it's the wrong wing. No one is here for a day."

I couldn't control it anymore. I turned towards her, and my voice cracked as I yelled, "what the fuck is going on here!?" I saw the fear creep to her eyes, and she started to turn her head, looking for help. When she turned back to me, I saw what she thought of me. What she saw. What I was. A monster.

I turned from her and ran to the end of the hall where I knew the stairwell would be. I took the steps down, two at a time, the duffel bag swinging on my side almost knocking me to the ground. I made it to the bottom floor and pushed into the outside world. The morning fog hung heavy, and the warming day had turned a brighter orange. I started running. Where was I going? I didn't care. None of this made sense. Where was she? Had she been there at all? Maybe she really was only a creation of my own mind, and she didn't exist outside of it. Why was Phil laying there in her place? How could he be? I just saw him. No that was weeks ago. No. Months? But that wasn't real either.

I brought my hand up as I continued to jog, and I slapped myself. Once. Then again. Harder. The sky was still orange and thick. Nothing still made any sense at all. My right foot stopped, like it stuck to something solid and clicked into place. Then my left foot lined up with it and froze again. Standing in the middle of the road with my feet held to the earth in invisible and immovable boots. My head turned first, followed by my shoulders and then my hips. Last to turn were those feet. It was as if they were unclicked from their locked spot for just a moment to turn before being locked back in.

I knew this street. I had been here before. There were houses that lined the street, each perfectly manicured lawn shining green against the houses that were all different shades of grey. The tears stopped falling down my face and my mouth opened as I stood staring down the block that I had been on so many times before. I started walking down the street, noticing the perfect grey cement beneath my sneakers. I turned as I heard a mower rev to life and saw an older man in one of the yards. His face was turned up and he was staring at me. He probably thought I was here to rob someone. Let him think that.

I turned back to the road and kept walking. I walked through an intersection and kept going. I could hear the birds chirping above me, but my eyes were already focused on something else. That house there. The one at the end of the street. It stood out from the others as it was painted a soft faded orange instead of grey. It didn't stick out in a good or bad way. It just was noticeable. I stopped and reached into the bag that hung by my side and pulled the unread book from it. I turned it to the back cover. She stood there. Younger than I had thought she had previously looked in the photo. But there she was standing in front of that orange house. I had found her. I put the book back in my bag. Tried to smooth down the jacket that I still wore even though I was sweating through the layers beneath it. Used my hands to smooth down the short hair on my head but left the stubble on my chin, knowing there was nothing I could do about that anyway. I walked the short distance so that I was standing directly in front of the house.

There were three small cement steps that led up to the front door. The garage was on the side, closed, but I saw two cars through the windows. I would have to explain to the husband how she is a friend. I would ask how she got out of the hospital so quickly and if she was going to live. Standing with one foot on the bottom step. I pulled up the other foot to match. Then another step up. And the third. I lifted my right hand, noticing the dirt that was pressed into the skin too late, and I pushed the little button as I heard the chimes come from within the house.

I COULD HEAR them talking behind the closed door. The door unlocked. And it was pulled from within to reveal a woman standing there. A woman that was not Elle. I didn't prepare for this. Why would I have? This was her house. The woman looked at me curiously, "How can we help you?" I saw the man standing behind her, protective against the dirty stranger that stood on the clean steps in their clean neighborhood. They waited while I searched for the words. I had been presumptuous that this was her house. That she would open the door. Might as well lead with the truth, "I'm looking for Elle... uh... Eloise." I caught the flash as it crossed her face but couldn't quite come up with the word to describe the expression. Then it was gone.

Her husband opened his mouth first, "Are you finding her because of her book? That's normally what we get. Someone wants an autograph, yeah?"

I shook my head as she followed up with a question, "Have you read her book?" I shook my head again, being honest without telling them that it lived deep in my bag. I had gone to sleep looking at the photo, still just now making the connection that she was the same as my Elle. He stepped forward and I saw them glance at each other before turning back towards me, "Why are you here?"

Fair Question, "I'm an old friend of hers. I thought this was her house. Did she move?"

The woman looked over at her husband again and he nodded. She turned to me and as she spoke it felt like I was floating further and further from her, "She died. Four years ago, around the holidays. I'm sorry that you didn't know before now." My head was shaking. I didn't start it and I couldn't stop it. They were talking to me through a tunnel, and I could feel his arms hold me up as I started to fall. The voices jumbled together, "Are you OK?" "I wonder how he didn't know" "Let's bring him inside" "Can you get him some water?" "I can't believe no one told him" "Do you think he knew the husband?"

I was sitting on a comfortable brown couch. The fabric moved just a little under my fingers as they shifted back and forth. The room spun and I was handed a glass of water to drink. I knew this room. This looked kind of like a room I knew at least. It was different. Where did I know a room like this? They were talking to me. What were they saying? I stared at her lips. Then his. Trying to make out what they were telling me. What was that? There was something about the previous owners of this house. She was Eloise. She's dead. The husband... what was that about the husband? He's not here. I took another drink of water. There was a box on the table in front of me. That wasn't there before. She was waving a hand at the box. What was she saying? I focused on her lips.

"When we bought the house, there was still so much stuff in it. Some friends of theirs came and took some things, and we gave some to charity, but we still have this box of items that no one took. It didn't feel right to toss it. You can take anything out of it if you want?"

My hands ran across the lid. It was larger than a shoebox but smaller than a file box. Maybe this held the answers. Maybe this is what I was searching for. If she was dead for years, how did I just talk to her? I shook my head to clear it and pulled the lid off the top of the box, leaning forward to look at the contents. The couple in the room sat in chairs across from me and this box of treasures.

I pulled out the first thing. A red stuffed animal. I turned it over and saw that it was a cartoonish little red bird. The stuffing still completely intact. Next was a little black box. I opened it to find the orange necklace that I had seen in the mall. It shined and sparkled like it had never been touched. I put the black lid back on and sat it next to the stuffed animal. There was a piece of paper. I didn't open it to see what it said but I sat it on the couch next to me instead of on the table, possibly to read later. I pulled out other things; an orange scarf which I lifted to my face to inhale the smell of her perfume that still lingered there; a few small toys and knickknacks. A small wooden duck. I had pulled out everything and reached my hand back into the dark empty box to make sure I hadn't missed anything. My fingers felt something small, and I wrapped my hand around it. The familiar object was heavy as I lifted it out and stared at it. Sitting in my hand as it had done so many times before. I rubbed the smooth surface of the rock with one hand as I reached into my pocket with the other. My rock was gone. This is my rock. No. That doesn't make any sense. I had never been here before. Why is my rock in this box? I tried to hide my shock as I slid the small rock down into my pocket where it had always belonged. I turned to the piece of paper that still sat next to me, folded closed. I unfolded the crinkled edges as the breath left my lungs completely. The whole living room and table full of items left my view and instead I was transported to memories I didn't know I had. They flew by my eyes in mere seconds, but each felt like hours.

She told me she was pregnant, and I ran to the store to buy something for our coming child. Something that would be completely us. I stood in the toy isle at the store and looked at the full shelves. Not knowing what to buy I started to leave the store empty handed. Right by the door I saw what I knew I wanted to buy. It was perfect. It was a little red stuffed bird that looked just like the cardinals that we would watch each morning from the back porch. They would swoop and fly above us, singing loudly. She laughed when I gave it to her, her green eyes shining with unshed tears. Tears that would fall when she lost the child five weeks later. The waterfall that we loved hiking around. Our little secret haven. The floor around it was covered with round grey smooth rocks. I had fallen and hurt my shin and she had picked up one of the rocks and gave it to me. I rubbed it twice and stuck it down into my pocket, "My lucky charm. It will go with me everywhere." We were lying in bed, the sun shining through the cracks in the blinds, and she would laugh at me as I would trace things in the freckles of her arms. Finding her in the grass while I was out reading one day. Her father had just hit her, and she was running away. To me. I fell in love with her that day. Learning she was dying. Closing off. From her. From the pain. Watching the machines keep her alive and then being pulled from the room as I yelled and screamed and fought. Trying to get back to her as they let her die. They let her die. I screamed at the Dr. "It's your fault she's dead." He told me that she didn't want to be kept alive by machines. She signed something. She never told me. Why did she never tell me? The world going grey as she was placed into the ground. The thing that I found that had made me happy. Lessoned the loss of my own parents when I was young. Now she was gone too. I looked down at the words in my hands. At the letter that ended with *I'm sorry. –J.*

I knew this letter. I wrote this letter. And then I left it sitting in the entry way right behind me with my ring. I looked down at my left hand and saw it there, shining gold against the finger. Had it always been there? I had left the rock on the note. That's what had been left. I remembered now. I whispered to the ghost that lived in this room, "Ellc."

I looked up at the oblivious couple that watched me and realized that there were tears streaming down my face. I smiled sheepishly, not wanting to tell them of my realizations. I packed everything back into the box except for the rock which stayed in its place. "I'll keep it with me. Always." I said to the ghost and the couple was smart not to ask what I meant. I pushed the closed box back towards them, the letter included, and stood. Tears still running down my face. I had to go. I had found what I was looking for. I had found myself. I had found my wife. My beautiful wife. I don't know why I lost her for so long but now she was with me. Forever. I knew now.

I thanked them both and turned to leave as they followed me towards the door.

I opened the front door to the sound of the birds chirping, a mower running, the world passing me by. My right foot made it out the door and into the light. A voice. Her voice. Whispered in my ear "It's not your time, my sweet man." I nodded and stepped down the stairs, feeling something that I couldn't quite describe. A feeling of being a whole person again maybe. When I opened the floodgates to the pain, in came everything else. The pain was heavy, and I could feel it moving through my body but as it went, it merged with the other pieces of who I had become over the past years. It joined the joy of remembering her smile. It melded with the names and faces of the people I had met before and after losing that smile. All of it coming together to transform my shell of a body into something else. Into someone... alive.

My back straightened. I felt the heaviness of new-found human emotions in my body, but it felt oddly light as I started walking towards the road. Someone called out behind me, "Hey!" I turned to see the couple standing in front of the door. Her voice was almost hesitant as she asked me, "What is your name?" I stood for a moment and thought about it. Deep breath in. And I answered her truthfully.

"My name is Jonathan. Jonathan Murray."

THE DEATH AND LIFE OF JOHN DOE

CPSIA information can be obtained
at www.ICGtesting.com
Printed in the USA
BVHW090212300722
643339BV00001B/1